THE
INHERITANCE

THE
INHERITANCE

Trisha Sakhlecha

PAMELA DORMAN BOOKS / VIKING

VIKING
An imprint of Penguin Random House LLC
penguinrandomhouse.com

Simultaneously published in hardcover in Great Britain by Century,
an imprint of Penguin Random House Ltd, London, in 2025

First United States edition published by Pamela Dorman Books, 2025

A Pamela Dorman Book / Viking

LIBRARY OF CONGRESS CATALOGING-IN-PUBLICATION DATA

Names: Sakhlecha, Trisha, author.
Title: The inheritance / Trisha Sakhlecha.
Description: [New York] : Pamela Dorman Books/Viking, 2025.
Identifiers: LCCN 2024018186 (print) | LCCN 2024018187 (ebook) |
ISBN 9780593832561 (hardcover) | ISBN 9780593832578 (ebook)
Subjects: LCGFT: Thrillers (Fiction) | Novels.
Classification: LCC PR6119.A377 I54 2025 (print) |
LCC PR6119.A377 (ebook) | DDC 823/.92—dc23/eng/20240510
LC record available at https://lccn.loc.gov/2024018186
LC ebook record available at https://lccn.loc.gov/2024018187

Printed in the United States of America
1st Printing

Designed by Alexis Farabaugh

To my number-one rival (and cheerleader) for life:

my brother, Rishabh

THE
INHERITANCE

I didn't think it would end like this.

The dense, black woods smother me as I run through them.

The pelting rain drowns out all sound except the pounding inside my chest.

A bramble twists itself around my ankle, its thorns digging into my flesh. I yank myself free.

There is no time to waste.

I run.

A crack of lightning pierces through the darkness and my eyes flick up to the winding path in front of me, to the faint outline of the house, its silhouette bleeding into the tree-choked horizon.

Where the rest of the family are asleep, safe from the storm, blissfully unaware of what's happened.

I take a sharp, quick breath and force myself up the path, my trainers pushing into the damp earth, leaving behind a trail of mud-sucking footprints.

Another crack of thunder as lightning rips through the sky.

I slow down as the house comes into view, illuminated only by the moonlight filtering out through the clouds. Disconnected images flash past my eyes. The celebration, the announcement, the hike.

The dead body.

I stop. I need to focus. I can't afford to make any more mistakes.

I wonder how long it takes for a body to go cold. For the limbs to go stiff. The lips to turn blue.

I force myself up the final few feet and ease the door open. I'm trying to decide what to do next but the choice is snatched from me.

I freeze as the lights come on and two sets of eyes take me in, flicking past the scratches on my face, skimming across the ripped jeans and the trainers that are no longer white, before coming to rest on the stains that not even the relentless Scottish rain has been able to wash off.

Blood.

But not mine.

I look around the room. How did this happen? The decorations that had felt festive last night look menacing in the pre-dawn light. The family photos we had laughed over just hours ago now seem saturated with foreboding.

The words are barely a whisper but they ricochet around the space, bouncing off the walls, filling my ears. An echo from the past.

What have you done?

In this family, there's only one cardinal rule. Family first.

Always.

I grit my teeth. I know what comes next.

I don't have a choice anymore.

Perhaps I never did.

1.

ZOE

I twist onto my side and burrow deeper under the duvet, trying to drown out the sound of Aseem's voice. He's been on the phone with his sister Aisha for at least twenty minutes, his words punctuated by the short sighs and long silences that I have come to associate with my husband.

Aisha's been swanning around in LA for the past three months. The last time we spoke, she told me she was extending her stay, which is why I'd been surprised when my mother-in-law told me that Aisha would be joining us on this week-long trip. Aisha detests family holidays—understandably so—and I find it hard to believe that she would willingly swap her Malibu villa for a week on a Scottish island, irrespective of how important this week really is. But I've long since given up trying to untangle the knot that is the Agarwal family, so when my mother-in-law, Shalini, told me that Aisha would join us in

London, I kept my disbelief to myself. Aisha was supposed to meet us at Euston station an hour before the overnight train to Fort William.

As expected, she didn't show.

Her phone was switched off and the airline staff were adamant that she had never checked in for her flight to London from LA. With no way to reach her, Aseem, his parents, and I boarded the train carrying between us a vast range of emotions; everything from panic, worry, concern, and irritation rolled up and tucked in between us as tightly as the theplas and parathas that my mother-in-law had packed into her carry-on.

"That is not the point, Aish." Aseem's voice drifts in through the thick duvet. "Do you have any idea how worried we were? The least you could have done is called."

A few beats go by and in the muffled silence, I let my breathing slow down, focusing on the rhythmic sound of the train pushing against the tracks, letting the shunt and roll of the carriage lull me back to sleep. My eyelids have just begun to feel heavy when Aseem speaks again.

"Oh, come on. You know how much this trip means to Mama. And Myra's been planning this for months."

I roll onto my back and peel my eye-mask away, acutely aware of the queasiness building in the pit of my stomach. Aseem is sitting next to me, eyes closed, head leaning back, but I can tell just looking at the set of his shoulders that he's anything but relaxed. With everything we have going on, it's a stance I've seen him assume far too often over the past couple of months.

Aseem's voice, when he speaks, is measured, and once again I am reminded of the inner calm that he's able to navigate back to no matter how chaotic his surroundings. His unflappability has always been the thing that I love the most about him. And often, the thing that frustrates me the most.

"It's an island, Aisha. You can't just rock up whenever you want."

I inch closer to him and tug the curtain open with my toes. Dappled sunlight dances across our tiny cabin as the train winds its way through the glen, deeper still into the Highlands. I am tempted to click a quick picture for Instagram, but I doubt I can avoid catching my own reflection in the window and if there was ever a day for a "woke up like this" selfie, it's not today. I've barely slept all night, I *know* my face will betray all the tell-tale signs of exhaustion and sleeplessness. I'm sure as hell not going to give the keyboard warriors who have been harassing me for months any more ammunition.

I imagine Aisha's voice on the other end, the unimpeachable tone she seems to reserve for her family, the charming excuses she always has tucked up her sleeve, and then I watch Aseem melt, as usual giving in to his little sister. It's annoying, yes, but there's never been any point arguing with Aisha.

If there's anyone in this family who can get away with murder, it's her.

"Fine," he sighs. "I'll handle things here. *This time.* How quickly can you get to the airport in LA?"

I sit up and curl one arm around my husband, pressing myself into him as I lean over to reach for the bottle of water on the fold-down table. Three years of marriage and I still can't keep my eyes—or my hands—off him. I snuggle up next to him, bottle of Highland Spring in hand.

I look at Aseem when he finally finishes the call, my eyebrows raised.

"She missed her flight," he says, running a finger along my cheek.

"And her phone—why was it switched off?"

Aseem shrugs, unwilling to reveal the details of whatever latest escapade his sister's been on. I don't press him on it. I'd rather get the *real* story—no doubt involving an entirely inappropriate man and a few bottles of tequila—from her later. "She's getting on the next flight out. But first," he says, pulling me close and kissing me. I feel the anxiety from earlier dissipate as his hand slips under my T-shirt and his fingers work their way up my back, massaging my neck, my shoulders . . .

The knock on the door feels so intimate, so startling, that we both jump apart. Almost on cue, my mother-in-law's voice filters through and Aseem scrambles out of bed, getting up to slide the pocket door open.

I remind myself that I love his attentiveness.

"Nashta?" my mother-in-law asks. Breakfast. One of the first Hindi words I picked up when I moved to Delhi. I ignore the flicker of irritation—it's barely seven a.m.—and climb out of bed.

It's just one week. I can do this.

"We'll be right there, Mama," I say.

I straighten my T-shirt and wriggle past Aseem into the en suite. I shower as best as I can in the tiny space, then squeeze myself into the pair of jeans and jumper I'd packed for today, carefully applying my makeup in the moving train. I dab on an extra layer of concealer, plaster on my best smile, and step out of the cabin, determined to make this work.

Despite the early hour, the dining car is packed. When Myra first suggested we take the newly revamped overnight train to Scotland instead of flying, I'd pictured the epitome of luxury and #slowtravel: mahogany paneling and tartan furnishings, observation cars with overstuffed sofas and table service. But the Caledonian Express is more *Slumdog Millionaire* than *Murder on the Orient Express*. We spot Mama and Papa at the far end of the carriage and thread our way through the group of Chinese students who seem to have no concept of personal space.

I slip into the window seat opposite my mother-in-law, watching Aseem as he pushes his way to the bar with our rather large breakfast order.

It's only when I tear my gaze away from my husband that I realize

Mama's eyes are on him as well. Other than the black kohl rimming her eyes, her face is devoid of any makeup, her skin dewy and almost translucent in the early morning light. I make a mental note to book in with her facialist—her biweekly appointments at Aura Spa are the only thing more sacred to her than her astrologer—and considering the fact that at sixty she can easily pass for a forty-five-year-old, maybe she's on to something.

"He looks tired," she says, turning to face me after a moment.

Of course he does, I want to say. Aseem took a step back from his own start-up and took over the family business when Papa had a stroke four years ago. Ever since then, he's been working himself into the ground trying to turn a product he has zero interest in into something profitable. But there's little point in saying anything. The company, PetroVision, and the petrochemicals it manufactures, is Papa's pride and joy, and the last thing I want to do right now is to upset him, what with his retirement and the transfer of the shares looming.

"He's been up since four a.m. talking to the consultants," I say instead. Though Aseem's been running the company since Papa's illness, Papa's still the chairman and, most importantly, the sole shareholder. It's important he realizes just how hard Aseem's working on this deal. "Something to do with the payment terms for the sale."

"Can't your lawyer handle all this while we're on vacation?" Mama says, looking up at Papa, her finely arched eyebrows giving her a look between worry and disdain.

"It's a three thousand crore deal, Shalini. The buyer is my oldest rival," Papa says, barely looking up from his newspaper. "And Aseem's the COO. So no, the lawyers can't handle this."

As Papa carries on about how he built PetroVision up from scratch, how he didn't even have an assistant, let alone a lawyer when he first started, I tune out. It's a story we've all heard countless times before.

Three thousand crores. Roughly three hundred million pounds, just fifty million shy of the King's estimated net worth. The King.

It's a number that would have seemed completely unfathomable to me just a few years ago.

A number that *still* gets my heart racing.

And judging by how quickly everyone agreed to this trip, I'm not the only one. Ever since Papa announced his retirement, we've all been waiting for him to reveal his inheritance plan.

I let my gaze drift back to the window, to the amber sun slanting across the snow-capped Munros. Once the sale is complete, Aseem won't have to play by Papa's rules any more.

We won't have to play by Papa's rules.

We'll finally be free.

The atmosphere in the carriage changes as we pass a particularly dramatic stretch. There's an audible holding of breath before people scramble to the right-hand side, cameras in hand. I press my phone up against the window to snap a few photos as the train skirts along the edge of a cliff, the slowly rising sun bathing the valley and the loch at its heart glittering orange. Despite the obvious beauty, there is something unsettling about the landscape, a harshness that makes it seem unforgiving. Hostile. I put on a goofy grin and scrunch my hair, making sure I look a little sleep deprived and scruffy, then take a few selfies. My #instaperfect life relies on my looking imperfect.

I scroll through the pictures and pick the two best ones, carefully tweaking the color and temperature before posting it on Instagram with the hashtags accidentaladult, offgrid, and discoverscotland. My followers love me for my spontaneity, but the irony is that I only found success as an influencer when I stopped being spontaneous and started paying attention to who my followers are and what they respond to: adulting. My followers are expat millennials with Peter Pan syndrome, so I've now got Excel sheets of hashtags and prewritten captions that give everything from fashion to travel a life advice spin. Everything about my seemingly off-the-cuff posts is planned to a military level of detail, snippets of my life tweaked and calibrated to appeal to my specific brand of followers.

It's exhausting.

But it's paid off. In less than two years, my account, Accidental Adult, has amassed half a million followers. I've progressed from being just another twentysomething trying to make it big online to being recognized and respected in the influencer space.

I'm busy responding to comments—close to a hundred in the space of five minutes—when Aseem returns.

"Did you close?" Papa asks him before he's even sat down.

"Not yet. Malhotra's being difficult about the earn-out period," Aseem says, carefully lowering the plastic tray with our hot drinks onto the table. He slides the second tray, stacked high with croissants and fruit pots, across the table before squeezing in next to me. He picks out Mama's breakfast—yogurt and some fruit—and places it in front of her before helping himself to a banana. "But I've straightened him out. We should have the paperwork tomorrow."

Papa nods. "We need to get this done. Keep checking in."

"I will," Aseem says between bites. "I'm handling it, Papa."

I reach for a croissant. I know as soon as I've had my first bite that I'm not going to be able to stomach the whole thing. I set it down on a plate and take a tentative sip of the orange juice instead as the conversation pivots back to Aisha.

I try not to dwell on how much the last-minute flights—first class, of course—would have cost while Aseem fills his parents in. Aisha will arrive at Glasgow airport tomorrow to find a chauffeur waiting for her at arrivals, ready to escort her to the port at Mallaig, from where she will be picked up and brought to the island. You'd think Aisha is a helpless teenager, not a twenty-seven-year-old "adventure-seeker" as she likes to call herself. I am half-expecting Papa to ask Aseem to stay back at Fort William so he can go and pick Aisha up himself, but he just sighs and turns back to his paper.

I glance up as an announcement crackles over the speaker and people start trickling out of the dining car. I gulp down the remainder of my juice and slide out of the seat.

Ten minutes to arrival.

This trip is meant to be a celebration. A family gathering to mark Papa's retirement and Mama and Papa's fortieth wedding anniversary. But the truth is we're all here for one thing and one thing only: the biggest piece of the pie. After the sale of PetroVision goes through, the family trust will be worth over three hundred million pounds. Up until now, Papa's been the sole trustee, doling out money to Aseem, Myra, and Aisha based on their needs and his whims. But thanks to a tax strategy that I can't quite wrap my head around, the terms of the trust are being amended to change it from a discretionary trust that Papa controls to a specific trust within which the shares of each of his three children will be fixed.

That's the real reason we've all dropped everything to be here. It's payday.

I push my shoulders back. Like Aisha, I'm not a fan of family gatherings, and if there is one thing that's more complicated than being on a family holiday, it's being on a family holiday on a Scottish island with no one to talk to except your in-laws and three hundred million pounds hanging in the balance.

But unlike Aisha, I don't have the luxury of bailing out. At least not yet.

I need to make this trip work.

My entire future depends on it.

2

MYRA

I squint as I carry the flowers into the kitchen, blinded by the unexpected winter sun pouring in through the picture window. I set the vase down on the dining table and rearrange the flowers one final time—freshly picked hydrangeas, lilies, and roses bristle against hawthorns and long tendrils of grass in a vintage crystal vase—the effect is spectacular, at once luxurious and rustic, much like the estate itself.

I pick out a few stray leaves from the vase and drop them in the bin, glancing briefly at the stack of unpaid bills on the kitchen counter. I shove the papers in a drawer for later, trying to ignore the words FINAL REMINDER and skim through my to-do list instead.

Welcome baskets
Fruit
Make up beds
Wrap presents
Wine delivery
Flowers

I cross off *flowers* and move from room to room, plumping cushions, straightening pictures, rearranging bookshelves, until every corner of the house looks perfect. Effortless.

I allow myself a brief moment by the living room window when I am done. The sunlight streaming in through the floor-to-ceiling windows is casting the room in a warm glow that, deceptive as it is, is wonderfully refreshing after months of gray skies and relentless rain. Beyond the glass, the icy waters of the loch glitter and sparkle in the midmorning sun.

I still find it incredible that I live here.

When Owen first showed me the advert, I'd rolled my eyes. We were looking for a townhouse in Edinburgh, somewhere we could start a family, not a private island that cost ten times as much, had no heating or Wi-Fi, and was a nightmare to get to. I couldn't understand why anyone would want to live in a place so completely cut off from the world. But over the next few weeks, I'd found myself returning to the listing again and again, poring over the details until I had them memorized. Three beaches, two lochs, an old boathouse, an eleven-bedroom main house, and six crumbling old cottages. Two thousand acres of wilderness.

It was nothing like what we were looking for. And yet, it was everything I wanted.

Where earlier, I'd seen two thousand acres of inconvenience and damp, I now saw open fires, long hikes, and vast open spaces for the kids to run through. I saw adventure. I snuck a glance at Owen, snoring softly beside me.

I saw hope.

Eighteen months and several lawsuits later, Owen and I were on a boat en route to our own island paradise. We'd spent a few blissful hours talking and discovering and planning, our ideas knotting together into a shared vision that shone so bright, it completely eclipsed the dark history we'd spent months grappling with.

By the time we met with the developer a week later, I knew exactly what I wanted. A hideaway that could rival Necker Island in its luxuriousness and Chatsworth in its charm. On the cards was a full refurbishment of the main house and the six cottages, a brand-new spa and infinity pool by the loch, a helipad, and a cluster of modern, self-contained apartments for the staff. The plan was to run the estate as a luxury retreat in the months that we weren't using it ourselves, and though we were stretching ourselves, neither Owen nor I was worried about the costs. It was far more important to get the vision right.

The vision that nearly five years later still lies half-developed before my eyes.

I turn at the sound of footsteps behind me. The housekeeper, Lorna, stands silhouetted in the doorway.

"The canapés are in the fridge and the lasagna is in the freezer. Fifty minutes should do it," she says, her Glaswegian accent still as hard to decipher as the first time I met her.

"Thank you," I say. "Has the wine arrived?"

I had given Lorna a long list of supplies to order in from the mainland last week. Everything from essential groceries and fresh fruits and vegetables to cases of wine and champagne and plenty of cold cuts and cheese to see us through the week. The food delivery arrived yesterday but the wine merchant had been running late.

Lorna nods. "Stu picked it up this morning. I've popped a few bottles of bubbly in the fridge and the rest is stacked in the cellar," she says, handing me the invoice.

I can't help but flinch when I see the bill. I take a breath, reminding myself that the small fortune that I've spent to host this holiday is not an extravagance. It's an investment.

And if it pays off, I'll never have to worry about money again.

I run through the invoice, checking to see that all the family favorites

I'd ordered have arrived. I'm halfway through the order summary when my heart sinks.

"What is it?" Lorna asks.

"The Pinot Noir."

She peers at the receipt.

Calera Mt. Harlan Pinot Noir 2016.

"I asked for the *2014* Pinot Noir," I add, silently cursing myself for trusting Lorna with the order. I love Lorna but her idea of a celebration is splurging out on some sweet potato fries and a bottle of Sainsbury's own brand Prosecco.

Lorna takes the piece of paper from me, tucks it into a folder full of invoices sitting on the marble coffee table. I resist the urge to straighten it so the corners line up. Technically, Lorna's an employee, the first person Owen and I hired after we bought Kilbryde, but over the past couple of years, she's become a friend. Quite often she is the only person I speak to all week. She knows more about my life now than some of my closest friends.

"These people are your family," she says. "They love you. They will not care what wine you serve."

"I know," I say. "I just . . . I need everything to be perfect this week."

The wrinkles around Lorna's eyes deepen as she fixes me with a look. "And it will be. Look how glorious it is . . . sunshine in March!"

Trust Lorna to always find the silver lining. "Are you looking forward to going back to Glasgow?" I ask her.

"Aye. It'll be good to see the lads. And my mother could do with a wee visit," she says, her face breaking into a smile as she fills me in on her plans for the week. Dinner with her son and his family, a trip to Edinburgh to see her newest grandchild, tea with her mother. It all sounds so simple. Uncomplicated.

I follow Lorna out through the kitchen and to the front door, where

Stu's loading her bags into the quad. I can't help but wonder if asking both Stu and Lorna to take this week off was a mistake. I dismiss the thought as soon as it occurs. Convenient as it would be to have the staff here to help, I don't want Stu or Lorna hovering in the background, hearing things they aren't supposed to. Or worse, letting slip one of the many small secrets I've kept from my family. I'd much rather slum it for one week.

"Right," she says, cocking her head. "Best be off or Stu won't be back in time to take you to the jetty. Sure you don't need anything else before I go?"

"I'll be fine," I say, forcing my lips into a smile. "Enjoy the time off."

I lean in for our usual double kiss but Lorna pulls me into a tight hug instead.

"Try to relax. Nothing's going to go wrong," she says, before spinning around and climbing into the quad next to Stu. I wait till they disappear from view before going back inside.

I'm not usually the nervous type but there is just too much at stake right now. Mama and Papa's anniversary. All of us together for the first time in ages. And a three hundred million pound payout to split between us.

There's plenty that can go wrong.

I take a deep breath and head back into the kitchen. I switch on the coffee machine, my mind going back to the phone call with Papa nearly a decade ago as I slot a pod of Aged Sumatra in. *The business is yours. Come home. Save it.* And I had. I'd dropped everything and flown to Delhi to fight the environmental damage lawsuit that had threatened not just to bankrupt the business but to completely annihilate it.

I indulge in another look out of the window as I wait for the espresso machine to spurt to life.

The layer of ice that has covered the loch for the best part of the winter is starting to melt, individual shards breaking off and floating on the surface, sparkling under the spring sunshine, their gleaming edges as sharp and lethal as a knife's edge.

We'd settled the billion-dollar lawsuit for a few hundred grand. Pennies, really. I'd saved the company, and our family, from financial and professional ruin. That's not something that's easily forgotten.

I *know* it's not.

So why does the knot of anxiety in my chest feel so heavy I can barely breathe?

3.

ZOE

Two chauffeur-driven Range Rovers are waiting for us outside the station. No sooner have we set off than Aseem and I turn to our phones, spending the two-and-a-half-hour-long, insanely picturesque drive to the jetty maximizing every last bar of 4G.

I still remember how people had looked at me when I quit my marketing job to focus on my Instagram account. You're going to be an influencer, they'd asked, the contempt barely concealed behind the wide smiles and knowing glances Aseem's family and social circle seem to specialize in. The response had bothered me, as had the unspoken conclusion that despite my assertions to the contrary, I was really no more than a bored twenty-five-year-old housewife. But less than two years and five hundred thousand followers later, I've proven them wrong. My work hasn't just provided me with a sense of community in a foreign country, it's given me a sense of purpose.

And yet, all it takes is one notification for my sense of pride to slip away.

NB_lurker wants to send you a message.

Fuck. *Fuck.*

I tap on the alert and reread the string of messages that has been haunting me for weeks, the sour feeling in my stomach growing stronger the further I scroll.

Par for the course, my agent had told me when I first mentioned the trolling, advising me to ignore the threatening comments and messages that come with being a woman on Instagram. And for a long time, that's exactly what I did. Growing up with an abusive father and silent mother is a remarkable way to develop a thick skin. I let the snide comments about my weight, my sartorial choices, my husband roll off me. But the mild trolling that started when I hit a hundred thousand followers has taken a darker, infinitely more sinister turn over the past couple of months. The messages don't feel like empty threats from strangers anymore. They feel intimate, a torrent of hate from someone who knows me or at the very least knows *about* me. I wake up more and more frequently from nightmares built on fragments from those messages, words and phrases twisting deep into my subconscious and reminding me of a past I've moved continents to forget. *Bitch. Cunt. I know what you really are. Stop selling yourself. Whore. Fraud.*

Outside our car, the single-lane track winding through deep valleys and thick woods has given way to open skies and sparkling turquoise waters. As we slow down and turn onto a steep gated path leading to the jetty, I force myself to put my phone away. I've spent far too many sleepless nights worrying about *NB_lurker*, unsuccessfully trying to work out who might be hiding behind the private account and anonymous profile picture. I will *not* worry about some random middle-aged man who doesn't even have the courage to use his real name. Every job has its limitations and in mine, the benefits far outweigh any drawbacks, nasty as they may be. When I first mentioned the trolling to Aseem, he said it was an indicator of my success as an influencer. He's right. The fact that people care enough to react with such vehemence means my content is doing what it's meant to: dividing opinions and creating conversations. It means that my voice matters. That I matter.

I reach for Aseem's hand and focus my thoughts on the week ahead. Myra's already warned us that other than a dial-up connection in her office, which is reserved strictly for business emails and emergencies, there is no Wi-Fi or cell signal on the island. For the next few days, I'll be on a forced digital detox, and come to think of it, perhaps that's a good thing. I can't afford any distractions, not right now, and ultimately, that's all that *NB_lurker* is. A distraction.

Though I grew up quite close to the borders, I've never traveled beyond Edinburgh, and as we all climb into a small boat for the crossing, I am reminded why. My idea of a holiday isn't stormy skies and gales so powerful they can throw you off a cliff, thank you very much. As mellow as the day looked from the safety of the car, the reality is quite different. The sun has disappeared behind thick clouds, bleeding all color out of the ocean and turning the water into a menacing slate gray. Frothy white waves rise up in front of us, constantly moving barriers that push us back a few feet every time we inch forward. At the front of the boat, the groundskeeper, Stu, is bent over the steering wheel, trying to exert some control over the boat as it lurches over one wave and jumps straight into another. There is something eerily familiar about the tattoo peeking out from under his jumper, a swirl of black ink dancing across the back of his neck. As he turns around to grab a bottle of water, I see him look me over. His eyes travel across my body, taking in my Barbour coat and Hunter wellies, resting on my face a beat too long before he slowly turns back to the wheel.

I am wearing a gazillion layers yet somehow I feel completely naked.

I clutch the side of the boat as it launches off yet another wave, an arc of water splashing inside it and inviting a surprised shriek of laughter from Myra as Aseem scoops a handful of the icy water and throws it back at her.

I try to laugh but it feels forced and I wonder if my face betrays my unease. The nausea that had kept me awake all night is churning in my stomach, worsening with every sideways lurch. Myra has consistently refused to share any progress pictures with us so I have no idea what to expect. If all goes well, we'll spend an idyllic week enjoying the wilderness. But if it doesn't . . . the nearest town is over a hundred miles away. There are no hospitals, no doctors, no emergency services that can get to us quickly. It's not lost on me that the remoteness that makes this island escape so attractive is also its biggest threat. Particularly considering its history.

"Are you okay, Zoe?" Papa asks, eyebrows knitted together above his Ray-Bans. His legs are angled awkwardly to his left, the boat too small to comfortably accommodate his larger-than-life frame.

Stu throws another glance my way, the contempt on his face obvious.

"Motion sickness," I manage to say between gulps of salty air. Aseem slides closer and rubs my back while Myra fumbles through the plastic box sitting at her feet. She tosses aside bandages and antiseptic wipes, pulling out, finally, a blister pack of antinausea medicine.

I swallow the small white pill, then lean back, resting my head on Aseem's shoulder, my gaze drawn to the jagged stacks in the distance, dark cliffs dotted with patches of green and surrounded by a shock of white.

"Look at that," Papa says. The pride in his words is undeniable, and I see it mirrored across the boat on Myra's face.

"There it is," she says. "Eilean Kilbryde."

———

This is quite the place, isn't it?" Aseem says as we step inside the house, which feels like a cross between an English manor house and Scottish castle in the best possible way.

"It is," I agree, casting a glance around the hall. With its grand facade and cascading rows of gables and turrets typical of eighteenth-century Scottish architecture, the effect when we came up the winding path to the house was mesmerizing, almost like stepping into a gothic fairy tale.

But while the exterior charms, it is the interior that stuns. The family has been a bit worried about Myra but, standing here, I can see why the renovation's taken so long and why she's been so reluctant to share any plans or pictures. A camera simply wouldn't be able to capture the full, jaw-dropping extent of the transformation. The wooden beams and double-height ceilings that I remember from the estate agent's brochure are still there, but the rest of the house is pretty much unrecognizable. The downstairs has gone from a series of small, stuffy rooms to a large open-plan space with polished wood floors, a huge granite dining table, and expensive-looking fur throws everywhere. The living room is separated from the kitchen and dining room by a set of stained-glass sliding doors; the only original feature save for the elaborately carved fireplace that sits opposite understated cream sofas and a marble coffee table. Huge sheets of glass have replaced almost the entire back wall. Sweeping views of the valley fill the windows, blurring the separation between the inside and the outside.

Before I met this family, I'd never been anywhere like this.

"It's a work in progress," Myra says as we follow her up the winding staircase. She turns to flash us a smile and once again, I'm struck by how different she looks. Gone is the sleek bob and perfectly made-up face. Myra's long brown hair is cut into subtle layers that soften the sharp angles of her face, and other than a hint of mascara that brings out the green-gold flecks in her eyes, her face is devoid of any makeup. It's clear that we've all been wrong. She didn't move here because she was having a nervous breakdown; she moved because she genuinely loves it here. "But I *am* proud of what we've done so far."

"You're on the first floor, next to me," she says to us as we walk down the corridor. "Mama and Papa are in the suite on the second floor and I'll put Aisha in the room across the hall." She stops in front of a mahogany wood door on the far end and pushes it open. "There you go."

My gaze moves past the enormous bed to the upholstered green velvet chairs and the window that stretches from floor to ceiling across the length of the room, overlooking a stunning view of the loch.

I breathe in the smell of Diptyque candles and fresh flowers. I've come a long way from the damp two-bedroom council flat I grew up in. How to go from social housing to luxury real estate: that's the advice I should be sharing with my followers.

I pull my eyes away from the window to take in all the little details of the room—the crystal vase with fat pink peonies, the gilded mirror over the fireplace, the stack of rare first-edition books on the dresser. #Instagold.

I realize with a pang of regret that I can't share any of this with my followers. Myra had been very clear about that in an email that was addressed to the entire family but directed mainly at me. She's planning a big reveal at the press launch, which means we aren't allowed to share anything on social media until the island is ready.

Our suitcases have already been placed on two identical luggage racks, courtesy of Stu. Thankfully, Myra's given him the week off, a fact that caused quite the furor when Papa found out, but I, for one, am relieved that he won't be here. I don't care how much Myra trusts him:

it makes me distinctly uncomfortable being on a remote island with a man I barely know.

I slide open the double doors opposite the bed to reveal the en-suite bathroom complete with his and hers sinks, a massive glass-encased rainfall shower, and the pièce de résistance, the claw-footed bathtub sitting opposite a picture window with yet another view of the valley.

I turn around to face Aseem. I shake my head. Myra must have spent an absolute fortune on redecorating this house.

"I know," Aseem says, reading my mind.

A box of chocolates is propped up against the cushions on the bed. Lindt Swiss Thins—Aseem's favorite. I pop the paper-thin chocolate into my mouth, enjoying the sensation of it melting on my tongue, before looking at the slim hand-bound book next to it.

A guidebook. Of course Myra made a guidebook. She thinks of *everything*.

I put it on the bedside table for later and sink into bed next to my husband. Dinner's at seven, which gives us the afternoon to recuperate.

"Not tonight, then?" I ask Aseem. I run my hand over the throw. Real fur.

"Not until Aisha gets here," he says.

After weeks of waiting, one more day will hardly make a difference.

And anyway, it's not the announcement I'm worried about.

It's what comes after.

4.

MYRA

I place the ceramic baking dish in the oven, then join Papa at the kitchen island. "The builders have promised me that they can finish the work on the cottages in a couple of months. Then I need to—"

"Something smells nice," Aseem says, cutting me off midsentence as he walks into the kitchen.

"Lasagna," I say, twisting around briefly to smile at Aseem before going back to the peppers I'm trying to manipulate into wafer-thin slices.

I glance at Papa. Even though he's made a full recovery, ever since I saw him lying sedated in a hospital bed, the fear that I will one day have to face life without my father hasn't quite left me. But looking at him now, his lean, six-foot-two frame looming over me, I realize he's just as sturdy as ever. Dependable. "Later," he says, patting my hand lightly. He twists open the jar of olives and tips it into a bowl. "Any updates, son?"

"I'm working on it," Aseem says.

I set the knife down, anxiety fluttering in my chest. I thought the deal had been finalized already.

"You need to keep an eye on this," Papa says, frowning.

"I know. We are on the one-yard line," Aseem says. "It's all happening tomorrow. I promise."

Papa looks at Aseem for a long moment before nodding. "Better take these to Mama," he says, picking up the bowl of olives and carrying it into the living room.

"Is there a problem?" I ask Aseem as he circles the kitchen island to take Papa's place.

"Just some discrepancies on the heads of terms," he says.

"Do you want me to have a look?" I ask. I'm conscious of how it sounds—a certain amount of back and forth on the heads of terms is to be expected, especially on a sale this big—but there is far too much riding on this deal to take any chances.

"It's fine, just housekeeping," he says. "Honestly, I've got our lawyers working on it. But I will need to use your office to send some emails tomorrow."

"Yeah, of course." I try to shake the worry away. "Whatever you need."

"What are these for?" he asks, reaching across the worktop and helping himself to a handful of cherry tomatoes.

"The salad," I say, swatting his hand away. I tip the onions, tomatoes, and peppers into the salad bowl, then set the knife and chopping board down to look at my brother. His hair is peppered with gray and his eyes are ringed with shadows, but he still has the deep dimples and sparkling brown eyes that I'd fawned over when Mama returned from the hospital carrying what I thought was my own living, breathing toy. I pick up a pomegranate from the fruit bowl and slice it open.

"Mama's worried about you," I say.

He smiles but doesn't say anything.

"As am I." The sound of Zoe's voice turns me around. She looks gorgeous, dressed in high-waisted jeans and a brightly patterned jumper that clings to all the right parts. Small topaz earrings—an engagement present I'd helped Aseem pick out—sparkle in her ears and her hair is bundled into a messy bun at the top of her head, highlighting her slender neck. I'd always been jealous of Zoe's hair—unrealistic as it was, I would've given anything to be a natural blonde—until Aisha told me that Zoe's natural color was as brown and boring as my own. The magnificent golden hair that I so envied was the result of a highly secret, fortnightly appointment at Toni & Guy.

"And that's my cue," Aseem says. He steals a handful of the pomegranate seeds that I've just scooped out before walking into the living room to join Mama and Papa.

"He's been working himself into the ground," Zoe says, coming to stand beside me. "But it's useless trying to reason with him, especially right now."

I offer her a small smile, then go back to preparing the dressing for the salad. Considering what Aseem's working on, it's no bad thing. I *need* this deal to happen, and soon. "He looks exhausted," I say, using the back of a spoon to crush the pomegranate seeds. "Is everything okay with you two?"

"Yes," she says, slowly. "Why?"

She looks so startled that for a second I worry I've overstepped.

"Just checking." I laugh, trying to mask the awkwardness with familiarity. I toss the dressing into the salad, then crumble some aged feta and sprinkle a handful of pomegranate seeds on top. "That's what big sisters do, you know."

If Zoe is annoyed, she doesn't get the opportunity to show it. A quick knock on the door draws my attention to the groundskeeper, Stu, who's standing silhouetted in the doorway carrying an overstuffed backpack and the distinct air of a man who has somewhere else he needs to be.

"Off already?" I ask.

"Aye. I need to get there for eight."

"Right. Give me one sec." I wipe my hands on the dishtowel and hand the platters of canapés to Zoe to carry into the living room. I wait until she's disappeared behind the sliding doors, then pull out the thick manila envelope I'd stashed in a drawer earlier and hand it to Stu. "First post tomorrow," I remind him.

Stu glances at the address briefly before shoving it into his backpack. He turns to leave, then hesitates. His voice softens. "You sure you'll be okay here on your own? I can—"

"I'll be fine. Just make sure you get this done."

Stu looks at me for a second then nods. "Nae bother. I'll text you in the morning."

I let out a small sigh before turning around, relieved that the family is too busy chattering away to have witnessed any of this.

I run through a mental checklist to make sure everything is in place. The lasagna is bubbling in the oven, the salad is ready, and the tiramisu is sitting in individual pots in the fridge ready to be brought out. I wipe the counter clean and look around. Perfect.

That was delicious," Papa says to a chorus of murmured agreements.

"I don't know how you manage to do it every time," Zoe says, tilting the clear glass ramekin to scoop out the last of her tiramisu.

I smile, unable to resist a satisfied glance around the table. Papa's leaning back in his chair at the head of the table. On the other end, Mama's sipping on her wine. Across from me, Aseem looks happily drunk, his arm draped around Zoe's chair. I push my chair back and carry the empty dishes into the kitchen. There was a time when hosting elaborate dinner parties came naturally to me, but I'm out of practice. I stack the dishes in the sink for later and reach for the sherry glasses and arrange them on a tray with the decanter of Palo Cortado.

This is my life now.

And whether I like it or not, there are things I need to do to hold on to it.

I carry the tray to the table and start pouring the sherry into the crystal glasses one by one, taking care not to get any splashes on the antique mirrored tray Lorna spent hours polishing.

"I don't have a Punjabi liver like the rest of you," Zoe says, shaking her head when I hold a glass out toward her.

I resist the urge to laugh. When I first met Zoe, nearly a decade ago, I'd been amazed by her capacity for alcohol. That girl can drink for England, Owen had muttered after a particularly heavy night out in Soho. But then a few years ago, she set up her Instagram "business" and it was as though she developed a new personality overnight. How "adulting" correlates with giving up alcohol I'll never understand. Literally every teenager I knew growing up couldn't wait to be an adult simply so they could *start* drinking without fake IDs and indulgent uncles.

I turn my attention back to my father. "Have you decided how you'll celebrate your retirement?"

"It's a way off still," Papa says with a shake of his head.

"Six weeks is hardly that far, Papa," I say, feigning exasperation. "I was thinking, there's that new resort in Maui. Private island. *Very* exclusive. You could go there."

"The Fitz Clarence property?" Aseem says.

I nod.

"Don't they only allow four guests at a time?" Zoe asks, eyes wide, reminding me just how new she is to this world.

"It's not a problem. I can give Jake a call," I say, looking at my parents. Jake's the CEO and an old friend from university.

Papa shakes his head. "My only focus right now is this deal. Once it's done, we can spend the rest of our lives relaxing." He looks at Mama. "Then my time is all yours."

Mama rolls her eyes but her unaffected manner hides layers of hurt. She's had to put up with years of canceled holidays and unrealized plans. "So you keep saying."

I take a small sip of the sherry, enjoying the taste of honeyed fruit laced with the sharp acidic lift. I'd forgotten how much I missed this, the conversation, the familiarity, the *normalcy*.

But then, nothing about this conversation or this whole reunion is normal, is it?

I try to keep my voice light, breezy as I circle back to the topic. "We should start looking at investment options. Are you still thinking of putting your share into real estate, Aseem?"

Is it my imagination or do I see Zoe flinch?

"I'm going to wait and see," Aseem says. "Ashok uncle was telling me it might be a good time to get back into hydroponics."

I glance at Papa. Hydroponics is Aseem's pet project and Papa's pet peeve. We lost a good few million the last time Aseem tried to "get into it." The only good thing to come from Papa's stroke was that it forced Aseem to give up his ridiculous projects and settle into a role he's at least somewhat good at.

"Ashok *always* thinks it's a good time to get into hydroponics but I've yet to see him turn a profit," Papa mutters. He pushes his chair back to stretch the entire length of his body. "That's enough shoptalk for one night. Now what's the plan for tomorrow? Aisha should be at the jetty by nine?"

I look into my glass, trying to hide my disappointment. This is a conversation I need to have. Soon. "Yes," I say. "I'll leave here at half-eight."

"Take Aseem with you," Mama says, adjusting her nose-pin.

"Aseem doesn't even know how to sail. You know I've done this boat-trip on my own dozens of times, right?"

"That's not the point. I don't understand why you gave the servants the week off when you knew we were coming. Stu could have gone with you," Papa says. "He seems like a dependable fellow."

"Everyone needs time off, Papa," I say, suddenly exhausted. I'd clearly overestimated my family's capacity to manage without help. "Anyway, I thought you wanted it to be just family."

Papa looks at me like I've lost my mind. I can't blame him. Domestic help is like furniture in India: essential but invisible. But invisibility doesn't guarantee discretion.

"I want to come." Aseem jumps in, before Papa can say any more. "It'll be fun. But hang on," he pauses, a deep frown appearing on his face. "You've got life jackets, right?"

I throw my napkin at him. "Shut up."

"Stop it, you two," Papa says, at the same time as Mama says, "It'll be nice to have Aisha here."

"We haven't all been together since—" Aseem's words fade into a silence that no one knows how to fill.

I take a breath. The last time we were together, my life was falling apart. "Since the funeral," I finish for him, my voice soft.

The moment drags. A knife scrapes against a plate. Someone clears their throat.

"You know Sonal's engaged," Mama says suddenly, her brown eyes bright as she leans forward. "The boy's from the Oberoi family."

"Good for her," I say. Nothing like a bit of family gossip to lighten the mood.

"It's been arranged," Mama continues. "We've always left you kids to make your own decisions, but I worry about Aisha."

I resist the urge to roll my eyes. Across the table, Zoe fiddles with her napkin.

Mama has always had an endless capacity to reinvent the past.

"Aisha needs stability. I think it's time we spoke to her," Mama says.

I don't need to look at Aseem to know that we're thinking the same thing. There is no one less likely to agree to an arranged marriage than Aisha. Heck, if she knew we were as much as talking about it, she'd cancel the trip immediately; the money, the family, the holiday be damned.

"Mama, no," Aseem sighs.

"I'm just saying—"

"It's actually not a bad idea," Papa says. He runs a hand through his hair, thinking. "She can't keep living this nomad life forever. And her choice in men leaves a lot to be desired. Remember Javier?"

Zoe and I exchange a glance. Aisha has quite the talent for picking unsuitable men, but with his dreadlocked hair and beady eyes, Javier could have put all her other *bohemian* boyfriends to shame. I don't think I saw him sober even once in the three months that that particular fixation took to wear off. Aisha had met him at a week-long juice retreat in the Algarve—an employee, not a guest I might add—and when it was time for her to return to London, she brought him back with her. I would have passed him off as yet another one of Aisha's less than remarkable flings, except that he tried to hit on both Zoe and me within the space of an hour at Zoe's birthday party a couple of months later. That night had ended with Javier leaving with a bloodied nose, Zoe trembling with rage, Aisha in tears and Owen and me trying to pick up the pieces. But if I'm honest, what happened that night was no bad thing. Without the wake-up call, God knows how long it would have taken Aisha to see Javier for the leech that he was.

"She doesn't have the best track record with men," I say, raising my hands to indicate I'm not finished. "But I can't see her agreeing to an arranged marriage."

Or being happy in one, I think. My little sister is many things but perfect bahu is not one of them.

"I think we should speak to her," Mama repeats, looking straight at me. "An arranged marriage doesn't mean she has to marry a stranger. It's just like being set up—"

"But by your parents," I say, looking at Aseem over the rim of my glass, hoping for a little reinforcement, but he looks away. He's never been able to say no to Mama. "I'm not sure about this, Mama," I continue. "She'll find someone when she's ready."

"Give her some time," Zoe says, plucking a handful of grapes from the platter in front of her. "Sometimes you need to kiss a few frogs."

"I don't know," Aseem says, leaning back in his chair. "You got pretty lucky the first time."

Zoe scowls at him before her face melts into a smile. She reaches out to touch his hair and I look away, embarrassed both by their tenderness and the stab of longing it inspires in me.

I steal a quick glance at Zoe. The trouble is, even if you find your prince, it rarely guarantees a happy ever after.

5

ZOE

Everything okay with you two?

The words whirl around my head as I climb up the curving staircase and slip into our room.

After dinner, Papa had suggested a round of cards. Not something I'd ordinarily mind—God knows I've had to sit through enough evenings like that—but between Myra's comment, the endless reminiscing, and all that bloody talk about arranged marriages, I was on edge. And the idea of spending another few hours, smile plastered on, pretending I didn't know that every single person on that table had tried to dissuade Aseem from marrying me . . . I had to get out, get away. I'd hoped that Aseem would come with me, but when I said I was ready for bed, he just shrugged and told me he'd see me later.

Less than six hours with his family and it's started already.

Everything okay with you two?

I go into the bathroom and reach for my makeup wipes, carefully swiping away the layers of foundation, my skin pale and blotchy underneath.

Myra likes to leverage her position as the eldest daughter in the family to justify her nosiness but even so, why would she ask me something like that? Unless . . .

I dismiss the thought as soon as it occurs to me. Sure, things have been a bit hard, the stresses of the last couple of years have taken their toll on us both, but Aseem and I are in a good place right now. A *great* place. There is no way he would have said anything to her. Not with everything else that's going on.

No, Myra's remark, and the way she kept sneaking glances at Aseem and me all evening, probably has more to do with her own loneliness than anything else. I feel a pang of sympathy as I think of everything she's been through. She's the perfect one, Aisha had whispered before introducing me to Myra. And for a while, with her brilliant career and her rock-solid marriage, she really was. To have it all fall apart so quickly, so brutally . . . perhaps that's why she's so committed to renovating this island.

It's all she has left.

I turn on the taps in the enormous roll-top bath and peel off my jeans and jumper, running a hand along the angry red marks on my stomach where the waistband has been digging in all evening. After what happened in London, perhaps I need to relax.

I flick through Myra's guidebook as I wait for the bath to fill.

Eilean Kilbryde (island of Kilbryde) is a tidal island on the dramatic west coast of Scotland. With two thousand acres of varied flora and fauna, it is a car-free and carefree wilderness heaven with a number of beautiful and varied walks along the Atlantic coastline. Until the middle of the eighteenth century, Eilean Kilbryde was populated with a number of crofters. At the end of the nineteenth century Iain Macquarie, the architect favored by Scotland's aristocrats, was commissioned to remodel the main house as a private hunting lodge.

Since then, the island has enjoyed an illustrious reputation, hosting aristocrats, artists, and writers and those wanting to shut themselves off from the world amid breathtaking surroundings. In the 1920s, the island was given to Lady Augusta Blair as a wedding present by her future husband. It remained with the Blair family until 2001, during which several renovations and improvements were made to the estate. The island has been owned by Myra Agarwal-Conroy since 2017.

The island's history has clearly been, if not rewritten, then glossed over. I'd spent a considerable amount of time reading about the island when Myra first bought it. Truth is, Kilbryde had been one of the islands at the heart of the Highland clearances that had torn through Scotland in the eighteenth and nineteenth centuries. While other, smaller islands were prospering by using the land for sheep farming, Kilbryde was running into losses. The laird, James Mackenzie, who Myra's conveniently forgotten to mention in her guidebook, decided to empty the island by resettling his tenants and starting over. His plan was simple: eviction would be swift and sheep and profits would replace people. The tenants had no choice in the matter—homes would be set alight if they resisted. But unlike other lairds who had used similar methods with great, if brutal, success, Mackenzie didn't have the money or the means to resettle hundreds of people and his tenants knew that. They refused to leave the island, assuming Mackenzie wouldn't burn their homes down if they were still inside. They were wrong. Entire families were killed; hundreds of people burned alive in their own homes.

I put Myra's guidebook away and take a picture of the mist rising from the pearly, claw-footed bathtub—the mandatory #bathgoals shot that I'm not allowed to share—then watch the bath bomb sizzle through the water as the small ripples breaking the surface slowly morph into a dense white fog. I slink into the bath with a sigh, my body practically melting with relief.

Aseem and I were supposed to fly to London a couple of days before the family holiday, but at the very last moment Mama decided to surprise us by tagging along for a shopping weekend. I had to cancel several meetings at the last minute, but that's not what left me feeling infuriated. With her there, the weekend in London became an extension of life in Delhi with all of our plans amended to accommodate Mama's whims. I suppose I should thank my lucky stars that Aseem made me cancel the couples' spa day at Raffles—even the thought of having my mother-in-law tag along for champagne and strawberries in a candle-lit spa is enough to make me shudder.

I sink deeper into the bath, enjoying the sensation of the hot water against my skin, the uneasiness slowly slipping away as my muscles unclench. This time, I'll take a leaf from Aisha's playbook: Aseem and I will stop in London before we head back to Delhi, but Mama will only discover our plans when we fail to board the flight back to India.

By the time I climb out of the tub, the water's tepid and my playlist's run out. Other than the soft whoosh of the breeze as it pushes against the window, I can't hear a thing. No sounds filtering up from the kitchen, no appliances whirring in the background, no noises from the street. This house is completely silent, void of the usual sounds of a family home. It's the kind of quiet that feels pervasive, heavy, as though it carries in it echoes of the island's history.

I dry myself off and reach for one of the bottles of body lotion arranged artfully along the windowsill. As I work the lotion into my skin, my mind goes to the brief conversation I overheard earlier. Myra's always been extremely guarded, particularly around the help. That's why her dynamic with Stu, the ease they have around each other, feels so odd. It's completely out of character. Unless . . . I can't help but wonder if their relationship is as professional as she'd have us believe. He's certainly attractive enough, albeit in a wrong-side-of-the-tracks way. I run through the past few hours searching for clues, but my interactions with Stu have been far too brief to reveal anything of value. Perhaps I should've made an effort to be friendly. Nice.

Nice. It's one of the things *NB_lurker* thinks I should be more of.

There are also plenty of things he thinks I should be less of.

I extinguish the thoughts before they can take hold. I will *not* let myself think about the messages. I won't.

Threats uttered behind a screen aren't real.

I put the lotion away and unfasten my hair, letting it tumble down to my bare shoulders. I don't know if it is a side effect of being constantly visible, *seen*, on Instagram but as I stand there, stark naked, the sensation of being watched returns. I press my face up to the glass but all I can make out are the shapes of the fir trees clustered against black sky and, amidst all that darkness, my own pale body reflected in the window.

I'm about to step away when I notice a movement. I cup my hands around my face and that's when I see it, something moving through the trees that line the loch. A flash of blue in the blackness, the color so bright, so unnatural that it can only be a person.

I back away quickly and wrap myself up in a towel.

I remind myself that there's no one out there. The five of us are the only ones on this goddamned island.

It must have been a trick of the light. Or the overactive imagination my mother always blamed everything on.

I pick up my nightdress and go into the bedroom, desperate to get out of the bathroom, which has gone from warm and welcoming to chilly.

Perhaps the menace I keep sensing comes from knowing what really

went on here, from understanding the bloody history that Myra's trying to wash away with bottles of L'Occitane toiletries and vintage
champagne. Perhaps it's because I understand that the wilderness that
people love about Scotland is the result of centuries of violence and betrayal.

Or maybe it's because I know that no matter how lively our gatherings and how heartfelt our claims about family and loyalty, when it
comes down to it, we all have our own agendas.

And when push comes to shove, none of us will hesitate to take what
we believe is ours.

6.

MYRA

"A re you sure you know how to work this thing?" Aseem asks, looking suspiciously at the motorboat that will take us to the mainland. "Maybe we should ask Stu to drive us?"

"Stu's not here," I say, climbing in and unspooling the thick rope tying the boat to the jetty. One of the first things I did when I moved here was learn how to drive the RIB. Stu's great, but I refuse to be on an island with no way of getting myself off it in an emergency.

If the past few years have taught me anything, it is to always have my own back.

I shield my eyes with my hand and look up at Aseem as he moves from one foot to the other, gaze flitting between the boat and the water lapping against it. I resist the urge to roll my eyes. As a boy, Aseem had been adventurous to the point of recklessness. But now . . .

Perhaps the joy, and the curse, of family is being able to see multiple versions of the same person in any given moment, the past, the present and the what-if: the version that might have existed if history had played out differently. I take a breath of the clean, wet air and toss the life jacket at my brother. "Get in, you wuss," I say, returning Aseem's worried look with a scowl that is only slightly mean.

I slip on my sunglasses and tilt my face up toward the rising sun as we set off, enjoying the unexpected warmth. If I didn't know better, I might have thought we were in the Med, not the Atlantic. I zip my coat all the way to the top. The wind is on our side right now but if there's one thing I've learned, it's that in Scotland the weather can turn in an instant.

"You know Papa hasn't stopped talking about you for months, right? Ever since you sent that promotional video over. At this rate you'll have half of Delhi queuing up for a booking before you even launch," he says.

"That's the idea," I say, smiling. Aseem's never stopped complaining about the soft spot that he insists Papa has for me. I laugh it off as usual, but I can't help but wish that he's right. Papa's favor carries weight and, with the sale looming, equity. "Jealous much?"

"Always." He grins back.

I'd paid a London ad agency a small fortune to put that video together: a montage of clips showing a young couple enjoying the island at its natural, untamed best before coming back to enjoy five-star luxury in the historic house.

I watch the sunlight dance across the water as we glide through it. The agency had suggested using a family—two cute kids to complete the picture—but there I'd put my foot down. I don't need a video of some picture-perfect family enjoying my island haunting me. My brain is more than capable of doing that unassisted.

Aseem's voice pulls me back to the present. "Are you still planning to open in the summer?"

Even the roar of the engine can't drown out the doubt in his voice.

The agency wants to follow the teaser video with a no-expenses-spared press trip in July before we open to the public in September. The plan is to have the house and all the cottages refurbished, the pool installed and the helipad and staff apartments ready by the end of May. Less than four months to go and all I've crossed off that particular list is the house.

The plan isn't working.

"Ideally, yes," I say. "There are nearly a hundred workmen scheduled to start at the end of the month. The architect has promised they'll be finished by May."

If I keep up the payments.

"That must be costing a fortune." Aseem frowns.

"It is, but it'll pay off." I turn my head slightly to look at him. With his hair slicked back by the wind and his eyes hidden behind gold-rimmed sunglasses, Aseem looks remarkably like Papa. The same wide nose, the same slight shadow that not even the closest shave can vanquish, the same business brain. The only thing missing is a mustache, the defining feature for most men of our father's generation that our generation did away with. "In fact," I add, "I was thinking, once the sale goes through, we should look at getting you and Aisha on board."

"On board?"

"As investors."

"I didn't know you were looking for funding."

I feel myself stiffen, thinking about the stack of unpaid bills and letters from the bank.

"I'm not. But this place . . . it's going to be a smashing success, Aseem. I can feel it." I pull my gaze away from the water and look him in the eye. "I don't want you guys to miss out."

Three hundred million pounds sounds like a lot of money, but there are taxes to consider and depending on *how* Papa splits the shares, it may or may not be enough. Having a back-up plan in place is the sensible thing to do. And it's not as if I'm trying to trick my siblings. Once the retreat is up and running, they *will* see returns.

"So you're planning on staying here long-term?"

I shrug.

"Myra," he says, touching my shoulder. "You could move back home, you know."

My face must betray my surprise because he backtracks immediately.

"Not with Mama and Papa. I meant that you don't have to stay here by yourself. You could come home. Move back to Delhi?"

Or to Edinburgh.

The unspoken words hang between us, as real and taut as the invisible string that binds us together.

"I've got a plan with this place, you know," I say. I'm going for breezy but I come off sounding defensive instead.

"I know you do," Aseem says, softly. "You can hire people to run the retreat or you could flip it, sell it to a developer. After the work you've done, you'll make a killing."

I tighten my grip on the wheel, seeking comfort in its solidity. Sure, my record over the past couple of years has been less than stellar, but is this really how little my own brother thinks of me?

"It's your life," Aseem continues. "But Myra . . . do you really *want* to be here, on your own? It's a fucking island in the middle of nowhere."

It's obvious what he's really asking is if Owen and I are finally over. But the failings of my marriage are not up for discussion. I chose this life. And come what may, I'm going to make a success of it.

"Look, there have been no more threats since we took possession, so where I decide to live is beside the point," I say, finally. "We both know that once I'm done, this island is going to be worth a hundred times what it is now." That part at least is true. "I thought you'd want in on that. But if you'd rather try hydroponics *again*, that's fine. It's your money."

I feel a flash of regret as my words land and Aseem's face darkens.

"Let me think about it," he says.

Translation: let me ask my wife. Mama's right, Aseem is far too easily influenced by Zoe.

Almost on cue, he brings her up. "Zoe had a bit of a scare last night. She thought she saw someone in the woods."

I raise my eyebrows. Zoe has always been a drama queen.

Aseem fixes me with a look. "We're the only ones on the island, right?"

"Uh-huh," I say, shifting my focus back to the water.

As the greenish smudge of the mainland comes into view, I switch gears and fix my thoughts on Aisha, the most uncomplicated of us siblings. Talking to her feels easy, Owen used to say, back when I still cared about what he thought.

Even from this distance, it's impossible to miss Aisha. She's dressed in a bright yellow puffer jacket and jeans. Somehow even at twenty-seven, Aisha can get away with dressing and, let's face it, acting like an eight-year-old. I exchange a bemused smile with Aseem. She's jumping up and down, waving at us with both hands, an image we're both achingly familiar with.

It's only as we're pulling into the slip that I realize that there's a problem with the image.

"What the fuck?" I say, looking at Aseem. His face shows the same combination of disbelief and outrage that's rippling through me.

I throw the line around the cleat of the RIB and yank it back, tightening the noose. I should have known she'd pull something like this.

"Let's give her a chance to explain," Aseem says, reading my mind, and I nod. Making excuses for Aisha comes naturally to us both, even if those excuses convince no one, least of all us.

The thing is Aisha *is* uncomplicated. But that doesn't mean she's predictable.

Or that she plays by the rules.

I suck in my breath and step on to the dock. There is nothing to explain.

Aisha isn't alone.

I arrange my face into a smile and pull Aisha toward me, startled by how different she looks up close. It's obvious how much weight she's lost, but it's not just how skinny she is; her hair is different too, longer than I've ever seen it with the ends teased into soft layers and streaked purple.

And then there's the smell. Tobacco.

"Who is he?" I whisper.

Aisha frees herself from my grip and wraps herself around the man who is without doubt responsible for these changes.

"Myra, Aseem, this is Gabe," she says, tilting her head back to look at him. He's tall, with hooded eyes and tanned skin that screams of long days spent lying in the sun.

Gabe glances from me to Aseem and back again, before holding his hand out for me to shake. "Gabriel," he says. "Aish has told me so much about you."

I look him over. He's handsome, all of Aisha's boyfriends are, but in his dark gray suit—complete with a tie and cufflinks—and Oxfords that are so well polished they'd put a boarding school master to shame, he looks like he's headed to a gala dinner in London, not a remote

Scottish island. For god's sake, Aisha, I want to yell out. Instead, I offer a polite smile. "I'm afraid we can't say the same."

"Babe, why don't I go get us all some coffees while you guys catch up," he says, taking the hint. He drops a kiss on top of Aisha's head before turning around. We watch him walk across the empty parking lot toward the shuttered kiosk.

"Who is he?" I repeat when he's out of earshot.

Aisha frowns. "I just told you." She hesitates for a second, then adds, "Gabe's my boyfriend."

"Why is he here, Aisha?" I ask.

"Wow. Okay," she says, taking a step back. "He's here because I wanted you all to meet him."

I force myself to take a breath.

"Is he staying?" Aseem cuts to the chase.

"Of course he's staying." Aisha looks around the empty parking lot, incredulous. "Where do you expect him to go?"

"You can't be serious." Aseem says, rubbing his face. "You know how much this week means to Mama and Papa."

"I'm here, aren't I?"

Neither Aseem nor I know how to respond. In the distance, I can see that Gabe's managed to persuade Michelle to open up. I can't see her expression, but I know from experience that she won't be impressed. Her Saturday lie-ins are sacred.

I glance at my phone, momentarily distracted by the text from Stu letting me know he's dropped the paperwork off at the Glasgow post office as promised. I zoom in to look at the delivery date on the proforma then shove my phone into my pocket. At least there's one person I can count on not to create any drama.

"Why are you guys making such a big deal out of this?"

"Because you lied, Aish," I say, unable to hide my frustration any longer. "You didn't really miss your flight, did you? And *Gabe*? This is my home. You can't bring some random guy here without checking with me first. I didn't even know he existed until five minutes ago."

"First, he's not some random guy. And second, what good would telling you have done? You aren't exactly rolling out the red carpet, are you?"

I sigh. "You know what, Aisha; I haven't got the energy for this right now. This is not about you or whoever your latest man is. This is about Mama and Papa. We're here to celebrate their anniversary."

"Sure, that's what this trip is about. Mama and Papa's *anniversary*," she scoffs.

I try to keep the annoyance out of my mind—and my heart—but Aisha can make it so challenging.

"You know what Papa's like about this kind of stuff," Aseem says, stepping in. "He wants this trip to be family only."

Aisha nods. "Right. Family only. That makes sense," she pauses. "So it's okay for Zoe to be here. Because she's family."

"Yes," Aseem says, ever patient. *Trusting.*

I know exactly where she's going with this and it's not going to be pretty.

"Only that's not how it started off, is it?" Aisha says, warming to her point.

I throw a quick glance at Aseem, but his face is unreadable. "That was different," he says, his voice tight.

"Why? Your secret girlfriend was attending every family holiday as my friend well before she was 'family.' At least I'm not lying to everyone about who I'm with."

"That's not fair," Aseem says. "You know why—"

"No, what's not fair is that you get to do whatever the fuck you want but I need permission to introduce my partner to my family."

Partner?

"Aisha—" I start but she cuts me off.

"Whatever, okay. I don't care," she says, sticking her chin out. It would be adorable if it weren't for the steely determination in her eyes. "This is the man I love," she continues, her voice low but strong. "And the only way I'm getting on that boat is with him."

7

ZOE

It's weird. To anyone watching, we'd look like a normal family. Food passes around the table as easily as the conversation, plates full with a mishmash of classic brunch dishes and invented family favorites, but there's an edge to the banter, a sharpness beneath the polite questions that feels as acrid as the ginger in Mama's egg bhurji.

I can feel Mama watching me as I stab a piece of spinach with my fork and lift it to my mouth. I'm sitting sandwiched between Myra and Aseem, with Aisha and Gabe seated directly across from us.

There's no getting away from it: Gabe is very good-looking. He's tall and muscular, with intense eyes and thick, honey blond hair that flops down to his forehead every time he looks down. He's taken his jacket off and draped it across the back of his chair, revealing a thick neck and a crisp white shirt. It's clear a lot of thought has gone into dressing "right" to meet his heiress girlfriend's family, but all his expensive suit does is betray how desperate he is to fit in. Not a look that goes down well with the Agarwal clan.

"Have long have you lived in California?" Papa asks, from his usual position at the head of the table.

"Just a couple of months," Gabe says. He's smiling but I can tell he's flustered. With his peppered mustache and low, deep voice that lends an air of gravitas to every conversation, Papa has that effect on people.

I help myself to some more juice while Gabe tells everyone his life story with a touch too much enthusiasm: he got a job in London straight after university, made some smart investments, then used the money to fund a move to Hong Kong. He met Aisha in Singapore over Christmas and after *six whole weeks* of long distance, packed up his bags and his "mega-successful" business, and moved to LA to be with her.

I have to admit, even I'm taken aback by that. Surely no one can wind up a business that quickly, let alone a successful one. And if they can, well, what's taking my husband so long?

"What kind of work are you in?" I ask.

"Finance. I grew up with two art historians for parents so typically I took the opposite route. I run my own financial management firm. Williamson Capital? We're one of the best performing investors in Asia, ninety percent returns this last quarter."

This makes Myra look up. "Ninety percent is pretty unusual," she says, fork and knife poised over a loaded pao.

"Not for us, it isn't," Gabe says, beaming. "I've basically transformed my fund into a personal investment vehicle. I specialize in high-risk, high-reward opportunities, so it's not for everyone, but I've already given my midterm investors over a two hundred percent ROI. The next five years are going to be even better. I'm in the middle of launching our American arm now."

I sit back and cross my legs. All the financial advisers Aseem's family works with come from the same stock. They start their pitch—and it's pretty obvious that's what this is—with a big speech about forging relationships and understanding the individual needs and wants of each investor, then focus on risk mitigation and asset preservation with some low-risk opportunities thrown in. Gabe's approach is different. Aggressive. I suddenly see why Aisha's drawn to him: underneath the well-cut suit is a gambler.

"That won't be easy," Papa says, frowning. "American finance is a tough industry to break into. All those old-money families . . . they don't always trust newcomers."

"I'm not sure that's true anymore," Gabe says. "If you can double or triple their money, people don't care where you come from. Whether it's old money or new, the key word in the business is money, right? That's all the mega-rich care about."

Aseem and I exchange a quick glance. Our distaste is reflected around the table. Gabe isn't wrong, but to state it so plainly . . . I don't think he realizes how crude he sounds. The only one oblivious to it is Aisha.

"People are still queuing up to work with him," Aisha says, happily munching away on some passion fruit. "Didn't Elon Musk's office call you the other day, babe?"

At least he has the wherewithal to look embarrassed. "We're closed to new investors right now, but if any of you are ever looking to diversify your portfolio, I'd be happy to help."

"You're entering a new market but you're closed to investors?" Papa asks, reaching for a grapefruit.

Gabe lifts his champagne flute to his lips, draining half the glass in one gulp. "At the level that we operate, I can only really handle four or five clients at a time." He pauses to swallow the remainder of his drink. "We have a ten million intake minimum. Quality over quantity."

"Is that so?" Papa says, his words sharper than the serrated knife in his hand. He slices the fruit in one smooth motion, two tiny drops of blood orange landing on the white tablecloth.

Gabe sets his cutlery down, opens his mouth as if to say something, then closes it again.

"Well, I think that's very impressive," Mama says before anyone can say anything. She smiles indulgently when Gabe nods. "And it's so sweet that you'd risk giving all that up to be with Aisha."

"Thank you," Gabe says, his relief apparent. "I love what I do, but all the money and success in the world is useless if you don't have someone to share it with. It's something my dad always says, family first, money second." He reaches for Aisha's hand, lacing his fingers through hers.

"That's a lovely sentiment. Raj started from scratch and built the business from the ground up as well, so I know exactly what the early years are like," Mama continues. It's a story we've all heard hundreds of times and I tune out as she goes on to explain how all Papa had when he started was ten thousand rupees in the bank and an idea. She wipes her mouth, then sets her napkin down and looks straight at Gabe. "Raj was so committed to making the business a success, he wouldn't even have *considered* stepping away or starting again somewhere else. It would've been too much of a risk and we certainly didn't have the money to squander away, not with little mouths to feed."

No one speaks. The sound of heavy cutlery scratching against delicate china reverberates across the table as everyone focuses on their food, unwilling to acknowledge the distinctly uncomfortable turn this conversation has taken. Or the part that Mama's played in it.

"Things are different now, Mama," Aisha says, shrugging. Next to her Gabe looks confused.

Mama pats her lips dry with a napkin before pushing her chair back and walking around the table to stand behind Aisha. She places her bony hands on her youngest daughter's shoulders gently, the two and a half carat diamond on her finger casting a pattern on the ceiling. "Oh, I'm sure they are, darling," she says, bending to kiss Aisha on the side of her head. "I'm sure they are."

8.

MYRA

It's hard not to spend the entire meal observing Gabe.

For someone who thought it appropriate to bring a bottle of Fortnum's own brand champagne to a family celebration, he certainly has no qualms helping himself to glass after glass of vintage brut.

I tear my eyes away from Gabe and look at Aisha. She's beaming, chair pulled close to Gabe, head resting on his shoulder. I do a quick calculation, working out the timeline of their relationship. Aisha met Gabe over Christmas. The rumors about the sale started doing the rounds in November, which means Gabe had plenty of time to do his research and orchestrate a run-in. It doesn't take too much of a leap of imagination to work out what his motive might be. Papa is the sole shareholder in the business and the press has spent months speculating about how he might divide his fortune between his children.

As have I, but that's beside the point.

Aisha might be fooled by his "chase love not money" spiel, but I've come across far too many men like Gabe to see it as anything other than what it is: a narrative constructed to reel Aisha in.

I take a sip of my coffee, savoring the bitter taste on my tongue.

I've spent so long looking after Aisha, trying to keep her safe, that to see her with this charlatan feels like a personal insult. But it's more than that.

None of Aisha's past boyfriends pretended to be anything other than what they were: opportunists who were openly and unashamedly taking advantage of her naivety and Papa's bank balance. But with his self-satisfied smirk and claims of running a successful investment firm, Gabe is different.

And that makes him dangerous.

M y suggestion to go on a walking tour of the island is shot down before I've even finished the sentence: Aisha is too tired from the journey, Zoe still has her mysterious jet lag, and Aseem needs to work. Instead we settle on a compromise: a short walk down to the loch followed by chai and taash in front of the fire. It's not quite the introduction to the island I'd originally planned, but it'll have to do.

"Let's go," I yell as I step from the porch into the cold bite of the early afternoon.

Mama's the first one out. "It's freezing," she says, pushing her hands deep into her pockets.

It is. The sun has slid behind a light veil of clouds and there is a sharpness to the day, a clarity that often accompanies a drop in temperature.

"You'll warm up once we start walking," I say. I close the distance between us and run my hands up and down her arms, her tiny frame lost in the thick puffer jacket she's borrowed from me. The action sparks a memory from a lifetime ago, when Mama would parent us, not the other way around. How quickly and irreversibly those roles had changed, along with Mama's entire personality. I can hardly remember the feisty, self-assured woman who never let her responsibilities rob her of an opportunity to have fun.

I share tidbits about the island's history and topography as we stumble over patches of uneven ground. A hush falls over the group as we cut through the pine trees and turn into a path that's so narrow and so steep we're forced to walk in a single file. Every now and then I stop to look over my shoulder, checking to make sure everyone's following me. I thought seeing my family would help, that surrounded by familiar faces I'd feel less lonely.

Instead I'm assaulted by outrageous longing.

Nothing could have prepared me for the rush of feelings last night, watching Zoe and Aseem so wrapped up in each other. Their tenderness made me nostalgic for a time when Owen and I had that. I'd checked finding a soulmate off my list an hour after my first date with Owen. It was that instant, our connection.

Our separation came just as quickly.

As the path widens and the loch comes into view, Papa catches up with me so we're walking side by side. I follow his gaze toward the small cross on our right. One of the many gravesites that dot this land.

"Has there been any more trouble?" he asks.

I shake my head. The lawsuit was just one of the battles we'd had to fight before we could buy this island. In the months preceding the completion, Owen and I had faced relentless opposition from the locals. Vigils, marches, threatening letters, we'd seen it all. The community—which hasn't lived here in decades, I might add—wanted Kilbryde restored but they balked at the idea of change. At one point, it got so bad Owen and I seriously considered withdrawing our offer. Thank goodness we stood our ground, though—the threats pretty much disappeared after we won the lawsuit.

"What is it then? You seem anxious," Papa says, his read on me as sharp as ever.

"Nothing. It's nice having everyone here." I lower my voice. "Well, almost everyone."

Papa laughs, a full, deep laugh that's so familiar, so comforting that it's all I can do not to bury my face in his shoulder and tell him everything.

But my father has never responded to weakness.

"I like it here," he says, after a moment. "It's calm . . . different."

"Good," I say. "You should spend more time here." I hesitate, then add, "In fact, I've been thinking, maybe you and Mama could come and stay for a while after you retire? It'll make for a nice change of pace."

"I think you and I both know your mama doesn't do 'nature' very well. She'll never be able to adjust to life without her hairdresser. She paid that crook fifty thousand rupees last week and I swear her hair looks exactly the same as before."

I laugh. Even I have to agree that five hundred pounds is a bit much for a cut and color. "I can set up one of the cottages for you, perhaps the one right next to the spa. With a hairdresser on payroll." I give my father a cheeky smile.

"You have always been the strategic one," Papa laughs. "But I doubt even the lure of a spa will cut it. Our family, our business . . . it's all evolving. And your mother . . ." He sighs, refusing to utter the words we all know are true.

Mama isn't adapting.

"So you're not going back to law?" he asks after a minute.

I shake my head. Returning to my practice means returning to Edinburgh. And I just . . . can't. "There's so much potential here." I look around at the acres of wilderness, at the loch with ribbons of mist floating above it, seeing both the space that exists and the future it represents. "You've seen the buzz a teaser video's created. I want Kilbryde to be the only name people think of when they think of a luxury island retreat."

"And what about Owen? I thought this was something the two of you wanted to do together."

"Plans change."

He sighs. Another sound I'm familiar with, only this one reminds me of all the ways I've disappointed him. "It's time to let it go, beta. Take him back."

I don't respond. I can't.

"Living here, hiding from your husband, your friends, giving up the career you worked so hard for. You're isolating yourself and you'll regret it. This might be different, but it's not sustainable. It's not you," Papa says. The sympathy in his voice makes the words sting even more.

Or perhaps it's hearing the truth, laid out so simply, that stings. I've spent the past two years wondering how my life has gone so spectacularly off the rails. I'm one of the top barristers in the country. I'm smart. I'm resilient.

Yet here I am. Hiding. Terrified of what I might find if I return to my old life.

I take a breath and turn to look at Papa as we come to a stop, the loch stretching out in front of us. I can hear Aisha's chatter in the background. Was there a time when I sounded that free? That relaxed?

Aseem looks like he's about to say something as he walks past us, then shakes his head and carries on along the shore, laughing and reaching out to steady Mama as she loses her footing. Zoe and Aisha go off toward the jetty, Gabe trailing after them.

"You're the one I've never had to worry about," Papa continues. "But right now, I'm worried about you. We all are."

I kick at the pebbles that lie along the bank, digging my toe into the damp earth, the mud coloring my trainers a dirty brown.

"I can't go back," I say. "I won't survive it if I do." My voice sounds clipped but right now, it's the best I can do.

"Myra, look at me." Papa lifts my chin, forcing me to look at him. "You can't go through life alone and Owen is a *good* man. The two of you had a good life together. Don't throw that away. You put all this pressure on yourself, but sweetheart, you need to realize you have nothing to prove and nothing to be ashamed of. Every marriage has its ups and downs."

"But—" I start but he silences me with a look.

"Mama and I will always be there for you, but Owen isn't going to wait forever. Promise me you'll think about what I've said," Papa continues.

A long beat passes. He raises his eyebrows.

Owen and I did have a good life together. We *were* happy. Deliriously happy. And then just when we were on the cusp of having everything we wanted, Owen destroyed me in ways that Papa can never understand. He took everything, every last bit of hope from me and left me hollow, a caricature of the person I used to be.

And for that I can never forgive him.

But that's not what my father wants to hear.

Papa's right: I have always been strategic.

"I'll think about it," I say.

"Good girl," Papa says, patting my cheek. He picks up a pebble, then swings his arm back and throws it into the loch in a perfect arc, the stone slicing through the water without so much as a ripple. Quick and effective, that's always been Papa's MO.

He turns around to face me. "Now what are we going to do about your sister and that idiot boyfriend of hers?"

9.

ZOE

Despite the awkwardness earlier, everyone seems to be on good behavior as we make our way to the loch. Myra and Papa are speaking quietly as they lead the group. Aseem and Mama are walking a few feet behind them, which leaves Aisha, Gabe, and me at the back, an arrangement I'm entirely happy with. I haven't had the chance to catch up properly with Aisha since she got here, and my curiosity about Gabe has only grown since brunch.

"I can't believe how long it's been since I've seen you, Zo," Aisha says. We walk arm-in-arm, our trainers slipping and sliding over thousands of shiny pebbles as we approach the jetty. "I feel like everything I know about your life comes from Instagram now. Or Mama," she adds after a moment's pause. "She does do an exceptional job of keeping me informed."

I laugh and give her arm a squeeze, realizing suddenly just how much I've missed her. There was a time when we were inseparable, when there was no topic off-limits, nothing we didn't share. When we first met outside City University, we were just two eighteen-years-olds trying to find our way to the freshers' orientation. But that initial awkwardness led to a friendship that was as intense as it was enduring, and back then we told each other everything. *Everything.* I was used to hiding behind a facade with everyone else, but with Aisha, there was never any point. She could see right through me right from the beginning. She's the only one who knows the full extent of my issues with my parents and the only one who's never judged me for it. She took on the mother-of-the-bride duties when my mother refused to fly to India two days before my wedding. When I wept for four days straight after my father died, she was the only one who understood that my tears were those of relief and that I wasn't looking for sympathy or condolence, just regular refills of wine.

"Things have just been so busy these past few months . . ." I trail off, guilt and regret niggling away at me. I flick a quick look at Aisha to see if she'll press me further, demand I come clean, but her gaze is focused firmly on the path ahead as we climb up the narrow steps.

"So Aseem mentioned the new brand partnerships. Chloe *and* Balenciaga? You must be so proud," she says instead.

"I am."

I fill Aisha in on the new campaigns and my plans for the next quarter, her excitement encouraging me to share more. Life in Delhi is far from easy, but despite all the hiccups and setbacks, I have achieved a lot and it's nice to hear someone finally acknowledge that.

We walk right to the edge of the jetty, then sit down on the wooden planks, our legs dangling over the glassy water. I twist to see if Gabe's behind us, but he's walked past the jetty, his mobile phone held out in front of him like a beacon as he attempts to find signal. There is something incredibly familiar about him, and yet the more I try to pin it down, the more it evades me. . . .

I unzip my pocket and look at my own phone. Nothing.

"You know everyone thinks you've started smoking because of

Gabe," I say, as Aisha pulls out a pack of Marlboro Lights from her jacket pocket.

"Of course they do." She unfurls the plastic wrapping and flicks the packet open with one quick, practiced motion. I shake my head as she holds the cigarettes toward me.

"Go on," she urges, flashing a grin the devil would envy. "We'll just blame it on Gabe."

I can't help but laugh. I've never smoked in front of Mama and Papa, but that's not what this is. "I'm trying to quit."

She rolls her eyes, then tips her head back and blows out three perfect rings of smoke. Aisha spent the best part of our first term at university trying to teach me how to blow rings, but I never quite mastered that particular skill. I enjoyed smoking, loved the quick release that came with exhaling a puff of smoke into a cold night, but blowing rings required something I just didn't have back then: patience. I spot Aseem talking to Papa from the corner of my eye. Almost a decade later, patience is something I still struggle with.

I turn my attention back to Aisha.

"Can you believe Myra's put Gabe and me in separate rooms?"

I laugh. It's ridiculous but I can one hundred percent believe it.

Aisha exhales a long plume of white smoke. She peels her eyes away from the water and nods toward the figures standing further along the shore. Mama and Papa are throwing pebbles into the lake, while Aseem and Myra cheer them on. "They don't like him, do they?"

I open my mouth to protest then close it without uttering a word. What would be the point?

"I need your support, Zo," Aisha continues. "You know my family, always wary of anyone who doesn't fit the mold."

I nod, remembering being on the other side. I'd known the Agarwals for years before Aseem and I started dating, but despite the fact that I'd become a regular fixture at their holidays and get-togethers as Aisha's best friend, when it came to accepting me as their future daughter-in-law, Mama and Papa needed persuading. A lot of persuading. A job that had fallen squarely on Aisha's skinny shoulders.

I look at her closely. Aisha is a textbook rebel. She enjoys provoking her family and though she'll never admit it, I've always thought that she picks her boyfriends based on where they might fall on Mama and Papa's disapproval scale. She enjoys the drama that comes with bringing an inappropriate man home. But this feels different. "So it's serious then, with Gabe?"

"It is." She pauses, stubs out her cigarette. "I didn't like him when we first met. I found him a little too . . . slick."

I nod. "I have been wondering how you fell for a guy in a suit."

"The suit is for the family, I fell for the package underneath." She smirks at me. "In all seriousness though, even dressed in normal clothes, he was just so keen. He actually wrote a list."

"A list?"

"Of all the reasons why I should have dinner with him. I agreed— just to get him off my back—and he took me to this fancy restaurant that you can only get to by chopper. And when we got there, there was a string quartet waiting. *On a first date.* It was all so extra. It was also bloody clever—I literally had no choice but to sit through the meal." She looks at me, eyes twinkling. "Uber doesn't do choppers yet."

I laugh. "I'm guessing by the end of the meal you were charmed?"

"Not the end of the meal, but pretty soon after. I've never felt this way about a man, Zo. When I'm with him, it's like everything just fits. He's so spontaneous and fun and he just does not hold back. And he makes me so, so happy." She looks at her hands, her voice wobbling slightly. "He reminds me of Ishaan."

"Oh Aish." I slide closer and wrap my arm around her, the gesture reminiscent of the long evenings we spent squashed together on the sofa, dissecting every detail of her conversations with her parents, strategizing ways to prove to them I was perfect for their son.

"If anyone knows how difficult my family can be, it's you," she says. "Talk to Aseem. Once he gets to know Gabe, he'll see how brilliant and charming and amazing he is. As will you." She fixes me with a look. "Please Zo, tell me you'll try?"

I shouldn't get involved, not when things are already so complicated.

But one look at Aisha, her big brown eyes shimmering with grief and longing, and any resolve I might've had melts. If anyone deserves to find happiness, it's Aisha. She has been through enough already.

"Of course I will," I promise.

The sun hasn't set yet, but the sky is mottled with dark clouds, and the woods, as we cut through them, are cloaked in darkness.

I loop my arm through Aseem's. "I saw you speaking to Papa earlier. Was that . . . ?" I look at my husband, hoping for some reassurance, but he's miles away. I tighten my grip on his arm. "Aseem?"

"Yes?" he says, his voice abrupt. "Sorry, I was distracted. What is it?"

I sigh. I know how much pressure he's under and the last thing I want to do is add to it, but this is an important week for both of us. Would it kill him to keep me in the loop?

I lower my voice an octave. "Did you talk to Papa?"

"Not yet."

I try to keep the disappointment from my face. Papa's always maintained that an undivided estate means an undivided family, but I think it's simply his way of controlling us. Though they'd never admit it, all three of his children crave his attention and his approval, and he enjoys the power it affords him. He likes pitting them against each other, enjoys watching them bend over backward to please him. Why else would he insist that the trust wouldn't be split equally or that he would only announce how the money is being split when the *time is right*?

Aseem managed to sneak a look at a draft of the distribution letter before we left Delhi. It's more than fair, but the trouble is I'm not sure if Aisha and Myra will see it that way. And the longer Papa takes to make the announcement, the higher the likelihood that one of them will do something to change his mind.

When Papa had the stroke a few years ago, Aseem had to give up everything—his own dreams, his career, *everything*—to step in. He took over PetroVision, looked after the family, and I supported him. Now it's time for them to support us.

"Is there a problem?" I speak slowly, trying to instill calm into my voice even as my brain races with all the ways this could go wrong.

The pause before Aseem speaks seems to stretch forever. "I think Papa wants to make sure the deal is as good as done before he makes any changes to the trust . . . which it is. They're sending me the paperwork this evening so I'll nip into Myra's office before dinner. It'll be fine."

I frown, unconvinced. "You look worried."

"I—" Aseem starts, shakes his head, then starts again. "I am worried, but not about the sale," he says. I follow his gaze a few feet to our right to where Aisha and Gabe are walking, hands clasped, dopey, teenage smiles on both their faces. Aisha looks smitten.

"Come on. He's not *that* bad," I say.

"He's obsessed with money."

I sigh. How to explain to someone who's never wanted for anything how large money looms in the minds of those who grew up without any? "He's an investor and frankly, he's probably nervous. Your family can be pretty intimidating, you know."

"Are you saying that guy is right for her? I mean, look at him. He looks like some sleazy marketing guy."

I take a breath. Sure, he's a bit overeager and there is definitely a humility problem there, but Gabe's been nothing but polite and attentive since he arrived. To most, it would look like he's making an effort. But the Agarwals aren't like most families, especially when it comes to Aisha. She could bring home Prince William and they'd still find him lacking. After what happened with Ishaan, it's understandable that they're so overprotective, but Aisha's right. Gabe deserves a chance.

Just like I did all those years ago.

"Remember when we first met?" I ask.

"Yes," Aseem says, but there is wariness in his eyes. He knows me too well not to guess where this is going. "You were beautiful and charming and completely irresistible."

"I was also broke, living rent-free in Aisha's spare bedroom, and working as a waitress. Gabe, on the other hand, seems pretty well settled."

"Or so he says. Anyway, our situation was different." His voice is even and low, but I can hear the frustration building behind it. Aseem and I rarely revisit our complicated history but that doesn't mean it's not there.

"Was it?" I press on. "It seems quite similar to me."

Aseem doesn't say anything, walking silently by my side. As we catch glimpses of the house through the trees, we pick up pace, all of us eager to get out of these dark woods. I stop walking and put a hand on Aseem's arm, forcing him to halt. I wait until everyone's out of earshot before speaking.

"Everyone thought I was using my friendship with Aisha to trap you. They were convinced what we had wasn't real. I know you think Gabe's got an agenda—" I pause, picking my words carefully, "—and there's a chance you're right. But Aisha is serious about him and there is also a chance that he's exactly the kind of man she needs. Just like your sister's working-class, smoking hot BFF was exactly what you needed."

He narrows his eyes. His gaze is cold, unnerving. "Not everything is about class, Zoe."

"That's not what I—"

"I think you're getting far too emotional about this. Gabe is not your problem to deal with. And there are far more important things we need to talk about right now."

The already freezing evening air seems to drop another couple of degrees. Aseem turns to look at his family. They are several meters ahead of us, the house shining like a golden beacon in front of them.

The trouble with keeping secrets is that you constantly worry about them being revealed.

I swallow. "What—"

Aseem twists around and cups my face between his gloved hands. "It's time. Are you ready?"

The panic takes a few seconds to dissipate. A smile spreads across my face as I realize what he means.

"Zo?" Aseem looks at me, hand stretched out.

I take his hand. "I'm ready."

10

MYRA

We end up back in the living room, all of us tired from the walk but hesitant to leave each other's company just yet.

I take one sip of what is meant to be masala chai—or Zoe's version of it—and set the cup down. Too much elaichi and not enough adrak. Surely the first step to *adulting* is being able to make a decent cup of tea.

I look at the cards on the floor and back again at the ones fanned out in my hand. I do the math.

"Aish, I'm calling your bluff." I pick up the top five cards and flip them over. Three queens, a jack, and an ace. "Ha," I say, pushing the cards toward Aisha.

"Hang on, no, I said three queens," Aisha says.

Gabe looks confused.

"I don't understand this game," Zoe says, even though we've been playing it for years. She's sitting cross-legged on the floor in front of me, her back pressed into Aseem's legs. "Why can't we play regular poker?"

We pushed the furniture to the edges of the living room to make space and yet Aseem and Zoe are welded together like a pair of newly-weds. It's nauseating.

"We're back to the old days, then. You lot bickering . . ." Papa says.

"And Aisha cheating," Aseem says.

"Don't pick on your little sister," Mama says, but Aseem shakes his head.

"You said five queens, Aish," Aseem continues. "If you're going to bluff, at least make it believable."

"Fine, whatever. Your turn, Myra," Aisha scowls.

Zoe looks at the cards in her hand and then back at Aseem. They're playing as a team. *Obviously.* "Actually," she says, placing the cards face down on the floor and then tipping her head back to look at Aseem, "we have an announcement to make."

I glance at Aisha but she just shrugs. It can't be about the trust. There's no way that Papa would let Aseem make *that* announcement. I look at Papa for confirmation but his eyes are elsewhere. In the corner, Gabe's helping himself to yet another glass of scotch.

For fuck's sake.

I turn my attention back to Zoe as she continues speaking. "Something that we hope will make this week even more of a celebration," she says.

I see a quick glance flick between Mama and Papa. Aisha leans forward.

I sit there frozen.

Zoe gets up and sits next to Aseem on the sofa, lacing her fingers through his. They look at each other for a brief moment, as if coming to a silent agreement, before turning to face us, wide smiles on both their faces.

"We're having a baby," Aseem says.

Time slows as I watch the news travel across the room, the slight chasm, the glance that Mama throws at me, so quick that if I didn't know better I'd have thought I imagined it, the sudden pressure of Ai-sha's hand on my knee, the way Aseem's eyes seem to stay on me throughout, before the spell is broken and we all remember to focus our attention on Zoe.

Zoe.

My reaction is automatic. A flash of hatred so sharp it's terrifying. My hand goes to my stomach, to the slight hollow I'd have killed for in my twenties. Sometimes I'm not sure whether it's more painful to remember or to forget.

I blink away the tears that seem to have sprung to my eyes as everyone crowds around Aseem and Zoe. I remind myself that this is my brother. My sister-in-law.

Papa congratulates Aseem while Mama cups Zoe's face in her hands. "Grandparents," Mama says. "This is the best anniversary present you could have given us, beta."

Aisha jumps up to squeeze Zoe into one of her ferocious hugs, which elicits a surprised laugh from Zoe and mock outrage from Aseem.

"Careful," he says. "That's my baby in there."

Aisha sticks her tongue out before pulling Aseem into an even tighter hug. "You're going to make a lousy father," she says, but her voice is thick with emotion. Even Gabe, who's reappeared by her side, looks genuinely happy as he congratulates Aseem and Zoe.

And through it all, I remain frozen, a reel of the best and worst moments of my life flashing in front of my eyes. The ultrasounds, the hospital visits, the first time I held her, the funeral. I force myself to snap out of it.

"I should've guessed," I say, wrapping my arms around Zoe. I try to mask my sadness with humor but I'm not sure it works. "You're never one to turn a drink down."

Zoe laughs. The joy on her face is gut-wrenching, but it's the look of worry on Aseem's face that pierces through me. I shake my head. Not now.

You okay? Aisha mouths, and I nod. I'm happy for them, I tell myself. As I should be.

"This calls for a toast," I say, busying myself with picking up the empty cups and saucers littered around the room. I stack everything on to a tray and head into the kitchen.

"Zoe, what would you like? Elderflower again?" I call out.

"Actually, I wouldn't mind some of that ice cream from last night," she yells back, her words echoed by a chorus of me too's from the living room.

Champagne with ice cream. *Vintage Dom Pérignon champagne with ice cream.* It's sacrilege but I haven't got it in me to say anything.

"I'm sure I've got another tub in the freezer downstairs," I say, setting the tray by the sink, grateful to have an excuse to go into the cellar.

To have a moment, just one moment, to pull myself together.

Is it too soon to know if it's a boy or a girl?" Aisha asks, pouring the champagne.

Zoe nods, scooping out the last of her ice cream before setting the bowl aside.

A conversation from years earlier begins whispering in my ears. I push it away.

"But you are going to find out?" I ask, even though I know they can't. Not unless they do it here in the UK.

"I think so," Zoe says. "I know it's tricky in India, but . . ." She trails off.

It's not tricky; it's illegal in India. Has been for decades.

"But it'll make shopping easier," Aseem says, by way of explanation.

"And you can start thinking of names," Aisha adds.

"Don't be silly," Mama says. "We need a kundli first."

Zoe shoots a quick glance at Aseem, her irritation obvious. I can't blame her. Mama's reliance on her astrologer is maddening.

"We'll set a room up for your mum in Delhi," Mama continues before Aseem or Zoe can respond. She turns her gaze from Zoe to Papa. "I'm sure Helen won't be able to stay away once her grandchild arrives. And we'll have to look at renovating the house as well."

A shadow flickers across Zoe's face. Her relationship with her mother has always been fraught and if I know Helen, she won't give a toss about a new grandchild. That woman is colder than the North Pole.

"I know the new place is almost ready, but you can't possibly raise a baby in a flat," Mama says, referring to the five-bedroom penthouse that Aseem and Zoe have been refurbishing for the past two years. "Children need a garden, space to play. And you'll need help. We'll get a nanny, of course, but you can't trust a stranger—"

"Shalini," Papa laughs. "Slow down. You're scaring the poor girl."

"It's too early for all that, Mama," Aseem says. "We've got a good six months to go, so let's make those decisions when we get to them."

As Mama starts telling Aseem about how far ahead you have to plan when it comes to babies, I turn my attention back to Zoe. She's smiling but her eyes are tensed, her shoulders pulled back as if she's bracing for impact. The joy I'd been so envious of moments ago has disappeared. She looks distinctly uncomfortable.

I catch her eye. *You okay?* I mouth.

She nods, widens her smile.

She holds my gaze for a moment, then looks away, staring intently into her mint tea.

I've known Zoe since she first befriended my sister, the pair of them two sweet but naive eighteen-year-old girls unsure of their place in the world. Zoe isn't overwhelmed. Zoe is hiding something.

11.

ZOE

I spend the rest of the evening lying on my bed, seething.

It's one thing for Mama to insert herself into her children's lives, quite another for her to presume to know what's best for *my* baby.

And that comment about my mother "not being able to stay away"?

She knows exactly how frayed my relationship with my mother is. She might have fooled Aseem, but not me. Her offer to prepare a room for my mum was nothing more than a dig, a sharp reminder that other than my husband, I have no one.

And right now, I don't even have him. Aseem's been holed up in Myra's office for hours working on the paperwork for the sale of the company.

I reach for my phone, desperately hoping for at least a bar of signal, but it seems my phone is as stubborn and uncooperative as my mother-in-law. I throw it on the floor in frustration.

It's times like this that I wish I could just pick up the phone and ring my mum, but the last thing I want to hear is *I told you so*. That's if she even bothers to answer the phone.

I'd been excited about spending a weekend in London with Aseem before the rest of the family arrived. It wasn't quite the long holiday I would've liked, but considering even a weekend away has been a struggle since Aseem took over PetroVision, it felt like a win. London is special to Aseem and me—it's where we first met, where we fell in love—but this weekend wasn't just about spa appointments and dinner reservations. There were things we needed to do in London, crucial pieces of my plan that I needed to put in place. That had all been sabotaged when Aseem's parents had announced that they had changed their flights so they could fly with us. It wasn't enough that we had to live with them, eat all our bloody meals with them, apparently now we also had to spend all our holidays with them. Suffocating doesn't even begin to describe it.

The only thought that's getting me through this week is that I'm not going to have to put up with this for much longer. Just six more weeks and everything will be different. All I have to do is stay calm and somehow keep all my anger and frustration bottled up.

Just six more weeks and all this will be worth it.

A knock at the door startles me out of my thoughts. "Who is it?" I call out.

"It's me." Aisha pushes the door open and strides in. She picks up my phone from the floor and throws it on the bed, her eyebrows raised.

"Don't ask," I say, hauling myself to sitting position.

"Okay." She flops down next to me, purple-tipped hair fanning out around her head. "I can't believe you didn't tell me." A pause, then, "Are you excited?"

I consider her question. Aseem and I had been trying for more than a year when I found out, so this baby is nothing if not planned. And yet, ever since those two lines appeared on the stick, there is a growing sense of unease in me. A restlessness. A constant worry. Am I excited? Yes, of course. But I am also so many other things. It's as though the world has shifted on its axis and now that I'm going to be a mother, I'm looking at everything through a different lens.

I'm also thinking about my own mother a lot more.

I reach for the simplest answer as a smile spreads across my face, just the thought of the baby enough to lift my mood. "I really am."

"I can't believe you're going to be a mum, Zo. I suppose that's the end of our partying days," Aisha says in mock despair.

I laugh. Our partying days ended quite some time ago. I've come so far away from that version of myself, I don't think I'd even recognize the person I was when I first met Aisha. "Yep. It'll be all happy meals and kiddie birthday parties from now on."

She rolls her eyes, looks at the ceiling. "I guess it'll be my job to make sure my niece gets a good, all-round education, seeing as her parents are such bores."

"Hey," I protest, flicking her lightly on the arm. My brain skips back to what she just said. "Niece?"

"I've got a feeling," she says, twirling a strand of hair around her finger.

My hand goes to my belly, feeling the small bulge that I've come to love with a fierceness that astonishes me. I've got a feeling it's a girl too.

Which makes everything I'm about to do even more important. My little girl will have everything I didn't. She will never have to worry about paying rent or paying for groceries. She will never have to fear for her safety in her own home. She's going to grow up feeling loved and supported and cherished.

She will have something I never had: choices.

Aisha flips on to her side to look at me. "So *have* you thought of a name?"

"Maybe," I say.

"Oh come on," Aisha moans.

I grin. It's easy to see why she gets away with so much; it's impossible to say no to Aisha. "Fiza," I say slowly. I love the lightness of the name, the way it rolls off my tongue.

"Fiza," she repeats. She closes her eyes for a moment as though turning the name over in her head. "I like it." She hesitates. "But—"

"But Mama and Papa won't? I know," I sigh. I've lived with them long enough to learn that Fiza is a Muslim name and my in-laws aren't half as liberal as they like to pretend they are. They want a vedic astrologer to pick the name, for fuck's sake.

"What does Aseem think?"

I lift my shoulders.

"You haven't told him?" Aisha asks, eyes wide.

"I've only just thought of it," I lie.

The truth is I haven't told him yet because I'm worried his reaction will mimic Aisha's. Or worse, that he'll want to run it past his parents.

Aisha sits up and I catch a glimpse of the black thread she wears around her left ankle. Kala dhaga. An ancient practice to ward off evil spirits. Mama put it on after the fire and as far as I know, she's never taken it off. "Is everything okay, Zo?"

"Of course."

She looks at me more pointedly than I thought possible.

I take a breath, not sure how to answer. "It's all a bit overwhelming," I say, finally. "Everyone has plans for a baby that isn't even born yet."

Aisha reaches for my hand and gives it a squeeze. "That's my family: over the top, meddlesome, intrusive. I did warn you."

"Don't get me wrong, it's sweet. And I love the family, you know I do. It's just a bit—"

"Much?"

I nod. If anyone can understand how I'm feeling, it's Aisha. She's struggled with her family as long as I've known her. "It has not been easy," I concede.

She frowns. "Nothing about my family's easy but you've always known that."

I sigh. Knowing something and living it are two entirely different things, as I've come to realize.

"Love is not the absence of boundaries. This is your baby, Zo," she says. "You decide how you want to raise her. If you aren't happy with how things are going, you're going to have to take a stand or you'll end up living a life you don't like. The baby isn't even born yet. . . . What happens when you need to pick a school or sort out childcare? Mama obviously wants to be involved, as do the rest of us, but it's up to you and Aseem to decide *how* involved. And that's okay. You know what I mean?"

"Thank you," I say, tears springing to my eyes. If only Aseem saw things the way his sister does.

Aisha reaches for the box of Ferrero Rocher chocolates on the side table and unwraps a truffle. "So what's really wrong?" she asks, fixing me with a look.

I hesitate. Aseem and I agreed we wouldn't tell anyone until it was a done deal. I don't want questions that I don't have answers to, he'd said. But I know it's more than that.

Just like Aisha can read my thoughts, I can read my husband's.

He's worried.

That's why this week is so important.

And why I absolutely cannot tell her.

The trouble is I am better at keeping secrets from my husband than I am at keeping them from my best friend.

I buckle. I tell her how lonely I am, how stifled I feel in that huge, eight-bedroomed house, how there are days I sit in my room starving instead of going down to breakfast just so I can have some time to think. Time to breathe.

"I've done everything that's been asked of me. I've changed how I dress, how I talk, what I eat, everything. *Everything.* I've tried, Aish, I really, really have, and it's still not enough. I feel like I'm being smothered," I say. "I can't . . . I just can't go on. You don't know what it's like to feel like you're being judged for every breath you take. I need space."

"Isn't the flat almost ready?"

"It's been ready for months." I throw my hands up in frustration. "But every time we try to move, there's a crisis. It's either Papa's heart or Mama's blood pressure or an astrologer claiming the month is inauspicious." I sigh. "And you know Aseem. He can never say no to them. I'm married to the man of my dreams but I've never felt so alone. I'm living in a country I can't understand and I haven't got one person I can talk to about it."

"What about your friends? All those other influencers? You have such a busy social life."

"They aren't friends, they're contacts. We hang out so we can get a bump in engagement from each other's followers. All my real friends are back in the UK." I look at Aisha. "Or California. I hate living in Delhi, Aish. It's suffocating and lonely and stressful," I say, finally admitting out loud everything I've felt for months. "People are so judgmental and so bloody intrusive. It's not the right environment for a family. Or for me for that matter. I'm losing my mind there."

I can see the cogs turning in Aisha's brain as her expression flits from sympathy to horror. "You aren't thinking of leaving Aseem, are you?" There is panic in her voice. Aisha's seen Aseem's and my relationship more closely than anyone else; she knows what we mean to each other. She gets it.

I fiddle with the box of chocolates, wrapping and unwrapping a truffle till the gold foil is tattered, little holes revealing where I've stretched the paper too far. Aisha is my best friend, but she's also my sister-in-law. And difficult as her relationship with them might be, she loves her family with a fierceness I've never understood. I don't want to put her in an impossible situation.

Aisha takes the truffle from me and tosses it to one side.

"Aseem's family, but so are you," she says, reading my mind. "Whatever it is, you can tell me."

I suck in a deep breath, then take Aisha's hands in mine, my grip on her so tight I can see my knuckles turn white. "You can't tell anyone. Not a word."

The color bleeds into the tissue, turning the paper scarlet as I bite down on it.

That's the problem with PR samples. You never know what you're getting.

I toss the stick of liquid lipstick into the bin and reach for my trusty Chanel red.

I'm wearing an emerald-green cashmere dress—Gucci couture—that skims over my hips, ending just below my knees. It's perfectly demure, until you look at the back, which scoops down dangerously close to my buttocks, the fabric grazing the elastic of my underwear. It's probably a little extra for a family dinner, but after my conversation with Aisha, I feel lighter.

And the dinner tonight is a celebration, after all.

I examine myself in the mirror, trying to decide how to wear my hair.

"Leave it down."

I look at Aseem's reflection in the mirror as he comes to stand behind me. "How'd it go?"

"Fine," he says, rubbing his forehead. "I looked into Gabe."

I sigh. Of course he did. "Was that really necessary?"

Aseem shrugs.

"What did you find?"

"He's nowhere near as successful as he claims."

"But?"

"But he seems legit. He interned in London. Morgan Chase. And his firm is garnering a bit of a reputation."

"Right," I say, too irritated to say *I told you so.* Of course my husband has been on a wild goose chase instead of finalizing the deal that is supposed to be our ticket to freedom. I finish applying my mascara, carefully coating each eyelash before turning to face him. "Did you give Papa the papers?"

Aseem takes the tube of mascara from my hand and sets it on the marble counter. He takes my hands, lacing his fingers through mine, and tries to pull me closer.

I resist, my irritation from earlier resurfacing. "Well?"

"I did."

I disentangle my fingers from his and turn around. I try to keep the exasperation out of my voice as I thread a pair of delicate gold hoops through my ears. "And?"

Aseem spent the entire afternoon in Myra's office, poring over the paperwork, hammering out the details with his consultant, then cross-checking everything with his legal team. The buyer, Malhotra, had finally met all of Papa's conditions—quite the feat considering the decades-old rivalry between them. But Malhotra's cooperation came with the proviso that we'd complete the sale in thirty days and that Papa would have no part in the handover and integration process.

Thirty days!

"Papa will make the announcement tonight," Aseem says, smiling.

I let out a long, low sigh, feeling every muscle in my body unclench as relief floods in.

This is it, the last hurdle. "How do you think Aisha and Myra will take it?"

Aisha's never taken any interest in the business or the way the trust is managed and though she is entitled, she's also fair. I doubt she'll raise any objections. As for Myra . . . she's always been generous, but that was when she made a few hundred grand in annual bonuses alone.

Things are different now.

Aseem turns me lightly by my shoulders. "You have made me the happiest man on the planet, Zo," he whispers. "And I'm going to do everything I can to give you the life you want."

I look into his serious, dark eyes. The first time I met him, my best friend's handsome, kind, generous older brother, I felt so safe I melted.

As he pulls me into his arms, I find myself melting again.

We stay like that for a long moment, breathing each other in, our hearts beating in unison. He takes a step back, then another, pulling me with him until we're standing in the middle of the enormous bathroom.

I look at him, eyebrows raised. He shrugs, pretending to look confused as his body starts swaying.

I throw my arms around his neck and press my body into his as we twirl across the marble floor, out bodies in perfect sync, moving to a beat only the two of us can hear.

I'm lucky to have him.

And now I'll have everything else I've always dreamed about.

12.

MYRA

I lean over the sink and splash my face with cold water.

I should be downstairs preparing dinner, but Mama insisted on cooking tonight's meal herself, rendering me and the paella sitting in the freezer downstairs useless. It's the first time I've seen all my children together in five years, Mama had said by way of explanation. She's overcompensating as per usual. She's trying to paint herself into a childhood that she missed out on, first because she was too busy hosting parties, and then because she was too broken to pay attention to the family she still had left. She's been in the kitchen for hours now preparing all our favorite meals.

Rajma chawal for Aisha.

Chicken tikka for Aseem.

And chole bhature for me.

It's a mismatch, but then so is our family.

I wipe my face with a flannel and glance in the mirror. Two days in and this reunion is already taking its toll.

I refuse to entertain the idea that my anxiety has anything to do with Aseem and Zoe's news. Or the fact that Aisha's managed to find the sleaziest finance guy on the planet and bring him home. No, my un-ease has to do with an acute sense that there is something that I should be trying harder to see.

Like any successful business family, we hold most of our assets and the income from the company in a discretionary family trust. Until now, Papa's always transferred money from the trust into each of our accounts, but the process is complicated and arbitrary. Given that the value of the trust is about to go up meteorically, it makes sense to change how the trust is structured so we all have control of our own money. I am, however, surprised that he hasn't told me how the shares will be distributed. I've always handled Papa's estate, and his caginess confirms something I've long suspected: my father no longer trusts me the way he once did.

But it isn't just the insult that stings. It's the whispered conversations Aseem's been having with Papa, the way he clams up every time I mention the sale or try to discuss investment options. And then there's Zoe. Her behavior these past couple of days has been far more peculiar than can be attributed to pregnancy hormones. She's been acting smug.

Naturally, Aseem's grown closer to Papa since he moved back to Delhi and there is no point in arguing Mama's dependence on her son, but I don't believe for a second that Papa would have discussed his plans with Aseem and Zoe before telling me. And yet, that is what it feels like.

Like they know something I don't.

I fling open the wardrobe doors and flick through the rail, stopping when I come to my favorite wrap dress in a rich burgundy. I run my fingers over the silky fabric, thinking about the last time I'd worn it. I still remember that night as clearly as if it was yesterday. I'd just won a huge case and after a difficult few years, Owen and I were finally back on track. It felt like everything was slotting into place and I'd walked into the bar feeling invincible.

I didn't know then that all it would take was one misstep for my life to shatter into a million pieces.

I push the dress to one side and pick out a gray silk blouse and trousers instead.

What I wouldn't give for the chance to retrace my steps, but no matter what anyone tells you, life is little more than a series of consequences, and mistakes are forever.

My mind goes to the emails and letters that seem to be getting shorter and sterner by the day. When we bought Kilbryde, we took out a five-year mortgage. The interest rates were at an all-time low and it made sense to take a mortgage out on the island. Saving the cash for the renovations would give us enough time and freedom to do up the house and the island exactly how we wanted, without having to worry about extending bank loans or meeting investor expectations. It was a good plan, but it was dependent on us keeping up the repayments. After everything unraveled, Owen doubled the amount on his direct deposit, trying to assuage his guilt by paying for the only thing I still cared about.

Three years later, he's run out of guilt and I've run out of money.

He canceled the direct debit three months ago, leaving our mortgage in arrears.

I look at the papers spread across my desk. The reminders from the bank, the letters threatening repossession, the unpaid invoices from the architect and the contractors, Owen's emails, each more frantic than the last. He's found a buyer, an overseas investor who wants to build a five-star hotel on the island. The offer stands at nineteen point five million pounds with a ten percent early completion bonus. It's more than what we paid, but it doesn't even begin to cover the work or the money I've put into restoring Kilbryde.

Nor does it take into account what the island means to me.

When I spoke to my financial adviser, she confirmed what I already suspected: because the island is in negative equity and I have no job to speak of, the bank won't even consider a remortgage application. If I don't come up with the money soon, this retreat and everything I've put into it will come crashing down.

I go to the window, the view of the valley broken by the plants that moved here with me. I trail my hand along the windowsill, quietly brushing my fingers along each of the seven pots, anchoring myself, reminding myself why I must do this. Everyone assumes that moving here, leaving my marriage, my career, my life behind must have been a gut-wrenching decision, but if I'm honest, it wasn't a decision at all. It was as simple, as thoughtless as breathing.

It was survival.

Perhaps I've been naive in waiting for Papa to initiate the conversation, in trusting that he would remember a promise he made me almost a decade ago.

I slap on some lipstick, fluff my hair, then step into the hallway, letting the door slam shut behind me.

I'm not going to leave my future to chance.

Not again.

I thought you might like a drink," I say, walking into my parents' bedroom just as Aisha's heading out.

"Thanks," Papa says, without looking up. He's sitting on the ottoman, his long torso hunched over his shoelaces.

I set his glass down on the small end table and perch on one of the armchairs. The suite runs along the length of the house with a spectacular view of the valley, and even at night, this room is the most impressive. I glance out of the window at the loch glittering in the moonlight. I squint, trying to draw a separation between the forest and the rest of the landscape, but all I see is endless shades of black, everything appearing closer, more tightly bound in the darkness. Zoe, however, claimed to have seen an intruder in all that blackness. Honestly, that girl and her drama.

I wasn't sure about giving Mama and Papa this room. Papa has only just recovered from his stroke, and the two flights of stairs are seriously steep. I was worried about tired lungs and achy limbs, but looking at Papa now, you wouldn't guess that he'd been bedridden for more than eighteen months. He's worked incredibly hard on rehabilitation and if anything, he looks fitter now than he did twenty years ago.

I nod at the hefty document wallet on the bed. "What's that?"

"Paperwork from legal. Your brother dropped it off earlier," Papa says, sinking into the other armchair. He lifts the glass to his nose and gives it a swirl, inhales. "Macallan." He takes a sip. "Ninety-nine?"

"You're losing your edge," I say. "It's a ninety-five."

"Ninety-five?" Papa repeats. He takes another appreciative sip, eyes twinkling. "You must really want something."

My skin flames. I force myself to smile back. "Sanjida is still head of legal, right?" I wait for Papa to nod, then continue. "I'm sure she's been thorough, but I can have a look at the documentation for the sale and the trust if you want. Double-check."

"That's not necessary."

"Are you sure? I mean, Sanjida's good but I did—"

"You trained her well," Papa cuts me off.

"But you *have* had the paperwork drawn up? For the trust?"

Papa's silence tells me everything. Sanjida reports to Aseem and if the paperwork's been drawn up, that can only mean one thing: Aseem, and by extension Zoe, knows how the shares are being divided. And I doubt that the thirty-five percent stake that Papa promised me would have them looking so smug.

The split, whatever it is, works for them.

I glance at the pair of medicine boxes sitting on the side table, each compartment stickered and clearly labeled in Aseem's handwriting. When did he take over organizing my parents' medication?

"Papa?" I press on, stung but not quite ready to give up.

He swirls the whisky, then knocks it back. "Don't let Gabe get his hands on this," he says, setting the glass down. He gets up and slips on his jacket, ready to join the rest of the family in the living room for drinks. "Shall we?"

I use my sleeve to wipe a speck of dust from the end table, unsure of how to launch into my request. Every bone in my body's telling me that Papa's going to announce his plans for the reconfiguration of the trust tonight. And once he's told everyone what he intends to do, it'll be even harder to ask him to make any changes.

I take in a breath and tilt my head up to look at him.

"Actually, there's something I need to talk to you about."

"Yes?"

"I might have underestimated the amount of work the island needs. The condition of the cottages is a lot worse than we originally thought. The builders have found subsidence and all the old plumbing and electrics are basically fried. The renovation is going to cost a lot more than I planned for and without my salary . . ." I pause, take a breath. "I'm not worried—"

Papa turns to face me. An eyebrow arches.

"I mean I *am* worried, but once the sale goes through, I'll be fine. It's just . . . it's been a few years since we spoke about it, so I wanted to make sure that nothing's changed."

Papa gives me a blank look. "Nothing's changed in terms of?"

"In terms of the way the shares will be divided. You promised—"

"I remember what I promised. How much do you need?"

Shame burns through me. To ask Papa to bail me out means finally facing up to the fact that I am no longer the independent, successful professional I worked so hard to become. But as uncomfortable as this conversation makes me, the thought that I might lose the island is worse. I swallow my pride.

"Forty million for the structural and building works and about twelve for the decoration and the interiors." I'm cringing so hard I can feel my insides clench.

"So you need fifty million? Give or take."

In all honesty, I need a lot more than fifty million but I can't exactly tell him that. I stand up. I need to get this over with. Once I have the money, I can find a way to make it work, cut some corners, stagger the payments.

"Slightly more than that, but yeah, give or take fifty million."

Papa takes no more than a few seconds to reply, but as I stand there, heart pounding in my chest, those few seconds feel like an eternity.

"Okay," he says.

"Okay?"

"Okay." Papa shrugs. He pauses, his face softening. "I know this sale and all the talk about the trust is . . . it's stressful. And you're all on edge right now, wondering who's getting what. But when have you ever had to worry about money, sweetheart?" Papa tilts his head to look at me. "Everything I've done, the business, the assets, the trust, it's all for the three of you. I have not forgotten what you did for the company, Myra." He frowns, continues, "We would not be here without you. So whatever you need, money, resources . . . you don't need to worry. I've always looked after you and I always will."

13.

ZOE

Even before I've stepped into the kitchen, I can hear voices filtering out and for a moment, that old feeling resurfaces, the sense of being an intruder, of waking up in a flat that isn't mine, having breakfast with a family that isn't mine, living a life that isn't mine.

Of being a trespasser.

I smooth my dress, running my hands over the soft wool, reminding myself that this *is* my life now, my family. And in a few short weeks, I'll never have to worry about feeling like an intruder again. I'll have the keys to the castle and everything that goes with it.

A wave of nausea rises up my throat as I walk through the kitchen.

Of course Aseem didn't tell Mama to go easy on the garlic.

I step through open double doors into the living room. A half-empty platter of canapés sits discarded on the white marble coffee table next to a couple of bottles of champagne.

Not only have they started before me, they're practically done. Typical.

"Finally," Aseem says, twisting to give me a quick kiss. He's standing next to Mama by the fire, his glass of champagne resting on the elaborate, pillared mantelpiece. "Mama was saying we should see Dr. Mehta as soon as we're back."

"Dr. Mehta?" I ask.

"He's an OB-GYN. He was Mama's doctor."

"He's the best in the country," Mama says. "A traditionalist. Only does C-sections, so you'll get none of the water birth or hypno-birth nonsense that these younger doctors keep advocating. I was up and about within days and even after three cesareans, barely any scarring." She pauses to take a sip of her champagne while I seethe silently.

What if I *want* a water birth?

"It's usually impossible to get an appointment with him, but his wife owes me a favor. I'll give her a ring and get you booked in for"—she raises her eyebrows, her question aimed at my husband—"August?" Aseem nods. "I'll ask pandit ji to suggest an auspicious date," she continues.

"Thanks, Mama. That'll be great," Aseem says, without so much as a glance in my direction or any consideration for the birth plan I've been agonizing over for weeks.

Tears sting my eyes. It's typical of Mama to presume she's in charge of my pregnancy. I should do what Aisha suggested, tell her off, take a stand. I don't.

Three hundred million pounds.

That's what I need to focus on.

I walk over to the drinks cabinet to examine my options. I could really do with a glass of wine, but I know exactly how my in-laws will react so instead I opt for the far more diplomatic choice of an elderflower cordial before joining Papa and Myra on the sofa.

I sigh as I sink into the plush velvet.

"Tired?" Myra asks.

"Exhausted," I say. "I feel like a nap pretty much all the time. How did you—" I cut myself off.

The burst of sympathy that Myra's half-smile inspires nearly has me in tears again. Bloody hormones. Papa shoots me a warning look.

"Where's Aish?" I ask, desperate to change the topic for both our sakes.

"Here she comes now," Aseem says, walking over to join us just as Aisha and Gabe make an appearance.

Aisha saunters over to join us, leaving Gabe to pour their drinks. "What did I miss?"

"Not much," Myra says, getting up. Dressed in a silk blouse and ankle-length trousers, she looks more relaxed than I've seen her all week. She looks like she's about to give Aisha a hug, but instead she wrinkles her nose in disgust. "Have you been smoking?"

"Of course not," Aisha says, not even bothering to disguise the lie. "I wouldn't dare."

"Be nice," Aseem mouths to Aisha before turning his attention to Papa. "Did you get a chance to look at the deal memo?"

"Not now, son."

"Okay. Sure. But we need to wrap this up by the end of play tomorrow. Malhotra's very keen to announce and our legal team—"

"I said not now." Papa's tone is sharp, and my heart swells as Aseem looks down, his face darkening. "I'm not paying our solicitors a hundred grand to boss me around."

"I'm starving," Aisha says brightly, the only one capable of defusing the tension. "Should we eat?" I shoot her a grateful look as she loops her arm through Papa's and steers him toward the dining room.

I don't get up immediately. I've been waiting for this moment for far too long to rush it. I take my time finishing my elderflower cordial. I set the empty glass on the coffee table, take a deep breath then follow the rest of the family into the dining room.

I slip into the seat next to Aseem. From across the table, Aisha beams at me. After our little chat, Aseem's been, if not friendly, then definitely far more civil to Gabe. It's clearly put Aisha at ease.

I turn to look at Aseem, barely able to keep the smile off my face as Papa stands up to make a toast.

"The past few years have been tough on our family, but to see you all pull together the way you did, to support your mother, me, each other . . . it has shown me that your mama and I did something right. I couldn't be more proud of you all." Papa looks at all of us in turn, his gaze softening as it lands on Mama at the other end of the table. "But seeing you here, together, what both Mama and I feel more than anything is gratitude. To Myra, for coming to our rescue once again and organizing this beautiful family holiday." Papa shoots a brief look at Myra, who beams back, before shifting his attention to his youngest daughter. "To Aisha, for tearing herself away from whatever beach she was sunbathing on to come here and help us celebrate in style. To Zoe, for giving us the best damn news we've had in months." Papa tips his glass in the air, eyes twinkling as he looks at me. I smile back, genuinely happy to be here, to be a part of this. He shifts his gaze to Aseem. "And most of all, to Aseem for everything he did to keep us afloat while I dealt with my health"—he waves his hand—"issue. Thanks, beta. I don't say it often, but the business, the family . . . we would have struggled without you at the helm. You stepped in when we needed you and I think it's only fair that we return the favor by letting you focus on Zoe and the baby now."

I lace my fingers through Aseem's under the table.

This is it.

"There's been a lot of speculation about the sale, numbers being thrown around, and I know you're all wondering what happens once I retire." Papa takes a breath, takes his time looking around the table. "I'm not going to sugar-coat it. The business is struggling. Has been for quite some time. And drastic measures need to be taken."

All of Aseem's hard work, all our patience, it's finally paying off. I don't even need to close my eyes to see it: the perfect, *perfect* life that I've always been denied, finally within my grasp.

"I know I look old," Papa continues, eyes crinkling, "but I feel young. I certainly don't feel old enough to resign myself to a life of early dinners and seniors' cruises."

He laughs, but there is something brittle about it, a dark undertone that makes me hold myself very, very still.

Myra flashes a quick look at Aisha before her eyes slide sideways. Gabe sits up, clearly sensing the change in tone. Mama takes the cream pashmina folded over the back of her chair and drapes it loosely around her shoulders. I glance at Aseem but his gaze is fixed on his father, his mouth set in a tight line.

Papa's expression turns serious. "When I started PetroVision, we were one of three petro-chemical companies in Asia. Now, there are more than fifty. And while some might think that the market is over-saturated, I think it's the perfect time for us to expand and take charge of the industry. Which is why I've decided to stay on for a few more years."

I feel every muscle in my body seize up. Little dots dance in front of my eyes.

Surely he doesn't mean . . . he can't. He wouldn't do that to us. To Aseem.

Several beats pass, and then everyone speaks at once.

"What?" Myra says.

"I've decided to stay on for a few more years. We'll reassess when—"

"Stay on . . . what do you mean? Stay on where?" Aseem speaks up.

"In the business," Papa shrugs. "As the head of PetroVision. As CEO."

"But—you're not—" I stammer.

"My test reports are absolutely fine. I'm fit and healthy and both my doctor and your mama have given me the green light for a phased return." He sighs. "Look, I know this might seem sudden, but I have been thinking about it for some time. And for all sorts of reasons that we don't need to go into right now, it's best for me to stay in situ. We'll run things the way we always have. As a family."

"You didn't tell me. The sale—" The words have barely left Aseem's mouth when Papa raises his hand to silence him.

"It's not a big deal. We haven't signed anything yet."

"But we've already negotiated. Malhotra agreed to all our terms—" Aseem says.

"I don't give a damn about Malhotra. The deal you've negotiated is not good enough. PetroVision will be worth ten times that once we expand," Papa says, impatience oozing through his smile.

"What about the trust? The reconfiguration—"

"Haven't you been listening, son?" Papa snipes back. "We aren't selling so we don't need to make any changes to the trust right now. Now, no more business on the table. To new beginnings." Papa raises his glass. "And to family."

We all raise our glasses, take a dutiful sip, but the air of celebration is gone.

Myra slumps back in her seat.

Aisha and Gabe exchange a confused glance.

Aseem looks like he's been punched.

And me, I push my shoulders back, feeling the tightness, the tension, the pure, unadulterated hatred. After everything we've done for the business. For the *fucking* family.

I look at Papa, the realization rising like nausea.

If he thinks I'm going to toe the line when I'm so close to having everything I've ever wanted, he has no idea who I am.

Or what I'm capable of.

14.

ZOE

I'm *staying on.*

The words are still ringing in my ears. Spoken so casually. As if he'd just decided to stay on at the office for an extra hour.

I'm staying on.

The sentence had not been uttered with the weight it deserved. There had been no acknowledgment of the fact that Aseem has given every-thing, *everything*, to the business.

Nor any consideration given to the fact that we have a life of our own, we have plans.

That this simple change of mind has repercussions that go far be-yond the billionaire's bubble that Papa exists in.

I'm staying on.

Five years ago, Aseem had been busy setting up his own tech start-up. He had the investors lined up, the office space leased. He had a whole future planned out that he was excited about.

That *we* were excited about.

Everything changed when Papa had the stroke. PetroVision was the family's main source of income and the Agarwals were agreed: saving it wasn't optional. Myra had settled the court case a few years ago but the company was still grappling with the reputational and financial repercussions of a long legal battle. The family knew what they were asking of Aseem. He couldn't possibly run a start-up and look after a business that was on the brink of collapse at the same time. While Papa fought for his life, Aseem fought for the business.

Aseem saved the company by sacrificing his own dreams.

And *this* is how Papa repays him.

"You don't think it's odd that he no longer wants the deal he was *desperate* to close until yesterday?" I stop pacing to look at my husband. He's sitting up in bed, the duvet pulled up around his waist. We've been arguing for hours, we're both exhausted, but I just can't let it go.

"Of course it's odd. It's *infuriating.*" Aseem rests his head against the headboard, tilting his face up to the ceiling and closing his eyes. "I guess he changed his mind."

"Why?"

"I don't know, Zoe. It's his company." The exasperation in his voice only winds me up further.

"That *you* kept from bankruptcy," I say, crossing the room to go to the window. It's completely dark outside, even the light from the star-spattered sky not enough to illuminate the dense forest.

Everything Aseem and I have is linked to the business. Except for the emergency fund I've been putting together over the past few years, we have nothing. No money, no assets, nothing. Even my health insurance is paid for through the company.

After years of pandering to his family's wishes, Aseem and I were going to use the money from the sale to finally build the life that we want. I think of the townhouse in Belgravia—six bedrooms that I've already picked out furniture for. I think of the business plan that Aseem's spent months perfecting, the office in Hoxton he's already made an offer on. I think of my baby and everything I want to give her.

And then I think of the last time I went to visit my mother in her flat, more than three years ago. The stench that had assaulted me when I stepped into the building, the corridors reeking of rotting food and urine, an unwelcome reminder of where I'd come from and where I had no intention of returning.

Not then, and certainly not now.

If Papa doesn't sell, Aseem will have no option but to stay on as COO. And I'll be trapped in Delhi forever, living in a gilded cage with my in-laws dictating every aspect of my life, and of my child's.

The thought wraps itself around me, its grip as suffocating as a tightly laced corset.

I spin around as Aseem flicks off the lamp and the room is plunged into darkness. "What the hell are you doing?"

"It's four a.m., Zo. What do you expect me to do?" He flips on to his side in the bed, his face turned away from me. "We can deal with this tomorrow."

He doesn't say it but I know what he's thinking. Aseem's always maintained that I'm too emotional, too easily wound up. It's a diagnosis that he's been reaching for a little too frequently since we found out I'm pregnant.

The words he doesn't say rile me further. This isn't hormones. I'm furious because I have every right to be. I march across the room and flick the lights back on. "Are you going to talk to your sisters?"

"This has nothing to do with them." Aseem sits up, rubs his eyes.

The plan was for Mama and Papa to retain thirty-five percent of the shares in the trust and split the remainder between Aseem, Myra and Aisha, thirty-five, fifteen and fifteen. It would have left Aseem and me with close to a hundred million after tax and Aisha and Myra with just over forty million each. Considering how much Aseem's put into Petro-Vision and this sale, it's a fair split, but I'm not sure if Myra would have seen it that way.

"Did you tell them how the money was going to be divided?"

"Of course not and neither did Papa. You know how private he is about this stuff. He didn't even want *me* seeing the paperwork in advance," Aseem says, waving my accusation away. "Papa built Petro-Vision from the ground up. It can't be easy for him to let it go, especially to a man who's always had it in for him."

"The company is in fucking shambles. He said so himself." I go back to pacing the room. "What the hell are we going to do?"

Aseem gets up and closes the distance between us in two long strides. "Hey," he says, putting his hands on my shoulders and pinning me in place. His grip is firm but his voice is soft. "Zoe, come on, calm down. This isn't good for the baby."

I shrug him off, spin around. I know that if I look at him, I'll melt.

"What's not good for the baby is being stuck in Delhi. You know how hard I've tried. I can't do it any more, Aseem. I deserve to be able to live my own life. We both do." I take a breath. "I am not going back there."

Aseem pulls me close, wrapping his arms around my waist from behind. I can feel the warmth of his body through my silk kimono.

He moves my hair to one side and lands a kiss on the side of my head. I feel my shoulders relax involuntarily. "I'll fix this."

"When? How?"

He doesn't reply.

"We don't have a lot of time." I press on. "If Malhotra pulls out—"

"I know. And I will talk to them, *all of them*, but you have to let me do it in my own way. I know my family."

And I know you, I think.

"I am not going back to Delhi, Aseem."

"Zoe." He pronounces my name with a sigh. "Do you trust me?"

I don't reply, letting the silence stretch and twist between us.

Aseem places his hands on my hips and turns me around. He tilts my chin up and looks me straight in the eye. "Do you trust me?" he repeats.

I nod, reluctantly.

"Then give me some time, sweetheart. We both want the same thing," he says, dark eyes filled with promise. He pulls me close and rests his chin on my head. "I'm just trying to make sure no one gets hurt."

15.

MYRA

I t's still dark when I step outside.

I lean my foot against a tree stump and stretch, pushing my heel in until I can feel the ripple of tension shoot up my leg. I finish stretching then take a breath of the clean, crisp air and begin to warm up with an easy jog. I'm still reeling from Papa's announcement last night, a mixture of shock, betrayal, and pure, unadulterated fury coursing through my veins, and I need the clarity that only physical exercise can provide.

The air is colder today, a dense fog resting low in the sky. I leap over a large puddle of frozen rainwater and cut through the pine forest, deviating from my usual path. I run past the site that had originally been earmarked for the helipad but after months of conflict still remains untouched. When we first discussed it, the architect told us was that the proposed site had minor historical significance, before assuring us we could push through any resistance from the planning officer. It was only when the council questioned the application that I realized that the architect had knowingly misled me. The "minor" historical signif-icance came from the fact that it was the site of a mass burial. We had inadvertently proposed building on top of dozens of unmarked graves. It's no surprise that the community was furious. Even Stu and Lorna, both of whom know better than to interfere, saw fit to object when they found out about our plans.

I push the thought away and follow the stream to the point where it tumbles over a large rock and plunges into the ravine underneath. I sprint across the small wooden bridge. The rain has washed away the track that shears down to the small loch, and I slow down as I duck through the branches, trying to find my footing on the carpet of fallen pine needles and ancient, moss-covered roots.

Papa likes to play things close to his chest and yes, sometimes that means his decisions take us by surprise, but he's not a liar and he's never broken a promise that he's made me before.

That's why I can't work out why he would tell me one thing and do another.

After hours of tossing and turning last night, I'd just about managed to silence my thoughts when Aseem and Zoe's voices started filtering through. Their endless arguing made sleep impossible, but more im-portantly, it gave me some measure of consolation.

At least I'm not the only one Papa kept in the dark.

The loch finally comes into view and I step through the gap between the trees that ring the dark pool of water. There are so many stories about this place, nearly every part of the island tainted by its bloody history, but to me, the small loch feels sacred. There are no remnants of old cottages, no left-behind statues or signs that anyone had even known of its existence. Its history is far more personal.

Owen had discovered this spot on one of his runs a few months after we bought Kilbryde and surprised me with a picnic lunch on our anniversary. We had lain on the shore, a blanket spread out over us as we looked up at the canopy of trees and planned the life we still believed we could have. That every now and then I allow myself to dream we can still have.

I reach out and grab a branch to stop myself from slipping on the mossy track. A layer of ice floats on the surface of the water. Hundreds of rocks surround it, their edges sharp and jagged. I know this island like the back of my hand, but what if I were to slip and injure myself? Even if my family realizes I'm missing, they will never know to look for me here. I'll probably catch pneumonia or freeze to death before someone finds me.

I throw a pebble into the lake and watch it slice through the ice and sink without so much as a ripple.

The small loch isn't marked on any map. No one knows it exists.

It's hiding in plain sight, like my own dark secret.

The sky is a blaze of pinks and oranges as I jog back toward the house. I'm reeking of sweat, my trainers are caked with mud, and my legs are so sore every step feels excruciating, but I feel light.

As a newly qualified lawyer still desperate for clients, I used to start every pitch telling potential clients that the biggest flaw in their legal strategy was that they were following the law. I used to call them out on their compliance and then once I had their attention, I'd go on to explain that of course I wasn't suggesting they do anything that wasn't above board, but I *was* suggesting they take the board and move it to a place that works for them.

That's how I built my practice: by going after what I want, by knowing how to work the law—and the situation—to my advantage. And by being ruthless.

I leap over a broken branch, my mind running through my options, when I catch a glimpse of one of the cottages through the trees. I stop and blink. It looks, just for a second, as if there is a silhouette, someone passing behind an illuminated window. It is a trick of the light, of course—the cottage has been unoccupied for years and I haven't got Zoe's penchant for drama—but it gives me pause.

Perhaps the problem is that I've been asking the wrong questions.

For weeks I've been obsessing over how much PetroVision will sell for and how much I'll get once the sale goes through, when instead I should have been questioning how serious Papa was about retiring in the first place.

I could talk to Mama. It's not inconceivable that she might know why he changed his mind, and more importantly, how to convince Papa to retire.

But for the longest time, the overarching refrain in our family has been, "Don't tell Mama."

Scraped your knee? Don't tell Mama.

Failed a test? Don't tell Mama.

Fought with your sister? Don't tell Mama.

My mother hasn't always been fragile. I remember my friends being in awe of her fierceness, but that version of her disappeared long ago. She is no longer the woman who would once drive me and my friends to a lecture that had the right wing's knickers in a twist. Or the one who insisted that family is a part of a woman's life, not the entirety of it. No, this woman is someone different. She is as delicate as a china cup that has been glued back together, too broken by the tragedies of our past to take any more, and shielding her is as much a part of the family contract as protecting Aisha.

Terrified you'll lose the only thing you still care about? Don't tell Mama.

I huff my way up the final few meters, my cheeks stinging from the cold and the exertion.

Judging by the snippets of conversation I overheard last night, Aseem and Zoe are just as desperate as I am. I can use that. Class action suits work because there's strength in numbers, and families are no different.

Growing up, when Aseem and I wanted something that Mama and Papa were set against, we banded together, often dragging a clueless Aisha with us. Mama and Papa could say no to one of their children, but when faced with all three, they almost always caved.

I think about the will I drafted for Papa a few years ago and my surprise when I realized he didn't want everything split equally between his children.

Class action suits aren't built equal, and neither are families.

I lift my hand in a wave as I approach the house. Mama and Papa are sitting on the patio bundled up in thick scarves and puffer jackets, steaming mugs of tea in their hands. I feel a twinge of anxiety at the sight, knowing what lies ahead.

"Hi. Happy anniversary," I pant, coming to a stop in front of them. I double over, resting my hands on my knees as I catch my breath. "Any chai left?"

So begins the complex dance of obligation and strategy. I look at Mama as she sets her cup down and goes inside. The sensation that runs through me feels a lot like disloyalty. I settle into the chair opposite Papa with a sigh, angling it so I can look at the slowly rising sun.

When we first bought the island, it was a passion project. Something for Owen and me to build together. Now it is a lifeline.

If anyone should be feeling guilty, it's Papa.

I love my father but Kilbryde is all I have left.

And losing it is not an option.

16

ZOE

I wake up to the sound of the shower running.

After our argument last night, Aseem and I made up with some pretty great sex. The kind of sex that had us reaching for each other with a desperation and urgency that reminded me of the early days of our relationship, when we could barely wait till we were indoors to rip each other's clothes off. To be honest, it's the kind of sex we've been having a lot of lately.

I haul myself out of bed and charge into the en-suite bathroom, discarding my silk nightie on the way. Aseem might grumble about my mood swings, and there is nothing sexy about morning sickness, but there is one side effect of pregnancy that we're both entirely happy with.

I swing the door to the shower open and step inside, wrapping my arms around my husband, pleased at the hardness I can sense even before he's turned around.

"Morning," I whisper, trailing kisses along the ridge of his shoulders.

Before I know it, he's spun me around and pinned me to the wall.

"Hi," he says, smiling. He touches his lips to my forehead. It is the most delicious feeling, Aseem's body pressing into mine. There is something about the contrast between the softness of his kiss and the roughness of his grip that leaves me quivering. If only he could press further, grip me tighter, perhaps we could fuse together.

We might argue, but underneath, it's all still there. We're fighting, but for the same things.

We're so engrossed in each other that we don't hear the bedroom door creak open.

We don't hear the footsteps cross the room.

We don't register Mama's presence until she's standing at the threshold of the bathroom, her face as white as the marbled floor.

My fingers tremble as I drop a tea bag into a cup, my nerves still frayed from the incident in the shower. The sight of Mama standing there left me flustered, but it's Aseem's reaction that I keep going over. He was mortified, of course, but after the initial shock had passed, he laughed it off.

"She didn't see anything," he said, stepping out of the shower and wrapping a towel around his waist. "And we should've remembered to lock the bedroom door."

The glass panels of the shower cubicle were misty enough to obscure most of what we were doing but that is not the point. Who walks into a married couple's bedroom without knocking first?

"I'm sure she knocked, but we were so busy doing"—he wiggled his eyebrows theatrically—"you know, we probably didn't hear her. Come on, it's funny. Where's your sense of humor?" He tried to pull me into his arms, but all that did was irritate me further.

So here I am in the kitchen, hands shaking as I tilt the kettle, hot water splashing all over the counter. "Fuck," I mutter as I set it down and look for a tea towel. All I want is a cup of tea and a moment alone.

"Top drawer to your right."

I don't need to turn around to know that the voice belongs to Gabe. I swallow my sigh. A quiet hour to myself is obviously too much to ask for in this house. "Thanks," I say, keeping my back to him. I take my time mopping up the mess, hoping that Gabe will take the hint, but he's clearly looking for conversation.

"I don't think I've ever seen such a tidy kitchen."

"That's Myra for you." I force myself to turn around and look at him. He's anchored himself to the kitchen island, legs stretched out in front of him. His hair, still wet from the shower, is slicked back, drawing my gaze away from his relaxed stance to his sharp features. "She's very organized."

"I picked up on that. She likes everything done a certain way, doesn't she? And she seems to be quite protective of Aish, more so than even her parents." Gabe laughs but there's a hollowness to it, as if he doesn't quite get why everyone's so over the top when it comes to Aisha. When I first met Aisha, I remember thinking it was odd as well, the way Mama would ring her every night to check if she was home, how Myra would sometimes visit unannounced, always under the ruse of a seminar that she would end up skipping to spend time with her sister. But once Aisha opened up to me, it suddenly made sense. After everything that had happened, of course they felt the need to protect her. I look at Gabe through narrowed eyes, trying to work out how much Aisha's told him about her childhood.

"The Agarwals are all extremely close," I say, by way of explanation.

"Are they? That announcement last night . . ." Gabe shakes his head, frowning. "None of you knew it was coming, did you?"

I give him a tight smile and make as if to move, but he's blocking my path.

I remind myself of my promise to Aisha. My foul mood isn't his fault. I force myself to make an effort. "What's your family like?"

"Oh, you know, typical middle class. Waitrose-loving mother, conservative father, a brother I barely see, a sister I see far too often." He shrugs, lips twisting into a wry smile. He tilts his head and fixes his gaze on me. "It must have been easy for you."

"Excuse me?"

"Fitting in. You knew the family before you met Aseem, didn't you? That must have helped."

It helped that I had a relationship with the family, yes. But as soon as they found out Aseem and I were dating, it was as though a switch flicked. Almost overnight I went from being Aisha's fun best friend who got on with everyone to a sly, conniving woman who was trying to infiltrate the family.

"To an extent, yes," I say. "And Aisha helped, of course."

"So I hear." He finishes the remnants of his coffee in one gulp. "Aisha told me you're trying to help. And . . . well, thank you. It means a lot to Aisha. And to me."

"Of course," I say, not entirely surprised by the sympathy and sense of kinship I feel toward him. I've been in his place; I know how difficult the Agarwals can be.

"You know, Zoe, you and I, we're really quite similar. Aisha told me that you were always very keen that the Agarwals accept you as one of them. I'm the same. The last thing I want is to take Aisha away from the people she loves. It's important to me to do this right, to become a part of this family."

"Why?" I ask, genuinely puzzled. By the time I realized how much the Agarwals resented me, it was too late, I was far too deeply in love with Aseem to step back. But Gabe and Aisha have only just met; he's seen how insufferable the family can be. He can still get away more or less unscathed.

"Why?" Gabe repeats. "For the same reason you were."

"Excuse me?"

Gabe pushes himself away from the island, sets his empty cup down in the sink, and comes to stand right in front of me. He's close enough that I can smell the coffee on his breath, but the queasiness building inside me has nothing to do with the smell. The air between us is dangerously electric, and I feel a jolt as our eyes meet.

The strong but subtle click of recognition.

"I mean I love Aisha. I want her to be happy," he says. He takes a step back and assesses me, his eyebrows meeting in a slight frown. "Why? What did you think?"

I never meant to fall in love with him.

I'd been living with Aisha for close to two years before I met Aseem. It was a Friday night, our winter term had just finished and instead of the club opening I was supposed to accompany Aisha to, I was in bed, nursing a cold and watching reruns of *The Good Wife* when the doorbell rang.

By that point I'd met every member of Aisha's family other than her brother. I'd spent several weekends partying with Myra and Owen, I'd been shopping with Aisha's mother, and I'd spent hours dissecting the drawbacks of the UK benefits system with her father. Unlike my mother, who I hadn't seen once since I moved to London, Aisha's family visited often. But they never stayed at the flat, preferring the luxury of the Four Seasons to spending the night on a sofa-bed and waking up to find little more than a pint of milk and stale eggs in the fridge.

So when I opened the door, barefoot and dressed in little more than a dressing gown, the last person I expected to see was Aseem.

I hastened to tidy up the detritus from Aisha's pre-drinks in the living room, using my sleeve to wipe away the light dusting of powder on the kitchen counter while Aseem wheeled his cases in. I might not have met Aseem before, but I could guess where he'd land on his sister's recreational drug use.

Seemingly unfazed by the state of the flat, Aseem told me there had been a mix-up with the dates on his reservations and the hotel didn't have a room available until tomorrow. Would it be too inconvenient if he spent the night at the flat?

I gawked at him. *Too inconvenient?* By that point I knew that the Agarwals had luxury boltholes that they rarely used across the world. They were practically rolling in money. But still, I was living rent-free in their two-million-pound Mayfair flat and *he* was asking *me* for permission?

I was charmed.

But I looked like shit. Truly. I made my excuses and went straight into the shower, helping myself to all of Aisha's nicest toiletries to rid myself of the sickly sweet smell that comes from having spent three days in bed.

By the time I returned, fresh faced and dressed in a chic shirtdress—also Aisha's—Aseem had tidied up the living room. There was a bottle of wine open on the kitchen counter and pizza was on the way.

I settled on to the bar stool across from him and looked at him over the rim of my glass.

I'd seen pictures of Aseem but they really didn't do him justice. He had the same deep brown eyes as Aisha, but while hers sparkled with laughter, his were filled with kindness. His dimples reminded me of his mother and Myra, and though there was mischief in his smile, there was also grace and empathy. His square jaw was a replica of his father's, but instead of the ruthless ambition I'd come to associate with Raj, as I referred to him then, Aseem's jaw spoke of a quiet determination. His entire face lit up when he told me about the tech conference he was there to attend. I already loved the family, their closeness was a reminder of everything I never had, but as one glass of wine turned to two, I realized just how charming Aisha's quiet older brother was.

Never have I been more grateful for missing a party.

And never have I fallen for a man as quick or as hard.

I don't remember exactly what we talked about that night. All I remember is the feeling I had when I looked into his face. Here was a man who would look after me. I could see it in the steadiness of his eyes, the sweep of his chest, the way he held himself, self-assured but not arrogant. I remember feeling lightheaded, woozy with relief and amazement. Aseem was everything I hadn't even known I wanted, the first man I'd ever really felt safe with. Did I mistake it for love at first sight? Maybe. Did it turn into love? Definitely.

Of course the money mattered.

Of course I wanted the lifestyle, the comfort, the *choices* the Agarwals had. Who wouldn't? But none of that changes the fact that I fell in love.

With Aseem, with Aisha, and with their chaotic, colorful, *connected* family.

If I had to describe my childhood in one word it would be lonely. I am a product of abuse at best, rape at worst. My mother didn't want me and she didn't make a secret of it. As for my father . . . my memories of him are limited to watching him beat my mother every night until I turned fifteen. Then his belt found younger flesh to torture and my mother realized she had been breeding a sacrificial lamb throughout.

Meeting Aisha and her family changed everything for me. I learned the meaning of family. I understood, for the first time, how class really works, how everything changes when you walk into a room knowing that you can buy the building.

Meeting the Agarwals gave me something to pine for and something to resent.

They represented everything I'd been denied my whole life: a family who cared about each other, who actually *wanted* to be together, and who had the means to live the kind of rich, easy life that I'd only ever witnessed from the outside.

I wanted in.

I wanted in so bad.

That first night, Aseem and I stayed up talking till Aisha returned home at three a.m.

The next morning Aseem told us that there were no hotel rooms available so we were stuck with him for the next week. Aisha was too hungover to protest and I was too triumphant. By the time Aseem's trip came to an end, my fate was sealed. I knew he was the man I would eventually marry.

Over the next couple of years, Aseem visited nearly every month. He always stayed at a hotel, and I invented a secret boyfriend so that I could sneak away to see him. Those were the best two years of my life.

I didn't tell anyone about our relationship. Not even Aisha.

Even as a naive twentysomething, I understood that people who are born with money are used to being in control. They're happy to let you enter their orbit, to share their good fortune, as long as they get to set the terms. Threaten to take that control away and they become defensive, fearful. Aisha never made me feel lesser than her, never treated me like a project, and yet there was a certain power she held over me simply by virtue of her place in the world. She set the terms of our relationship from day one. My role was to follow. I didn't know what would happen if the scales tipped and some of that power shifted to me, and I was too scared to find out.

It wasn't just me though. Aseem wanted to keep our relationship a secret as well. He said he wanted to keep us protected, safe in our little bubble for as long as was possible.

The tint of my glasses was so rosy, so full of hope, I never thought to ask what we needed protection from.

It wasn't an accident.

Nothing about this week—the things we said to each other, the things we did to each other—has been an accident.

Love, money, control: each of us had an agenda. A motive.

And each of us was prepared to do whatever it took to get what we came for.

I just didn't think I'd be prepared to—

My gaze flicks to the window as a streak of lightning lights up the landscape, showing the island for the menace it really is. A place haunted by death and violence that no amount of time can erase.

If there's anyone who can fix this, it's Papa.

Papa. My heart stops.

I think again of the body on the beach.

Papa can no longer fix anything.

We all went to a lot of effort for this reunion. It could have been the start of a new chapter for all of us, a chance to heal old wounds.

Instead Papa pitted us against each other.

He used us to further his own agenda.

And considering how much was at stake, is it really a surprise that it ended in murder?

17.

MYRA

The atmosphere is stilted as we sit down to the breakfast I've spent hours preparing to everyone's tastes. Papa's announcement from last night is like a gaping hole at the heart of the table.

We deal with it in typical Agarwal fashion: we pretend nothing is wrong.

Papa approaches his breakfast with laser focus; Mama fusses over Aseem; Zoe insists on having poached eggs then spends fifteen minutes pushing them around her plate. Even Aisha looks tired, her usual brightness toned down several notches as she nurses her hangover. Only Gabe seems unaffected, oblivious to the mood at the table as he talks nonstop, telling us about "the most amazing, life-changing retreat in the middle of the Amazon rainforest."

At least he's not on the champagne this morning.

"Ah, you lifesaver," Gabe beams at Zoe as she returns with a fresh pot of coffee. "I'm desperate for caffeine."

My gaze flits from Zoe to Aseem. My brother and his wife have always been one of those couples who can go from having a flaming row one minute to being totally loved up the next, so I'd assumed they would have made up by now. But the cloying tenderness I'd witnessed yesterday is gone. Instead there's a tension between them that's only made more obvious by how attentive Zoe's being toward Gabe. Aseem sips his coffee silently while Zoe quizzes Gabe about all the countries he's traveled to and Aisha tries to work out where they might have crossed paths.

Just listening to them is exhausting.

My irritated glance finds Papa's across the table just as Mama cuts Gabe off midsentence and turns to Aisha. "How's work, beta?"

Aisha's been working at a luxury travel agency for just over a year now. She once described the holidays and retreats she organizes as *Eat, Pray, Love* with private jets and butlers, which sounds pretentious even to me, but the important thing is that it makes her happy.

And pays for her rather expensive lifestyle.

Aisha fiddles with her napkin, folding it into a perfect square only to unfurl it again. "I quit, actually."

I set my fork down. With the constant travel and unbelievably fussy clients, most people would hate that job, but not Aisha. It's as close to her dream job as possible and she loves it. Or at least I thought she did. I flick a quick glance at Gabe but he's looking down, suddenly fixated by the plate of egg bhurji in front of him.

"Why?" I ask Aisha at the same time as Mama speaks. "When?"

"It's been a couple of months." Aisha looks uncertainly from Mama to me, shrugs. "It was always meant to be a temporary gig. And I was *miserable*." She turns to Gabe for reinforcement. "Wasn't I?"

"She really was," Gabe says, reaching for the juice.

"We'll find you something else." Papa sets his napkin down and looks at Aseem, ready to deputize this latest task. "Ajay Shukla was talking about launching a travel show. I'm sure he'll need a producer."

Ajay Shukla owns one of the largest media conglomerates in Asia and Papa owns a ten percent stake in his business.

Gabe's glass pauses momentarily on the way to his lips.

"I've already got something lined up in LA," Aisha says, scooping out a large spoonful of peanut butter and spreading it on her toast. She glances at Gabe then continues, "Gabe's friend is planning to open a yoga retreat and he needs a business development manager."

Aseem raises his eyebrows. Our baby sister has many redeeming qualities, but a head for business is not one of them.

"Wow," I say.

"I know!" Aisha beams, mistaking my surprise for excitement. "I've been talking about doing something in the wellness space for ages. I was thinking I'd start small—a day spa or soul cycle studio—but Gabe suggested I dream bigger. And the very next day, his friend calls to ask if he knows anyone suitable." She takes a breath, looks at Gabe, her excitement obvious. "Isn't it incredible?"

"It is," Zoe says. "How long is the contract?"

"I've bought a stake in the business so I'm hoping she'll stick around for a bit," Gabe says. "But it's up to her really. Can't hold this one down too long."

"No, you can't," Aisha says, smiling. "But between the retreat and the position Gabe got me on the Met board, I'm going to have my hands full."

The Met board?

I narrow my eyes. It takes a serious amount of influence to get on the Met board, and if Gabe can make that happen for a girl with next to no experience, I can't help but wonder if I'm wrong about him. I glance at Papa. Perhaps Gabe is that rarest of things, a man whose only agenda is love.

Argh. The sappiness of that thought is enough to leave me cringing.

I straighten my placemat and rearrange my cutlery as the conversation drifts back to holiday destinations.

"We're thinking of doing Europe in the summer," Zoe is saying. "A short break before the baby comes."

"Do you know where?" Aisha asks. "I can help you book something."

"We haven't really discussed it yet, but I'm definitely thinking a beach holiday. Somewhere nice and chilled?"

"And easy to get to," Aseem adds, nodding.

"Portugal?" Aisha asks at the same time as Gabe says, "How about Greece?"

I freeze.

"Gabe," Aisha says, quickly shaking her head.

Gabe holds up his hands. "I know the Greek islands are a bit passé, but hear me out. There are some gorgeous new properties on the mainland. Really top notch, lots of pri—" He pauses, taking in Aisha's stricken look.

Mama's face has paled over her egg-white omelet.

We don't talk about Greece. Ever.

"I'm sorry. I didn't think—I mean, it's been nearly twenty years, right?" Gabe says, visibly flustered.

She told him?

No one speaks. For a second I feel bad for him.

Then I want to kill him.

Mama sets her cutlery down, her hands trembling, then gets up and walks out of the kitchen without a word. Life changed for all of us after Greece. But Mama? It changed her.

Gabe looks around the table, his gaze leaping from one face to the next. Aisha places a hand on his arm. Papa looks ready to punch him. "I'm sorry," Gabe repeats. "I didn't mean to bring it up. I can only imagine how hard that must have been . . . especially for you, Aseem," he continues.

Metal screeches against wood as I push my chair back and get up.

Strangling Gabe at the table is not an option, so instead I strangle the conversation.

"Zoe, will you help me clear?" I say. "We're done, aren't we?"

There are murmurs of assent as I begin stacking plates on top of each other.

Gabe pauses midbite then hastens to put his fork down as I reach for his plate.

Aisha looks at me, her brown eyes pleading, full of apology, but I used up my reserves of compassion a long time ago.

I look away, furious. When she decided to tell the man she's known for less than six months about what happened in Greece, she should also have told him to keep his mouth shut. She should have taken the time to explain to him that there's a reason we don't talk about Ishaan.

Even the mention of what happened to him has the power to annihilate us all.

18

ZOE

Every family has a few topics that are impossible to discuss without reopening old wounds. The ones that lurk beneath every conversation, never acknowledged but ever-present.

In this family, that topic is Ishaan: Aisha's twin brother, who entered the world exactly three minutes after her and who died, aged eight, while the family was holidaying in Greece.

It's the tragedy that nearly twenty years later still haunts the family.

I remember how horrified I'd been when two years after we first met, Aisha finally told me about the accident. Even though she was just a little girl when it happened, her recollections of the fire were visceral, her account of what it did to her family gut-wrenching.

The flames that killed Ishaan might not have touched anyone else, but his death left a mark on each of them, shaping not only their choices but also their personalities. It's the reason why Mama's so fragile and Myra's such a control freak. It's why they're so protective of Aisha: she's the twin who survived.

Accidentally or not, I cannot believe Gabe brought it up.

"Are you okay?" I ask Aseem as soon as we're back in our bedroom.

He doesn't say anything, just kicks off his shoes and goes to sit on the edge of the bed.

I lock the door and sit down next to him.

"Do you want to talk about it?" I ask, even though I know the answer already. Aseem's always avoided discussing what happened to Ishaan. No matter how many times I ask, all I get from my husband is silence. Today's no different.

I put a hand on his knee, my worry for my husband briefly loosening the knot of fury that's been twisting inside me. Like Aisha, Aseem was just a kid when it happened, but he doesn't see it that way. He was babysitting the twins when the accident happened and he still lives with the guilt of not being able to save his baby brother. In some ways, they all do.

Another family might have got help, gone for counseling, or at the very least, discussed it among themselves, but the Agarwals are far too posh to indulge in honest conversation. They responded to Ishaan's death by never talking about it. Ever.

"Aseem?"

"You should change," he says, looking at the silk dress I have on. "I told Myra we'd help with the cake."

The cake for Mama and Papa's big anniversary dinner. Call me petty, but after Mama's intrusion and the stunt Papa pulled last night, I really don't feel like spending a few hours rolling out fondant for them.

However, I can't deny that with my parents-in-law out of sight, it'll be the perfect opportunity for Aseem to talk to his sisters. And if I'm there I can steer the conversation where it needs to go.

I get up and go into the bathroom. I change into jeans and a sweat-shirt and pull my hair into a ponytail. By the time I return, Aseem's moved to the armchair, laptop balanced on his knees. His face brightens when he sees me, all signs of the tension from earlier gone. "Ready?" he asks as he slams the laptop shut and gets up.

Sometimes it feels like I've married a complete stranger.

Turns out we're helping with more than just the cake. Myra has the quite the feast planned for the evening and though she's done a lot of the preparation beforehand, there is an incredible amount of work still to be done.

Gabe cuts half a dozen strips of prosciutto before making a flimsy excuse and leaving the rest of us to labor on. Myra's whipping up the batter for the cake, Aseem's working on the goat cheese and prosciutto wrapped breadsticks, and somehow, Aisha and I have ended up in charge of manipulating fondant into delicate little roses.

It doesn't take long for the conversation to land on Papa.

"I don't understand why he would spring something like that on us," Myra says. She looks at Aseem. "You've been working on the deal for what, six months now? Why go along with it if he didn't want to sell?"

I bite down on my lip. I can think of half a dozen reasons, starting with the fact that he's a narcissist control freak who *always* does stuff like this. Yet somehow they never expect him to.

"I don't know, but coming back . . ." Aseem pauses as he spreads goat's cheese on a slice of prosciutto. "It's not a good idea. He's been out of the loop for years now."

"He did build the company, Aseem. I'm sure he can catch up," Aisha says.

"I'm not so sure," Aseem says. He finishes wrapping up a breadstick and places it on the baking sheet. "The business isn't what it used to be. We're out of touch, we haven't diversified and our profits . . . Our position in the market is precarious. And then springing an announcement like this . . . I don't think either of you realize what it takes to keep PetroVision afloat."

"I think I have a fair idea, thank you very much. I did win the lawsuit."

"And nearly bankrupted us in the process," Aseem retorts.

Myra smirks. "Oh sorry. Would you have preferred jail time?" She chooses an egg from the carton in front of her and cracks it with one firm tap. She prizes it open, taking her time transferring the yoke from one half to the other, separating it from the white. She looks up after the white's run off, seemingly having found her way back to the issue at hand. "You're worried about the valuation?"

"No, that's not what I meant. I don't care what happens with the business; we can sell it, keep it, whatever, but Papa can't take on so much responsibility again," Aseem says.

"You don't *care* what happens with the business?" Aisha echoes.

"Stop it, Aish. I'm worried about him. Maybe the two of you have forgotten what it was like when—" Aseem stops midsentence, his voice thick. "He nearly died. The doctors *told* us it was stress induced."

"He looks fine. And he did say he's spoken to the doctor," Aisha says, tentatively.

Myra scoffs. "And you believe him? It obviously has to do with Malhotra. Perhaps *someone* should have worked harder to find a buyer who Papa hasn't spent years competing with."

Typically, Aseem pays no heed to the obvious—and *completely* unfair—dig, and for a few minutes we all work silently, the only sound the whir of the stand mixer as Myra whisks the egg whites.

"What happens if Papa stays on?" Aisha asks, twisting semicircles of pale-yellow fondant into dainty roses.

Aseem looks up. "To the deal?"

She nods.

"Malhotra isn't interested in a merger," Aseem says. "If Papa stays, he'll walk."

And take his three hundred million pounds with him.

I roll out the last of the fondant, then reach for the paring knife. "He can't actually stay on though, can he?" I say, voicing the thought that's been running through my mind all morning.

"He can do whatever he wants," Myra replies. "But I agree with Aseem, I don't like the idea of him putting himself under that much pressure. It's not good for him."

Relief flutters through me.

"I don't know. Papa gets his energy from working. Retirement is probably his idea of hell," Aisha says. "Why are we having this conversation anyway? It's his life, his business."

"We're having this conversation because we care about him," Aseem says. "And because his decision makes zero sense. He's been pushing for this deal for months."

I stop carving and look up.

"Why are you all so fixated on *why* he changed his mind? That's irrelevant. It's already done." Aisha looks straight at Myra. "What does his will say?"

"Seriously, you don't want to talk about Papa but you want to discuss his will? What is the matter with you?" Myra sets the spatula down and looks at each of us in turn. "Should we talk to him? All three of us together?"

"What? No! I don't want to talk about any of this," Aisha says, pressing the petals together into a perfect little rose. She sets the flower down and wipes her hands on the kitchen towel. "Gabe warned me about this, you know."

"Gabe *warned* you?" Myra's tone is sharp.

"He guessed something like this might happen. And he was right. Always about the money in this family."

"It's not—" Aseem starts but Aisha cuts him off.

"Yes, it is."

"Do you think maybe Gabe's trying to manipulate you?" Myra says.

Aisha scoffs. "Sure, *he's* the one trying to manipulate me."

"What's that supposed to mean?" Myra says, arms crossed in front of her.

"Oh come on, I'm not completely clueless. I know how you operate," Aisha says, looking from Myra to Aseem. "You think I can't tell what you're trying to do here? You are so desperate for Papa to sell the business and hand over our inheritance that you're trying to manipulate me into siding with you. Both of you."

Myra takes an audible breath. She rests her hands on the counter and leans forward to look Aisha in the eye. "We aren't trying to manipulate you. We're having a discussion about what's best for Pa—"

"It's his life! Whatever he wants to do is what's best for him," Aisha spits. "I'm out." She throws the kitchen towel on the countertop and walks off.

Myra makes as if to follow her but Aseem holds up his hand. "Give her some time to cool off," he says.

Myra nods, then starts spooning the batter into the cake tins. "We need to get her away from that leech," she mutters. She scrapes the last of the batter out with her spatula, then looks at me. "Has Aish said anything to you about him?"

"Only that she thinks it might be serious. I think we should give him—" I catch Aseem's eye, notice the slight shake of his head and backtrack. "I think we should be careful."

Aseem gives me a quick nod before turning to Myra. "About Papa. Are you sure talking to him together is the best idea?"

Myra frowns.

"It might come across like an attack," Aseem elaborates. "Maybe we should take it in turns. You speak to him first, get the lay of the land, and then I'll go in and talk numbers."

It's obvious that he's trying to avoid a confrontation with his father but in this instance it might actually be a good thing.

Papa dotes on Aisha, but Myra's the one he trusts. He'll listen to her.

"Okay," Myra says, sliding the cake into the oven and slamming the door shut.

I pick up Aisha's kitchen towel and examine the carnage underneath. All but one of the roses she and I so painstakingly assembled have been crushed.

19

MYRA

By the time Aisha returns, wearing an embarrassed expression and the brightest pink trainers I've ever seen, I've finished decorating the cake; the carrots, parsnips, and potatoes are chopped, peeled, and dressed; and the port sauce is bubbling away on the hob. I slide the venison and wild mushroom wellington I've just finished wrapping into the fridge, ready to go into the oven later. I've planned a rather elaborate menu for tonight and, as with anything, preparation is key.

"You could win *Bake Off* with that thing," Aisha says, coming to stand next to me. I follow her gaze to the cake.

A vine of pale yellow and lilac roses twists around two tiers of vanilla sponge covered in ivory buttercream. I turn my head from side to side, trying to alleviate the tension between my shoulder blades, then get started on the sandwiches I'm preparing for lunch. I enjoy hosting, but I'm not crazy. Lunch is a simple picnic of freshly picked mussels and smoked salmon sandwiches down by the beach.

"Look, I'm sorry about earlier," Aisha says. "I was—"

"On edge?"

She nods. I'd guessed as much. It's odd for Aisha to get so worked up about the business, odder still for her to defend Papa. Her reaction earlier, the defensiveness of her words doesn't make sense in isolation, but in the context of the conversation Gabe started earlier, the picture completes itself. The mention of Ishaan—it does that to us. A therapist would probably say it's because we've all repressed our memories of that time, but I'm not so sure.

Whenever I get anxious, the memories come back, intense and insistent. The sounds first. Mama's howl. The wail of the sirens. The squeak of my shoes on the ICU floor. Then the smells. Petrol. Smoke. Disinfectant. Finally, the visuals make an appearance, clicking into place with a brutality that doesn't seem to lessen with time. The real ones and the ones I've imagined, my brain filling in the gaps. The bag that was too big for such a tiny body. The flames that took one twin and spared the other. Owen's face when he told me what he'd done.

Flashes from two different scenes, memories that are separated by decades, yet inextricably linked in my brain. I blink the images away and squeeze Aisha's hand. If the mention of something I never even witnessed can send me spiraling, I daren't imagine how much worse it must be for her.

Aisha rests her head against my shoulder for a brief moment before straightening up. "He means well," she says, her eyes searching mine for compassion I do not have. Easy as it is for me to forgive my little sister, my benevolence doesn't extend to her boyfriend. She picks up a slice of bread and starts assembling a sandwich. "You'll see."

Papa's sitting in the living room, thick book in hand, patio doors flung open. He looks up when my shadow obscures the midmorning sun.

"Any good?"

He flips the book he's reading so I can look at the cover. It's a compilation of essays documenting the shifting tide in Indian politics. "Utter nonsense. You need to get Wi-Fi installed here."

I roll my eyes. The whole point of coming to a remote island is to disconnect, but that's a nuance that's lost on my father. Papa likes everything, from his morning chai to his postdinner whiskey, with a side of the news.

I lower myself on to the sofa across from him. I'm under no illusions that this conversation will be pleasant, but Aseem and Zoe are upstairs, Mama's in the kitchen, and Aisha and Gabe are outside. I'm unlikely to find a better moment to launch into this discussion.

And if Owen's emails are any indication of things to come, I'm running out of time.

"That was quite the announcement last night," I say.

He raises an eyebrow, then returns to the book he clearly has no interest in.

"Aseem and I are worried," I say, undeterred.

"About?"

"About you, Papa. You've only just recovered and—"

"I told you I'm fine."

"—and Aseem thinks you staying on might mess up future valuations of the company."

"You know better than to trust everything your brother says. What do you think?"

"I think we've got a really good deal and it would be unwise to walk away. We nearly went bankrupt a few years ago."

Papa shrugs. "Peaks and troughs."

I cross my arms in front of my chest. I'd forgotten how difficult Papa can be. How unrelenting. "Fine. Keep it for sentimental reasons until you run yourself into the ground trying to save a business that's no longer viable."

"No longer viable?" Papa scoffs. "You have no idea, beta. And I didn't build all this up to have that rock star Malhotra waltz in and butcher it."

Malhotra. I knew it.

Before Jayant Malhotra became the CEO of Wren Alloys's Indian division, he was Papa's right-hand man, his mentee. When he left, he took some of our biggest contracts with him, something Papa's never forgiven him for.

Papa's anger is justifiable, but turning three hundred million pounds down to further a personal vendetta isn't just foolish, it's irresponsible. I tell him as much.

Papa puts his book down, finally bothering to look at me. "Why are you so worried about this?"

I answer his question with one of my own. "Are you going to tell me what you're actually planning?"

He shrugs, gives me a half-smile, as if he's indulging a child. "Lots of moving parts."

"But it's real? You are going back just so you can show Malhotra up?"

Papa sighs, his expression turning serious. "Myra, I don't give a toss about Malhotra. I care about my business. In five years' time, there will only be one independent petrochemical manufacturer left in India. I want that to be us. With our connections in government, that *can* be us. But not with Aseem at the helm. Maybe if you were to come in . . ." He shakes his head. "Your brother doesn't have the grit or the imagination for what I have planned. He's too soft. And too far under his wife's thumb."

"Fine. Whatever. But why did you lie to me? You promised me you were going to retire and give me—"

Papa raises his hand in objection. "I didn't promise you I was retiring. I promised you I'd look after you. Two completely different things."

"What does that even mean? I'm in trouble, Papa. I need that money."

"Why is it so difficult for you to—"

Papa stops talking midsentence, his words cut off by a sound so familiar and so horrifying, it makes my stomach flip. The scream that pierces the air is unidentifiable, yet we've both heard it enough times before to know that it can only belong to one person.

Aisha.

20

MYRA

apa's right behind me. Mama, Aseem, and Zoe arrive at the scene seconds later.

"Where is she? What happened?" Mama pants.

I twist to look at Mama, then take a step to my right so she can see what I'm looking at: Aisha and Gabe emerging from the fringes of the forest.

She's okay.

She's okay.

Already, my breathing softens, but I'm confused.

Because Aisha doesn't just look fine, she looks delighted.

We crowd around her, all of us speaking at the same time, asking Aisha what happened, if she's hurt, if she's okay.

"I'm okay," Aisha laughs. "I promise. I've just had a bit of a shock."

She reaches her hand out to pull Gabe into the tight knot we've formed around her.

"Actually, not a shock, a surprise," she says.

There is a flash of excitement in her eyes.

I freeze. I know, in that moment, exactly what she's about to say.

I should have seen this coming.

"We're engaged!"

Engaged. The word lingers. Sinks in.

"You're engaged?" My voice sounds distant, like an echo. Or perhaps a memory.

"Yes!" Aisha holds her hand out toward me, beaming. "Isn't it *gorgeous?*"

I look at the ring on my sister's hand. It's a classic Art Deco design with a blinding three, maybe three-and-a-half carat cushion-cut diamond. It's exquisite. The sort of thing you'd find in a Christie's catalog. Every suspicion I've had about Gabe comes back to me as I peer at Aisha's hand, trying to work out if the ring is an antique heirloom or an excellent fake.

"So?" Aisha prods, looking from me to Mama, and back again. "What do you think?"

"It's stunning," I say, forcing myself to gush for the sake of my little sister. I glance at Mama, certain she's thinking the same thing as she reaches for Aisha's hand, tilting it so she can inspect the diamond.

"Beautiful," Mama says.

Aisha moves to hug us both at once before remembering to pull Zoe in.

"I hope you don't mind," Gabe says, looking sheepishly from Mama to Papa. "I didn't mean to upstage your big anniversary, but I wanted to propose to Aisha with her whole family around. And I just knew that she'd love the idea of us getting engaged on the same day that you got married."

I resist the urge to roll my eyes.

"That's not the thing I mind, Gabriel," Papa answers stiffly.

Gabe frowns, raises his hands in apparent defeat. "I know, I know. I'm sorry I didn't come to you first, but you know what Aish is like. She thinks it's such an antiquated tradition; she would've hated it if I'd asked for your permission. But," he says, breaking into a nervous grin, "for what it's worth, I want you to know that I think Aisha is the sweetest, kindest, most generous woman I've ever met and I'm going to do everything I can to be worthy of her. Nothing is more important to me than making her happy. I didn't ask for your permission, but I am hoping you'll give us your blessing? And some tips. Forty years is a long time."

A nice speech, but something about it doesn't ring true. It's too slick, just like the man delivering it.

As expected, Mama defuses the tension. "The most important tip I can give you is to always keep Aisha's family on side," she says, smiling.

My eyes find Aseem's. It's not just the fact that with his claims of building a multi-million-pound business from scratch, then leaving it behind to follow his heart, Gabe has set off a series of alarm bells. Even if I'm wrong about him—and Aseem's initial research into him certainly suggests I might be—there is the fact Aisha's known him for less than six months. As far as I know, she's never even met his family.

"This is all quite sudden, isn't it?" Aseem says, reading my mind.

"Doesn't feel sudden to me," Gabe says, a little too earnestly. "I knew the moment I saw Aisha that I was going to marry her. I picked the ring out a week after we met. If anything, it's been agonizing having to wait for six months."

Once upon a time, I might have been taken by the romance of a story like this, but not anymore. I think about Owen's proposal, the trek up to the ski lift, the pretense of a lost binding, the ring sparkling amidst a blanket of snow.

Owen swept me off my feet. Which is why, when a few years later the rug was pulled out from under me, I was bereft. Instead of the solid ground I was expecting, I found myself standing on a cloud of empty promises.

People assume it's the bad memories that terrorize me, but if I'm honest, it's the good ones that are far more brutal.

I'm pulled back to the present as I suck in a breath of the chilly air, relishing the slight tremble behind my ribcage as my chest rises. Mama, dressed in just a thin jumper and chinos, is complaining about how cold she is, Zoe and Aisha are talking excitedly, and Papa is looking at me, his expression one of worry.

Papa and I hang back as everyone starts to move inside.

After Ishaan, Mama sank into a depression so deep she'd sometimes stay in her bedroom for days. Aseem was still just a child, all of twelve years old, so looking after Aisha became our responsibility, Papa's and mine.

We both know that it'll be down to the two of us to avert this particular disaster as well.

"What do you think?" I say, keeping an eye on the group through the patio doors as they move through the living room and into the kitchen.

"I don't trust him," Papa says, simply.

I rub my arms, suddenly cold.

As if this week isn't hard enough as it is.

"About what we were discussing earlier—" I start, but Papa cuts me off.

He pushes his hand through his hair. The frustration on his face is obvious, and the shame it triggers in me expected. "The trouble with you, Myra, is that you can get so blinkered that you completely miss the bigger picture. You seem to have forgotten that PetroVision is my company, and I can do whatever the hell I want with it." He draws a long, steadying breath. "Including giving my daughter fifty million when she needs it."

"But how—"

"How is not important. It's choreography." His face softens. "Have I ever let you down, beta?"

I hurry to bat the unwanted tears away even as relief ripples through my entire body.

"I need you to stop worrying about the money and start thinking about the family. We need to stick tight. Tighter than ever now," Papa continues.

I turn my attention to the kitchen window to observe the tableau assembled inside. Everyone's gathered around the dining table as Aisha chatters excitedly to her captive audience. I study Gabe as he circles the table, pouring champagne, dropping a kiss on Aisha's head, inhabiting my kitchen with an ease that is unnerving. He catches me watching and as our eyes meet, I force myself to smile, appear polite, but his face stays frozen. There is no smile, no acknowledgment. He just stares.

I think of my panic when I heard Aisha scream, the deep-in-my-bones belief that Gabe had hurt her.

No matter what he says or how besotted he appears to be with Aisha, I know in my gut that he's not right for my sister.

"Just because Gabe didn't lie about his career doesn't mean he's a good guy. It means he did his homework. I'm telling you, this man has an agenda," Papa says, his words echoing my worry.

I tear my gaze away from Gabe and look at Papa.

"We need to protect our family," he says.

21.

ZOE

I'm not dressed for the walk.

We're having lunch on the beach, which seemed like a lovely idea when Myra first suggested it, but like most things in life, the promise doesn't live up to the reality. The mood dampens somewhat as we pass a cluster of burned cottages. The beach, one of three on the island, is a couple of miles away and, though the hike through the forest and up the hillside is straightforward, it's hard work. By the time we reach the pristine white sands, my leather boots, which the sales assistant at Harrods assured me were made for hiking, are giving me blisters, bits of seaweed and broken shells have attached themselves to my jeans, and underneath my fluffy cashmere jumper and Barbour coat, my skin prickles with goosebumps.

To be fair though, Myra has gone to a lot of effort. She's pulled out deck chairs and blankets from the beach hut and arranged them in a wide arc around the campfire. A couple of picnic baskets sit on a striped towel, and we've all been handed small plastic buckets to collect mussels. It's like something out of an Enid Blyton novel. Except that unlike George and co., our whispered conversations and knowing glances hide things far darker than childhood pranks and old-fashioned xenophobia.

I've never been foraging before and it's only when we're right by the water, waves crashing beneath our feet, that I realize that the jagged black stacks of rock I'd admired from afar are heaving, moving colonies of mussels.

Fish trapped in their own shells, isolated yet stuck together.

Kind of like this family.

"Ew," Aisha yelps as Aseem drops a long piece of seaweed on her head. He throws a large handful of mussels into the bucket at her feet, before going back for more.

Just the thought of cooking them, of tossing the slimy, squirmy things into a pot of boiling water, is enough to make me gag. I walk back to the beach hut and sink into one of the deck chairs.

The rest of them follow a few minutes later, carrying buckets full of more mussels than we can possibly eat, but it's about the sport, I suppose. If you can call it that.

Everyone seems to be in a good mood. Aisha's discussing wedding lehengas with Mama, Gabe's busy taking pictures, Papa and Myra are debating tide timings and water levels, and Aseem, diplomatic as usual, is dipping in and out of both conversations.

The normalcy is so artificial it takes my breath away.

As if Aisha's surprise engagement hasn't thrown them all into panic mode.

As if at this very moment, they aren't all silently plotting Gabe's exit.

This picnic is little more than a performance, an announcement to no one watching that the Agarwals are a close-knit, wholesome, *happy* family.

When I first met them, it was this closeness that struck me the most. The whole family seemed to move as a single organism, connected even when they weren't together. I'd go to lunch with Mama and Aisha and get drawn into a discussion about Myra's latest case; I'd visit Myra in Edinburgh and she'd spend half the time talking about Aseem's start-up. They consulted each other on everything, but what surprised me the most was the fact that not only did they know exactly what was going on in each other's lives, they *cared*.

I'd never seen anything like it.

It took getting married and living with my in-laws for me to realize that the closeness I so envied cloaked a vein of darkness that ran so deep it was embedded in their DNA. My husband's family uses love as a shield, an excuse to justify everything from their insecurity and nosiness to outright intrusion.

I take a sip of my Diet Coke as a fresh wave of nausea roils my stomach.

Papa pulled me aside earlier to tell me that he's counting on me. He wants me to talk to Aisha, to help her see that Gabe isn't right for her, that he'll never be able to assimilate into the family.

I had to bite my tongue to stop myself from reminding him that Aseem and I have been counting on him too. And that Aisha is an adult, entitled to make her own bloody decisions.

Myra begins opening the picnic baskets and starts laying the food out. "There's sourdough to go with the mussels," she says, nodding to Mama, who's using a sharp knife to yank the barnacles off, "and smoked salmon sandwiches for anyone who's squeamish."

"That'll be me," I say, eyeing the platter of sandwiches.

I've barely finished speaking when Mama interjects, frowning. "Those aren't for you, sweetie. Salmon isn't good for the baby."

Oh, for fuck's sake. I love salmon. I twist to look at Aseem for support but he refuses to meet my eye. I turn to Myra—she knows better than most how to deal with Mama's ridiculous pregnancy rules—but all I get from her is an apologetic smile. "I think Mama made you something special," she says, handing a Tupperware box to Mama.

Mama opens it with a great deal of ceremony. She places the contents—five fist-sized balls—on to a paper plate and hands it to me. "Gondh ke ladoo," she says, by way of explanation. "My mother-in-law made these for me during all my pregnancies. These little treats are packed with all the nutrients you need right now."

I'm trying to keep an open mind, I really am, but the misshapen blobs on the plate don't look anything like the melt-in-the-mouth, delicately flavored sweets I've eaten before. I stick a fork in one of them. Solid, sticky, and, as I take a tentative sniff, disgusting.

I clamp a hand over my mouth as the urge to gag takes over.

I set the plate down and reach for my Diet Coke.

Mama tuts. "All that artificial sugar . . ." She trails off, the passive-aggressive comment enough for me to set the can down. She picks up the fork and lifts a large brown morsel to my mouth. "Here, have a taste," she urges.

It takes everything I've got not to push her way. "Maybe later."

"Shalini, do you remember you refused to eat them the first time as well?" Papa says. He looks at me. "But one taste and she could not get enough. I swear, some days, all she ate was these ladoos."

Papa's attempt to defuse the tension earns him a smile from his wife, but I'm not as easily swayed. "How can I forget? You teased me about it incessantly, claimed the kids would end up becoming halwais," Mama says. "Confectioners," she adds for my benefit.

On the fire, the mussels hiss and spit in their pot, the smell of the fish cooking in their own juices making me even more nauseous. I take another, rebellious sip of my Coke. The only person allowed to tell me what to eat—and what *not* to eat—is my doctor.

I reach for the plate of sandwiches, ignoring the look Aseem shoots me. My fingers have barely grazed the edge of the plate when Mama swipes it away.

"For fuck's sake. What's wrong with you?" I say.

"Zoe," Aseem says, his tone sharp, abrasive. He darts a horrified glance at Mama.

"What?" I snap.

Myra leans forward and places a pacifying hand on my arm. "It's okay. If you don't want to eat it, you don't have to."

I feel my whole body sigh with relief.

"Thank you," I say, looking at Myra, both surprised and touched by her support. At least someone has my back, even if it's not my husband. Or my best friend, who is inspecting her ginormous ring with unprecedented focus.

"Apologize to Mama," Papa says.

"Excuse me?"

"Rehne do. There's really no need," Mama says.

"*No need*? Baat karne ki tameez nahi hai isme," Papa snaps back.

I stare at him. I can deduce what his words might mean, but more than what he may or may not have said, it's the switch to Hindi that infuriates me. In my in-laws' hands, even language is a weapon, one they deploy at choice moments to alienate me further.

"I think what Papa means," Myra intervenes, looking from Papa to me, "is that Mama went to a lot of effort to make these for you."

So much for having my sister-in-law's *support*.

"Well, maybe next time she should ask me first," I bite back.

I haul myself out of the deck chair and brush the sand off my clothes.

"What are you doing?" Aseem finds his voice.

"I'm going back to the house," I say.

A glance passes between Myra and Papa. Aisha stares into her glass like it holds the secrets of the universe while Gabe looks at me, his expression unreadable.

And Mama . . . all that wounded bird look does is rile me further.

"Come on, Zo. Is that really necessary?" Aseem says.

"Yes, it's *necessary*," I spit out. "I'm exhausted. I'm hungry. I'm cold. And I want to lie down."

I could remind him my doctor's told me to make sure I eat well and get enough rest, but I refuse to justify my decision. No matter what they all think, it's not normal for Mama to intrude into my life, my pregnancy, my fucking *shower*.

I cross my arms, pushing my hands up into my coat sleeves.

"I'm leaving," I repeat.

Aseem looks at me, then at Mama and Papa, eyebrows furrowed.

"Okay," Mama says, nodding.

That single word, the *permission-granted* tone, unravels me.

"I was talking to my husband."

Mama's eyes widen, her face freezing in an expression of shock as my words land. She looks away, finally getting the message. Papa makes as if to get up but Mama's hand on his knee stops him.

"Zoe." Aseem pronounces my name with a sigh, his voice both exasperated and resigned at once.

"Yes?" I lift my chin, waiting for him to say he'll accompany me. I'm not a damsel-in-distress, far from it. And I don't expect him to share my unease about the island and its morbid history. But I am his wife, I'm pregnant, and he made me a fucking promise. If he doesn't have the spine to stand up for me, the least he can do is walk me back.

He sighs. Again.

"If that's what you want." He shrugs and picks up a sandwich. "I'll see you later."

22.

MYRA

We try to gloss over Zoe's behavior, but no amount of small talk can fill the embarrassed hush that follows her departure. Zoe knows how much Mama cares. She knows *why* Mama feels things as deeply as she does. Would it have killed her to have a tiny bite of the ladoo? Considering how generous Mama and Papa have been, surely politeness is the bare minimum they're owed.

"Does she always behave like this?" I ask Mama as we wrap up the leftovers. I keep my voice low, conscious that Aseem's only a few feet from us. I watch as he douses the campfire with water, then begins burying the embers in sand, his mouth set in a tight line.

Aseem looked mortified at Zoe's rudeness but there was something else too: a resignation that tells me that this kind of behavior is far more frequent than I might've expected, especially considering how hard Zoe used to try to please Mama.

Of course that was back when she was trying to impress her future mother-in-law. Things are different now.

Mama picks up the beach towel and shakes it off. "It's probably just hormones. You know what—" She pauses, sighs. "She's always been different. Difficult. But you know your brother. Patience of a saint. He'll never say anything to her, especially not now. Maybe once the baby's born . . ." Her words lack conviction. We both know that once the baby's born, Aseem will do whatever he can to keep the peace with her.

When something's bothering Zoe, she makes it known, loud and clear, but no matter how unhappy Aseem is, he never admits it. He bottles it all up, suffering silently until it's physically impossible for him to contain it any more.

That's what Ishaan's death did to him; Aseem retreated into himself. More than twenty years later, it feels as though we're still waiting for him to re-emerge, to catch a glimpse of the carefree, spontaneous boy he used to be.

That's why I'd been so relieved when I first found out that he was seeing Zoe.

Papa had rented the usual chalet in Verbier for the season. After a lot of maneuvering and shuffling of calendars, we finally found a week when we could all be there. Owen and I flew in from Edinburgh, Aseem took the red-eye from Delhi, and Aisha hopped on a plane from London. Though Zoe wasn't invited per se, she was always welcome, and as usual she tagged along. It was one of those rare family holidays when things actually felt easy. Uncomplicated. The weather was perfect and, other than Aseem, who's always preferred lie-ins to early morning ski runs, we were all on the slopes two, sometimes three times a day.

When, two days into the trip, Zoe, who rarely lasted more than an hour on the slopes anyway, stayed home with a migraine, none of us gave it much thought.

If the ski lift hadn't shut unexpectedly, we likely wouldn't have returned to the chalet until after lunch. And I definitely wouldn't have the image of Zoe's buttocks imprinted on my brain.

Mama, Papa, Aisha, Owen, and I crowded into the dining room while we waited for Aseem and Zoe to get dressed, all of us talking at once, our reactions a mixture of shock, anger, and indignation. When Aseem finally appeared, dressed and decent, his cheeks were flushed with embarrassment and his words rushed. This wasn't how he meant for us to find out, he said, but it was serious. It turned out that they'd been dating secretly for nearly three years and Aseem was so smitten, he was thinking about proposing. With Mama and Papa's blessing, of course.

After the initial shock passed, I'd been pleased. Aseem's previous girlfriends had been a perfect fit on paper—sophisticated, beautiful, used to a life flitting between high society dinners and elaborate family get-togethers—but they were also mind-numbingly boring. Zoe was easy-going in a way that Aseem could never hope to be; there was a simplicity to her that felt refreshing. She was independent, ambitious, and most of all, *fun*, which I thought was just what Aseem needed.

Mama and Papa did not feel the same way. They were convinced that Aseem was making an irreversible mistake. As far as they were concerned, Aseem and Zoe were too different, their lifestyles and temperaments ill suited to each other.

Voices were raised, accusations slung, but ultimately it came down to this: Zoe had been brought up in a single-parent household. She had no siblings or cousins to speak of and no notion of what it meant to be part of a family, let alone a big, extended Indian one. No one could deny that she had been a huge support to Aisha, but Papa was worried that Zoe wouldn't be able to integrate into our family or the circles we moved in. It was one thing to live with Aisha in her Soho flat and come along for family holidays, quite another to marry Aseem and move to the family home in Delhi, he argued. How would a working-class white girl adjust to the change in lifestyle? Would she be able to learn the hundreds of traditions and live up to the expectations that come with being part of a family like ours?

Papa's concerns were valid, but Aseem was adamant.

In the end, Papa relented and six months later, at another family holiday, Aseem proposed to Zoe. For a while at least, it seemed as though Mama and Papa had been wrong. Zoe moved to Delhi two months before the wedding and made the transition from friend to wife and daughter-in-law with remarkable ease. The only resistance came from Zoe's mother, who, for reasons I cannot fathom, refused to attend the wedding. In the three years since, aside from the usual hiccups that come with marriage and family, by and large their relationship has seemed perfect.

Now I'm not so sure.

I busy myself with stowing things away in the beach hut, while Aseem and Gabe carry the deck chairs inside and stack them to one side. The wind is up already and the ocean, which was calm just an hour ago, hurls itself against the rocks in an explosion of foam, before sliding back to gather force for another assault.

"What's that about?" Aseem says, coming to stand next to me. I follow his gaze to where Papa and Aisha are standing, clearly in the middle of an argument. They're only a few feet from us but the sound of the waves makes it impossible to hear what they're saying. Their faces are turned away but I can tell just looking at Aisha's posture, from the tilt of her chin and the curve of her spine, that she's not happy with whatever Papa's saying.

"Best guess? Her fiancé," I say, rolling my eyes.

Aseem shakes his head. "It's pointless. She's not going to budge."

I nod. Though she comes across as spontaneous and fun-loving, when it comes to the things and people she loves, Aisha can be notoriously stubborn. It's the one thing all three of us have in common: we each have invisible lines we won't cross, positions we'll defend no matter the cost. As laid-back as she is, on some things Aisha cannot be moved. It seems Gabe is one of them.

"Zoe thinks we should give him a chance," Aseem says after a moment.

"Yeah, but Zoe would think that, wouldn't she?" I say before I can stop myself. The regret is instant. Aseem already has enough to deal with when it comes to his marriage—he doesn't need me adding judgment to the equation. I pinch my eyes. "Sorry, I'm exhausted. I just meant she's always a bit blinded by Aish."

"Aren't we all?" he says, his voice resigned. "Do you know what Papa's thinking?"

I shake my head. "Only that he wants Gabe—"

Aseem clears his throat, stopping me just in time. "All done?"

"Yep. Deck chairs stacked, door locked," Gabe says, closing the distance between us in two quick strides and handing me the key. He looks out toward the water. "This really is a wonderful property. So much potential. It's making me think about buying an island myself." He pauses, looks around. "Something less conflicted though. They really did make your life hell, didn't they?"

"It wasn't that bad," I say, my voice clipped.

"I'd have thought death threats is about as bad as it gets," Gabe responds. "I have to admit, I wouldn't have had the nerve to invest here, especially with the community opposed to redevelopment. But then I suppose a return on investment isn't the deciding factor in a place like this."

I grit my teeth, tell myself not to rise to the insult, but Gabe is making it very hard.

"Actually, ROI is pretty much guaranteed in a place like this," I bite back.

Gabe raises his eyebrows. "I'm sure you know what you're doing," he says, his words as insincere as the smile I'd like to wipe off his face.

How dare he stand here, on *my* island, and insinuate I don't know what I'm doing?

"But if you ever need someone to crunch the numbers for you, I've got a team that specializes in luxury real estate."

"I'm okay, thanks," I say and for once, I mean it. I'm worried about Aisha and appalled by Zoe's behavior with Mama, but ever since my conversation with Papa earlier, it's as though nothing can touch me. I have just over thirteen million due on the mortgage. If I pay that off from the fifty million from Papa, that'll leave me with thirty-six million, which will just about cover the backlog of invoices and pay for the most essential works—the refurbishment of the cottages, the electrics and plumbing, and at least a couple of the staff apartments. Enough to get the retreat up and running, albeit at a smaller scale than I originally planned. There is still the staggering cost of maintaining Kilbryde to be considered; just the utility bills, taxes, salaries, and gardening expenses can inch up to six figures a year. But once Papa's scaled Petro-Vision, that'll be just a drop in the bucket. I might not have the money in my bank yet, but for the first time in a long time, I feel safe. Looked after. Without the constant worry fogging my brain, there is a clarity to my thoughts that makes everything feel simpler.

"Sure," Gabe says, returning my half-smile with one of his own. He looks from Aseem to me, his eyebrows knotted as if he's debating something. "You know, all I want is to make Aisha happy. After everything she's been through, she deserves that, doesn't she?"

His audacity is staggering. Of course she deserves to be happy. And that is why I need to find out everything about *you*, I think.

23.

ZOE

I've been walking for at least thirty minutes. The path that seemed straightforward earlier is starting to feel more and more challeng- ing by the minute as I stumble through the trees, trying to find the fork in the woods that leads back to the main house.

I rotate slowly, trying to work out if I've missed the turning, but find- ing my way out of this goddamned forest is proving to be impossible. The criss-crossing paths all look the same and the trees are so dense there's barely any light, even in the middle of the day. I stop and stare at the skeletal ruins of a large cottage. I peek through the arch that must have held a door. There is no roof and the walls that remain are black and charred, crumbling into the earth. The size and layout makes me think of a public building, a school in all likelihood. I shudder, my mind going instantly to Ishaan. If this is the damage a fire can do to a building, what chance did a little boy stand? I spin around and walk in the other direction.

Why Myra chooses to live here is beyond me.

I'm so busy looking for the turning, it takes me a few minutes to realize my phone is vibrating. Somehow, deep in the middle of this forest, I have signal.

I have signal!

I stop and pull out my phone, scared to move even a centimeter for fear of losing reception. It's only when I see my screen light up with hundreds of notifications that I realize how desperate I am for a peek into the real world, how much I crave the connection with people who see me for who I am, not just Aseem's wife. I perch on a felled log and scroll through my Instagram greedily, looking at all the new likes, replying to the comments, savoring the attention, the admiration, the *recognition*, until I go into my inbox.

My stomach twists.

One new message from NB_Lurker.

For fuck's sake. Can't I escape him even for a few days?

I click it open. Even through a screen, the venom is palpable. I push to my feet abruptly, cursing myself as I stumble over a patch of uneven ground.

A slight movement catches my eye and I put my phone away, suddenly aware of the harshness of the landscape. My hearing is amplified, my heart beating both incredibly fast and not quite fast enough the longer I stand there. Listening. To the quiet rustle of the leaves. The distant echo of the waves. The low murmurs of the tall Scottish trees swaying.

And the sound of scuffling coming from my right.

Something or someone moving in the underbrush.

I peer into the trees but even during the day, the forest is cloaked in shadows. At first I think it's a fox, only it doesn't sound like any fox I've ever heard. I stop breathing, listening fiercely. The scuffling stops. A dull thud follows.

But it's the sound of leaves crunching underfoot that prompts me into action.

That is the sound of a person.

"Who's there?" I call out.

The noise stops.

It feels as though every leaf on every tree is holding its breath.

"Hello?"

All I can hear is the distant echo of the waves and the sound of my own voice. Nasal. Nervous. *Weak.*

No wonder Mama thinks she can push me around.

No wonder *Aseem* thinks he can push me around.

I move forward, one panicked step at a time, my eyes darting from left to right, trying to untangle the trees from the shadows.

It happens so quickly I almost miss it.

A silhouette shooting past the trees and disappearing into the shadows.

I spin around and run down the path, retracing my steps. A branch snags on my jacket, the fabric ripping as I yank it free. The mud sucks at my feet, as if trying to keep me here. I force my legs to go a bit faster, my worries about running into a ditch or tripping on a branch no longer as pressing as my need to get back to the house.

I am vaguely aware of the loch to my right, which means the steep path leading up to the house can't be much further now. My heart is beating fast, my legs burning up, but the fear, the sheer, total panic rising through me pushes me forward.

I *need* to get to the house.

A sudden fork in the path shows me that I am at the turning. I flick one quick look over my shoulder before I turn the corner and the house comes into view, its big glass windows mirroring the landscape.

I run up the gravel path and through the porch, my lungs screaming with effort as I step inside and slam the front door shut behind me, re-lief flooding through me as the bolt clicks into place.

What was that?

That sound could only have come from a person.

Illogically, it's the groundskeeper, Stu, that I think of. I remember the way his eyes had swept across my body.

Except I know that's impossible. Stu left.

I *saw* him leave.

But I did see something. *Someone.*

Didn't I?

I go into the kitchen and across to the window, sweat trickling down my chest. I press my forehead into the cool glass. The path coming up to the house is deserted, a pale gray snake leading to the forest I'd run through.

Myra warned us about the wildlife on the island. Enough deer that once a year they need to be "managed," she'd said. Foxes and boars. Pine martens. The sound—and the fleeting silhouette—could have been any of them and jumpy as I was, I'd panicked.

I don't need anyone to tell me that a stray animal is a far more likely suspect than some random intruder chasing me through the woods. Perhaps it's inevitable that I feel watched, given the message I just read.

I squeeze my eyes shut, thinking about the message, finally allowing myself to acknowledge where the panic is coming from.

> **Enjoying the wilderness? Don't think for a second that
> going off-grid will help you. No one can escape their past.
> The island you're hiding on is proof of that.**

I'm good at ignoring trolls. I've made an art form of letting mean-ingless threats roll off me; I know these messages are little more than the products of an insecure mind.

One of the first things my agent told me to do when I signed with her was to never ever give away my exact location. There are all sorts of creeps online, she said.

I've been careful not to name Kilbryde in any of my posts. I haven't dropped so much as a hint about visiting an island.

In fact, I've purposely been vague about which part of Scotland I'm visiting, intentionally misleading my followers by asking for recommendations around Inverness.

And yet somehow, *NB_Lurker* knows exactly where I am.

24

MYRA

D amp wood creaks beneath my feet as I push open the door to my makeshift office. Despite the layers of insulation we added in to the cottage, the narrow corridor is icy, cold clinging to the stone walls. Pulling my scarf tight around my neck, I go into the front room and turn on the electric space heater.

I switch on the iMac and settle into my chair, irritated by the disappointment that creeps in every time I come in here. As though somehow, the dark, damp cottage might have magically transformed into the bright, double height space I once used to work from.

Aseem had scrolled through Gabe's website and social media yesterday. I was hoping there might be inconsistencies in Gabe's story, but all Aseem's research did was corroborate it. Gabe exaggerated the scale of his success, but he *is* the founder of an up-and-coming investment firm. And if his LinkedIn profile is any indicator, a rather well-connected one.

With the picnic over and the family safely back at the house, I finally have the time to do a little digging myself.

I log into Facebook and wait for Aisha's profile to load on the gratingly slow dial-up connection. Perhaps Aseem hadn't found anything because there was nothing to find. Perhaps Gabe is exactly who he says he is and I'm the one who's got it all wrong. My heart twists as a picture of Aisha and Gabe lying on a patterned blanket at the beach, heads close together, fills my screen. There is a strange mixture of arrogance and earnestness in his smile, and his eyes, dark behind his lightly tinted sunglasses, seem to challenge me. I run my knuckle back and forth across my lower lip, thinking of his little speech about giving Aisha the happiness she deserves, his claims of running a successful business, his offer to help with developing the island.

Something is off balance. As a lawyer, running background checks was as much a part of my job as advising on legal strategy. After you've vetted hundreds of people, peeled back the layers of countless lives to expose truths, you develop a sense for the liars. The trouble with Gabe is that his story's too perfect, too slick.

Owen would tell me I'm being cynical, but if there's one thing I've learned it's that the people with the shiniest, glossiest appearances are almost always the ones with the most to hide. They're the ones whose secrets are dark enough to give you nightmares.

Prime example: me.

I type Gabe's full name into the search bar, then click into my inbox while I wait for the results to load.

There are a couple of reminders from the bank, yet another email from Owen that I don't care to read, and an email from my old flatmate, Lisa, inviting me to her baby shower. Her tone is enthusiastic but cautious. Distant. Like she's trying to approach a wild animal.

I cannot find it in me to reply to her email.

I cannot bring myself to tell her that when I lost my family, I also lost all that was good in me. That I'm terrified by the anger and hatred that rips through me every time I see a woman announce her pregnancy. Even if that woman is my former best friend. Or my sister-in-law.

Gabe. That's who I need to focus on.

I navigate back to the browser just as the page is blinking into life.

The search has pulled up several Gabriel Williamsons, but none of them look even remotely like Gabe. As I wrack my brains for another detail about Gabe, it hits me just how vague he's been about his background. He told us he has two siblings, but not their names. He said he grew up in a middle-class family, but not where. Even his social media profiles only go as far back as university. I'd assumed that was because social media wasn't as big back then as it is now, but I wonder now if this is the crack in his story I've been looking for.

I run through every conversation, every passing comment, finally landing on a nugget that I'm hoping will help. I'm sure Gabe said something about an ex-girlfriend with charitable ambitions.

I type in Gabriel Williamson + girlfriend + charity and scroll through the results, hundreds of them.

I trawl through page after page of social media profiles, articles, Companies House listings, and news pieces.

The only reason I pause on the fifth page is because the headline is so cringeworthy.

THE LADY AND THE BARTENDER: INSIDE A MODERN LOVE STORY

It's an article in a now out-of-print regional paper chronicling the "tasteful" engagement party thrown by Lady Sarah and Mr. Alfred Harrison-Dees for their only daughter, Annabel, and her fiancé, Gabriel Williamson, bartender and son of local plumber Tim Williamson.

I sit up. This can't be right.

Gabe's father is a *plumber*?

I try to keep an open mind as I skim through the details of the event and scroll down to the picture that shows Gabe with his arms wrapped around a dainty, impeccably dressed blonde woman in her early twenties. According to the article, Gabe met Annabel while volunteering as a bartender at a charity event. Sparks flew and three months later the young couple were engaged to be married. The tone of the article is largely positive, commending the Harrison-Dees for being among the modern aristocrats breaking down the barriers of Britain's class system and presenting Gabe and Annabel's engagement as nothing short of a modern fairy tale.

But something about the whole landed-gentry-welcome-working-class-son-in-law narrative seems a bit off. I scroll through the rest of the pictures from the night, stopping when I get to a picture of Gabe with Annabel's parents. I click to enlarge the photo and peer at the faces. The Harrison-Dees are smiling but there is a detached wariness in their eyes, the slight distance between them and their future son-in-law more telling than the elaborate celebration. Gabe has the same earnest expression that I've witnessed countless times over the past twenty-four hours, but there is something else there, too. An air of self-congratulation, which suggests that to him Annabel was little more than a conquest. A means to an end.

A quick search on Annabel Harrison-Dees confirms what I already suspect. Gabe and Annabel never married. Two years after her engagement to Gabe, Annabel married the aristocrat hotelier, James Fitzroy, in an intimate ceremony covered by *Tatler*.

So much for championing social mobility.

I close my eyes and lean back in my chair as I try to make sense of it all. The *Tatler* article covering Annabel's wedding is peppered with names of her previous boyfriends but makes no mention of her ex-fiancé. On social media, there is little evidence to suggest that Annabel and Gabe even knew each other, let alone that they were engaged. There are no posts announcing their engagement, no awkward group photos or holiday pictures, no tactless messages from friends about their subsequent breakup.

I compose a short message and send it to Annabel along with a friend request, but considering her last public post was three years ago, I'm not holding out much hope.

No one wants to stay connected to their ex, but the fact that other than a society piece in an out-of-print newspaper there is nothing that connects Gabe to Annabel suggests that they both went to a lot of effort to erase all traces of their relationship from the public domain.

Then there is the timing. The article covering Gabe and Annabel's engagement dates back five years. Right before Gabe moved to Hong Kong and set up his business. Which begs the question: How did a plumber's son with no background in finance find the capital to set up a hedge fund in one of the most difficult markets in the world?

25

ZOE

I sit in my bedroom seething. In the hour or so since they all returned from the picnic, Aseem hasn't even bothered to come up to
check on me, let alone apologize. And if the sound of laughter filtering up from the living room is any indication, he's in no hurry to
either.

Meanwhile, I've spent the past few hours staring at my phone, dissecting a message from a man who doesn't even have the courage to
use his real name. It's pathetic.

I hate that *NB_Lurker* is getting to me so much. I've never been the
sort to worry, never been the type to fret over a passive-aggressive
threat. Even when I was waitressing for sleazy middle-aged men, I
could shake off the inappropriate glances and unwanted attention before I'd even taken off my apron. I would never have given a second
thought to this sort of thing back then.

I swing my legs to the side of the bed and get up.

NB_Lurker's messages are just the product of a life that's as empty as
his threats and I refuse to waste another minute thinking about him.

I walk into the living room to a tableau I'm entirely familiar with.

Papa has a book in his hand and his feet up, Mama's massaging coconut oil into Aisha's scalp while she flicks through a magazine, and Aseem and Myra are huddled together on the window seat, two mugs of chai in front of them. The only one missing from this Kodak family moment is me. I can't help but bristle at the thought that much of that is by design.

"I thought you'd be asleep," Aseem says, looking at me, his gaze on me as sharp as it's ever been.

"I had a nap," I say, trying not to sound too defensive. I turn my attention to Aisha. "Are you up to much?"

Aisha smirks. "Yep. Just heading to the spa. And then maybe a trip to the cinema." She clocks Myra's expression, sighs, then adds, "No, I'm just here for a nice, chilled afternoon with the fam-jam."

Myra rolls her eyes. "Oh, quit moaning. Why don't you go check out the lighthouse? It has some incredible views." She flashes me a quick smile, shrugs. "You might get some nice shots, Zoe."

I force myself to take a breath. Nice shots that I can't fucking post.

"Fancy another hike?" Aisha says.

We walk in silence, stopping every now and then to consult the map Myra gave us as we were setting off.

I ignore the niggle of fear that reappears every time I hear the crunch of gravel or the creak of a branch. Animals. Just animals moving through the woods.

"Why the fuck couldn't she have installed Wi-Fi?" Aisha says after we've circled the same path three times. "Or bought an island with goddamn cell signal."

I take the laminated piece of paper from Aisha, frowning at the tiny letters on the map. "I think we should go that way," I say, pointing to a gap in the trees on our right, a small clearing that I hope will get us to the coast. "That should lead to the cliffs, so the lighthouse can't be too far off?"

Aisha shrugs and we start walking.

If there's anyone who understands how suffocating being a part of this family can feel, it's Aisha. But even with her there are some topics that are strictly off-limits.

A few weeks after Aseem was finally allowed to propose to me, I took Mama out to lunch. The awkwardness that arose after the family discovered my relationship with Aseem had never really been addressed, and I wanted to remind Mama that I was still the same person she'd known, and liked, for years. I wanted to prove to her that I was worthy of not only her son but also her family. I booked a table at the fanciest restaurant I could afford, a little Italian bistro on a tree-lined street in Kensington, the one all the bloggers were raving about. I had agonized over the menu in preparation, planning out exactly what we would order, where we would sit, and even calling ahead to make sure they had her favorite wine in stock.

I remember the sinking feeling I had when Mama entered the restaurant. She offered me her hand—dainty, soft, and entirely unexpected after years of warm hugs. Her eyes swept across the room, taking in the entire space in one quick glance, her reaction condensed to a monosyllabic "oh." That initial response set the tone for the rest of the afternoon. Our conversation that day was dominated by Mama telling me interminable details about every aspect of Aseem's life. She went through the minutiae of his day from the moment he woke up to when he went to bed. She detailed his progress at work, the colleagues he most liked and the ones he couldn't stand, the friends he sought advice from and the ones he avoided, the office spaces he was considering and the areas he loved. She told me about his love for cats—the one thing

I'm allergic to—and asked if I knew that he wanted four children, two boys and two girls. She spoke of his dreams of bundling up his menagerie of cats and kids into the car to show them all the wonderful places she'd taken him to as a boy. And on and on it went. The entire conversation was designed to show me how intimately embedded she was in her son's life and how little room there was for me, all done with perfectly coiffed hair and the sweetest of smiles.

I'd been hoping this lunch would strengthen my relationship with the woman who had so far been more generous and kind to me than my own mother. Instead, I'd spent two and a half hours feeling like I was losing a contest I hadn't entered.

When I mentioned it to Aisha later, I expected her to roll her eyes, then open a bottle of wine to commiserate. I'd spent dozens of evenings listening to Aisha rant about her parents and now that I could finally contribute to these discussions, I was oddly excited, like I was finally a proper member of the family. But the response I got from Aisha was more than just unsympathetic, it was downright hostile. She didn't understand how anyone could take offense to anything Mama said. It was the first time I'd seen the flash of steel beneath Aisha's happy-go-lucky exterior, a protectiveness that told me exactly where she stood when it came to her family.

As we walk through the woods now, I'm desperate to dissect the events of the afternoon, but it's futile trying to get Aisha to support me over her family, even though that's exactly what she expects of me.

Even so, I need to make my side of the story known. "About earlier, I wasn't trying to be rude to Mama, it's just that—"

"It's all right, Zo," she interrupts, surprising me. "If anyone understands how things can spiral with one comment, it's me. In fact, there's something I need to tell—" A gasp. "What the fuck is this?" she continues, hands on her hips. I follow her gaze to the small clearing amidst the tall grass. Small cobblestones ring an area that can be no more than a hundred meters in diameter.

I step into what looks like a ceremonial circle and walk over to the single paving stone at the center. It's engraved with a distinctly familiar crest of looped lines and elaborate motifs, underneath which is a single sentence: *In memory of those who were never identified but will forever be remembered, cherished and in time, avenged. Clan MacBrodie.*

The Clan MacBrodie used to be one of the most powerful Scottish clans until the clearances, when they became victims of what many now refer to as genocide.

I turn to face Aisha. I imagine I look just as stricken as she does.

We're standing on a site of mass burial.

26

MYRA

G abe is standing by the French doors, thumbs hooked into the pockets of his jeans, looking out over the quickly darkening valley.

"Do you think the girls will be all right?" he asks. All traces of the beautiful weather we'd experienced earlier have disappeared. Thick black clouds mottle the sky, heavy with the threat of a storm. Gabe looks at me directly, his gaze tinged with worry. "Maybe I should—"

"Aseem's gone to fetch them," Papa says from across the room. "I wanted a moment to speak with you alone. Drink?"

"Sure," Gabe takes his hands from his pockets and folds them across his chest. He looks at me, still perched on the window seat, his expression puzzled.

"Oh, don't mind Myra," Papa says, walking briskly to the drinks trolley in the corner. He pours whiskey into two glasses and hands one to Gabe before sitting down in the armchair. My own drink—a bottle of sparkling water—dangles from my fingers. I'm doing my best to appear relaxed even as tension pushes through my veins.

Gabe takes a large sip of his whiskey, his eyes drifting back to the window as he speaks. "Even in the evening, this view is still incredible. So expansive." He pauses, letting the low rumble of thunder fill the room. "I hope Aisha and I can build something like this one day." He swirls his drink before lifting the glass and finishing it in one swallow. "Mind if I have another?"

"Help yourself," I say. If draining my three-hundred-pound bottle of Macallan will help us get rid of Gabe, so be it.

The glass bottle clatters against crystal as Gabe pours himself a large measure, then sits down on the sofa across from Papa.

"Is everything okay?" Gabe asks, his voice uncertain.

Papa looks at him, his face blank, expressionless.

A moment passes, then another. Gabe runs his hands through his hair, looking from Papa to me then back again, clearly unnerved by the lack of response.

Growing up, Aseem and I were always more scared of being subjected to one of Papa's cold silences than of being yelled at. Aisha never had to face either.

"You tell me," Papa says, finally.

"I—I'm not sure what you mean?"

"Gabriel, I love my daughter, both my daughters, very much. Maybe someday you'll understand what it feels like to love someone more than you thought possible—"

"That's how I feel about—"

Papa holds up a hand.

"I love both my daughters but I worry about Aisha the most. She is fragile, always has been. She cannot handle more heartbreak."

"I will *never* let that happen," Gabe says, his expression earnest. He lets out a short sigh, then sets his glass on the coffee table and leans forward, elbows pressing into his knees. "Aisha is everything to me. I wouldn't have moved my business, my whole *life*, halfway across the world if she wasn't. All I want is for her to be happy."

"I appreciate that. I really do." Papa presses his palms together, nods once. "Myra?"

I push off the window seat and go to sit next to Gabe. I can smell the whiskey on his breath as I sink into the sofa. Our knees knock together as I angle myself to look at him. I speak quietly, keeping my tone firm but neutral. "We would like to offer you a four percent stake in the business. At the current valuation, that's twelve million pounds. Based on the latest projections, in ten years' time, it could go up to one hundred, one hundred and fifty."

Any reservations I might have had evaporate as I watch the greed pass over his face. People like Gabe deserve to rot in prison, but this is the next best alternative.

"One hundred and fifty . . . million?"

I give him a sharp nod and reach for the thick manila envelope sitting on the side table. Gabe looks confused as he flicks through the agreement I drafted earlier, his eyes darting from left to right, trying to look past the legalese to decipher the meaning.

I take no pleasure in spelling it out for him. This money is part of my inheritance and the last person I want to see it go to is Gabe. But if paying him off will keep Aisha safe and Papa happy, so be it.

"Half the shares will be transferred now and the remaining half in twelve months' time, assuming you abide by the conditions."

His head jerks up. "The conditions?"

I tap the document in front of him. "It's all set out in the agreement here, but essentially we'll need you to leave tomorrow morning."

Gabe frowns, confusion creasing his features. "Leave for where?"

"Anywhere you want. When Aisha gets back, you'll tell her that you mistook infatuation for love. You can tell her you can't see yourself fitting into the family or that you've realized you aren't ready for a commitment, whatever you want. We'll sort out the flights, first class, of course. If you need anything from her villa, we can organize for your belongings to be shipped to you as soon as practicable. After tomorrow, you will have no contact with Aisha, no phone calls, no emails, no accidental run-ins or meetings, nothing. If at any point in the next year, Aisha sees you or hears from you, or if she discovers anything about this conversation or that you've got any interest in the family business, the contract will become void. As for the shares, you're free to do what you want with them after the twelve months are up. Do you have any questions?"

He looks down at the document and back up again. "I don't think you understand. I love Aisha. This isn't about the money."

"I'm sure it isn't," I say, getting into my stride. "If you were to get married, there will naturally be a prenuptial agreement. Aisha's interest in the family trust, all her assets, and any current or future interest she has in the family business will be ring-fenced. The family won't be making any investments into any businesses you or Aisha set up. In effect, that means you will not have access to anything, not even her current account or credit card. In the event of infidelity, divorce, separation, or," I swallow, "if anything were to happen to Aisha, her estate, life insurance, savings, and any profit from current or future investments will revert to the family."

I let it sink in. From across the room, Papa gives me the slightest of nods.

"I *love* her," Gabe protests, his voice rising. "Don't you get it? She is everything to me."

I was prepared for Gabe to demand more money, but the emotion in his voice catches me off guard. Something about this moment transports me back to a conversation I've spent years trying to forget. I steel myself, reminding myself that love is just a word, one that men reach for when all their other excuses fail. Gabe has been lying to Aisha from the moment he met her.

I do my best to keep my voice level. "Then you'll want to do what's best for her, won't you? Gabriel, I genuinely don't see your engagement lasting more than a few months. The two of you come from different worlds and sooner or later, Aisha will see that. This way, you get to save both of you the heartache and set yourself up for life."

"You aren't going to get a better offer, son," Papa says.

Gabe pushes the papers back into the envelope and gets up. "Aisha warned me," he says. "But you people, you're something else. You act like you care about her but have you even stopped to consider what she wants? We make each other happy." He pauses and looks at me, his eyes full of contempt. "Not that you'd know what that's like."

I push to my feet, feeling the final threads of self-control snap against his audacity. "Right. Because I'm sure what Aisha wants is to marry a man who's been lying to her. Your parents are art historians, are they?"

Gabe blinks, a flash of panic passing over his face. "How do you—" He stops abruptly, hooded eyes fixed on mine.

"How much did Annabel's family pay you?"

He sucks in a breath. "It's not what you think."

I cross my arms across my chest. "Isn't it?"

Several beats of silence pass.

Gabe holds my gaze; I don't look away.

I am vaguely aware of movement outside, the low crunch of gravel, the muffled echo of voices, but it's the sound of the front door slamming shut that snaps me out of the moment.

"We're back," Aseem calls out. I hear the sound of footsteps traveling through the hall and toward the kitchen.

I lower my voice, inject it with confidence. "You and I both know how much Aisha hates being lied to. When she discovers the truth

about your father, about Annabel, she is going to call off the engagement. The way I see it, you have two options. You can take what we're
offering and use the money to grow your business, or you can stick
around and be penniless instead. Your choice." I take a step back as
Aisha walks in, followed closely by Zoe and Aseem. "Good, you're
back. We were starting to get worried."

"It's freezing outside," Aisha says, rubbing her hands together. Her
smile disappears as she picks up on the tension in the room. "What's
going on? Gabe?"

Gabe's posture softens in her presence. "Papa and I have been talking shop. I've been trying to explain to him that the best investments
are about values, not money," he says, pulling Aisha close and kissing
her full on the mouth. It's the kind of kiss that leaves Aisha flushed and
the rest of us embarrassed. But it's not just the performative quality of
the kiss that grates, nor is it his casual use of the word Papa.

It's the challenge in his voice that gets to me.

I feel the strange blink of dislocation, a sense that the dynamic has
shifted.

"What's that?" Aisha asks, looking at the envelope in Gabe's hand.

There is a moment of complete silence as Gabe glances at the envelope, then drops it on the sofa. He turns to Aisha. "Nothing you need
to know about. *Yet.*" My stomach shrinks into a tight knot as Gabe rubs
his hands up and down Aisha's arms, like he's trying to warm up a
child. "There might have been some chat about wedding venues. . . ."
he continues, his tone light, teasing.

Aisha's face lights up. It's heartbreaking. "Oh?"

"Myra has some interesting ideas, but I've given her lots more to
think about," he says. He twists to look at me, his eyes narrowing as his
words land. "She wants the best for you, but I'm not sure your sister
knows you as well as I do."

27

ZOE

I traipse upstairs after Aseem. I am exhausted after the hike, every bone in my body screaming with the effort, but this day is far from over. We're all supposed to get dressed up and assemble downstairs at seven sharp for the big celebration: Mama and Papa's anniversary. We're supposed to sit down for an elaborate meal and spend the evening playing happy families. It's hard to think of anything I want to do less, but in this family, that's what we do. We smile over overpriced champagne and salty caviar. We keep our plates full and glasses topped up, all while sharpening our knives under the table.

Christmas at Sandringham would be easier.

I peel off my jumper, the cashmere heavy and damp against my skin, and drape it over the radiator. Aseem, Aisha, and I got caught in the rain on our way back, but it's not the cold spreading across my skin that I'm worried about.

Aseem and I have barely said two words to each other since this morning, but furious as I am, I can no longer wait for him to reinitiate the conversation.

Aseem goes into the bathroom without so much as a glance in my direction. "Do you want to shower first?"

I follow him into the bathroom. "Did you speak to Papa?"

"Not yet," he says, unbuttoning the top of his shirt and pulling it over his head. He drops it on the floor on top of his trousers.

I look at Aseem in the mirror, distracted momentarily by the shape of his body, my eyes tracing the angled lines defining his chest and shoulders. Gabe's already discussing investment options with Papa and Myra won't be far behind, if she hasn't staked her claim already. And yet my husband, who has spent the entire day with his parents, is waiting for some impossibly perfect time to claim what is legitimately ours.

"Has Myra spoken to him?"

My question is met with an indifferent shake of his head. "She's been busy trying to deal with Gabe."

I perch on the edge of the bathtub while Aseem fills me in, past, present and future blurring into one as I think about Mama's behavior with me this morning, the evening that's stretching out before us, the years and years of innocent smiles and persistent interference that I still have to endure. "I can't do this."

"What?"

"This. Everything. I'm exhausted."

He steps out of his boxers and wraps a towel around his waist, his gaze softening as he turns to look at me. "It has been a bit much, hasn't it? How about we skip whatever Myra has planned for us tomorrow and have a proper lie-in instead?" He crouches down in front of me and takes my hands in his. "Just the two of us."

As easy as it will be to say yes, I resist. This is what he does every time. He uses our time alone as a balm but refuses to address the larger issues at play. "I think we need more than a morning to ourselves, don't you? The picnic—"

"Don't worry about the picnic. We don't need to talk about that right now," Aseem says, kissing my fingers.

I extract my hands from his and grip the edge of the bathtub. "I think we do."

It's Aseem's turn to sigh. He shakes his head, shrugs. "If that's what you want. I didn't want to say anything when you're feeling . . ."

Angry. Belittled. Ridiculed?

". . . hormonal, but you can't speak to Mama like that."

My mouth drops open.

"She was really worried when you left. And hurt. It doesn't have to be tonight, but you need to apologize to her."

"What?"

"I know she can come across a bit . . ." he frowns, searching for the right words, "insistent sometimes, but you know that's just Mama's way of showing she cares. She's so excited about the baby and all she wants to do is help."

I tighten my grip on the bathtub and force myself to breathe. It's true what they say about every marriage being a compromise. Although Aseem and I rarely compromise equally, the fact remains that for our marriage to survive, we need to be a team. A unit comprising Aseem and me.

Not Aseem, his mother, and me.

I've tried time and time again to put myself in his shoes, to see things through his eyes and come to some sort of understanding of how a grown man can be so blind to the actions of his mother.

I can't do it. And right now, I'm not sure I even want to try.

"She's not trying to help, Aseem. She's trying to take over my pregnancy."

"Sweetheart, no. All grandparents like to be a part of these decisions. She probably thinks it's what you expect of her. Don't build this up into something it's not." I stare at Aseem. His voice is soft but the accusation in his tone is unmistakable. He thinks I'm overreacting. "And after everything she's been through . . . you can make more of an effort, can't you? She *is* my mother."

There it is. The trump card Aseem brings out every time we argue about his mother. Just because we don't talk about it doesn't mean that any of us are ever allowed to forget what happened to Ishaan. Or more crucially, what that did to Mama. How one incident reduced her from a famously independent woman to someone so fragile a gust of wind might break her.

If only all of our past tragedies could insulate us from the inconveniences of our present.

I'm about to tell him as much when I hear the muffled sound of a sneeze being stifled. We exchange a glance, both of us realizing at the same time that whoever is in the hallway can probably hear us.

A tentative knock follows.

I fling on my dressing gown as Aseem goes to open the bedroom door.

His face breaks into a smile at the sight of his mother. She walks in clutching a tray with two brightly patterned porcelain mugs and a small bowl of blanched almonds.

"Haldi ka doodh," she says, setting the tray down on the dresser. "I didn't add any sugar to yours," she adds, looking at me.

The obvious display of consideration only irritates me further.

Her eyes linger over my tousled hair and mottled face before drifting over to the bed, where my outfit for the evening, a dress from Sabyasachi's fall line, is laid out. "Is that what you're wearing?" she asks, her diamond nose-pin catching the light from the chandelier as she tilts her face up to look at me.

"You don't like it?" Try as I might, I can't keep the challenge out of my voice.

"It's gorgeous," she says, her voice dripping honey. "I was just thinking how nicely my diamond and pearl earrings will go with that color. I was going to wear them tonight but you're more than welcome to borrow them."

"That's so kind," Aseem says to his mother, before turning to me. "You love those earrings, don't you Zoe?"

I don't, but I know how much his mother does. It's an olive branch and one that I really should take. "I do. Thanks, Mama," I say. I close the distance between Aseem and me and loop my arm through his. "But I think I'm going to wear the studs you gave me last month," I say, smiling at Aseem before directing my gaze to his mother. "I've been saving them for a special occasion." Mama's smile freezes and mine widens. She has no idea what I'm talking about. "Aseem commissioned them from your jeweler in Antwerp the day we found out we were pregnant."

"How lovely. I'm sure Aseem chose well." Mama claps her hands together. "Now, I'd better go check on Papa. Don't let that milk go cold," she says, closing the door behind her.

"That wasn't so hard, was it?" Aseem says. He hands one of the mugs to me.

"She was eavesdropping."

"You don't know that," Aseem says, as usual blind to her ways.

I put the mug down and lean against the dresser. I'm not sure what bothers me more, the fact that Aseem can't see through his mother, or that he can't see how deeply this charade affects me. "I cannot spend my entire life arguing with you about your mother," I say, circling back to the conversation Mama interrupted. "I want out."

He sits down on the edge of the bed, hands positioned on either side of him as if he's bracing for impact. "I know and it might take a little longer than we thought, but we *will* make the move—"

I throw my hands in the air. "How? How exactly will we *make the move* when you refuse to speak to Papa about it? Myra has this bloody island, Aisha's got her villa. We've got literally nothing. We can barely afford a flat in Delhi without Papa's help. Which you refuse to ask for."

"Come on, Zo, you know I'm trying. This week's been difficult. With Aisha's engagement—"

"Stop. Just stop. If it's not Aisha, then it's Myra or Owen or the company or your parents. It never ends. I'm your wife, Aseem. We're starting a family together. At what point do I become the priority?"

"That's not fair."

"Not fair?" I scoff. "Not fair is you telling me you have my back and then acting like I don't even matter. It's you spending the entire trip fussing over your parents." I close my eyes, trying to fight the tears that are threatening to spill over. I force myself to take a deep breath and place my hands on my stomach, feeling the slight bulge, trying to reassure myself as much as the baby I'm doing this for. I look at Aseem through a blur of tears. He's hunched over, his shoulders curling in on himself. "Do you even care about me? About us?"

He looks at me then, clearly torn between his family and me, and I feel a stab of guilt, the emotion catching me off guard. There are many things I've questioned about my marriage and my choices, but the one thing that's kept me grounded through it all is knowing that what Aseem and I have is real. I know how much he loves me. When it's just the two of us, when Aseem isn't worrying about how his mother might feel or what his father might say, things are great. Perfect.

Our problems start when the whole family is together.

I turn and walk to the window. I know I'm pushing him, but what else can I do? I can't raise this baby alone. And I refuse to raise her with my in-laws second-guessing every decision I make.

I feel Aseem's body slot into mine as he comes to stand behind me, his arms twisting around my waist. He breathes deeply, his exhale landing on my neck. A sigh masquerading as a kiss. "You *know* I care. I love you. I can't live without you. You are—" his voice cracks "—everything to me. *Everything.*"

We stand like that for a long moment. Outside, the trickle of rain we'd got caught in has turned into a full-blown storm, the wind howling as it pushes through the trees, forcing them to sway and bend in its service. Aseem's grip on me tightens as a streak of lightning pierces the sky, momentarily bathing the forest in stark white light, highlighting details I'd barely noticed before.

I disentangle myself from my husband's arms. I take a step closer to the window.

The longer I look, the more I see. I take a deep breath.

"If you can't live without me, you know what to do."

28.

MYRA

S tarted early, I see."

"Liquid courage and all that." I fill another cocktail glass with gin and slide it across the kitchen counter toward Aseem.

He takes a sip, winces. "A touch of vermouth might be nice."

I shrug. The relief I'd felt after my conversation with Papa is long gone, the tension in my stomach worsening with every passing hour. Gabe's reaction to my offer has left me gobsmacked. I can't fathom what he's playing at and the not knowing sickens me.

"Do you need help with anything?"

"No," I say, following Aseem's gaze around the room. It's not quite the set-up I might have had in Edinburgh, but I've done my best under the circumstances. The table has been set with my finest china, monogrammed cutlery sits next to vintage crystal glasses, and the napkins match the pristine white tablecloth. The centerpiece is a simple assortment of wildflowers and candles. Understated. Elegant. *Economical.* On the sideboard, family photos in antique brass frames nestle between fairy lights, chronicling the handful of cherished memories we roll out again and again as a family. The photo frames are a last-minute addition and the only element of the decor that feels a bit off. They're a touch too sentimental, reminiscent of the kind of Instagram-ready events Zoe attends, but I know Mama will appreciate the effort. "It's all under control."

Aseem raises his eyebrows. "If you say so. Listen, before everyone else shows up"—he pauses, clears his throat, his hesitation telling me not only what he wants to discuss but inadvertently how important it is to him—"did you speak to Papa about the sale?"

He does an impressive job of sounding neutral, but it's already too late. Even without the long pause, his expression gives away everything his words are trying to conceal.

"He doesn't want to retire, Aseem."

"I know, but—"

"And he's hell-bent against selling. He thinks the deal you negotiated is impressive—"

Aseem scoffs, looks up at the ceiling. "We aren't going to get a better offer."

"—but the timing's off," I continue. "Papa thinks we should be scaling up instead."

"Scale up?" Aseem shakes his head. "Wow. Okay. What do you think?"

"What do I think in terms of . . . ?"

"In terms of next steps. He's obviously not thinking straight. Should we talk to Mama?"

I sigh. Finish my drink. Resist the urge to pour another. "I don't know. I don't think . . . He said there are only a handful of independent petrochemical companies left and the way the market is going, someone is bound to emerge as the leader. He thinks that could be us. He wants to expand into Southeast Asia—"

"Expand? You must be joking. Has he even considered the logistics, the funding, the sheer infrastructure we'd need to expand?" Aseem pushes his hands through his hair, his frustration obvious. "Papa always does this. He gets an idea in his head and he just . . . he ignores the practicalities. We don't have the means to expand. And he would see that if he wasn't so obsessed with outmaneuvering Malhotra."

"I don't know what to say. He isn't going to retire and he's definitely not going to sell. To Malhotra or to anyone else from what I gather."

Aseem folds his arms. "And you're okay with this?"

I let out a long breath, trying to find the right words. "I don't know. He's doing a lot better, he's fit. I mean, you saw him today. You and I were more wrung out from the walk than he was. Who's to say that going back to work won't be good for him?"

"Good for him? Fuck's sake, Myra. He's sixty-eight. Do you have any idea what it takes to run this business?"

"Oh, piss off. I've been doing his legal work for years. I probably know more than you do." I take a breath, force myself to calm down. "Why don't you speak to him? He's talking about making a few strategic acquisitions, repositioning the business with a sharper focus on emerging markets. To be honest, it sounds inspired and if we can pull it off, I think it could be good for us. As a family."

"As a family?"

"Yeah."

I see a flicker of something in his eyes—disbelief perhaps—but he conceals it quickly. "I see," he says, narrowing his gaze. He drains his drink and goes to put the glass in the sink. "Fucking typical."

"Excuse me?"

"It's my fault," Aseem says, swinging around to face me. "I should've seen this coming. Even if he manages to find the funding for these acquisitions, which frankly, I don't see happening, there is no way Papa can pull this off alone and he obviously doesn't trust me to do it."

"That's not true," I say, my skin burning under his gaze.

Aseem's always had this way of looking at me, looking through me. It makes me feel like he can read thoughts that I'm not even comfortable with myself. I take the matchbox and go to light the candles on the table.

"He's offered you something, hasn't he? That's why you've changed your mind all of a sudden. What is it? COO? General counsel?"

"Don't be paranoid. You know I don't want anything to do with the business. My life is here. On Kilbryde."

"Money then. A protected role in the trust? Shares?"

"Aseem, you're being crazy. Papa's always been ambitious and there's a lot that PetroVision can still achieve." I rearrange the candles, checking that each one is equidistant from the other before lighting them one by one. "Why are you so keen for him to sell, anyway? It's not like you've got some brilliant second career waiting."

His expression tells me I've touched the nerve I thought I would. He's always been sensitive about his progress in his chosen career, or lack thereof.

"The point isn't why I want to sell. We have got an incredible deal on the table and I—"

"And you've worked really hard. I get it. But I don't know what you expect me to do. It's not like Papa listens to anyone. And frankly, I've got much bigger things to worry about right now." I take a breath, remind myself that my little brother is going through a difficult time right now. "Just take it easy, okay? Papa's insistent that this has nothing to do with Malhotra, so find a way to string the lawyers along for a few more weeks, see how this all plays out. Who knows, Papa might change his mind again." I drop the spent matches in the bin and put the matchbox back in the drawer. I lean against the counter and look at Aseem. "The only thing he's thinking about right now is Gabe. It's the only thing I'm thinking about. I don't know what to do."

Aseem closes his eyes, sighs. "Do you think he's trying to negotiate?"

"He says he doesn't care about the money. He didn't bat an eyelid when I mentioned the prenup," I say pointedly. Zoe, on the other hand, did more than bat an eyelid. She refused to sign the prenup and in the end we relented.

"Is there a chance . . ."

"What?"

"Could we be wrong about Gabe?"

I shake my head. "He's definitely got an agenda. I can feel it in my bones; he's not right for her."

Aseem rubs his face, lets out a long breath. "We have to talk to Aisha, don't we?"

I take a moment to consider what he's saying. We could tell Aisha everything I've discovered about Gabe. Perhaps we could lay out all his lies and try to convince her to take a step back.

It will never work, not with Aisha. "You know how she'll—"

"Talk to me about what?"

I spin around at the sound of Aisha's voice. She's wearing a velvet dress with a sweetheart neckline and tie-up straps. Her hair is pinned back, the purple streaks pushed to one side with two mother-of-pearl barrettes. The overall impression is one of innocence, naivety. I swallow.

"A baby shower for Zoe," Aseem says.

Aisha looks at Aseem, then me, her eyes darting between us, before settling on me. "Bullshit. First, Zoe will have a godh bharai, not a shower," she says, rolling her eyes. "Second, that's the last thing the two of you would ever discuss." She hoists herself on a bar stool, the ridiculous diamond on her finger glinting under the pendant lights. "What were you talking about?"

Aseem looks at me, eyebrows raised. I nod. He's right. We have no choice.

"We're a bit concerned that you and Gabe might be rushing into things," Aseem says.

"This again? I don't understand why you guys don't like him."

He holds his hands up. "I never said that."

"You didn't need to. It's obvious enough," she says, twisting the ring around her finger.

"It's not that we don't like him," I say. "It's just that we don't really know him."

"From what you do know, what is there to dislike?"

I sigh. Aisha sees the best in people. Looks for it. It's one of the reasons I've always had to watch her back.

"Nothing," Aseem says. "Nothing at all. It's just . . . it's all rather sudden, isn't it?"

"You just met him and now you're engaged," I add. "It feels like things are moving really quickly and I guess I'm—we're—just wondering why the rush? You've only known him six months."

"Mama and Papa got married less than three months after they met each other," Aisha counters.

"That was different," I say. "Do you *want* an arranged marriage?"

She rolls her eyes. "Just because the two of you took years to make up your minds about your spouses doesn't mean I have to. Nothing about marrying Gabe feels rushed to me. I feel like I've known him my whole life. Can't you guys just give him a chance?"

Aisha looks at Aseem, then back at me. Her eyes are beseeching, her eyebrows pushed together. It's a look I remember well from when she was little. Giving in to Aisha, putting her at ease has become such a fundamental part of my muscle memory that saying no to her hurts. Physically hurts. I swallow the lump in my throat and remind myself that I'm doing this for her.

"He's using you, Aish."

"Don't be such a hypocrite."

"Excuse me?" I say, just as Zoe slips into the room, quiet as a mouse. As if this isn't humiliating enough as it is.

"You heard me," Aisha snaps back. "Gabe's not the one asking Papa for fifty million."

Aseem's gaze whips up. "What?"

Aisha nods at him. "To hold on to this"—she waves her hand around—"treasure fucking island."

Aseem scoffs. "Knew it."

Resentment rises in my throat, but I swallow it.

"It's an investment," I say. "I'm going to pay him back."

"Like you paid him back the last time?" Aisha challenges.

I refuse to take the bait. "I looked into Gabe."

"Of course you did. What is the matter with you?"

"Aish, come on. We're just trying to look out for you," Aseem says.

"Fine. What'd you find?"

I take a breath. "He's been lying to you. He's been engaged before—"

"To Annabel," Aisha says.

I nod quickly to cover my surprise. "And about his background. His father's a—"

"Plumber?" she says, beating me to it.

I take a step back, my fingers reaching for the counter behind me. "You knew?"

"Yes, I knew. We have an honest relationship, not that *you* would know anything about that," Aisha says, her gaze fixed firmly on me. "I told him to lie."

"What?" Zoe says at the same time as I say, "Why?"

"Because," she throws her hands up. "I knew exactly how you would react."

"How?"

"Like *this*. Like the fact that we were all born with silver spoons makes us better somehow," she says. "Why is it so hard for you to believe that he's in love with me?"

"Because I know what people like him want," I say. "How do you think a plumber's son, a boy who went to state school and worked as a bartender, found the funds to set up a hedge fund? He targeted Annabel and now he's targeting you."

"And you have proof of this?" Aisha asks, giving me a look that is at once defiant and accusing.

I hold her gaze. "I don't need proof."

"No, that's always been your thing, hasn't it?" Aisha spits out. "Despite what you might believe, you don't know everything, Myra. *Gabe* broke it off with Annabel, not the other way round, because she was sleeping her way through London high society just like all the other toffs. He took out a loan to start his company. Started from scratch like Papa and built his business from nothing. He's done well because he works hard and he's ambitious. But unlike some of us, his life doesn't revolve around how much money he has in his bank. He actually cares about stuff."

"And you believe him?"

"Oh my god," Aisha says. "*Yes*, I believe him. I believe him, I trust him, and I will marry him. No matter what you say. Fucking hell, Myra. If you weren't so goddamn frigid, maybe you'd still have a marriage. Heck, maybe you'd still have—"

"Aisha!" Aseem says.

"What?" Aisha says, coming to stand in front of me.

I take a step back and force myself to breathe. Every ounce of my energy is going into remaining calm, into not doing something I might later regret.

Aisha leans forward, her breath hot on my skin. "It's true. It's not fair to blame Owen when his wife has a heart of stone."

I feel the air leave my lungs.

I've been holding it in for days. Weeks. Months.

I push her away with so much force it leaves me trembling. "Fuck you, Aisha."

29.

ZOE

The living room is miserable with small talk. There's still an hour to go until dinner and the high spirits from yesterday have been replaced by something darker, more dangerous. It's not just the wariness that always rears its head after a few days together, but an air of competition that feels fierce, volatile even. We have all returned to our natural pairs, our allegiances on display as though battle lines have been drawn. Mama and Papa are talking in low murmurs, sneaking glances repeatedly at Aisha, who is perched on the armchair, draped around Gabe. Standing next to me, Aseem is frowning into his drink, his face set in an unreadable expression. Even Myra, who has always had a robustness about her, is on edge.

I watch her go around the room, briskly topping up glasses, her usual warmth laced with an undeniable sliver of ice, but it is the way she walks past Aisha, refusing to even acknowledge her, that tells me just how deep Aisha's words cut. Myra's fury always takes the form of a cold indifference, but I've never seen it directed toward her sister before. Not that I can blame her. Aisha lashes out when she's hurt. Normally everyone indulges her, but tonight she crossed a line.

I take a sip of my elderflower cordial, then lean close to my husband. "Did Myra talk to Papa?" I whisper, twisting my arm through his.

At first I'm not sure if he's heard me. I'm about to repeat myself when he swivels his head, dark eyes narrowing on me.

"For fuck's sake, Zoe," he says, pulling himself out of my grip. "Can't you let it rest for even one minute? I'm doing my best here."

His words have the effect of a grenade being dropped in a mausoleum. The room goes impossibly quiet and I sense rather than see five heads turn in our direction. I take a step back, my face flooding with color.

Gratitude floods through me when Aisha saunters over.

"Trouble in paradise?"

I stare at her, confusion mingling with hurt.

"Geez, relax, I'm joking," she says, taking in my expression. She scowls at Aseem. "I did warn you he can be a prick."

I attempt a smile, trying to keep up the pretense that my little disagreement with Aseem was just that: a minor tiff in an otherwise happy marriage, but it's obvious I'm not fooling anyone. I drag my thumb across my phone's screen, for want of something to do while Aseem and Aisha snipe at each other.

I look up as Gabe walks over. He's dressed in a classic black tuxedo, complete with gold cuff links and dress shoes. It's obvious he's making an effort to fit in, but even dressed in the most expensive dinner jacket, Gabe can't quite match Aseem's polished ease. His bow tie is too symmetrical, the satin of his lapels too shiny. The effect is oddly disconcerting, like watching an amateur actor who's just landed his first role in a West End production. I have the sense that I know him from somewhere, but once again the feeling is fleeting, gone before I can even begin to pin it down.

I shiver as a gust of wind throws itself against the window, rattling the leaded panes and pushing a draft of cold air into the room.

"Just fluctuation because of the storm," Myra explains, as the lights in the room flicker. She raises her glass. "I think it's time for a toast."

What started as drizzle a few hours ago has turned into a full-blown storm, the thick curtain of rain rendering the landscape outside almost invisible, a blur of dark shapes against an even darker sky.

I turn my attention back to Myra.

"Go on, beta," Mama says. She's dressed in a deep red sari. The silk rustles as she wraps the pallu around her shoulders, a gesture that I've learned means she's anxious. Papa towers next to her, dressed simply in a chunky cardigan and black jeans.

"Do you remember how obsessed Aisha was with fairy tales when she was little?" Myra says, speaking directly to her mother. She waits for Mama to nod, before continuing. "There was this one book with Snow White on the cover—she took it *everywhere*. Refused to read anything else for months. She loved the stories about princesses and white knights and their happily ever afters. I was thinking about it the other day and I realized, I never read any fairy tales growing up."

"We did get you some books, but you threw them out," Papa interjects, putting his hands up.

Myra nods. "Sounds about right. Those stories never appealed to me." She plants her gaze on Aisha as she says this and even though the words are uttered with a smile, it's clear they're meant as a dig. "Those fairy tales were too artificial compared to what I saw at home every day." She holds Aisha's gaze for a moment before turning to Papa. "Now, you clearly don't have the coloring to be a white knight"— everyone laughs—"and I know no marriage is without its hiccups, but to me, the love, the commitment, the hard work I saw you put into your marriage and our family every single day, despite all the ups and downs, to me that is the real fairy tale. That has always been my benchmark. And I just want to take a moment to thank you . . ."

Papa shakes his head. "Sweetheart, you don't need to——"

"No, Papa, let me say this, please. We have not had the easiest time as a family, and I can see now that the three . . ." Myra swallows, her voice wobbling. "The three of us haven't always been as grateful as we should've been. But no matter what we did, however badly we behaved, however loudly we argued, you have always been there, ready to clean up whatever mess we got ourselves into. You've saved us, again and again. You showed us how to keep going even through the impossible. Aseem, Aisha, and I are lucky to have you as parents and I . . ." Myra pauses, her raised glass frozen midair, as the lights flicker again, this time accompanied by a resonant buzz. I glance toward the window. As the lights dip again, I think I can pick out a vague outline amidst the pitch-black darkness outside.

I find my eyes returning to Gabe. He's standing next to Aisha, one hand resting on her lower back, fingers caressing the top of her but-tocks. I should look away, but the fact that I can't quite place where I know him from is bothering me now. I watch as he steps away from her and reaches for a fresh bottle of champagne. It's as he pops it open that it clicks into place.

The Groucho. He worked as the bartender for a couple of months around the same time that I was waitressing there.

The satisfaction of piecing it together dissipates as soon as I remem-ber the rest and I realize, with a sinking feeling, that Myra and Papa are right about him.

I glance at Aisha, already dreading the moment I'll have to break it to her.

"And I would like to . . . I'd like to . . ." Myra continues, only to stut-ter to a stop, her eyes moving between the chandelier and the window as the lights blink a few more times before going out altogether, plung-ing us into semi-darkness. The light coming from the fireplace only adds to the eeriness, as shadows leap and dance across the walls in tandem with the flames.

We all fall silent, suddenly aware of the ferocity of the storm raging outside, listening to the rain hammering against the endless panes of glass, the sound as relentless and unforgiving as a hundred bullets going off at once.

"Shit," Aisha says at the same time as Aseem says, "There's a generator, right?"

"Myra?" Papa says, but Myra's frozen in her spot, her eyes fixed on the window.

The room is cloaked in shadows and where the landscape outside was a blank darkness before, I can now see the massing silhouette of the trees against the slightly luminous sky. I can make out the branches dancing in the rain, their sinewy forms reflected twice in the double glazing, and as I take a step closer to the window, I'm certain that I can see, inside the building on the right, a flash. Blue and yellow.

I pull in a sharp breath, all thoughts about Gabe set aside.

I walk to the patio doors, press my forehead into the glass, and cup my hands around my face to look out into the night. I turn to Myra, my voice shaking. "Is that . . . ?"

But she's frozen, her face still, her fingers wrapped so tight around the stem of her champagne flute that I'm surprised it hasn't snapped yet.

I stand there, momentarily riveted by the sight.

Flames licking at glass.

"The outhouse," Myra says finally, her voice little more than a whisper. "It's on fire."

30

MYRA

I spring into action, my champagne flute falling and shattering as I yank the patio doors open and rush outside. There is a fire extinguisher on the porch.

I am vaguely aware of Aseem behind me, conscious of the memories a fire—even a small one—ignites. But I haven't got time to stop and think.

The outhouse is connected to the garage, which is connected to the main house, and if the fire spreads . . .

I pull the side access door to the outhouse open and run into the front room. Flames soar, licking the walls, inching toward the timber I'd asked Stu to stack before he left in case we needed more logs for the fire.

I pull the safety pin and aim the nozzle of the extinguisher toward the base of the fire, swaying from side to side as I squeeze the handles together with as much force as I can muster. The air sizzles, the flames dampening within seconds. A small plume of smoke rises from it, a final flame flickering before the stream from the extinguisher suffocates it.

I set the extinguisher down, catch my breath.

Behind me, Aseem coughs.

I turn around. My voice is soft as I speak to him. "It was just faulty wiring," I say, nodding toward the socket at the base of the wall. "We're okay. Let's go."

We walk out in silence. After Ishaan, Aseem developed a phobia of fire. Just the sight of a candle was enough to induce a panic attack. He's come a long way from that, but the fact that Aseem followed me inside, despite his fears, is testament to the goodness of my brother.

I pull the door shut behind us and turn to him. With the flames put out, we've lost what little light we had. "Let's see if we can get the power . . ." the words die on my lips as I notice the movement in front of us.

The figure of a man approaching the house.

The breath freezes in my throat. One glance at Aseem confirms it.

This is not my imagination. This is real.

With every step he takes toward the house, his features slot into place one by one until the picture is complete.

Aseem squeezes my arm. "I'll wait for you inside."

Deep down, I knew this was coming. I knew I'd have to come face to face with him, but this is not how I imagined it would be. Not with me standing guard outside the house with the rain needling my face and panic hammering my ribcage. Not with my family gathered together, waiting to kick off a celebration I can no longer be bothered with.

I rub the space below my collarbone as the pressure in my chest worsens, the tightness reaching for my throat.

None of this is how it's meant to be.

I move toward him, shining the light in his face, the beam from my torch pulling his features into focus. The umbrella he's carrying is bent out of shape and despite the oversized raincoat he has on, I can see that the clothes underneath are drenched.

"What are you doing here?" I shout over the sound of the rain.

He stops and runs a hand over his face, flicking drops of water away from his eyes. I no longer have the ability to read his mind, but there is no mistaking the smile on his face. He looks between the house and me, then throws his head back, his laughter drowned out by the sound of thunder as a streak of lightning pierces the sky.

"Saving you, by the look of it," he yells.

I try to ignore my mounting alarm as he closes the distance between us in a few quick strides.

I could kill him.

I very nearly did kill him.

I force myself to take a step back, all the fear, the fury, the pure, un-adulterated hatred I've been trying to bury for the past three years rising up all at once.

"You shouldn't be here," I say, but my words are lost in the storm whipping around us and I'm left staring into the face of the only man I've ever loved.

The only person I've ever truly hated.

My husband.

I'm soaked before we've made it halfway back to the house. Wind and rain whip my face. The hem of my dress is heavy with water, the fabric slapping my legs as we walk through the front porch into what was once the gunroom.

I push my hood down and blow on my hands, thawing them out as I step into the small, dark vestibule. I feel around the wall, looking for the light switch while the man who stole the light from my life pushes the large oak dresser to one side.

"Why haven't you had this fixed yet?" Owen says, crouching down in front of the ancient fuse box.

"All of this needs to go," the electrical engineer I'd called in from Edinburgh a few months ago had said, shaking his head in amazement at the state of the unit. "This wiring is older than me," he'd laughed, before turning serious. He pointed to a jumble of wires leading to a single breaker switch. "See all this, it's a botched DIY job. They've overloaded this circuit here and I bet none of these wires have been properly earthed. It's an electrical fire waiting to happen."

He'd recommended a complete overhaul and he was right, as evidenced by the incident tonight. But his quote for rewiring all the electrics on the island came to a eye-watering forty-nine thousand pounds. Money that I couldn't spare, then or now.

I wipe my hands on the towel I keep here for exactly this purpose, then squat down next to Owen.

"Let me . . ." he starts as I angle the flashlight toward the grid of rusty switches and naked wires.

I reach around him and push the switch back up, flooding the room with light.

"Well," he says, pinning me in place with those icy blue eyes. "At least it still works."

I return his gaze, quietly taking in the changes to the features I once knew by heart: the sharp jaw, the signs of gray around his temples, the deep lines around his eyes and mouth that seem to have appeared out of nowhere. He looks older, but that's not what leaves me feeling unsettled. I'd always been drawn to the kindness and laughter in his eyes, the openness in his smile.

All of that has vanished, replaced by an unreadable weight that feels as heavy and punishing as the storm we've found ourselves in. How he managed to sail here in this weather is beyond me.

I stand up. He follows my lead and takes a step back, reinstating the distance between us.

I can't stop looking at that bag, at the tiny drops of water glistening on the initials I'd had specially engraved. I force myself to take a deep breath.

"Why are you here?"

The air between us feels charged, heavy with a mix of emotions I haven't got the courage to unpack.

"You haven't been responding to my emails." I don't answer and as he bends down to unzip his bag, I realize he doesn't expect me to. "I can't keep putting things off any longer," he says, pulling out a thick manila envelope and holding it toward me.

I shake my head, take another step back as I realize what he means. My back presses into the wall, the cold penetrating deep into my bones. "We had an agreement."

He narrows his eyes. "Yeah, we did."

"I just need . . ." The words die on my lips. I can hear footsteps outside. The haze in my mind crystallizes as the sound gets closer. "You need to leave. You can't . . ."

The door swings open.

"Owen," Papa says, his face breaking into a huge, devastating smile. "I thought that was you. What a brilliant surprise." He moves forward as if to pull Owen into an embrace then stops at the last moment, a frown appearing on his face. He shifts his attention to me. "Aseem said the fire was electrical. Bad wiring?"

I nod, not trusting myself to speak. Strains of voices carry in from the living room, reminding me that there's a dinner, a celebration that I'm meant to be hosting.

"Right. Well as long as it's been safely put out," Papa checks, looking from Owen to me. He's doing his best to act normal. "Are you two planning on coming inside or will we have to freeze ourselves out here?"

I glance at the envelope in Owen's hand. Its edges are scuffed and there is a deep crease running down the center, the paper bent and bruised from being crammed into a tight space. I take the envelope from him and lift my gaze to meet my father's.

"Owen just came to drop some papers off," I say. My voice sounds unnaturally high-pitched. I try to lower it, try to keep the tremor out of it. "He isn't staying."

Owen stuffs his hands into his pockets, rocks back on the heels of his shoes, his chin pointed downward. Fat drops of water slither off his coat and land on the floor.

At least he has the grace to look embarrassed.

"Nonsense. He's come all this way," Papa says. He turns to Owen. "You have to stay for dinner. Shalini will be thrilled to see you."

"I don't think—" Owen begins, but Papa cuts him off with a wave of his hand.

"I'm not taking no for an answer. Especially not in this weather."

The air in the room constricts, the already small room suddenly stifling. I look at my father, examining his face. I know what he wants. He's made it abundantly clear that he thinks I'm making a mistake, that I should give my marriage another chance, but Papa would never try to force anything on me. He can be stubborn but he's not thoughtless.

"It's just a little rain," I say, even as the wind howls outside, making the small square window rattle in its frame.

"Don't be ridiculous, Myra. I'm not letting your husband get on a boat in the middle of a storm."

That's how he got here, I want to say.

The sound of thunder cuts through the room as if to illustrate Papa's point.

"Now go and dry off, both of you, before you catch your death."

I follow my husband and my father into the hall reluctantly. Papa stops, turns to look at Owen. "It's good to see you, son."

Owen nods. "Thanks, Pa—" I glare at him. "Thank you."

We stand quietly for a moment, both of us watching Papa as he walks away, waiting for the kitchen door to swing shut and the sound of his footsteps to fade.

"They're all here," Owen says, his words more a statement than a question.

"We're celebrating my parents' anniversary." I swallow. "And Aseem and Zoe are expecting a baby."

I see a flash of something—regret or shame perhaps—flicker across Owen's face, but he turns away before I can decipher it. "I'll leave as soon as the rain stops, but we still need to talk. I can't hold things off for much longer."

Still a liar, then. Some things never change.

I cross the hall and walk toward the staircase.

He starts to follow me, then stops. "Is our—is the room—"

"Everything you left here is in the downstairs guest room," I say.

I stop when I'm halfway up the stairs. I don't turn around. My voice, when I speak, is ice.

"I don't need you to save me."

Owen's sigh fills the hall. His words pull at a string that I thought had snapped long ago.

"No," he says, his voice soft. "You never did."

31

ZOE

"What the hell are you doing?" Aisha protests as I loop my arm through hers and drag her into the hallway.

"I need to talk to you," I say, pulling her into the cloakroom. I lock the door, then turn around to face her. "I've been trying to work out why Gabe seems so familiar. I just remembered something."

"Okay," Aisha says slowly. "Enlighten me."

"Remember when we first met? After the freshers' orientation at university, I brought you to the Groucho. I used to work there as a waitress during our first term." I wait for her to nod, then continue. "Gabe was there too. Just for a few weeks. He was covering for the bartender."

Aisha shrugs as if to say so what.

"I'm pretty sure he met you. Or saw you there at the very least."

Aisha sighs. "For fuck's sake, Zo. Not you too. I've had enough conspiracy theories for one night." She tries to push past me to leave but I have her cornered. There is no part of me that is enjoying this conversation, but I care about her too much not to level with her. Aisha might not believe any of her family—and with good reason—but she listens to me. Or at least she will when I'm done.

"Annabel was a regular there too."

This gets her attention. Finally.

"You know her?"

I nod. "Not any more, but I knew her pretty well back then. She used to go by Annie." I close my eyes for a brief second, her face flashing before my eyes in a before-and-after reel. The Annie before Gabe: radiant, fun, and always smiling. And the one after: broken. I can't let that happen to Aisha. "They'd only been seeing each other for a few weeks when he proposed. Her friends couldn't stand him, her family were dead set against their relationship, but Annie was completely besotted. Refused to listen to anyone, tore up the prenup her father had made. It was all very dramatic, like they were star-crossed lovers. She was all in and the way she made it sound, so was he. I don't think I've ever seen anyone look happier. Then a couple of weeks before the wedding, she came into the bar in a total state. Turned out he'd been cheating on her the whole time."

"Don't be ridiculous," Aisha says. "*She* was cheating on *him*."

I shake my head, the memories from that time rushing back now. "No, she wasn't. He broke her heart, Aish. And he stole her money. After our regular bartender came back, Gabe was out of work. He was struggling to get by so she gave him her bankcard for emergencies. After she confronted him about the cheating, he cleaned out her account. He didn't even tell her before he left for Hong Kong, just took off. Literally days before the wedding. It was a huge scandal."

"That's impossible. Gabe would never do that."

I shake my head. "Annie told me all this herself. He's not who you think he is, Aish."

"You're lying," Aisha snaps.

"I have no reason to lie. He's using you."

"He's got more money in his account than you or me."

I suck in a deep breath. Why is it that the unbelievably wealthy are blind to what being rich actually means? "It's not about the money, Aisha; it's about what the money represents. Gabe is ambitious. He knows that after a point success is about the circles you move in. It's about reputation and connections. That's what he wants from you. He's using you to climb up the social ladder."

Aisha's face is rigid with anger. "How dare you? Just because we're friends doesn't mean you can say anything you want. You couldn't even afford to pay rent when I met you. You used to live off my leftovers, for fuck's sake. And look at you now." She leans forward. "Designer clothes, diamond jewelry, *esteemed social profile*. The whole fucking package. And even that's not enough. I'd call you a leech, except even leeches fall off after they've had enough. But you . . . you just take and you take and you take. If there's anyone here who's used me, it's you."

32.

MYRA

Standing in my room, in the room that was once ours, I am hollowed out. Crippled by the outrageous longing that years later still holds me hostage.

Serendipitous. That's the word I used to reach for to describe how Owen and I met. A word and a meet-cute straight out of a Richard Curtis film.

Friday night at my friend's flat in London. Susanna and I had met a few summers ago in Aspen and instantly bonded over our shared love of nineties pop music and modern American literature. I was visiting her over the holidays and I was completely out of place at her party.

When Owen approached me halfway through the evening, I stepped to one side, assuming he was aiming for the drinks table I was standing in front of. I'd been pleasantly surprised when he refreshed his drink, then turned to me and introduced himself. Owen Conroy, a medical student who grew up in a small town in Scotland. He had known Susanna since they were toddlers.

The more we spoke the more I realized just how much we had in common. We had both traveled the world with our families, we were both fiercely ambitious and driven by a desire to make our mark in the world, him by becoming a surgeon and me by becoming a lawyer. It was the first time either of us were living away from our families, and as much as we missed the comfort of home, we were both relieved to finally have a blank slate to start from. Even our birthdays were within a couple of weeks of each other. My heart stopped, just for a second, when he told me he was the eldest of four siblings. I'll tell you which one irritates me the most if you promise not to judge, he whispered conspiratorially, even though his voice was thick with emotion.

We spent the entire evening chatting, the conversation flowing effortlessly without any awkward pauses, but the world didn't fall away beneath my feet. My stomach wasn't flipping cartwheels. There were no quivering hearts or butterflies. There was just this sense of solidity, a comfort I hadn't known before. I liked him. Or at least I liked the feeling of being with him.

It had been less than a year since Ishaan's accident. I didn't like talking about him, didn't like revisiting the most horrific day of my life or describing the blanket of guilt and grief that felt so heavy that some days I woke up feeling like I couldn't breathe. For some reason, I told Owen about Ishaan, about the boy who had been so naughty, so full of mischief and joy and laughter, it was impossible to take your eyes off him. And yet, we did take our eyes off him. Seeing the horror flash across Owen's face, knowing he could unwrap the layers of regret and hurt and longing without me having to spell it out, it pierced a hole in that blanket. A small fissure to let the air in so I could breathe again.

It was only when I slipped into bed hours later that I was able to identify what I'd felt staring into those intense blue eyes: relief, as though all the tension I'd been holding for weeks and months had just suddenly melted away.

I didn't expect it to lead anywhere and for a while, it didn't. We were miles apart, pursuing highly competitive degrees in two of the best universities in the country, me at St Andrews and him in Cambridge. A long-distance relationship was not an option. I erased him from my memory, until six months later Owen texted to say he was visiting St Andrews and he was wondering if I might be free for a drink? Halfway through the drink that turned to dinner that turned to coffee, I excused myself to call the boy I'd started seeing a few weeks previously: it was over. Owen had been offered a place at St Andrews and he was planning to transfer after the end of year exams. It was so simple it almost took my breath away; there were no games, no coyness, just a sense of coming home.

Which is not to say it was perfect or effortless.

We argued, even back when there wasn't much to argue about, and I worried that, despite all our similarities, we were fundamentally different. I saw the world as a threat, expected the worst to happen, possibly because the worst *had* happened. Owen, however, saw life as an adventure. For the longest time, I hoped that some of his optimism, that complete faith he had in the world and his place in it, would rub off on me. I'd known within five minutes of meeting Owen that I could trust him with my life. If he believed that everything would work itself out, perhaps it would.

I handed him not just my life but my whole world, trusting him to hold it all together when I couldn't. And just when I thought I could let go, he let it drop.

I allow myself a moment, then throw the envelope on the bed and start to undress, the delicate satin fraying as I pull at it, fighting with a zipper that refuses to budge. I twist in front of the mirror and yank it down, desperate to get out of the dress that suddenly feels too tight.

I stand there in my underwear, looking at who I have become: a woman with sunken cheeks and circles under her eyes. A woman who looks more exhausted, more beaten by her past than she cares to admit.

I spin around, my attention going automatically to the bed I still sleep in. The bed in which I still have the nightmare that masquerades as a dream, where I'm woken not by bad memories but by the sound of little feet stamping on wooden floors, where the bed never feels empty because it is full of warm bodies. Full of love.

The bed is still warm but not with love. It's soaked with blood.

That dream, it's paralyzing.

And yet, it's the prospect of a dreamless sleep that terrifies me.

Because before the blood comes the laughter, the gurgles, the feeling of a tiny fist wrapped around my finger.

Those nightmares are all I have left. And it's all Owen's fault.

I pull the duvet off the bed. I rip off the bed sheet and hurl it across the room, every ounce of politeness and reserve draining out of me as I press my face into a cloud of white bed linen and scream and scream and scream.

33

ZOE

Owen's here. Despite the initial awkwardness, his unexpected presence changes the dynamic, brings a lightness to the atmosphere as we all slip into a familiar rhythm, our attentions seized by the one man we all unequivocally adore.

"I hear congratulations are in order," Owen says, walking around the coffee table to wrap me in a hug.

"Thank you," I say, shifting gently out of his reach and tilting my face to look at him. He's dressed simply in a dinner jacket and a roll-neck jumper. There are flecks of silver in his hair and deep lines surround those sharp blue eyes, but the signs of age only make his already attractive face more arresting. Owen may not have won the genetic lottery like the Agarwals, but he has that rare quality that makes it impossible to turn away from him. While my husband's and his siblings' movie-star good looks can sometimes alienate, with his perpetual five o'clock shadow and easy smile, Owen has the opposite effect. His attractiveness is more subtle, rooted in his signature charisma, an effortless, easy charm that is the trademark of an Old Etonian. He is equally if not more privileged than the Agarwals, but there is a polish to him that none of my in-laws can replicate. Meeting Aisha and her family showed me what money looks like. Meeting Owen for the first time? It was a lesson in class. His wealth always seemed invisible until I realized what to look for: the furniture and watches that were inherited instead of bought, the pieces of art that were on loan to the V&A, the access to people and places that a checkbook can never buy.

I looked him up when Aisha first told me about him, back when we were still speculating if Myra's boyfriend of eight years would ever go down on one knee. His father, Sir Norman Walter Conroy, is the twelfth baronet of Ballikinrain, a peerage that Owen will inherit along with the townhouse in Edinburgh where he currently lives, the family home where he grew up—a *wee* castle near Inverness—and half a dozen listed properties in Scotland and Ireland. And yet, he works full-time as a trauma surgeon, choosing to work twenty-hour days instead of flitting between vanity businesses and ski resorts like the rest of his kind.

I've always wondered if their ambition was what brought Myra and Owen together. They both have a keen sense of purpose, a need to find their place in the world, though admittedly over the past few years, Myra's ambition seems to have shrunk to encapsulate only this island.

"You look incredible as always, but how are you feeling?" Owen says, holding me lightly by my elbows. That's the other thing about Owen. Coming from anyone else those words might have seemed superficial, but there is a sincerity to him, a sense that he is genuinely interested, that has always put me immediately at ease.

"I'm good," I say. "Aseem's spoiling me rotten."

"As he should," Owen says. He gives my arms a reassuring squeeze and I wonder if he can see through my manufactured happiness.

I smile, try to appear sincere. "You need to tell me all about your trip to . . ."

The words die on my lips as Myra walks in, followed by Aseem.

"Right," she says, her voice cold. "Dinner?"

There are murmurs of assent. We all file into the dining room and as chairs are scraped back and glasses refilled, the buoyancy, the *relief* that Owen's unexpected presence has inspired is sucked right out of the room.

I'm not sure when she found the time to do this but Myra's pulled out all the stops tonight. The table is set with filigreed bone china plates so fragile I worry even a slight scrape might result in a crack. Monogrammed silver cutlery that marches up one side of the china and down the other is reflected in the stemmed crystal glasses. The assortment of flickering candles and tea-lights cast soft shadows on our faces, and the smell of wildflowers mingles with the delicate aromas drifting in from the open-plan kitchen. It's incredible. Absolutely gorgeous.

And yet all the beautiful setting does is highlight how awkward and strained the mood is at the table. Aisha sighs as she stabs a piece of the venison with her fork, the sound of her exhale loud in an already tense silence. Aseem reaches across the table and pours the last of the champagne into his glass, beating Gabe to it. His mouth is set in a straight line, his expression strangely absent. Only Mama and Papa seem relaxed, talking quietly to Owen about his work, his life in Edinburgh, and everything in between. I sneak a glance at Myra. She's sitting next to me, barely looking up as she nudges a fondant potato with the tines of a fork.

Despite everything that Myra and Owen went through, it came as a shock when she announced she was going to move to Kilbryde full-time. For all her nosiness, Myra is rarely forthcoming about her own affairs. We all knew she'd been struggling, but Myra has always been a trooper; carrying on through the worst is what she does.

The news came by way of a group email. A short paragraph that told us little more than the basics: she couldn't stand being in Edinburgh anymore. She needed a change of scene and she'd decided it was time to take a break from her law practice and focus on developing Kilbryde. Myra had been with Owen for nearly fifteen years at that point. Their lives were knotted together so tightly—their friends, their home, their careers—she said she felt like a ghost haunting her old life in Edinburgh. I understood that. Mama and Papa suggested she move in with them, with *us*, temporarily, but she refused. I understood that, too. She needed space and distance to heal, both of which are in short supply in India. She would never be able to outrun the sympathetic glances and thinly veiled pity of Delhi's gossipy high society. But her decision to move here, to live alone on this island in the middle of nowhere, completely cut off from the world, this I do not understand. Myra left Owen because he had an affair, and yet her behavior suggests she's punishing herself. For what, I do not know.

The sound of my name turns my attention to the other side of the table.

"What's that?" I ask Aisha.

She rolls her eyes, fixing me with a bored expression. "This she hears."

I raise my eyebrows.

Aisha cocks her head to the side, just the slightest bit. "I was just saying that instead of banning social media on the island, Myra should look at getting a few influencers on board before the launch."

"It's too soon," Myra says, barely looking up. "I don't see the point of inviting influencers when the island isn't ready. They'll just rip it to shreds under the guise of an honest review."

"That is so not how it works. Right, Zo?" Aisha says, shaking her head. I stare at her, my fork suspended midair. I know that look, the wide-eyed innocence that Aisha feigns before the scathing remarks come out. In some ways, she is remarkably like her mother, the expert sniper whose bullets come doused in honey.

"Influencers aren't journalists. They don't care about honest reviews," Aisha continues, not waiting for me to respond. "They're basically the sluts of the online world. Hashtag will-do-anything-for-cash." Her gaze lingers on me for a second before sliding sideways to Myra. "I guess that's another item to add to the invoice you'll be handing Papa."

I lock the door, hands trembling, and sit on the toilet, unable to take my mind off Aisha's words. She's being catty because I dared to point out that her prince charming is really just another charlatan. That's all. But hashtag will-do-anything-for-cash? It's too much of a coincidence.

It started with a comment.

> If only your brand partners knew how you truly operate.
> Nothing about your life or your fame is "organic" and the
> world deserves to know that. #perfectlyfake #perfectlyslutty

The criticism was in response to my post promoting an international beauty brand's new #perfectlyauthentic range of inclusive, cruelty-free makeup. The brand had shared my video talking about its "invisible" foundation with its eighteen million followers—a brilliant result by any measure. It was my first collaboration with a brand of that scale and one that I knew had the potential to lift me to the topmost tier of influencers.

I've based my brand on authenticity, on being real. The vitriol wasn't just hurtful, it was threatening to undo the very foundations I'd so carefully built.

By then, I was used to my follower count and engagement rates rising and falling based on how glossy or not my hair looked, how relatable or funny my caption was, how heartfelt I appeared in my videos, and how perfectly imperfect my life looked from the outside. I was used to the odd comment or DM telling me off for being insensitive or superficial. I understood that no matter how many times I tweaked the slant of my posts, there would always be someone who thought I was doing it wrong. I was used to adjusting everything from the tone of my captions to the shade of my lipstick to appease my followers. I was used to getting it wrong more often than I got it right.

What I wasn't used to, what I'm still not used to, is people sending me vicious threats because they think my life looks "too easy." Or because they assume that I've somehow cheated my way into becoming an influencer.

Admittedly, the notion that my rise as an influencer is entirely organic or that I just stumbled into Insta-fame is fiction, one that my agent and I carefully and strategically crafted, but that doesn't mean it's not bloody hard work. Building and sustaining a loyal following takes skill and commitment and yes, strategy. I spend hours precision-planning hashtags and captions. I've built a network of influencer friends to swap tags with. I regularly engineer situations to make product placement seem organic. When my follower count grew from three hundred to three thousand, I was pleasantly surprised. When it grew from three thousand to thirty thousand, I knew my method was working.

When I crossed the fifty thousand followers milestone, my newly appointed agent sent me to a seminar on trolling and online abuse. Don't engage, never reply, block and report, the speaker advised. For over a year, I followed that mantra to the letter.

Until that comment dropped.

SamBar87's words accusing me of being fake garnered close to a thousand likes in just fifteen minutes.

I lost it. I deleted the comment.

That was my first mistake.

Within minutes, a torrent of hate appeared on half a dozen of my recent posts.

I went back to the speaker's advice. I blocked *SamBar87*'s profile and reported it to Instagram.

The next morning, *NB_Lurker* was born.

That was three months ago.

Since then *NB_Lurker* is everywhere. In my comments, in my DMs, replying to my stories and commenting on every post I'm tagged in.

It's the level of detail he goes into that terrifies me. I've read about trolls who become obsessed, but I find it hard to understand why a complete stranger would go to such lengths to intimidate me.

NB_Lurker's account is private, but the fact that he has no posts, zero followers, and he follows only one account himself tells me everything I need to know.

The account exists purely to troll me.

I unlock my phone and go to my inbox, scrolling through the dozens of messages he's sent me over the past few months. I stop when I get to the one I'm looking for. A response to the video I'd shot in collaboration with a mindfulness platform talking about the ethics of being an influencer and the importance of creating honest, meaningful content.

> Why do you insist on acting like there's anything ethical about your business? It's tiresome. Everyone knows all you care about is the money. #hypocrite #willdoanythingforcash

Will do anything for cash.

The exact phrase that Aisha just used.

I've long suspected that *NB_Lurker* isn't a total stranger. There's an intimacy in the way he talks about me. I know him, or rather he knows me. For weeks, I've been stressing about the sexual undertone to his threats because his messages are strewn with words like rape, slut, whore. But what if the misogyny is a front?

I place my phone on the marble counter, Aisha's taunt ringing in my ears.

What if *NB_Lurker* is actually a woman?

I peel off my clothes, my bra and underwear landing in a puddle on top of ripped jeans and a jumper that is streaked with blood, until I'm standing in the small bathroom stark naked.

I stare into the full-length mirror, unable to turn away from my own reflection.

There's blood everywhere. In my hair, around my nose, under my nails.

I rub my hands together. Despite the warmth of the room, I am shivering.

I turn on the shower and step into the stream of scalding hot water, wincing as it hits my skin, every inch of my body burning.

I can still smell it. The metallic, sharp scent of the blood mingling with the earthiness of the soil. The faint odor of feces. I rest my hands on the wall and bend over, heaving in the tiny glass cubicle, but all that does is make me even more nauseous.

I press my forehead into the shower screen, watching the water run off me. Crimson. Like a particularly heavy period. Bits of leaves, mud, and moss circle the plug, filth turning the gleaming white shower tray grotty. I grab the body brush sitting on the shelf and start to scrub, pressing the bristles into the creases and crevices of my body, behind my ears, underneath my nails, vigorously sloughing off the layers of mud and grime until every inch of flesh is raw and mottled. I run my hands over all the scrapes and bruises, feeling the sting as my palms press soap into the cuts, fingertips pushing against torn skin.

There is a perverse satisfaction in the stinging pain, a sense of penance.

I rest my head against the tiled wall and close my eyes.

I should never have agreed to this reunion.

I force myself to turn off the water and step out. It's almost four in the morning, only a couple of hours until the sun rises and the others start stirring from their beds.

I dress quickly, bracing myself for what is to come, running through the list of things I need to take care of. The body. The alibi. The evidence.

I need to get my story straight.

34.

ZOE

I return to the kitchen to find everyone gathered around the table, ooh-ing and aah-ing over the cake. It's yet another family tradition, the anniversary cake, and we all cheer as Mama and Papa blow out the candles before feeding each other a tiny morsel. More champagne is poured, pictures taken, memories revisited. Alcohol seems to have loosened everyone's tightly knotted shoulders, the tension easing as the evening wears on. Even Papa looks relaxed, his face awash with happiness as Mama recounts their first meeting. It's a story we've all heard countless times before, and I tune out as Mama describes the brief introduction at a mutual friend's wedding that led to a forty-year marriage. All of nineteen and already primed for an arranged marriage, Mama had been tasked with welcoming the groom's family and friends, showering them with rose petals as they walked in. She paused for a split second when Papa walked in. Here their narratives differ. She says Papa said she was too pretty to be one of the flower girls as he approached her. Papa denies this completely, insisting all they had was a stolen glance before he pointed her out to his older brother, who jumped into action. Connections between the two families were dug up and a week later, under the watchful eye of their parents, grandparents, and neighbors, Mama and Papa had their first proper conversation. Three months later, they were married.

"I knew even before she said hello that I'd found the love of my life," Papa says now, his voice thick with emotion as he drapes an arm around Mama.

This is it, the perfect time to speak to Papa.

I glance at Aseem, but he's standing in the corner, absorbed in whatever Myra's telling him.

I could pull him aside, remind him of the promise he made me, but I'm not sure he'll appreciate the interruption. Aseem might need to be prompted into action when it comes to his family, but he doesn't like to be reminded of it. I've learned over the years that I can only push him so far before he turns on me. And who knows, I think, looking at Aseem and Myra as they huddle even closer, he might be talking to her about the sale of PetroVision right now.

Someone changes the music to Bollywood and Aisha, more drunk than I've seen her in a long time, starts twirling around the room. The double doors between the dining area and the living room have been slid open and Aisha utilizes the large open-plan space as her personal dance floor.

She has always been a fantastic dancer. There is a looseness to her, an ease in the way she inhabits her body, that makes her movements appear fluid. She seems utterly oblivious as I watch her, both mesmerized and repelled. She stumbles, champagne spilling out of the flute and on to the mantelpiece as she rights herself. How many times have I danced with her, both of us lost to the music, completely unaware and unconcerned about our surroundings? I think back to our university days: the gigs, the all-nighters, the impromptu house parties. I never knew how an evening would end—our lives were dictated by Aisha's whims—and yet I never complained. Why would I? She was spontaneous. Fun. Adventurous. And she was my best friend.

My chest tightens as I think about the messages on my phone. She can be snarky, and admittedly our communication has been a bit off lately, but Aisha is still my best friend. There's no way she's an Instagram troll.

Aisha comes to a stop in front of me midtwirl. She grabs my hand and pulls me to the center of the room. "Remember when we used to go clubbing?" she says, a little breathless as she dances me around the room, forcing me to move my body in sync with hers, our movements mirroring each other's as much out of habit as instinct.

"I miss this. I miss us," she says.

My face softens, some of the tension dissipating as I throw my head back and move in time with the music. The chandelier spins. "Me too."

"I'm sorry for being such a bitch," Aisha says quietly. "I didn't mean it. I just . . . this week . . . it's tested me in ways I can't even begin to explain. You're wrong about Gabe, but I shouldn't have said that stuff. It was cruel and unnecessary. I'll do better, okay? I'll *be* better."

I nod, realizing how ridiculous my worries are. Aisha's always had a temper and a tongue so sharp it can slit you in half. But she has a good, kind heart, and she's always had my back. Always.

I can sense the heat of Aseem's gaze on me as I close my eyes, feeling the music pulse through me. I push my hands through my hair. Aseem has no natural rhythm but he used to love watching me dance, back when we still went dancing. I dance with a little more intention, hips swaying from side to side.

Let him watch. Let him remember.

Owen's voice pulls me out of my trance. "There she is. I knew you were hiding the real Zoe somewhere." He winks at me before turning to Aisha. "Can I bum a cigarette off you?"

"No! What would my dear sister say?" Aisha widens her eyes in mock outrage, before bursting into laughter. She plants a kiss on my cheek, then loops her arm through Owen's. "I'll join you."

I watch for a moment as they slide the patio door open and huddle under the narrow awning, the orange embers of their cigarettes glowing bright against the black sky.

Owen is far too good-natured to be crass or insensitive, but I'm willing to bet my life that he's the latest recruit in Papa's campaign to get rid of Gabe. And considering Aisha's fondness for him, the one most likely to be successful.

I look around me. Myra, Aseem, Mama, and Papa are in the dining area, looking at the pictures on the sideboard. Even though it's still early, not even nine p.m., I am exhausted. I'm eyeing the sofa, wondering if pregnancy is a legitimate excuse for curling up in the middle of a party, when Gabe comes over, drink in hand.

"I was enjoying that little dance. Very sexy."

I stare at him, unsure if I heard him right. "What did you say?"

He leans in, dropping his voice an octave. "You heard me."

I feel a flush creep up my neck. His eyes are glazed over and it's clear from the slight drawl in his voice that he's drunk. I laugh, trying to get past the inappropriateness of his comment. "I think you're confusing me with your fiancée. Aisha's just stepped outside," I say, nodding toward the patio.

I take a step back, aware that I'm dangerously close to the fireplace. The heat radiating up my legs is no match for the outrage spiking my heart. I shoot a look across the room, my anxiety easing as I catch Myra's eye.

"Everything okay here?" Myra says, walking over and planting herself next to me. She places a hand on my back and steers me away from the fire, the gesture both reassuring and nostalgic, but her eyes are on Gabe.

His lips curl into a smile. "Perfect. I was just looking for my fiancée," he says, before heading toward the patio.

"Zo?"

"Yeah," I say, distracted by the scene unfolding beyond the glass doors. Aisha twists to beam at Gabe as he steps outside, slotting her body into his as he wraps an arm around her.

"What was he on about?" Myra asks.

I pull my focus away from the patio and turn to look at Myra. I've spent enough time around drunken men to know that Gabe isn't as drunk as he might like me to believe. He knew exactly what he was saying and he enjoyed saying it, enjoyed watching the heat creep up my face. I should tell Myra, but if I do, she will tell Aseem and I know how that's going to end. My husband is the most sanguine, calm person I've ever met, except when it comes to things like this. The last time someone tried to hit on me, Aseem gave him a broken nose and a couple of cracked ribs. We were lucky the man didn't press charges.

Gabe was being a jerk, which isn't all that surprising. I just hope Owen's able to drill some sense into Aisha.

Plus there are far more important things that I need to discuss with Myra.

"Nothing," I say now. "Mama and Papa look so happy, don't they? The photo frames were a brilliant idea." I look toward the dining area, where Mama is still standing by the sideboard. Something about the display, the way the pictures sit amidst the fairy lights, makes me distinctly uncomfortable.

"You know how much she loves looking at family photos," Myra says.

"Don't we all?" I say. "I meant to ask, did you manage to speak to Papa at all?"

Myra frowns. "I thought Aseem would have told you."

I feel myself stiffen. "Told me what?" I try to keep my tone neutral.

"I did speak to him. Papa isn't going to retire and . . ." Myra sighs, clearly annoyed about being the one who has to break it to me. "I think it's for the best, actually."

The words wrap around me like a corset, pushing panic into my throat.

"But all that stress . . . his health," I say.

But Myra's eyes have already left my face, her attention seized by something else. "You should talk to Aseem," she mutters.

My gaze finds Aseem's across the room. He raises his eyebrows.

My mouth is set in a straight line, my hands clenched at my sides. A silent answer to a silent question.

You promised.

Very slowly, his gaze slides off me. He dips his head and turns as usual to his mother, bending down to whisper something in her ear before slipping out of the room.

Fucking typical.

There is a knot of tension in my jaw as I walk over to the sideboard. I look at the photo from the family holiday in the Maldives, my eyes drawn to the tanned faces smiling up at the camera. Aseem had proposed to me on that trip, popping the question in the privacy of our villa, surrounded by hundreds of candles and nothing but the sound of waves. The picture was taken moments after we'd announced our engagement at breakfast the next morning. It was the happiest day of my life. Our lives. And yet I'm not in that picture.

I examine the dozen or so pictures that make up this nauseating display of family milestones. I am not in a single picture. I know Myra well enough to understand that the oversight won't have been intentional, but that only makes it hurt more.

I've been trying for years to become a part of this family, and yet the longer I know them, the more I realize that they'll never include me; they don't even see me.

I worry now that my husband's vision is so focused on his parents, so blurred by the tragedies of the past and their expectations for the future, that he's stopped seeing me as well.

Or worse, he's stopped caring.

I look at the picture at the heart of the arrangement. Mama and Papa on their wedding day.

I take a step back, realizing suddenly what this elaborate display of gilded picture frames and twinkling lights reminds me of.

A fucking shrine.

35

MYRA

I slip out of the kitchen and go upstairs, eager to escape Zoe's incessant questions. I have enough to deal with as it is; I cannot immerse myself in what is clearly Aseem's problem, not when I have so much to contend with myself.

I glance over the legal notice Owen served me with this evening. I have four weeks to buy him out or he'll sell Kilbryde. It's no choice at all.

The first time it happened, I was stoic. I went back to work the same afternoon, poring over a case file while blood gushed out of me, soaking the thick pad the nurse had pressed into my hands. I comforted myself with statistics, reminding myself that one in three pregnancies results in a miscarriage. A rite of passage. I should have expected it, really. And now that I'd got the miscarriage out of the way, statistically, it couldn't happen again. It meant that the next time I got pregnant, the hope would be real. It would be bulletproof.

The statistics didn't help. The next time it happened, I was bereft. But again, I was optimistic. What were the odds of a twenty-something, healthy woman having two miscarriages in a row? "Sometimes the body knows before we do when a pregnancy's unviable," the doctor said, "think of it as your body's way of saving you from having to make an impossible decision later on." I nodded. Smiled through the tears. Third time's the charm, I said. My doctor agreed.

I tried so hard to put a positive gloss on things, to keep going despite the grief, to keep trying, believing that I could change biology through sheer will and bloody-mindedness, that when it happened again, just seven weeks into my third pregnancy, I crumbled. I wasn't prepared for the aching loss, the complete lack of logic or sense. Most of all, I wasn't prepared for the calm with which Owen handled it when I told him.

I begged him to start trying again, but after the third miscarriage, it wasn't just my husband who was hesitant. My body was, too. I couldn't get pregnant. It took three years and six rounds of IVF for our luck to turn around. Three years by the end of which I could barely recognize myself. But none of that mattered because I was pregnant. Each of my past miscarriages had happened early in the pregnancy so when I crossed the ten-week mark it seemed destined.

Then five days into my eleventh week, I woke up with a wetness between my legs and the tart, metallic smell that told me it was happening again. I was curled up on my side when Owen woke up. He carried me to the bathroom, held me close as I lay there, willing my body to stop, to find strength to keep my baby.

Oddly enough, that final miscarriage did bring us closer together. Gone was the unspoken blame, the insinuation that I was putting us through this, with my insistence on round after round of IVF. This time, when I bought a plant pot, instead of looking away, Owen stood with me as I carefully placed what remained of our baby in it.

And for a while at least, he became the man I'd fallen in love with.

He was loving and tender. He wept with me when the specialists told us that I'd never carry a baby, that another round of IVF was not an option, that we needed to start thinking about surrogacy and adoption. "You've had four miscarriages in seven years," the consultant said, "your body is trying to tell you something."

The consultant recommended one final test to check my levels of NK cells: natural killer cells. It turned out I had too many. The diagnosis cemented one of my deepest fears: instead of acting as a shield, my womb was killing my babies.

I was killing my babies.

I don't think Owen fully understood what that diagnosis did to me, but I know he tried. He tiptoed around the conversation for months, and finally, I was the one who brought up the topic of adoption.

It was the only way to bring some joy back into our lives.

I was used to irregular periods ever since the IVF started and between buying the estate and completing the paperwork for the adoption agency, I barely even realized when I missed my period.

And even when I did, I didn't even think to take the test. The consultant had been very clear: you can be a mother, but you'll never give birth.

I had hardened myself.

I was more than three months late by the time I made an appointment with my gynecologist. I was prepared to be told it was early menopause, another item to add to the long list of my body's failings.

I was too stunned to speak when she told me I was pregnant. I walked out of the exam room and into the waiting room on autopilot. Time concertinaed and fragmented in ways I cannot fathom. Someone must have called Owen because he was crouching in front of me, still in his surgical gown and scrubs, splashes of a stranger's blood on his sleeve.

I held up the little piece of paper for him to see.

Twins. I was carrying twins.

Neither of us dared to say it, but we both knew that this time it was going to work. I was already in the second trimester. Without even realizing, I'd crossed that twelve-week milestone that had until now evaded me.

And the fact that it was twins . . . It was a sign from a god or universe that I had previously never believed in, a chance to right what had happened in my family decades ago, to finally heal. I convinced myself that everything in my life had been leading up to this, that all the miscarriages and the heartache were a test, a preparation for what was to come.

I suppose in some ways it was.

Mourning someone who never got the chance to exist is a strange thing. After each miscarriage, there was a blankness to my grief, a sense of unknowing that was wrapped up in all the missed opportunities, the possibilities of what might have been.

That final pregnancy . . . I wasn't grieving a possibility. The twins were real. They had names, personalities. I had held them in my arms. I remember the look on Jay's face, the way his little forehead was scrunched up like he was surprised to see me. And Misha. She was the fighter, a little fireball of energy and will. I can still feel the weight of her tiny body in my arms, simultaneously as light as a feather and as heavy as a rock grounding me, reminding me that motherhood was the biggest responsibility I'd ever have. There was a sense of inevitability to it, to knowing that I would carry that weight as long as I lived, that from that moment on, I would worry about everything all the time. From choosing a nappy to choosing a school, every decision would be a source of stress and anxiety. It was a pressure I was prepared for. A pressure I had craved for years.

I would give anything to feel that fear, that worry, that weight again.

Losing Jay and Misha left a hole in me. Learning of Owen's betrayal turned that hole into a crater. A crater that swallowed my marriage, my career, my sense of self, everything I believed in.

The knock on the door pulls me back to the present.

"I was just coming to find you," I say, opening the door and stepping to one side to let Owen in.

He looks at the papers spread out on the desk, nods. "It's a good offer."

"Maybe, but I'm afraid your trip's wasted. I'm not agreeing to this."

"For fuck's sake, Myra, I cannot keep up the payments anymore."

"No, it's not like you can afford it," I say, my voice bitter as I stand with my back pressed against the wall. "The family castle doesn't run itself."

Owen squeezes his eyes shut, pinches the bridge of his nose. His voice is cold, devoid of any emotion. "I've had the bank ringing me every day for weeks. There's only one way this ends. This is the best possible outcome."

"For you, maybe. You know what this place means to me."

He looks up and I see it then, the indifference flashing across his eyes as he stares at me, revealing a glimpse of the person I discovered behind the charming aristocrat. "I'm sorry it's come to this. It hasn't been easy for me either, you know. Everything changed after you came to live here."

After you came to live here. How easily he skims over it. His coldness, the obvious lack of regret reaffirms my decision. The doubt that has been plaguing me for days disappears.

"I'm buying you out," I say, relishing the look of surprise on his face.

"How?"

"That's not really your concern, is it? You want out, I'll buy you out.

It's as simple as that. You are not going to take one more thing from me. I won't let you."

"I would never—"

Indignation prickles through me, its glint as sharp as a blade's edge. "Yes, you would. You did. You didn't even tell me before stopping the payments. What next? Are you going to send bailiffs knocking?"

"That's not fair," he says, shaking his head. "I've been doing my best to reach you. It's not my fault you refuse to answer your phone or your emails."

"Don't pretend you don't want to hurt me."

A shadow passes over Owen's face. He shifts his weight. "I'm not trying to hurt you, Myra. I'm trying to do right by you."

"I'll instruct my solicitors next week, they can reach out to your guys to agree to a number as part of the settlement."

He looks at me, a question in his brow.

"I'm filing for divorce. The paperwork is already on its way to your office." I spell it out for him, already anticipating the hurt on his face, but his expression remains unchanged. He looks at his feet, then back at me. There is the sense of everything clicking together as I finally get it. He's moved on. The realization is like a punch to the stomach.

"There's someone else," I say. "That's why you came, isn't it? It's why you stopped the payments."

Owen shifts his gaze to the window. Outside the rain has reduced to a soft patter. "I should leave," he says, turning to open the door, then twisting back to look at me, one hand still on the doorknob. "You know what, Myra? If you keep pushing people away, you don't get to act surprised when they actually leave."

36

MYRA

Owen and another woman.

Another woman.

It's a shock, that's all. I've gotten so used to living here by myself that I forgot that Owen is still out there in the world, meeting people, doing things. Of course he's met someone.

It's one of the things I hate about him, his ability to laugh, joke, carry on as if what happened to us is little more than a blip in an otherwise extraordinary life.

After the funeral, Owen stayed at home for weeks. From cooking to checking my stitches and monitoring my medication, he did everything he was supposed to, but we'd lost the ability to comfort or sustain each other. I could barely climb out of bed, let alone hold a conversation. Words, laughter, kindness became scarce as loneliness crept in. I rarely left my room, spending every day doing the same thing: going over the past few weeks with a fine-tooth comb, trying to find the exact moment when it all unraveled. I always came to the same conclusion, stopped at the exact same moment.

I'd taken the day off work so I could finish getting the nursery ready.

Although I still had nearly three months to go until my due date, I didn't want to leave it till the last minute. The walls had been painted and the cribs assembled, but there was still a lot to do. I hummed as I moved through the room, unpacking boxes, hanging up pictures, arranging Jay and Misha's soft toys and clothes in their wardrobes. Despite the fact that it was springtime in Scotland, sunshine was streaming in through the windows of our Edinburgh townhouse, the harsh glare turning the loft room into a sauna. Owen was supposed to install the blinds weeks ago. I picked up the head rail and examined it, turning it over to look at the mechanism. It was a simple clip frame. The decorators had already fixed the brackets on to the windows, all I needed to do was snap the clips into place and attach the roller blind. I pushed the small stepladder against the wall and climbed on it, clips in hand.

This is where it gets blurry.

I must have faltered, fallen. I must have called out for help. I must have crawled across the room to reach for my phone.

All I remember is the look on Owen's face as he knelt down beside me on the floor, his arms wrapped tight around me as he cradled me, telling me over and over again that everything would be okay, reminding me that he was right there with me. Then came the sirens, the rush to A&E, the surgeon's face as he told me what was happening.

It was too soon. Only twenty-eight weeks. My babies weren't strong enough. Pointless objections tumbled out of my mouth.

The twins were in distress. They had to get them out so they could breathe.

I woke up in a hospital bed with a hollowness in my belly and a husband who refused to meet my eyes.

They had got Misha out in time. She was in the NICU, breathing into a tube, but breathing nevertheless. A real fighter.

But Jay had been in an awkward position, the umbilical cord

wrapped around his neck. He was already gone by the time they got to him.

A nurse brought him to me. Someone had bathed him and wrapped him in a patterned white and blue blanket. He was wearing a knitted hat that was far too big for his tiny head. But he was still perfect. I held him for what felt like hours, refusing to dwell on the deep purple lips, convincing myself that my baby boy was just sleeping.

With Misha, it was different. Her eyelids fluttered as I lifted her out of the giant glass box. I detected what I thought was a small smile behind the tube. But as I held her against my bare chest, I could tell she was suffering; every breath she took needed monumental effort. Misha spent three days in the NICU but even with the best will and all the tubes in the world to help her, at just twenty-eight weeks, her lungs simply weren't strong enough to keep her alive.

I am not sure of the sequence of events or the precise details of that week or the ones that followed. Every morning, I woke feeling lost and alone. Every morning, I tried to rewind time, fixating on the moment when everything changed.

The moment when I pulled the stepladder across the room, that's the one that haunted me. That still haunts me.

If I'd just waited.

It was that moment I was thinking about when, exactly eighteen days after we lost Misha, I climbed out of bed and walked across the hall to the nursery. I stood with my hand on the doorknob, willing myself to open the door, to look at the bright yellow room and ask myself if it had been worth it, when I heard the sound of laughter float up the stairs. It was nearly midnight. Owen wasn't in bed, but then he rarely was. I had painkillers to numb myself, but Owen didn't. He found his respite in mindless television. But this wasn't TV laughter. These were voices I recognized. My husband and my sister.

They were in the kitchen, a half empty bottle of tequila and two shot glasses sitting on the counter in front of them. Owen was laughing so hard his entire face had gone red.

That's the detail that stuck with me. Eighteen days after Misha died, he was laughing.

I stood watching them for ages, in a nightdress stained with breast milk, before Owen turned around.

His laughter stuttered to a stop.

His gaze darted to Aisha's face before coming back to settle on mine, his eyes saturated with guilt.

A month later, it all unraveled. He tried to explain it away, reminding me of our history, trying to leverage our past to save our future, but it was pointless.

In the space of two months, I lost two tiny lives, my marriage, and in all the ways that mattered, myself.

Which is why my reaction today makes no sense.

It doesn't matter that Owen's moved on. My marriage has been dead for years, all I did today was acknowledge it.

I have broken the last remaining link with Owen to stop him from destroying the thing I still care about. I won. I should be relieved. Hell, I should be jubilant.

I hear footsteps on the landing, a door opening and closing, then a knock.

This time it's Aseem who looks in, a serious expression on his face. I wave him inside.

"Owen just told us he's leaving," Aseem says, leaning against the desk.

I don't say anything.

"What happened, Myra?"

"The storm has settled. He has no reason to stay."

"You know that's not what I mean. Divorce—really?"

I sigh. "You heard Aisha. My marriage has been over for a long time."

"Aisha's an idiot. And you're not being honest."

I shake my head as I reach for the closest thing to an explanation—not the whole truth, but not a lie either. "Owen's been pushing me to sell the island. That's why he's here, to serve notice. He stopped paying for the mortgage a few months ago. And without my salary, it's been . . . hard."

"Jesus. That's why you asked Papa for the money?"

I nod. "I need to buy Owen out. I can't lose this island, Aseem." I swallow. "I won't survive it if I do. I know you worked really hard on the PetroVision sale and you must have your own plans, but this place is all I have left. Putting off the sale might mean we can't all cash out right now, but if Papa can pull off scaling the business, in a few years' time, we'll have two, three times what we have now."

Aseem looks at me for a minute, his expression unreadable. "How can you be so smart and so naive at the same time?" He pulls in a breath, then looks at me with something resembling resolve. "Papa isn't going to give you the money. He can't. Why do you think he offered Gabe shares in the business when he's never considered transferring shares before, not even to his children?"

I open my mouth to object, but something stops me. I sit and listen, filled with a familiar mixture of disbelief, outrage and helplessness as Aseem spells it out for me.

"You know what Papa's like: he goes into every situation assuming he'll win. There is a chance that he can turn things around at PetroVision, but it's a very, very slim chance. Five percent, if that. Papa keeps talking about scaling up, which is never easy, but in this current climate?" He shakes his head. "Eight petrochemical manufacturers have gone under in the past eighteen months, another five are going into administration. Papa's entire plan hinges on acquisitions; all he's thinking about is what bringing in one of those companies will mean for us. But he hasn't considered the regulatory hellhole we'll have to navigate to make that happen. It'll soak up all of our resources. We'll be bankrupt before we even get to a place where we can make any offers."

"I don't understand," I say, genuinely confused. "We've made acquisitions before and we've never had problems. I know the profits haven't been quite where they need to be, but Papa said we were doing okay."

Aseem sighs. "We're far from okay. We've been in negative equity for years. We've taken on so much debt that there isn't a bank in town that will even talk to us now. That's why I've been trying so hard to sell. It's not about me or what I want, it's about staying afloat and selling while we still can." He pauses. "The valuation that Malhotra's offer is based on is inflated."

The reality of what Aseem's saying travels through my body like a current. "You doctored the books?"

"I made some tweaks, things that can be explained away as mistakes or oversights. Malhotra wants to embarrass Papa; that's the only reason he hasn't spotted it. I approached him because I know how deep their rivalry runs. Malhotra is too busy congratulating himself. That's why this sale is so critical, Myra. We aren't going to get an offer like this again. Any other buyer will buy the business for parts."

I look at my brother, seeing suddenly not the businessman or the expectant father, but the boy who has always shouldered more than his share.

"This is what I was trying to tell you earlier," he continues. "Papa has offered you money he doesn't have. The reality is that we barely have enough liquidity to keep the lines running. There's some money in the trust and Mama and Papa have their personal accounts but—"

"But it's not enough?"

I feel a surge of anger rush through me. Papa never intended to give me the money. It was a ruse, a means to control me.

"Papa sent you to see me, didn't he?"

Aseem dips his head. "He wants you to give Owen another chance."

I shake my head. "I can't."

"What really happened between you two?" he asks, eyes fixed on mine.

"You know what happened."

My entire family witnessed the coldness between Owen and me in the weeks and months after the funeral. I dodged their questions for as long as I could, blaming the stress, the grief, the trauma, but in the end, I told them the only thing that I thought would put an end to the questions: Owen was having an affair. I figured they'd all be furious on my behalf and that with one lie I could bury the truth forever.

As I look at Aseem now, I realize I was wrong. My parents and sister might've believed me, but my brother clearly doesn't.

He crosses his arms across his chest and looks me in the eye. "Don't give me that bullshit about an affair again. It's hard enough navigating this family as it is; I thought you and I didn't have secrets."

I feel my jaw clench.

"We all have secrets, Aseem. Even you."

37.

MYRA

By the time Aseem and I return downstairs, the party in the living room has diminished, the evening suddenly quiet. Owen's bag is sitting by the patio doors, his coat flung over an armchair as he says his goodbyes.

I watch from the kitchen as he wraps Aisha in a tight hug.

I used to love Owen's ease around my family. I loved the fact that he had relationships with each of them that existed outside our marriage, but as I watch them now, his closeness with Aisha irks. She's my sister. Surely, she should be on my side.

They should *all* be on my side.

"I'll talk to her," Papa says, as Owen moves to stand in front of him. His voice is loud enough to carry across the room. "She's not thinking clearly."

Owen throws a glance in my direction before turning back to Papa. "Thank you, but I don't think there's anything left to discuss. It's time we . . ." He trails off, shaking his head before continuing, his voice bitter. "At least she gets to keep the island."

Anger boils through me. I turn to Papa, my eyes full of challenge. He meets my gaze but doesn't hold it, turning to drape an arm around Aisha instead while Owen talks to Mama.

I fill a glass with water and take a sip, my head buzzing with confusion. I can draw things out, delay telling him, but once Owen discovers that I can't afford to buy him out, he will move forward with the buyer.

"Hey," Aseem says, placing a steadying hand on my elbow. "We'll figure it out." He looks out of the window, frowning. "Are you sure it's safe for Owen to take the boat?"

The rain has reduced to a drizzle, but after a storm like that, the water will still be rough, the undercurrents strong. If Owen gets caught in a bad wave . . .

He can't sell the island if he's at the bottom of the ocean.

The thought is as dark as it is fleeting but it leaves my skin tingling. "Owen's good on the water. He'll be fine."

"I told you to cancel Stu's holiday."

I can't keep the irritation out of my voice. "I told *you* we don't need him."

"Don't need whom?" Owen says, coming over just as Zoe walks in looking rather spaced out.

"The groundskeeper. Myra stupidly gave him the week off or he could've taken you back," Aseem replies. "The storm looks quite bad, Owen. I don't think you should take the boat out on your own."

Owen shrugs. "I'll be fine. And anyway, the groundskeeper is still here. I saw his boat next to the jetty when I came."

I sigh. Even I can't be this petty. "In that case, if Stu's back, he can take—"

"Stu still works here?" Owen interrupts, a note of alarm in his voice.

"Yes." I tilt my chin up. I hated it when Owen told me what to do and I can't help but rub it in.

"What is Stu still doing here?" Owen says, looking at me closely. "I told you to fire him." Sharper now. He's angry, his jaw set in a tight square.

"Well, I didn't," I snap. "I like Stu, not that it's any of your business."

"Fucking hell, Myra, do you have to be so difficult all the time? You didn't read the file I sent you, did you?"

Owen takes his phone out, scrolling furiously until he finds whatever it is he's looking for.

He practically throws the phone at me. I glance at the document on the screen. It's a scanned copy of a letter of reference. I skim through it, searching for whatever it is that's causing so much drama. The letter is brisk and to the point, but largely positive, much like Stu. I look at Owen. There is a part of me that's enjoying this, a part of me that's vindicated seeing him so worked up, perhaps even wondering if his anger hides a layer of jealousy. "I don't see a problem."

"Look at the name at the bottom. Stu's short for Stuart," Owen says, his eyes drilling into me. "Lachlann Stuart MacBrodie."

It takes a moment for it to snap into place and when it does, I realize what I've done.

Fuck. *Fuck.*

When Owen and I first decided to buy the island, we assumed any difficulty we faced would be by virtue of my nationality. Scots are famously suspicious of foreign investors and, since the property was currently owned by the Scottish Historic Buildings Trust, we were worried they'd be all the more likely to reject our offer. But after a decade of failed redevelopment efforts, Scottish Historic Buildings were desperate to sell, and because of Owen's family name and history, they were willing to make allowances for his Indian wife. They accepted the first offer we put in—under the asking price but generous considering the

estate had been on the market for over a year—and we moved to exchange stage within a matter of weeks.

That's when the problems started.

Though Kilbryde was unoccupied, several of the original islanders'
descendants lived nearby on the mainland and they wanted to put in a
community bid to buy and redevelop the island themselves. A noble
thought and one with precedent, but they didn't have even a fraction of
the amount needed. Their petition was dismissed almost as soon as it
was filed, and after what seemed at the time a small hiccup, we started
moving forward with the process once again.

But that was just the first battle. The islanders were unmovable: they
wanted progress and spoke of creating jobs and advancing the econ-
omy. But when it came down to allowing the investment that would
create that progress, they threw obstacle after obstacle in our way, gal-
vanizing everyone from the press to the local council to stop us.

We suffered it all: planning objections, months-long delays in paperwork being moved from one desk to the other, hit pieces in the local
press likening us to the eighteenth-century lairds who prioritized profits over people. Threats popped up in the post with alarming regular-
ity, all of it culminating in a lawsuit which, once again, the islanders
lost. It wasn't surprising. They were disputing our bid to buy Kilbryde
without any evidence of a competing offer. Legally they didn't have a
leg to stand on, and morally it made no sense. Did they really think
the island sitting empty for another ten years and becoming more and
more derelict was a better outcome than us injecting some life into it?
All their lawsuit did was cost them money they didn't have and delay
our bid by a few months.

In the end, as much as those early threats had shaken me, I put them
out of my mind. All those years in corporate law had desensitized me.
I was used to threats being issued in the heat of the moment only to be

forgotten the next week. Owen, however, didn't see it that way. He insisted we hire private security and run every member of staff we hired through an agency—a ridiculously expensive agency that overpromised and underdelivered. We ran through seven different groundskeepers in three years.

It was our housekeeper, Lorna, who suggested we speak to Stu. "He's a local lad," she told me on one of my weekend visits. "Young but keeps himself to himself. I think he was working down south for a while but his family's from round here. Seems rather taken by the idea of living on an island."

When we interviewed Stu a couple of weeks later, both Owen and I were instantly impressed. He was keen, asked insightful questions about Kilbryde, and, most importantly, he was happy to live here full-time. He had experience running a large estate and seemed genuinely pleased to see the small cottage that would function as his living quarters until the staff apartments were ready. Owen and I hired him on the spot. After the string of impossibly high-maintenance groundskeepers we'd had through the agency, we were so relieved to have found Stu that neither of us stopped to consider why a young, twenty-something man would want to commit to a life of complete isolation.

I'm sure we completed all the paperwork, asked him for references, but I can't recall actually checking them. I was six months pregnant at the time so we had bigger things to worry about and if I'm honest, there was never any need. With the previous groundskeepers, I felt like we were pandering to their endless demands: more equipment, better Wi-Fi, longer holidays. Stu was different. I got my accountant to set him up on the payroll and then left him to it. Every time we visited, the estate looked a little tidier, better cared for, and Lorna couldn't stop singing his praises. "Dependable lad, this one," she told me a few weeks after he started. "Dinnae talk much but he gets the job done."

When I moved to the island full-time, it gave me comfort to know that if ever there was an emergency, Lorna and I weren't totally alone.

A few months after I moved here, Owen rang me, insisting I fire Stu. He'd just gotten around to checking Stu's references and he didn't like what he saw. Owen's bossiness, the assumption that he still had any right to tell me what to do, only incensed me further. I hit delete on his email almost as soon as it landed.

As I look at the faces around me now, I wish I hadn't.

Lachlann Stuart MacBrodie was the leader of the islanders' group, the one who had led the campaign against us. He'd published lengthy blog posts, written to MPs and council members, and circulated petitions. I never met him, never so much as saw his face, but for months he made our lives a living hell. He'd done everything he could to stop us buying Kilbryde, including, in the end, sending me threatening letters.

It was hardly surprising when our solicitor discovered Lachlann had a history of intimidating behavior. A history that we used to win the case, in what the *Herald* described as a "typically upper-class, cutthroat move to snatch the land from its rightful owners and privatize it."

Never mind that the "rightful" owners didn't have the capital for even a two percent deposit, let alone the ten percent that most mortgage lenders required. No, according to the papers, Lachlann was right: I was stealing from the community. Somehow while all the articles acknowledged that Owen and I were buying the island together, they placed the blame squarely on my shoulders: the entitled brown woman stealing from the good white folk.

The final straw came when two days after the court dismissed their case, Lachlann went on live radio. He drew comparisons to the Highland Clearances, comparing Owen and me to James Mackenzie, the laird who had burned islanders alive to take control of the island. He was so out of line that the radio presenter was forced to abruptly cut the interview short, but not before Lachlann made his final threat: history has a way of repeating itself, he said, and he would hate to see Owen and me suffer the same fate his ancestors had.

Despite my fortitude, that particular threat left me feeling uneasy. I'd worked with men like Lachlann before, men who were so consumed by their self-righteousness that they couldn't see past their own vendettas. I understood that men like him either ended up killing someone or getting themselves killed.

Owen and I were anxious enough that we flew to Dubai the following week. We told each other it was a much-needed break after the stress of the last few months, but we both knew it was more than that.

"Is he dangerous?" Mama asks now.

The family is gathered around the kitchen island, Owen's departure delayed as we fill them in.

"I don't know," I say, honestly.

Until today, I haven't had any reason to think about Lachlann Mac-Brodie or his threats. There hasn't been a peep out of him since that radio interview. I assumed that the nasty threats were a by-product of his wounded pride and when it didn't get him anywhere, he'd moved on.

How was I to know that he'd moved, quite literally, to my island? I scan the faces around me but it's Zoe my gaze is drawn to. She's gone completely white.

She opens her mouth to speak, then shakes her head, as if she's struggling to find the words. "Earlier, when I left the beach, did any of you come after me?" Her eyes skitter from left to right, darting from Gabe and Aisha on one side to Aseem and Mama on the other.

I see the way Aseem's eyes narrow at her question. I place my hand on his. Whatever's going on between the two of them can wait.

"We all left the beach together a couple of hours later," I say, looking at Zoe. "I went to the office and everyone else came back to the house. Why?"

"Someone followed me through the forest."

"What? Why didn't you say anything?"

"I was so tired, and on the first night, when I saw movement outside my window, Aseem didn't believe me so I thought I imagined this as well, but now . . ." She shakes her head.

"Did you see a face?" Owen asks, with far more compassion than I can muster.

She shakes her head. "I didn't see anyone today," she pauses. "And it was too dark to see a face that first evening, but whoever it was was wearing electric blue. A jacket or a hat maybe?"

My blood runs cold. Owen and I used to joke about Stu's electric blue jacket, back when we still spoke to each other.

I acknowledge the thought that's been niggling away at me. I'm certain I locked the outhouse after Stu left and yet, when Aseem and I went in to extinguish the fire, the door was unlocked. I glance at Owen, one look enough to know that we are both thinking the same thing.

The fire in the outhouse was no accident. It was Stu.

Lachlann, not Stu, I remind myself now.

The man who threatened to kill me on live radio.

38

ZOE

Time seems to shrink and stretch as plans are made then abandoned. Unsurprisingly, it's Owen who makes the decision.

In all the years that I've known him, I've never seen Owen agitated. He's objective, rational, and calm, exactly the kind of person you want in charge in a crisis. I suppose there's very little that can faze you when you spend your days attending to a constant onslaught of trauma cases. Being faced with death on a daily basis must harden you.

Perhaps that's why seeing him now, pacing the length of the room, is so unnerving.

"We need to find him," Owen says, coming to a stop in front of the kitchen island. "The man threatened to kill Myra, for god's sake. Zoe's seen him lurking around the house. Whatever he's planning, he's one step ahead of us. We need to find him and we need to get him off this island before he hurts someone."

It's the fear in his voice that does it. The mood in the room changes in an instant, quiet panic working its way through the group like creaking ice.

Papa turns to me, his unspoken accusation damning. I swallow hard.

Why didn't I say something sooner?

"He's probably in his cottage," Myra says, nodding tightly. She pushes to her feet. "I'll go."

"Absolutely not." Papa's voice is firm. "You aren't going anywhere."

"It's my island," Myra says, her voice sharp.

"Sit down." Papa commands, without so much as a glance in her direction. He turns to look at Owen and Aseem. "Are you boys okay to head out?"

Fear leaks through the space between my ribs as I watch Aseem get dressed. He's rushing, his movements quick as he steps out of his suit and into his jeans.

"I don't understand why you need to go. Owen knows Kilbryde better."

"Come on, Zo. It'll take Owen all night if he goes alone. I have to go."

"No, you don't. You don't have to do anything." My hands close around his shirt as I pull him to me, forcing him to stop and look at me, to remind him what is at stake. All of the blame and anger that's been simmering between us has disappeared, our resentments put into perspective in the face of actual physical danger. "Stay here with me. Send Gabe."

Aseem disentangles himself from me. "I trust Stu more than I trust that guy."

"Fine then, let's call the police."

"And tell them what? That one of Myra's employees is on the island? I know how that call will go." He throws on a thick jumper, before perching on the ottoman to put on his boots. He looks up at me, fingers still tangled in his laces. "Owen is panicking, but think about it: Stu's been working here for years. If he wanted to hurt Myra or burn down the house, why would he wait till her family was here?"

"To avoid suspicion? To make it seem like one of us did it? Don't forget he's not even supposed to be here right now."

"So he decided to come back from holiday early. There's no shame in being a workaholic," Aseem says, but his joke falls flat. He gets up and places his hands on my shoulders. "Breathe."

I do as I'm told, but fear and frustration are circling me. Stu's already tried to start a fire. What if he attacks Aseem or Owen? I'm spiraling, but I can't help it. Even the idea of something happening to Aseem is paralyzing.

"We're just going to have a chat with him, that's all. There's absolutely no need to worry. I'm sure there's a perfectly reasonable explanation for everything." Aseem presses his lips to my forehead for a long moment before pulling back to look at me. "It's been a long evening—why don't you go to bed?"

I pull a face. We both know that's not going to happen.

"*Okay*, so have a lie-down, relax. I'll be back in no time. And we'll talk about everything else in the morning, okay? We'll sort it out, all cards on the table. This week . . ." His voice cracks, weighed down by the stresses of the last few days. "I love you, Zoe. I don't want to argue anymore."

"Me neither. Promise me you'll be careful?"

"Always."

I press my face into his chest, momentarily calmed by his confidence.

But as I watch my husband walk out of the room, the fear returns. His shoulders are tense, the muscles across his back and neck pulled taut, his entire body stiff and wooden.

He's just as scared as I am.

39.

MYRA

I wouldn't have heard them if I hadn't sneaked back upstairs, furious at Owen for taking control, livid at Papa for ordering me to stay at home like some little girl, but most of all disgusted with myself for letting them—both of them—call the shots.

I go straight to my room and fling the wardrobe open.

Kilbryde is still my island and I will bloody well do what I like.

I'm pushing my head into my jumper when I pick up the sound of voices. I yank it down and push the sleeves up to my elbows. I can't make out the words but I can detect the tone. Two people arguing.

I follow the sound along the corridor, stopping outside the slightly ajar bedroom door. Through the small gap, I can just about see Aisha and Gabe. She's standing with her back to me, hands on her hips, and Gabe is leaning against the windowsill, looking contrite.

I frown and take a step closer.

"I can't believe you'd say that. I saw the way you were looking at her earlier."

"What are you talking about?"

"You know what I'm talking about. And don't think I don't know what really happened with Annabel. Zoe told me everything. After all that we've been through, after everything I've done for you, the lies I've told . . ." Aisha says, her voice heavy with tears. She sounds defeated, drained of the endless energy and enthusiasm that has always been her trademark. "The whole purpose of coming here was to convince my family about you, but maybe they're right."

"What happened with . . . I don't know what Zoe told you, but whatever it is, she's lying. She's just trying to break us up like the rest of them. You know everything there is to know about me. Babe, I love you. I'll do anything for you. You know that," Gabe pleads.

"And yet, you don't want to be with me."

I hold myself very still, listening intently. Their relationship is obviously not as straightforward as Aisha would like us to believe. A wandering eye, perhaps even an affair: there are fault lines there that she's been hiding from us, perhaps even from herself. Aisha's need to rebel has always clouded her judgment, but is it possible that she's finally come to her senses and seen him for the parasite that he is?

"I do. There is nothing I want more than to spend my whole life with you. But not with your family—" Gabe starts but Aisha cuts him off.

"My fucking family," she says, pushing her hands through her hair. "They do this every time. It was stupid of me to expect anything else."

I tense, listening harder now, simultaneously furious for Aisha and at her. Why is she so desperate to be with a man when she knows he's a cheat?

"They're . . . vile. Toxic. I can't believe they had me doubting you. I don't want anything to do with them anymore," Aisha says, decisively. She walks to Gabe, her face tilted up to his, beseeching. "Let's just go to a court and get married."

Gabe seems to hesitate for a moment before shaking his head. "We aren't in Vegas, babe. That's not how it works here." He places his hands on her shoulders. His voice softens. "And don't you want your family there when we get married? I don't want you to have any—"

He stops midsentence, his gaze shifting from Aisha to something behind her.

By the time I realize I've been spotted, it's too late.

The door flies open, giving me barely enough time to rearrange my expression, let alone turn around or walk away.

There's nothing to do but admit it.

"I heard yelling," I say, frowning. Aisha's face is streaked with tears, her nose red and mottled. "What's wrong?"

Aisha looks at me for a long moment before stepping to one side, giving me a proper look inside the room. There are clothes everywhere, strewn across the bed, flung over the chair, heaped in a pile on the floor.

"We're leaving," Aisha says.

I spot the suitcase lying open on the bed. "Why?"

Aisha sighs. A long, deep sigh that leaves me feeling deeply unsettled. "Do you really need to ask me that?"

I try again. "I'm just asking out of—"

"We're leaving because I'm exhausted. I've tried and tried and tried and I'm done. I was so excited for you all to meet Gabe, I thought it would be different this time. But you just couldn't give him a chance, could you?" Her voice cracks. "You've done some terrible things, Myra, but I honestly thought you'd draw the line at trying to buy your own sister." She pauses, draws in a long breath. "Twelve million? At least I know now what I'm worth."

The words have the impact of a slap.

Anger boils through me as I look at Gabe behind her. "You *told* her?"

"He didn't have to," Aisha says, walking around the bed to the dresser. She picks up the manila envelope and throws it at my feet.

The contract.

I take a step toward Aisha, flinching at the speed with which she visibly recoils.

"You know, for a moment I actually believed that you guys were discussing wedding venues. I was so relieved that you'd finally accepted him that I didn't even stop to think how unlikely it was. But then, earlier, when you and Aseem said all that stuff about Gabe, when you made all those accusations . . . I had to see for myself what was in this."

"You don't understand—"

"I understand perfectly. You keep accusing Gabe of wanting to marry me for money, but you're the one who tried to put a number on me." She tilts her face to the ceiling as she blinks back the tears. "Is it really so hard to believe that someone might actually love me for who I am?"

The hurt, the pain in that last sentence pierces through me. I place a hand on her arm but she shrugs me off. "Aisha, no, of course not."

She draws a breath, steel entering her voice. "Or is it that you're jealous? Is that why you keep trying to ruin my life?"

I'm expecting anger, I'm expecting tears, but Aisha's quiet fury throws me off balance. "Ruin your life? Everything I did, I did because I love you. All I've *ever* done is try to protect you."

"Tell yourself that all you want," Aisha says, shaking her head, "but the truth is you've done nothing but sabotage every single relationship I've been in. I just wish I'd seen it sooner. You can't stand to see me happy, can you? You want me to end up like you. Alone, miserable, and barren."

My skin flames. She's trying to hurt me, but no matter what she says or does, I can't walk away.

It's the curse of family, I suppose. Stuck together even in misery.

She gathers a bunch of clothes in her arms and drops them into the open suitcase, while Gabe continues to linger uncomfortably in the background.

He should be the one leaving, not her.

"Everything okay here?"

I swing around to find Zoe standing on the landing behind me.

She's discarded her movie-premiere dress in favor of leggings and a thick jumper. She's scrubbed her face clean of all makeup and her hair is piled high in a bun on top of her head. The change in her appearance is so dramatic, I can't help but do a double take.

She steps through the open doorway and examines the mess, looking from Aisha to Gabe and back again. "Aish?" she prompts. "What are you doing?"

"We're leaving." Aisha says. She throws a pair of trainers into the case, then turns to look at Zoe. "Turns out there are no lows you all won't stoop to. My best friend is making up stories, my sister's trying to buy me. What next? Are you going to have a go at Gabe with an axe?"

"You know it's not like that," Zoe attempts.

Aisha shakes her head, her expression hardening as she looks at Zoe and me. "All I know is that there's nothing left for me here. I don't want anything to do with you, either of you."

"Aisha, come on, you can't just leave," Zoe protests.

"Watch me."

I sigh, my patience wearing thin. Aisha sees the world through a lens that remains focused on her at all times. Perhaps it's unrealistic to expect anything else from her. For years we've let her believe that she is the sun that all our lives revolve around, but would it kill her to be a little less self-involved and a little more considerate?

"How exactly are you planning to leave?" I say. "You don't know how to drive a boat and I'm certainly not going to take you, not like this."

The words come out sounding harsher than I intended and the shift in Aisha's features is immediate. Her head snaps up, her eyes darken. "Owen promised me he'd give us a ride back if it gets too much. Did you really think I'd come to a family holiday without an exit plan?"

Something in the way Aisha is looking at me niggles, but I can't place it. I push my unease aside. My first impulse is to walk away, focus on the far more pressing problem that is Stu, but I need to fix things with Aisha. I don't want to let this horrible argument fester. "Everything I did—"

"You did for me, I know. You can't just keep repeating one line."

She shifts her weight, her stance like that of a boxer poised to deliver a devastating blow. "Do you know why Owen is here?"

Her words stir a fist of anger in me but I don't say anything. But that niggle reappears as I consider her question. Why is she asking me about Owen? Why now?

I glance at Zoe but she just shrugs.

Aisha just said that she only agreed to come here because Owen told her he'd bring her back, but that means . . .

Aisha pouts, the tears and hurt replaced by the sharp wit that is her trademark. "Next time, take a look at yourself before you try to tell me how naive I am. Papa asked Owen to come. He's determined to get the two of you back together. You refuse to talk about what happened so Papa decided the best way to remind you how happy you were was to ambush you." A pause. "I've known for weeks," she continues. She flicks a glance at Zoe. "As has Aseem."

I stare at my sister. Her words wash over me like a wave, overwhelming me for a few torturous seconds before receding, leaving me breathless and unsettled.

"Hurts, doesn't it?"

"You're lying."

"You know I'm not," Aisha says. She narrows her gaze. Sticking the knife in isn't enough. She goes for the flourish, the twist that we Agarwals excel at. "But you understand, right? Everything Papa did, he did because he loves you."

40

ZOE

I refuse to get drawn into the family drama surrounding Aisha and Gabe. They're fixating over the money that they're convinced Gabe will steal, but what the Agarwals fail to understand is that Gabe wants the clout and respectability that come with being an Agarwal. He already has the money, now he wants the privilege. Why else would he refuse to elope with Aisha when he has the chance? Or turn down twelve fucking million. As for Aisha, it's obvious that she's in no mood to listen and if I'm honest, right now, my BFF turned sister-in-law is the least of my worries. If she wants to run off and marry the man who is clearly using her as a social ladder, then that's on her.

Aseem's been gone for over an hour and I can feel my heart pounding against my chest. The storm that had seemed to pass without incident has returned with renewed force, raging so fiercely it feels like it's trying to command our attention. The rain is hammering down, the trees groaning and swaying under pressure from the wind, but cocooned inside the house, we're all still trying to convince ourselves that all is calm, all is well.

I get to my feet, unable to contain myself any longer. Mama's been reciting the Gayatri Mantra nonstop for the last hour and, rather than create a sense of calm like it usually does, the cure-all Hindu mantra is only riling me up further.

I pace to the patio doors, then swing around and stride back. It's raining so heavily it feels like there's a sheet of perspex between the house and the landscape, shapes blurred together.

"Maybe we should call the police," I suggest, circling back to the conversation I've initiated half a dozen times by now.

"Let's give it another half hour," Papa says, looking at his watch. "If they aren't back by then . . ."

If they aren't back by then: they might have had an accident, they might have slipped in the woods or got caught in the storm; they might have found Stu, they might have been killed, or they might have killed him. My mind races with possibilities, each worse than the one before, but it's the last two I keep circling back to.

Aseem is not the kind of man who loses his temper or likes throwing his weight around. He is not the kind of person who loses control. He is the most reasonable, cool-headed person I know.

Except when one of his own is threatened.

I've never been able to forget the incident at my twenty-fifth birthday party. Aisha had organized a small party in her flat to celebrate, the guest list limited to just three couples: Myra and Owen, Aseem and me and Aisha and her latest boyfriend, Javier, who was doing a spectacular job of getting on all our nerves. We were irritated, but no more than usual, and by and large the evening had been lovely but uneventful.

Until the caterers left and the shots started. Several rounds of tequila later, Javier had abandoned his spiritual snobbery in favor of something far cruder, giving us a glimpse of the pervert he really was.

I've seen Aseem lose his temper less than a handful of times, but when he does, it's terrifying. All of his logical, considered thinking flies out of the window and he turns into someone else. Someone who has no handle on reality.

One inappropriate comment. That's all it took. Before any of us knew what was happening, Aseem had punched Javier full in the face. So hard that Javier's head snapped back, bottles of vodka and tequila smashing as his body crashed into the drinks trolley and landed on the parquet floor.

It was all so sudden, so unexpected that we all just stood there, too stunned to react.

Until Aseem was standing over Javier, beating the shit out of him.

If Owen hadn't pulled him off when he did, Javier would've ended up with more than just a broken nose and a few cracked ribs, and Aseem would've probably ended up in prison.

All Javier did was insinuate that he fancied me. He made a disgusting joke about a threesome involving him, Aisha, and me.

Stu has made real, actual threats to kill Myra.

What if, in all his anger and indignation, Aseem does something stupid?

Aseem is fit, but he's no match for Stu's bouncerlike frame. And for all his weight training and marathons, Owen's never thrown a punch in his life.

Oh god.

I pace, suddenly furious at Myra. It's her bloody-mindedness that's got us here. Who moves to an isolated island and then hires someone without a proper reference check? As if that's not bad enough, even when Owen tried to point out her mistake, told her Stu was dangerous, she refused to listen. And now she's sitting upstairs, sulking. The arrogance is astounding.

"Zoe," Mama says startling me out of my daze. "Sit down, beta. You need to look after yourself. Think of the baby."

I nod but the last thing I can do right now is sit down. Every cell in my body is alive with fear and worry.

My stomach clenches as I peer out through the glass doors, but all that greets me behind the thick curtain of rain is complete darkness.

41.

MYRA

I suck in my cheeks and walk down the stairs, steeling myself against the strain of voices filtering into the hallway.

It's the one thing I've learned from Mama: even if the world around me is collapsing, I can put on a brave face and carry on.

It's what we do, we Agarwals.

After I bought the island, I put the stories of murder and deceit out of my mind, refusing to dwell on the violence that had taken place here, telling myself that the island's bloody history was in the past, and Owen and I were its future. But perhaps I'd been wrong to think that the past is something that can be escaped or glossed over, be it the island's or my own.

No matter how alluring the promise of reinvention, our histories are like our DNA, too deeply embedded in our identities to ever be completely erased.

Zoe's voice pierces through the kitchen door. She wants to call the police. I can hear Aisha banging around upstairs, noisily packing her bags, an announcement to no one listening that she doesn't give a fuck about our family.

I should go inside, tell Papa about Aisha, offer to make a round of tea.

And yet, I find myself frozen, unable to take the few steps I need to cross the hall and push the kitchen door open.

Unable and unwilling.

I am too exhausted to lie, too tired to keep playing the dutiful daughter and supportive sister, too spent by the effort of trying to look after my image, my family, and my property all at once.

I force myself to take a few steps forward. At the very least I need to warn Papa that Aisha knows what we did.

Papa flew in to see me a few days after I told the family that Owen and I were separating. It was an entirely unexpected visit and seeing him on my doorstep forced me to change out of my pajamas and step out of the house for the first time since the funeral. Everything about that day is blurry, from the shock of seeing my father on my doorstep to the quiet panic of trying to find a clean pair of jeans, but Papa's words as we stepped out of the house and into the icy Edinburgh morning have been imprinted on my mind ever since. He told me that all he cared about was my happiness and if moving to the island would make me happy, he'd support me. I believed him. I trusted that, despite his affection for Owen, he would always be on my side.

Papa knows exactly how I feel about Owen and he invited him here anyway. He promised me money he doesn't have. He's the person I trusted most in the world and he lied to me. Manipulated me.

Family first. It's always been our motto, the only compass we've been taught to rely on.

Well, fuck that.

This is what happened.

By the time they wheeled me into the hospital, I'd lost too much blood and Jay and Misha were in distress. My original birthing plan went out of the window as I was rushed in for an emergency C-section.

I remember the surgeon assuring me it would be okay. He knew me and not just as a patient. He was Owen's friend, a man who knew not just my medical history, but also my personal one. He would look after me. I remember Owen telling me he would be there the whole time, watching from the gallery while his friend and colleague brought our babies into the world. I was safe. My babies were safe.

But Jay and Misha weren't safe.

And though I didn't know it, I wasn't safe either.

Six weeks after I came home, Owen finally told me the truth.

After they'd taken Jay out, my uterus didn't contract and shut the blood vessels off like it was supposed to. I was losing too much blood and if they couldn't stop it, I would bleed to death.

They tried everything, uterine massage, balloon blast, before finally resorting to stitches to stop the bleeding but they were worried the fix was only temporary.

They could watch and wait or they could be proactive.

I'd already lost Jay, and when Owen signed the consent form, he stole from me the one thing that he knew I wanted more than anything else in the world. Any hope that I could ever be a mother.

He agreed to a hysterectomy.

He didn't hesitate. He took the decision without asking me, without considering what it would do to me.

That was when he still loved me.

I know without a shadow of doubt that he won't hesitate this time either.

If I can't buy Owen out, he'll force me out, no questions asked. And my father will help him do it.

I know what they both deserve and it certainly isn't my loyalty.

The thought is like a current running through the darkest crevices of my brain.

The thought stills me. It angers me.

More than anything else, it terrifies me.

42.

ZOE

Three hours. That's how long they've been gone. Night has fallen and we *still* haven't called the police.

I pace the length of the room, pausing in the kitchen to look at Mama, my fury now focused on my parents-in-law. Mama's preparing yet another round of chai that no one will drink. Papa's sat at the table, setting his book down to check his watch every few minutes. They're both acting as though they're worried and yet they're the ones who sent their only son out to confront a man who threatened murder. Who does that?

I cross the room and peer out through the glass doors, desperation making me even more fidgety than usual. Is it my imagination or is that a beam of light cutting through the forest?

I squint, trying to make out if the blurred blob I can see through the dark sheeting rain is the shape of a person.

I'm sure it is.

I search the landscape for another shape, another man, but whoever this is, he's alone.

He's hurrying toward the house, stumbling with each step, the beam from the torch bouncing up and down as he runs.

"I see someone," I say, without turning around.

Within seconds, Mama and Papa are behind me. Mama tries to jostle me out of the way but I stand strong.

I am paralyzed with fear and panic and hope, a single thought running through my head. I love Owen, but let it be Aseem.

I don't need to look at their faces to know that my parents-in-law will be making the same mental bargain with a god none of us believe in.

Aseem. Please, God, let it be Aseem.

As he comes closer and his familiar features fall into place, I feel my whole body shudder with relief. I slide the door open to let him in. He's soaked, his teeth chattering with the cold, but he's here. He's here and he's alive.

I pull him into a fierce hug, practically knocking him over as I throw my arms around him.

"I'm okay, I'm okay," Aseem whispers. His voice is like a balm soothing my frayed nerves and, after a long moment, I let him pull away.

But the relief is short-lived. I only have to look at Aseem's face to know that something terrible has happened.

Mama's telling Aseem to sit by the fire to warm up and asking Aisha, who's come downstairs having heard the commotion, to bring him a cup of tea.

They all seem to be speaking at the same time, except Papa.

"What happened? Where's Owen?" he asks his son, his voice cutting through the chaos in the room.

"He's not back yet?" Aseem says, alarmed. "I thought . . . I don't know where he is. We split up so we could cover more ground. I went to Stu's cottage and the office, Owen went to look in the boatyard and check the cottages on the other side of the island. He should've been back here by now."

"Did you find Stu?" Aisha asks.

Aseem shakes his head. "No, but the fire in his cottage was on. That's why it took me so long. I figured Stu would be nearby so I thought I'd check the surrounding area."

Papa frowns. "Why would he be outside in this weather?"

Aseem sidesteps the question. "I think we need to . . ." He pauses, looks across the room. "Where's Myra?"

"Upstairs. I'll go get her," Mama says, turning around and walking out of the room.

We all turn our attention to Aseem as he pulls out a plastic bag from the inside pocket of his coat. It's crammed full of papers. He shakes the water off, then tips the bag upside down, showering the coffee table with papers. "I found these on his desk."

I kneel down, spreading the slightly damp sheets out with my hands, trying to make sense of what I'm seeing.

Drawings, dozens of them. Maps, floor plans, layouts.

Some hand drawn, others architectural, but all marked. Littered with tiny crosses in red.

The breath catches in my throat as I realize that several of the crosses sit right on top of the gravesite Aisha and I had stumbled across on our hike. I glance at the crest on one of the maps. It's the same pattern Aisha and I saw at the headstone earlier. What's worse, I realize, it's the same elaborate swirl that runs across the back of Stu's neck. That's why his tattoo looked so familiar.

"What is this?" I whisper.

"I don't know. I don't understand why Stu—Lachlann—would have these," Aseem says. "I picked up as many as I could, but there are dozens more. His desk is crammed full of this stuff."

THE INHERITANCE

"It's bloody creepy, is what it is," Aisha says. "He's obviously obsessed, maybe a bit unhinged, but that doesn't necessarily mean he's dangerous, right?"

I look at her, surprised. Does she not remember what the inscription at the grave site said about revenge?

I look up to see my fear reflected on Aseem's face.

"I don't know what it is exactly, but he's planning something. No one goes to such lengths without reason." He pauses, frowns. "Where the hell is Myra?" he asks again just as Mama walks through the door, her face white.

"Myra's not here," Mama says.

Papa frowns. "What do you mean she's not here?"

"I mean," Mama says, her voice punctuated with panic, "*she's not here*. Myra isn't upstairs, she isn't anywhere. She's gone."

43

MYRA

For a while I walk blindly through the woods, desperate to put distance between my family and myself. I pull my hood up over my head and wipe the rain away from my eyes. Anger and indignation burn through me.

I refuse to be the person who cowers behind her own front door.

Or her soon-to-be ex-husband.

I angle the torch in front of me, but even with the glare of a hundred thousand lumens, I can barely see more than a few meters ahead. The wind and the rain whip at my face, stinging my eyes, as I dodge and weave my way through the trees.

As I turn left, cutting through the pine trees and walking toward the small loch, I think of the lit-up window I saw when I was out running this morning. I didn't think much of it because that part of the estate has remained untouched since I bought the island. The cottages on that side are still boarded up, derelict ruins that have been uninhabited for decades. There are no services there, no gas, no electrics, not even running water. I'd assumed the illuminated silhouette I'd seen was the result of a trick played by the sun as it moved across the horizon, its glare reflected in a panel of glass or a piece of metal. But as I consider it now, I am more and more certain that I didn't imagine it.

I slip and stumble, my boots failing to find purchase on the mossy ground, until I finally reach the point where the forest ends and the path opens up, running parallel to the coast. I inch down slowly, placing one foot after the other, only too aware of the sheer drop on my right. One misstep and I'll be hurtling to my death. In better weather, I might walk all the way along the top of the cliff to get to the cottages, but the wind is up, laying the grasses of the machair flat. On the cliff, I'll be blown off my feet. It'll take longer but I think I'll be better off walking along the beach, sheltered by the huge stacks of black rock.

I stop when I get to the beach, relief mingling with dread. I've seen Stu here before, cooking over a campfire or sitting on a rock looking out across the water, but tonight the sand is flat and wet, devoid of any footprints. No one has been here since the rain started. I walk close to the cliffs as I make my way toward the steep steps on the other end that lead to the machair and beyond that, the cottages.

It hits me now that I know nothing about Stu. I have no idea what he does on his weekly visits to the mainland; no clue what he does alone in that little cottage of his every night. I've placed my trust—and my safety—in the hands of a stranger.

Stu's always blended into the landscape, and I thought his unobtru- siveness, the way he's happy to just disappear into the background, was a testament to the strength of his personality, but it occurs to me now that his entire personality is manufactured, a pretense that he puts on for my benefit.

There are too many gaps in my knowledge so I do what I've been trained to do. I consider the situation as I would if it were a case brought to me by the chambers' clerk, objectively and without prejudice. Ir- respective of what Stu claims, what excuses he uses to build his defense, the irrefutable facts of the case are plain to see: he threatened me with violence, lied about his name, and misled me into hiring him, gaining access not only to the island but also to me, the woman against whom he led a very public, very besmirching campaign. And then, to add to his threats, he set the outhouse on fire.

Motive, opportunity, and priors. If this were a case brought to me by a clerk, it would most certainly be accompanied by a dead body, a charge for murder, and, knowing Stu, a not guilty plea.

In my desperation to wrest control from Owen, I'd unwittingly handed it over to the one man I should have done a background check on.

Stu must've been laughing at me this whole time.

Despite the cold, sweat trickles down my back as I climb up the steps that twist up the other end of the cliff. Every step up is a monumental effort, the already steep climb made worse by the pushback from the wind.

I stop and catch my breath when I finally make it to the top. At least it's stopped raining.

I glance at the machair stretching out in front of me. Another few yards to the right and I should hit the path that leads to the cottages.

"Myra?"

I whip around at the sound of my name.

Owen. He's standing a few feet from me, his face unreadable. "What are you doing here? You're supposed to be at the house."

"I could ask you the same question. I thought you and Aseem were going to check his cottage."

There is a note of challenge in my voice, but Owen doesn't rise to it. He shrugs, unconcerned. "We decided to split up, cover more ground. I've checked the cottages; Stu's not there."

I circle around Owen, moving toward the path that leads to the cottages.

His hand shoots out and quick as a flash, he grabs my arm, pulling me toward him. "I just told you I've already checked the cottages."

I twist out of his grip. "Then you won't mind if I check again."

"You think I'm lying?" He takes the tiniest step back, his eyes flashing with shock. "You really don't trust me, do you?"

I laugh. A cold, mean laugh that I would've thought myself incapable of just a few years ago. I glance at the sheer drop behind Owen. It's not the only thing I'd have once thought myself incapable of. "Can you blame me?"

"For fuck's sake, Myra. We can't keep having the same argument. It's been three years, let it go."

"Forgive me if it's a little hard for me to 'let go' of my dead children."

His expression darkens. I see the shock on his face, then the hurt, and I'm alarmed at the ripple of satisfaction that runs through me. Is this what I've become? Someone who enjoys wounding other people just to lessen my own pain?

"You know that's not what I meant."

"I don't know anything about you, Owen. Not any more. Maybe your girlfriend—"

I stop midsentence, my attention seized by a flash of electric blue in the distance.

Stu's about fifty feet away, moving quietly across the machair in front of us. He's clearly looking for something or someone, his head swiveling from side to side as he moves through the grass, every step bringing him closer to us.

I am considering lifting my torch, calling out to him, when I notice it.

The outline of something solid at his hip; a piece of metal held in a plastic case. It glints every time a sliver of moonlight leaks through the clouds.

One look at Owen confirms that he's seen it as well.

A holster.

He has a gun?

Alarm sweeps through me as I realize how exposed we are, standing on top of a cliff, armed with little more than words and righteous indignation.

The thought is a punch in the gut: this isn't a courtroom; my words have no power here.

I should've waited at the house, insisted we call the police or at least wait till the morning before trying to find a man so manipulative that he's been living here under a false name, planning God knows what. The stupidity of my actions astounds me. *History has a way of repeating itself.* I understand suddenly why he chose those words, why he started the fire in the outhouse, and why he's waited so long to take his revenge. His entire clan was decimated in the clearances, and now *my* entire family is here on the very island where that happened.

Not only have I endangered myself, I've endangered my family.

What was I thinking?

I glance at the steps I just climbed up. Stu hasn't spotted us yet, but even if we move quickly, there's no way that we can make it down without him seeing the beam from our torch. And if he follows us on the steps . . . I look at the sheer drop below. He won't even need to use his gun.

The decision is taken out of my hands.

"Myra?" Stu yells, lifting his hand and pinning me in place with the circular beam of his torch as he walks toward us.

In front of us the machair stretches out for miles, a large, flat expanse with nowhere to hide. Behind us, the cliff.

For all the vastness of the landscape, we are trapped.

"Lachlann," I yell back, my voice loud but shaky. They might not have the impact of a gun, but my words are all I have right now. "What are you doing here?"

It's too dark to make out his expression but I can hear the laughter in his voice, his tone derisive, mocking. "So you finally figured it out."

44.

MYRA

For a moment, I stand there, motionless, staring at Stu as he walks toward us.

"Owen? Is that you?" he says.

There is no change in his demeanor, nothing to suggest he's violent or vengeful. He behaves exactly like the man I know. Brusque, bordering on rude, but harmless.

Except that he has a gun. Somehow the fact that he isn't pointing it at us, that he doesn't feel the need to point it at us, makes it all the more disturbing.

"Stay away from her," Owen says, taking a step forward.

Stu says something but his words are distorted in the wind, leaving behind only the tenor of his voice, urgent and dark. My heart races as he rushes forward, closing the distance between us in seconds.

I steal a look at Owen, a jumble of emotions swirling inside me. Panic, confusion, regret. Is this it? Is this how it ends for us, shot down by the man we defeated in court nearly five years ago?

"What's going on?" Stu says.

Something about his insolence, the way the greeting rolls off his tongue so casually, prompts me into action. I find my voice. "You're not supposed to be here. You're supposed to be on holiday." I am surprised by how calm I sound, how confident and in control, when I am none of those things.

Stu raises an eyebrow. "Aye, I suppose I am," he pauses, watching me, waiting for me to question him further. He gives a half shrug and continues, "I didn't have anywhere to go so I came back."

A sick feeling rises in me.

"You lied to us," Owen says.

"I didn't," Stu says, shaking his head. "Lachlann is my given name but I go by Stu, always have." He smirks, lips curling into a twisted smile. "Though I must admit I was a little surprised that you didn't pick it up in the paperwork. I'd have thought a lawyer and a doctor might have been more, what's the word, detail-oriented? But I figured you either didn't catch it or you didn't care."

His response reminds me of the carelessness with which his threats were delivered before we bought the island, the ease with which he insinuated violence. "Didn't care? You threatened to kill me."

His smirk deepens, ratcheting up my unease. Which I suppose is what he wants. "Stranger things have happened."

"Why did you come here?"

"I wanted to live here, see what it was like." Stu swings his arm out, making a large arc with his hand. "This land, it belongs to my ancestors, but none of us have been allowed to set foot on it for the best part of a century. My great-grandfather was born here. His father was the clan chief, but when the laird decided he wanted to clear the island, there was nothing he could do."

I hold my breath, waiting for him to continue. I remember my solicitor telling me that the man leading the community bid had links to the island, but I didn't realize he was a direct descendant of the chief, that his family had been victims of the fire. That changes things. Puts his anger, which until now had seemed purposeless, into perspective. Next to me, Owen goes still.

"Honor and pride don't hold up in front of money, but I don't need to tell you that. My great-grandfather was the only member of the family who made it out alive. He was just a little one, seven or eight, and he was forced to watch his entire family, his entire community, burn to death. Can you even imagine what that must've been like? How it scarred him for life?"

I feel a pang of sympathy for him, my thoughts going instantly to Ishaan. To what Aisha was forced to witness as a child. I might not have seen the fire myself but I am all too familiar with the trauma of it, how long the pain lingers, how deep it cuts.

Stu points into the distance. "Their remains are buried right there, by the lighthouse. Where you were planning to put your precious helipad."

A shiver runs through me at the mention of the helipad.

"That's not happening any more," I say. "I'd never—"

"Only because you couldn't get planning permission." The smirk leaves his face, leaving behind a cold, blank expression. His eyes narrow. "I spend a lot of time walking the land, trying to imagine what it might have been like if the laird hadn't set the entire village on fire. Did you know that there are only five of us left? One of the most powerful clans in Scottish history and now we're on the verge of extinction. All because a foreigner decided he knew what was better for our land than the people who'd tended to it for centuries." He turns his wrath on me. "What you're planning, it will change the landscape, the entire topography of the island. You're talking of building foundations so deep it'll change the quality of the soil; half the forest will have to be razed just so you can live your 'back to nature' dream."

"How do you know all this?" I demand.

"I downloaded the plans from your desktop," he says, as if it's completely normal to break into your employer's computer and steal confidential information.

"Is that what you've been doing this whole time?"

"Not the whole time. Two people are not enough to run an island, let me tell you that. But aye, I've been looking into it. You're making a mistake."

My throat tightens as Stu takes another step forward. Behind us, the sea roars, waves beating into the cliffs, the tide now back in.

I can barely force the next words out but we need to find a way to move forward, literally.

"You should know the police are on their way."

A look of confusion passes over his face. "Police?"

"They know everything, the threats, your history," Owen says, picking up on the seed I've planted. "If anything happens to either of us, the ownership of the island will pass to our families. If you kill us, all you'll do is land yourself in prison."

"*Kill you?*" Stu looks stunned, speechless. He's looking at the sky, shaking his head. "Jesus. Fuck. No. *No.* Look, I was furious that you'd won and I wanted to give you a scare. I would never . . ." Stu starts laughing, so hard that he has to bend over, resting his hands on his thighs as he catches his breath, then straightens up. "Oh lord, you think—you genuinely think I'm here to kill you?"

"You have a gun," I say.

"As should you. We live on an island with a hunting tradition."

We stand there, staring at each other. Owen and I exchange a quick glance as Stu's hand twists to his side and unclips the holster. I'm not sure who reached for whom, but I'm incredibly aware that my hand is wrapped around my husband's.

"Jesus, relax," Stu says, his eyes skimming our faces. "This is a hunt-ing pistol. I only use it to manage the pigeons. It's barely good enough to kill a deer. Trust me, I couldn't kill you with this if I tried."

He tosses the gun on the ground and raises both palms in the air as he takes a couple of steps back. "Also, let's just establish that I don't *want* to kill you. I'll admit things got a bit out of hand, but all those threats were meant to do was give you a scare and put you off from buying the island."

"You started a fire—"

"That was hardly a fire and for the record, I didn't set it." Stu gives me a sympathetic look. "I love this land, far more than you can imag-ine. I've seen what you're planning. I think the drawings are flawed and you're obviously running out of money, but what you want to do with the island, the whole retreat thing, that has potential. I was going to come to you with this later, once I had something concrete to show you, but well, fuck that." He laughs unhappily. "Look, I shared the plans with a few mates. The English guys you're using, they're ripping you off. Charging you two, three times what the work's worth and de-stroying the island in the process. You need someone who knows this land and who can honor its history. My mates are from around here, local lads who understand the landscape and its limitations. They can do a far better job, for a lot less money. And that way you'll be putting money back into the community, not giving it to a bunch of corporate builders who don't give a shit about the heritage or conservation." He shifts his weight from one foot to the other, looking anxious. I feel like, for the first time, I'm seeing him for who he is, not a threat, not a duti-ful employee, but a man on a mission. "I've seen how you operate. You can be a bit gullible but much as I hate to admit it, your heart is in the right place. You might not be from here, but you obviously love the land. You wouldn't have lasted this long if you didn't."

I should say something but I don't know what to do, what to think. "You don't want to kill me?" The words are out before I can censor them, think them through.

There is a moment of complete silence. Stu crosses his arms over his chest and tilts his head, deadpan. "Not unless you would like me to?"

45

ZOE

There was a moment, right after we realized that Myra was missing, when the room descended into chaos. Tensions were running high and voices were raised even higher. Papa and Aseem wanted to go back out to look for her. Mama and Aisha wanted Gabe to go with them. And me, I was so adamant that Aseem not go out again that I gave him an ultimatum: if he went, I'd go with him, putting myself and our baby at as much risk as he was insisting on putting himself in. Decorum, politeness, respect—it all went out of the window as we argued. We were all so engrossed in defending our positions that no one heard the front door bang shut. None of us noticed that the woman everyone wanted to rescue didn't need rescuing, not until she was standing in the middle of the room, her own voice raised, demanding to be heard.

The relief was palpable, a collective exhale followed by a sense of anticlimax as Myra and Owen told us about their encounter with Stu. It turns out that not only was he not dangerous, he was actually trying to help. All he wanted was to give local tradesmen the opportunity to restore their ancestral land and make some money in the process.

Barely an hour later, Stu's probably back in his cottage and we're all gathered in the living room: Myra's on the armchair, a blanket draped over her knees; Owen's standing next to Papa by the fire, nursing a glass of brandy; Aisha is on the floor, snuggled in a blanket with Gabe; and Aseem is sandwiched between Mama and me on the sofa. Our voices are still raised, the adrenaline is still coursing through our veins, but the mood in the room is drastically different. Jubilant. Grateful, even. Relief has dissolved our defenses and even Aisha, who couldn't wait to get away from the family just hours earlier, seems to have mellowed.

I think I catch a flash of annoyance in her eyes as she sets a cup of masala chai in front of Myra, but the expression is fleeting and by the time she sits down next to Gabe, her face is set in a smile. There is no further talk of leaving, at least not tonight. Even the tension between Myra and Owen seems to have thawed a bit.

I turn to Aseem. I want to say something, apologize for all the arguments and misunderstandings of the past week, remind him just how much he means to me, but I can't find the words. Instead I inch closer to him and lace my fingers through his.

"I'm okay," he whispers, the tightness of my grip communicating everything I can't articulate.

I twist to look at him. My nerves are frayed from the fear and anxiety of the evening and I am overcome with a strange sense of nostalgia. I don't want this night to end. It feels as though this, right now, is all there is.

When I lean into him to kiss him there is just the hint of resistance—his family's watching—but then his lips begin to move against mine and I get the sense that the world is slowly returning to its axis.

More logs are thrown into the fire, several rounds of chai made and Scotch drunk. There is a sense of comfort and camaraderie as we sit together until well past midnight, the conversation meandering from one topic to the next. We listen as a misty-eyed Mama recounts memories from a time when her days revolved around looking after four cute but impossibly demanding children. Owen tells us about his stint in Afghanistan, how amidst the magnitude of trauma and loss, he'd sparked a friendship with a young patient who, despite losing his entire family in a shelling, managed to see the world with joy and optimism and that, by the end, this was the only thing that kept him going. Myra tells me about the time Aseem launched headfirst into an inflatable pool and Papa reminds her that she's thinking of the wrong brother. There is an air of nostalgia and serendipity as timeworn stories are brought out and family jokes repeated. Even though no one says it, it's obvious we're all thinking the same thing: it's ridiculous that we've spent the week arguing over money and property when really we should have been celebrating each other, celebrating life.

How little it takes to put things into perspective.

At some point the cards come out and before I know it, Gabe, Aisha, and I are the only ones left in what ends up being a fantastically raucous round of poker.

I squint at my cards and then at Gabe and Aisha in turn, trying to work out whether or not I should go all in. Not for a second do either of their expressions waver. Excellent liars, the pair of them.

I look at my cards again. I toy with a coin from the stack sitting in front of me. I consider my options.

Fuck it, life's too short.

I do it. I go all in.

I win. I throw my hands in the air, laughing, acutely aware of how disproportionate my sense of pride is but I'm too happy to care.

I sweep my winnings into my corner, turning to look at Aseem, but the spot behind me is empty.

I find him in the kitchen with Mama. They are sitting at the breakfast bar, stools pulled together, heads almost kissing. They're talking in murmurs. The scene is so intimate I take a step back. Something resembling a cough makes its way out of my throat.

"Zoe," Aseem says, his head jerking up with a jolt.

"Is everything okay?" I ask, looking from my husband to his mother. Mama's face is streaked with tears and she's clutching Aseem's hand so tight I can see the whites of her knuckles.

Aseem prizes his hand away gently. "Mama had a bit of a scare tonight, that's all."

I nod. We were all worried sick when we thought there was a killer on the loose.

"Zoe, come on," Aisha calls out. "I am not going to let you win this one."

"Coming," I holler before turning to Mama. "A round of cards might help?"

"Nahi, beta. Maybe next time." Mama gives me a watery smile but there's a glint in her eye that hardens me to her tears.

I head back into the living room, keen to see if my luck will hold for another round.

I settle on to the floor cushion across from Myra and Papa, and pick up my cards.

Three aces. I have the winning hand.

And yet, as I sit there, cards fanned out, my best poker face on, I have the distinct sense that I've already lost.

46.

MYRA

I bring a stack of fresh towels into the guest bedroom and set it on the bed.

"Thank you," Owen says. I nod.

Even I can't ask Owen to leave, not at one in the morning and not after the night we've had.

"About earlier. I—I'm sorry. I didn't mean—I think about them—our babies—every day. It's the first thing I see when I wake up. I thought I could dull it with work but even when I was in Afghanistan, even when there were bombs going off . . ." His voice breaks.

I nod. I don't trust myself to speak.

All of us struggled with Ishaan's death but none of us have lived with it the way my mother has. She told me once, years later, that she never got over losing Ishaan, and I knew the moment that Owen told me about Jay that I'd never get past his death either. That day is a blur to me, but I remember the look on his face as he crouched next to my hospital bed. The touch of his hands as they smoothed my face. The wetness of his tears mingling with mine as it sank in. My heart will always ache. But it's only now as I look at him that I realize so will his.

"I will never regret anything more than not hanging up those blinds. If I'd just . . ." Owen says. "I'm sorry, Myra. I'm so, so sorry."

"So am I." I look at my feet, my heart softening as I realize that the sequence of events that torments me also torments him, that I wasn't the only one who was grieving in those early days, not the only one who needed support. "I presumed that you weren't hurting and I shouldn't have—I should've done more. I'm sorry."

"We both did the best we could," he says.

I turn to leave but there is something else that's bothering me. Something I haven't quite been able to put my finger on until now.

"Papa called you here, right?"

His eyebrows shoot up.

"Aisha told me."

It's his turn to look down.

"Your father can be very persuasive. I didn't think coming here would work, but I went along with it because I didn't see any other option. You haven't been taking my calls. And I thought . . . maybe if I came over here . . . There is no one else, Myra, there can never be anyone else."

It clicks into place. Owen has never been driven by money. My husband has many faults but stinginess or greed is not one of them. He would never have stopped paying his share of the mortgage to hurt me. This is all my father's doing.

"The mortgage. Was it his idea?"

Owen looks confused for a moment before nodding. "He thought the fear of losing Kilbryde might make you reconsider things between us. I'm not proud of it but I was desperate enough to go along with it. I thought . . . I didn't realize how far you were from that point. Divorce?" He shakes his head. "I know I hurt you. I know I did something you never wanted, and if that means you can never be with me, that's okay. But if there's one thing I've realized tonight, it's that I can't live with you thinking that I hurt you on purpose. I can't go to my grave thinking that.

"Myra, you could have *died* that day. When they told me how much blood you'd lost, all I could think was we've already lost Jay, we've lost so much, I cannot lose you. I wanted children, I wanted you to be a mother, but the idea of you dying so we could have the chance at a family . . . I *needed* you to live. My only thought in that moment was doing whatever I could to keep you alive. Maybe that was selfish, but can you honestly say that if you were in that position, if it was Aisha or your mother on the operating table, you wouldn't have made the same decision?"

I can't answer but my eyes are filling with tears. Because I know as well as he does that there is only one answer to that question.

"I knew that you didn't want a hysterectomy. I knew what it would do to you, to us, but I signed the consent forms knowing that I'd rather have you hate me, I'd rather have you file for divorce than die because I couldn't do what was needed. That's the pact I made with myself. I've spent the past three years hoping that maybe in time you'll see things differently, but if leaving me is what makes you happy . . ." He pulls out the envelope I gave him earlier from his bag and hands it to me. "I've signed these. I'll transfer ownership of the island to you. All I've ever wanted is for you to be happy."

I'm not sure who makes the first move but as I look at him I realize we're barely centimeters apart.

"We had it all, you and I," he says.

I nod, the tears now streaming down my face. I place a hand on his chest. "We did."

I don't know how long we stay like that. It's all so familiar—the smell of him, the way my head slots into the hollow beneath his collarbone, the way his hand curves around the nape of my neck when finally our lips meet.

I pull back to look at him, my fingers tracing the contours of his face.

"Are you sure this is what you want? There are things we can try. Counseling, therapy . . ."

We were happy and for a brief time, we had it all.

I take a step back, my hand finding the doorknob through the blur of tears. It doesn't matter that my heart still aches for the life we could've had.

We are not the same people any more. I am not the same person.

"Goodbye, Owen."

47.

ZOE

Aseem's the first one to call it a night and I follow shortly after, leaving the rest of the family outraged as I throw in my cards midgame to join my husband upstairs.

"Hey," he says as I step into our room. The room is cloaked in shadows, lit only by the slight glow of the moonlight. Aseem is standing by the window, staring out into the darkness.

"I thought you'd be asleep already," I say, softly. I ease the door shut and walk up to him, wrapping my arms around his waist.

"I couldn't sleep. This week . . ." he says, pinching his eyes.

I nod. I can hear the worry in his voice, the vulnerability, and it breaks my heart to admit that I'm responsible, at least in part, for his stress. I've spent the last six months worrying about money, about getting our dues, but this evening, the threat of losing him has shifted something in me. I feel lighter, less anxious about the practicalities of life and more focused on the joys of it. I'd be a liar if I said I haven't enjoyed having access to the Agarwal family fortune, but the money is only a fringe benefit; the star attraction has always been Aseem. My Aseem. The one person I'd go to the end of the earth for.

Aseem peels my hands away and turns to face me. His sigh reverberates through his entire body. "We need to talk, Zo."

I nod. I can see now what I've done to him, the pressure I've put him under, and I hate myself for it. "Before you say anything, I've been thinking . . . I was wrong, Aseem. We don't need the money. As long as we have each other, as long as we're healthy, and happy, that's all that matters. Okay, so you won't be able to start your business immediately and maybe our children won't grow up with a nanny each, but who cares? We'll be together and we'll be free to live our lives the way we want."

"Zoe, I—"

"No, let me finish, please. I know I've been fixating on this deal but the truth is, I don't need a big house or fancy lifestyle. The only thing I need is you. You and our baby. That's it. As for the rest . . . We can get jobs, rent a flat in the suburbs, ask my mum to babysit, whatever. I know it'll be different to what you're used to, but this could be the opportunity you've always wanted. You can finally strike out on your own. It'll be an adventure, toughen us up," I finish, a little breathlessly.

Aseem looks at me, his eyes filling with tears. "Zo, we can't . . ."

"It's okay." I put my hand on his chest, my own voice thick with emotion. "Do you remember how happy we were before your parents found out about us? Everything was so simple. So effortless. I want us to go back to that. I don't care what Papa does with the business, not as long as I have you."

Aseem squeezes his eyes shut, shakes his head. "No, that's not . . . you don't understand. We can't move," he says. "I can't leave my family."

I drop my hand, take a step back. "What?"

"I've been thinking too. This week, everything that's happened, it's made me realize that I can't just walk away. My parents have looked after me my whole life and now that they need me . . . They're getting old, Zo. Papa's recovery is far from over and Mama doesn't show it, but she's struggling." He pauses, finally lifting his gaze to meet mine. "You're right, the money is irrelevant. I need to look after my parents and I can't do that from London. It's not fair."

His words are like a blow to the center of my chest. I feel shocked, deflated, and then when it finally sinks in, furious.

"*Not fair?*" I shake my head in disbelief. "We made a decision. Together. We agreed that moving to London is what's best for our family."

He takes a sharp breath in. "I don't know what to say. I have a responsibility here and moving to London . . . it's just not an option, not right now." He pauses. "Look, I promised you that things will be different and they will. We'll move into our own place as soon as we get back and as for the other stuff, I've already spoken to Mama. She's going to take a step back. Give us our space."

"You spoke to Mama?"

He nods. "Yes, and she's completely on board—"

"She is completely on board with you giving up your own dreams to become her glorified carer?"

Aseem's expression hardens. He crosses his arms across his chest. "It's not like that."

"I don't see either of your sisters uprooting their lives to move to Delhi."

"That's different."

"Why? They're Myra and Aisha's parents too, aren't they?"

Aseem shakes his head, exasperation lining his features. As if I'm the one being unreasonable here. "I know it might not seem like it, but I am doing my best here, Zoe. I love you. More than anything else in the world. If I could leave, move to London, I would." He drops his gaze. "But I can't do it. I cannot let my parents down. Not again."

"And yet you have no problem letting me down," I say, outrage and indignation rising in my throat like a slick of bile. "When your dad had his stroke, we dropped everything so that you could be there for him. Of course we did. But right now? Your father's fine. And even if he wasn't . . . When are you going to realize that your parents don't give a shit about you? They were quite happy to send you to your death—"

"Oh, come on . . ."

"They literally asked you to go confront a violent criminal."

"What else were we supposed to do? Wait? Or maybe you'd have preferred it if we sent Myra or Aisha," Aseem spits out. "Please don't make this harder than it needs to be, Zoe. We have a good life in Delhi. And you might not realize it, but we will need support when the baby comes."

I stare at my husband, suddenly realizing what I'd witnessed earlier. The tears, the drama: it's so obvious I can't believe I didn't see it coming. I press my fingers into my temples and close my eyes, buying myself a moment to think before I look straight at him, fury making my voice tremble. "This isn't about your parents. This is about your mother and what she wants."

"Don't bring Mama into this."

"She's already in it. She's been in it since the day she found out we were together. You told her we were planning to move to London, didn't you?"

He doesn't respond but one look at his face is confirmation enough. I throw my hands up. "I can't keep having the same fight over and over. I finally have the chance to have the kind of family I've always wanted. I am not going to give that up just so you can pander to your mother's wishes."

"No one's asking you to give anything up. Mama—"

"Your mother is interfering. She's inserting herself where she's not needed."

"You're being ridiculous."

"No, I'm being honest, something I should've been years ago. I get that you have this really special, weirdly twisted relationship with your mother, with all your secrets and whispers and in-jokes and whatnot, but I am your wife. I am your wife, Aseem. Me. Not her. Honestly, sometimes I think . . ." I shake my head.

"What? Go on, finish the sentence."

I look at him, take a deep breath.

"Your relationship with her, this hold that she has on you . . . It's not normal."

"You're going to tell me what a normal relationship looks like?"

"What the hell is that supposed to mean?"

"You have no idea what it means to be a family. You pretend you care about people but it's all fake. Meaningless, like your Instagram posts. How often do you speak to *your* mother? You didn't even go to your own father's funeral."

"How dare you." Of all the people in the world, Aseem knows exactly what my father put me through. He's the only one who knows how often my mother used to hide in the bathroom, knowing full well that without her there, I was the one who would have had to bear the brunt of my father's anger. He knows where the deep loathing for my mother comes from. He's seen the scars I carry.

"Fuck. *Fuck.*" Aseem rushes forward, reaching for my hands. "I'm sorry, I shouldn't have said that. I'm just—if you knew how much I owe them . . . the things Mama has had to endure because of me. I'm trying to do the right thing here, Zo. For all of us."

"Not for all of us," I say. I push him away and march to the dresser to pick up the jumper I'd discarded hours earlier.

"What are you doing?"

I ignore him. I throw the jumper on and shove my feet into my boots, cursing as the zip catches the skin above my ankle.

"Zoe, please. Let's talk about this calmly."

"You've made your decision. I need to make mine," I say, turning around. "This is not the life I want." I am trembling as I say this, fighting back the tears but determined to get the words out. I'm desperate for him to believe I am serious about leaving. Desperate, still, for him to choose me, to stop me from walking out.

I'm already at the door when he jumps into action. His hand shoots out and grabs my arm, fingers digging into my flesh. He twists me until I am pressed up against him, our faces inches apart.

"You can't just walk away," he says.

I try to wriggle out of his grip but the strength of his fingers takes me by surprise. I am pinned in place, the sharp pain shooting up my arm no match for the anxiety spreading through my heart. We've argued before but this feels different, more dangerous. It reminds me of the fights I witnessed as a child.

"Let me go," I say, trying my best to keep my voice level.

He doesn't budge.

"Aseem, you're hurting me. Let. Me. Go."

A few beats pass as we stare at each other, then he drops my arm. Steps back.

"Please believe me when I say this, Zo: I know you think I'm choosing Mama over you but I don't have a choice. Not really."

"There's always a choice, Aseem," I say. "It's a shame that you're making the wrong one." Anger turns my voice bitter but it feels wrong, as though my fury is misplaced. I walk to the window, the pitch-black darkness outside more welcoming than the environment in this room.

I think back to what he said earlier: I can't let them down. Not again. *Not again.*

"That's it then? You're going to leave me?"

There is something about the way he says it, the flatness of his voice, the tone of defeat laced through his words, that makes me spin around.

Aseem is sitting on the ottoman, shoulders stooped, arms wrapped around himself, as though he's trying to shrink into himself. It feels as though, for the first time ever, I can really see my husband, not the assertive, quietly confident man I fell in love with but someone far more vulnerable. A broken man who is still grappling with the burdens of his past, who believes that life is simply giving him his dues.

I can't believe I didn't see it sooner. He isn't acting out of duty or love for his mother. He's acting out of shame. Guilt. And even though it makes no sense at all, I have a gnawing feeling I know what this is about.

"Yes. Unless you tell me what's really going on."

"I already told you. I need to look after my parents."

I force myself to breathe. Inhale. Exhale. "You said you owe them. That Mama's had to endure things because of you. What aren't you telling me? If you're going to ask me to sacrifice my dreams for you, the least you can do is tell me the truth."

He lowers his head into his hands.

"Aseem?"

Silence.

"It's about Ishaan, isn't it?"

My words are met by more silence, but as I look at the tears in Aseem's eyes, at his quivering expression, I know I'm right.

Time seems to stretch as we stare at each other, neither of us wanting to say something that we can't come back from, until I can't take it any more. Anything, anything will be better than not knowing. Anything will be better than the things I'm imagining.

I take a deep breath and look right at him.

"What did you do?"

48

ZOE

I fucking knew it.

Ishaan. That's what it always comes back to in this family.

I listen as, for the first time in the five years that we've been together, Aseem finally tells me about the incident that has defined his life.

"You don't know what it's like," he says now. "To know that you are the reason your brother died. To live with that guilt, every day." He shakes his head. "We were spending the school holidays in Greece. Papa had gone to London for the day, Myra was off somewhere with her friends, and it was just Mama, Aisha, Ishaan, and me. We were supposed to spend the day at the beach, but Mama had a migraine. She asked me to take the twins to the pool so she could lie down for a few hours."

I sit down next to him on the ottoman.

"Aisha was easy but Ishaan was a handful. He was so naughty, always doing things he wasn't supposed to. I didn't want the stress of looking after him in the hotel pool so I took them to the play center instead."

I already know all this but I nod encouragingly.

"Ishaan was thrilled. He loved that play center. He was quite a hyperactive kid and in many ways, that play center was perfect for him. It was this tiny, dingy room but it was crammed full of toys and books so he was always discovering something new to play with." He smiles at the memory. "Aisha and Ishaan got engrossed in some game as soon as we got there. They were like that, the two of them, always lost in their own world. Our rooms were on the other side of the hotel complex but I thought if I cut through the gym, I could check on Mama and be back within five minutes tops. I didn't think the twins would even notice and Mama had looked so ill, I wanted to make sure she was okay."

"So you went to check on Mama?"

I didn't know this before. It adjusts the picture somewhat. I didn't know that Aseem had left the twins alone. I thought his guilt came from the fact that he hadn't paid enough attention to what Ishaan was getting up to and that by the time he did, it was too late. But thinking about it now, it makes sense. That's why Aisha never mentioned Aseem when she described the fire to me originally. He wasn't there. I can imagine him as a boy, so responsible, so considerate. He would've wanted to make sure his mother was okay. He would've felt the burden of responsibility on his shoulders with both Papa and Myra absent.

Aseem nods. "When I got to the room . . ." He stops, looks at me. "Is this really necessary?"

I ignore his question. "She wasn't there?"

Aseem pauses, his face taking on a pained expression. "She was, but I could see that she wasn't sick. We had an argument and I left. I was so angry, I completely forgot about the twins. And by the time I remembered . . ." He breaks off. "It was too late. The entire room was in flames. Mama tried to go in but they wouldn't let her. One of the porters managed to pull Aisha out in time, but Ishaan . . . We were forced to stand outside and watch. I could hear his screams. I could—I could smell his flesh burning. I kept trying to go in but—if I'd just done what Mama asked . . ." He pulls in a breath.

I sit next to him, just the thought of what he had to witness enough to bring tears to my eyes. The more he tells me, the more I feel the ground shifting beneath my feet. Something's niggling at me but I put it aside. I am appalled by everything he's telling me, by the realization that he blames himself so very deeply, and yet I am compelled to keep pushing him to talk.

When he speaks again, I can hear the anguish in his voice, and even though his face is turned away from me, I know the tears are already running.

"Children under ten weren't allowed in the play center by themselves. The staff would only open it up if an adult or older child was present. Mama lied for me. She told the police that I only left the room after she arrived so the inquiry was focused entirely on her. The things they put her through, Zo, the accusations they made . . . And afterward . . . I was a mess for years. If it wasn't for Mama, I don't know what I would've done. She had to put her own grief aside so she could look after me."

We stay like that for a long time, my heart breaking as I watch my husband grapple with guilt so heavy it seems impossible that he's been carrying it for nearly two decades. There is a strange sense that pieces of the puzzle that never quite fit are realigning themselves, and I can finally understand where Aseem and his mother's codependent relationship comes from. I should feel a level of satisfaction in having finally solved the puzzle that is the strange and toxic Agarwal family dynamic, but mostly I feel thrown off balance.

For years, I've been telling myself that Aseem and I are a team, that he needs me as much as I need him, but I can see now that I was wrong. Aseem will always be loyal, first and foremost, to his mother.

He will always choose her over me. Not out of love or duty, but out of guilt; guilt over something that should never have been his responsibility in the first place. But it isn't just the fact that Mama left a twelve-year-old boy in charge of a pair hyperactive twins that's bothering me. Aseem can fly off the handle sometimes, but underneath it all, he is the kindest, most considerate person I know. Even as a boy, the fact that his mother wanted a few hours to herself wouldn't have antagonized Aseem to the extent that he could have stormed off and forgotten about the twins. There has to be more to it.

"What did you and your mother argue about when you went back to the room?"

He looks up, surprised, shakes his head. "I don't—it's irrelevant."

"No, it's not," I say. "Why were you angry with her?"

Aseem sighs.

"Tell me."

"She was with someone," he says heavily. "A friend of Papa's. He used to visit quite often. Sometimes when Papa was there, but mostly when he was away."

I frown, confused, until it clicks. My eyes widen. "She was having an affair?"

He nods. "She didn't notice me in the doorway at first, but then . . . No one wants to see their mother like that and . . . I didn't know what to do, so I . . . I just left. Mama came after me but I was so shocked, I ran away. I didn't want to listen to her. By the time we got to the twins, it was too late. If I hadn't left the play center, if I'd just done what Mama asked me to . . ." He looks up at me and I can see not just the man, but the little boy who has been forced to carry with him guilt that isn't his. That shouldn't be his. It's heartbreaking. It's infuriating. "That's why I can't leave," he says. "I destroyed my family once, I can't do it again, Zo. Don't ask me to do it again."

49

ZOE

T ea. Something to calm our nerves. That's what I tell Aseem, but the truth is that I need to think. I need to find a way to reframe the narrative that has defined how I've seen my husband and his family for years.

I also need to make a decision.

I go into the kitchen and even though it's well past two a.m, I slide a capsule into the coffee machine, drumming my fingers on the countertop while I wait for my coffee to finish brewing. I need the clarity of thought that only caffeine can provide. I stir in a couple of spoons of sugar, then slide the glass doors open and step on to the patio. The slap of cool air would normally be a source of pleasure but it does little to soothe my nerves. I stare out into the darkness, the stillness and impenetrable silence of the landscape only serving as a reminder of the remoteness of Kilbryde and the cruel indifference of the family I've spent years trying to become part of.

What a bloody waste of time that was.

For as long as I have known her, Mama has projected the image of the perfect wife, the selfless mother, concerned about nothing more than the wellbeing of her family. Her children.

When we first met, I thought it was endearing, the way Aseem spoke about his mother. It was obvious, even in those early days, that he was something of a mama's boy, her favorite by a long shot. I attributed their closeness to their shared grief—Aisha was too young to remember what had happened, but Aseem and Mama had witnessed something unimaginable together—when in fact it came from their shared secret. Mama's made it clear, time and again, how protective she is of her son, and yet instead of helping him process his guilt, she's purposely let him believe that he is responsible for Ishaan's death.

To use your own child as a human shield and make their life about serving you . . . The cruelty is staggering.

I rock back on my heels, the gravel crunching beneath my feet. I've been out here, on the patio, for at least twenty minutes. Aseem will be wondering what's taking me so long. I should return upstairs, find a way to help my husband through this, but I don't want to go back in there until I've sifted through my thoughts and worked out how I feel about this.

I take a sip of my now lukewarm coffee and look up at the thin sliver of light that is the moon.

What I want to do is call Mama out. I want to confront her with the truth and watch her try to wriggle out of it while the rest of the family watches. I want to take that precious reputation of hers and crush it like a used-up can. But to do that, I'd have to betray Aseem's trust, and that's something he will never forgive me for.

But if I do nothing, Aseem and I will forever be slaves to his mother's whims. Aseem will keep bending over backward to please her while the guilt eats away at him, and I'll be forced to put up with her interference for the rest of my life. Because no matter what Aseem says, no matter where we live, she will find a way to insert herself into our lives, of this I am sure.

A swell of panic rises, hot and quick.

I can't fucking win. Not unless I leave and attempt to forge a life without Aseem, and what would be the point of that? I love my husband; I'm having his baby. My life is with him.

I kick at the ground, sending pieces of gravel flying into the darkness.

I am so lost in my thoughts I barely even notice when the kitchen lights behind me go on. It's only when the patio door slides open that I realize I am no longer alone.

"Is everything okay?"

I don't reply. I don't even turn around.

"Zoe?"

I shrug off the hand on my shoulder and twist to look at my mother-in-law. She's clutching a blister pack of painkillers in one hand and a glass of water in the other.

"My head is killing me and I need to eat something before I can . . ." She trails off, offering an explanation I never asked for. She frowns. "You seem unsettled."

The note of concern in her voice only angers me further. I manage a tight smile. "I'm fine."

She lifts her glass to her lips and takes a small, precise sip. That's my mother-in-law: always proper, even when she's ruining lives.

"You should get some rest," she continues.

I don't say anything, just take a sip of the coffee that's now gone cold.

"I can see that you're upset, beta. Don't you think it would be better to talk about it instead of"—she pauses, waves her hand at me—"burying it with caffeine?" She sighs and fixes me with a look, her brown eyes sharp and steady. "I know you kids think I don't know anything about anything, but I can tell when something's wrong. I might be Aseem's mother but you know you can tell me anything, right?"

I can feel my muscles tensing. I can't believe there was a time when I would've fallen for her nonsense.

Her expression turns serious. "Is this about London?"

I don't say anything, but my expression gives it away.

"I thought as much. You have to remember that I brought up four kids. You plan and plan and plan and you *think* you know what you're doing, but once the baby comes . . ." She shakes her head. "You have no idea how exhausting it is. Hospital appointments, interviewing nannies, dealing with nap times and baths while also monitoring your own diet and the baby's feeding schedule . . . it all adds up. You are going to need a lot of support and I can do that for you. I *want* to do that for you. But you have to let me." She leans forward, taking the coffee cup from my hand. "And that starts now. You're young and healthy but you can't be careless when it comes to your pregnancy. Stress isn't good for you or the baby. And neither is coffee."

Her behavior is so out of line, I am left speechless. I've always believed that she isn't consciously malicious, just unimaginative when it comes to other people's lives, but I can see now that I've underestimated her. She's enjoying this. She thinks by convincing Aseem to stay in Delhi she's won. This conversation isn't about her trying to share wisdom or advice or whatever the fuck she might dress it up as. It's an opportunity for her to gloat.

I meet her gaze, thinking of all the times she's made me feel lesser than her. Of all her little cruelties, always packaged as kindness or concern. I think of the half-concealed sighs and loaded looks, the jokes that were always edged with malice. The realization that I no longer need to put up with it is exhilarating. I might not be able to confront her but I certainly don't have to put up with this superior attitude, not any more. "You don't get to do that," I tell her. "You don't get to tell me how to live my life."

"Oh sweetheart, that is not what I'm doing. I just want to help," she says. "When I had Myra, I was completely unprepared for how overwhelming my love for her was. The urge to protect her, it was all-consuming. All I saw was danger everywhere. But here's the thing, Zoe, what none of the pregnancy books tell you is that it never goes away. It doesn't matter how many children you have or how old they are. It's primal. I'd sooner die than let anything happen to my children."

"And yet you didn't die, did you?"

She freezes.

"Where *were* you when Ishaan died?"

The words spill out before I can clamp down on them. "You like to act like this saint. But I see you; I know who you are. I know what you—"

"*Enough.*"

I freeze at the sound of my husband's voice. He's standing at the threshold, his face obscured by shadows. I don't know how long he's been there but I can tell from his posture that he's heard enough.

I force myself to swallow. "I was just—"

"I said, enough."

I am chilled by the menace in his tone, such a contrast from the vulnerability I'd witnessed just hours earlier.

He steps on to the patio. I scan his face, my eyes searching for something recognizable in his expression, but it's as though a switch has flipped.

We stare at each other for a moment, then he walks past me.

"Where are you going?" I take a step forward, my anger, my words to Mama, everything forgotten. "Aseem, wait."

He turns around, holds up a hand. I can see fury in his face, but it's tinged with something else. Fear. As though he is afraid of what he might say. What he might do.

He walks into the darkness, his last words suspended in the thick fog that's set in all at once.

"Don't follow me."

50

ZOE

Of course I follow him.

I go after him, trying my best to keep up, but the ground is boggy and Aseem has always been a fast walker.

The trees seem to inch closer as I make my way in the dark, the path narrowing as we go deeper into the forest. Behind me I can hear the faint echo of his mother's voice. She's calling out to her son, begging him to stop.

As am I.

"Aseem, wait," I yell. I run and close the gap between us, reaching out to clutch his arm when I'm close enough. "Please. Wait. Talk to me," I pant, my words coming out in gasps as I catch my breath.

There's a ringing in my ears, a strange tinny sound. I can barely stand but my grip on him is strong. He is forced to turn around and look at me.

"I trusted you."

I am expecting anger, I am expecting fury, but the naked vulnerability in his voice is unexpected. I release him, hot tears pricking my eyes.

"I didn't say anything," I whisper.

"You didn't need to. You really think Mama won't know what you were talking about? She's not an idiot. I swore to her I'd never tell a soul. It's all she's ever asked of me. And you—you . . . After everything she's been through . . . Do you have even a shred of empathy in you?"

"That's not . . ." I pause, distracted by a thump behind me. I spin toward the noise but all I'm met with is silence. Aside from the distant sound of the stream, the forest is quiet. Even nature, it seems, is holding its breath.

It seems, for a moment, like we are the only two people in the world.

"I think you're overcompensating—"

"*Overcompensating*? My brother died, Zoe. Because of me. He didn't get to finish school, didn't get to have a girlfriend, go to university, fall in love, nothing. Mama didn't get to see him achieve any of the milestones that we take for granted. That is on me. I put her through that. It's irrelevant what she was and wasn't doing. I was in charge of the twins. Looking after them was my only responsibility that day and I fucked up. Nothing I do will ever make up for that and if you can't understand that . . ." He shakes his head. "I trusted you. I told you the worst thing I've ever done and you betrayed me."

I feel the wind whip around us. The guilt and shame in his voice are horrifying. She did that. To her own son.

Standing there, in the dark, I can finally see what I never saw before. I used to think that she was thoughtless, but I realize now that it goes deeper than that. Mama uses Aseem's guilt to absolve herself. She's been making unreasonable demands of him for years and keeping him close because witnessing his guilt is what allows her to bury her own. Nothing will ever be enough for her. Aseem could cut his heart out and give it to her and she'd still be asking for his kidneys. It will never end, not until she faces up to what she did, until she admits that the only person responsible for Ishaan's death is her. And until Aseem sees that, he will never be free to live his own life.

We will never be free.

"I lost my temper but I would never betray you, not in a million years," I begin, softly. "But you need to understand that what happened that day . . . the fire, it wasn't your fault. You were just a boy, Aseem. A child. Mama should not have left you alone."

"You think I don't know all this? Sure, I was a child, but Myra and I started babysitting when we were ten! That's what happens in Indian families—we step up and support each other; not that you would understand that."

With that Aseem turns around and starts walking off.

"No, you do not get to turn this into an *Indian* thing. Mama should not have left you alone with the twins. It was irresponsible and it was selfish. And then to let you carry all that . . . for so many years. Can't you see? She has been using you. She's been playing on your guilt and your goodness to protect herself. She doesn't care about you."

"And you do?" He stops, spins around. "You think you know what's best for me because you've known me for what, five years?"

"I know what's best for you because I love you," I say. "I can't see you like this. You deserve better."

A moment passes. Somewhere in the distance I hear a fox wail. Or perhaps an owl.

"You really take me for an idiot, don't you?"

"What?" I feel an unexpected twinge of nerves, a deep knowing that I can't predict what happens next, not any more. We've come too far for that.

Aseem's lips twist into a sneer. "I know about your secret stash, Zoe. If anyone's using me, it's you."

I open my mouth to speak, then shut it again, as I try and make sense of his words. He can't possibly mean what I think he does.

"How much have you pilfered over the years? Five, six hundred grand?" He shakes his head. "Did you genuinely think I wouldn't notice that money keeps disappearing from the company account?"

The air between us freezes. I force myself to breathe. Inhale. Exhale.

"You've got it all wrong. That money—it's for us. Our future. You don't draw a salary. I was trying to protect us—"

"Spare me the bullshit, Zoe. Those brands you claim to work with, they don't even know you exist. You've been stealing from me so you can buy designer bags and then pretend you got them for free. All for what? So a bunch of strangers on the internet think you're cool? It's pathetic."

"That's not true. I've built a name for myself," I say, trying to convince myself as much as him.

"I can't do this," he sighs. "You're delusional. You can't see beyond yourself."

I stare at him, alarm sweeping through me, my panic growing in speed and intensity.

"I've been so in love with you, so desperate to get this to work, I've been ignoring all the red flags. I'm just a fucking ATM to you, aren't I? And the money is one thing, I don't care about the money, but to talk to my mother like that? To threaten her? Mama was right. You can take a girl out of the gutter and put her in a castle, but the stench will always be there. You're so blinded by the money and the lifestyle, you can't see that we are first and foremost a family. I should never have married you."

"You don't mean that," I say, my heart breaking.

He looks at me for a long moment. "I do. I'm done."

"No," I whisper.

"You can have the fancy lifestyle you've always wanted. The money, the house in London, all of that. But you and me? We're done."

"No," I repeat, louder now.

"And just so we're clear, there's no fucking way that I'm letting you raise my child. I am not going to let you . . ."

He goes on speaking. On and on and on, listing all of the things I've got wrong, parroting words that have no doubt come from his mother. He isn't in a rage. The anger, the fury from earlier is gone. He is absolutely in control, speaking in a voice so calm, so considered, it terrifies me.

"No," I shout. "If you even *think* about leaving me—I'll tell everyone. I'll tell them what really happened. I'll tell them Mama was having an affair. That's what killed Ishaan. Instead of looking after him she was busy fucking your dad's friend."

My words fall into a long silence. A single sob escapes me.

What the fuck have I done?

This is the man I love. The only man I've loved. I can't lose him, not over *this*. "I'm sorry. I shouldn't have—I love you, Aseem. I can't—"

"You threaten my mother again and I'll kill you," Aseem says, speaking so softly I have to crane forward to hear him.

There it is, that hot breath of fear. I stare at him, warning bells ringing in my head, reminding me of a past I thought I had long escaped.

From the moment I first met him, I've felt safe with Aseem. I've had the sense, a deep knowing, that nothing can go wrong as long as he is with me.

Those first few months, when our relationship was still a secret, we would spend hours in bed, just talking, my head nestled in the crook of his arm, his fingers stroking my hair. I'd wake up every morning comforted by his warmth next to me, thanking my lucky stars that I'd found a man who wasn't a monster, who would look after me, look out for me, no matter what.

I should've known better. I really should've.

I grew up watching my father kick and scream, and my mother, a five-foot eleven-inch woman, shrink into herself. My father's rage was a constant presence in our house, but the violence was rarely brutal. It was the unpredictability of his anger that was petrifying. He could be livid and never lift a finger and equally, the smallest comment could send him over the edge, turning a simple meal into a war.

I grew up watching my parents argue. I know that abuse doesn't always follow a pattern. I know that anger can look different in different men and yet I ignored all the signs.

When I met Aseem, I saw in him everything that I'd once hoped to see in my father. I saw safety, security, kindness, love.

I saw what I wanted to see and I ignored the rest.

Aseem's rage doesn't announce itself before the first strike. His fury is quiet. It creeps up on you, but once it shows itself, there's no controlling it.

I understand finally how my mother always knew things were going to get ugly before my father had even said a word. How she knew when to lock herself in the bathroom. It wasn't the violence or the yelling, it was something else, something darker in his eyes.

As I look at my husband, I see it.

And for the first time since I've met him, I'm truly horrified.

I try to ignore my mounting alarm as I realize that I only have seconds, not even minutes, to show Aseem that all of this is a terrible mistake.

We are in love. We are starting a family. We are happy.

But I am also scared. Terrified of this version of my husband.

The forest seems to creep closer and closer, the landscape shrinking around me.

Before I can even stop to think I'm spinning around, walking, then running away from him, away from his fucked-up family, away from it all. I'm tearing through the forest. My legs feel leaden, my breath short. I can barely see through the tears but still I run.

Only when I can't hear the sound of feet following me do I stop. I bend over, hands on my knees, panting, my breath harsh and jagged as it tears through my chest. I thought he loved me. I thought he would, when it came down to it, choose me.

I don't know how to fix this. If I *can* fix this.

The breath slowly returns to my body and with it the fear. Every nerve ending in my body is alert. My only thought is that I have to get out of this goddamned place.

I can figure the rest out later. I look around trying to orient myself. My ponytail has loosened. The breeze sends strands of hair flying across my face so that everything I see appears broken.

I need to get back to the house and find Owen. He's the only one who won't try to force anything on me.

"You shouldn't be here."

I spin around. A hot bolt of terror shoots through me. I take a step back.

"Don't—Don't come near me. I'll tell everyone. I'll tell them everything."

Aseem moves so quickly I barely have time to process what's happening. Barely have time to breathe when I feel the sharp pain on the side of my head.

Bright stars dance before my eyes, but even as I struggle to maintain my balance, I know they aren't real. My lungs hurt, my throat feels constricted. I try to scream but all that comes out is a strangled noise.

My hands reach out, grasping at air, searching for something—anything—to cling on to.

But I'm falling.

A wetness on my head. Sticky. Metallic.

I think of my baby, of the future I wanted to give her.

Falling. Falling. Falling.

I've made mistakes, I've done some stupid things, but never out of malice.

All I've wanted my whole life is to be loved. To find someone I could feel safe with. To have a family that was different from the one I grew up in.

This is not how things were supposed to end.

51.

MYRA

Something wakes me.

The faint hum of the boiler kicking in, the pitter-patter of the rain hitting the already boggy ground, or perhaps just a sense that something's coming.

I listen to the quiet, hearing nothing out of the ordinary.

The clock on my bedside table tells me it's five a.m., too early for anyone to be awake.

Yet there is something off about the silence. I can't explain it but I can sense something's not quite right.

I slip out of bed and pad to the window, drawing the curtain to one side. The sky is beginning to brighten, but the landscape is dark and undisturbed.

I reach for my robe, tightening it around my waist as I move to the other window, looking at the island, *my* island, from different vantage points. I watch the clouds drifting peacefully across the almost-black sky, as though they hadn't been waging war just hours ago.

I realized at some point last night that I'll need to tell everyone, not just about the divorce but about the transfer of the ownership. No more begging Papa for money or asking my siblings for handouts dressed up as investments.

Not in my wildest dreams could I have imagined that Owen would give me everything I wanted without a single objection, and now that he has, I don't know how to react. Even the most amicable divorces get messy once us lawyers get involved, my tutor used to say. Property, gifts, stocks and shares—people always find something to bicker about and rarely is it about the asset itself. No, it's about the pain. The opportunity to inflict one last wound on the person they once vowed to cherish forever is far too gratifying for most people to pass on. It's not sadistic; it is human to want to hurt. Like picking at a scab; sometimes the only way to dull pain is by causing more, and nowhere is this more apparent than in family law. I've always stayed away from it, not because I don't want to get caught up in the never-ending cycle of pain and hurt, but because in some ways I'm addicted to it.

I should be celebrating right now. I've spent months worrying about how I will save the island, plotting, planning, scheming, contemplating the most unimaginable things and hoping against hope that I won't have to implement any of my more drastic schemes. Now that Owen's offered me everything I've been working toward, I should be thrilled.

Yet all I feel is a kind of hollow displacement.

I'm so deep in thought that I almost don't see it at first, the movement between the trees, the sliver of a shadow moving slowly, slyly.

I feel my throat go dry. My heart somersaults in my chest.

I should get someone, do something.

But I stand rooted to my spot.

That is my brother.

And he's covered in blood.

52.

AISHA

I've always thought of myself as a good person.

I've always believed that if I spotted a crime in action or saw someone do something truly heinous, my conscience would kick in. I'd take a stand. Do the right thing.

Turns out the definition of the "right thing" can change when the victim is your best friend and her killer your brother.

I was out smoking when I heard the sound of my brother's wails rip through the forest. I've never run as fast as I did in that moment, only to come to a grinding halt when I saw what it was that had induced that horrifying sound.

Aseem's back in the house now, slumped in the corner in the kitchen, sitting in almost exactly the same position as the one I'd found him in, except there is no body in his arms, no one left for him to cradle. His wife, his dead wife, is still out there in the woods. Alone. Lying on the ground.

"What the fuck happened?" I'd yelled when I found him, covered in Zoe's blood. "What the fuck have you done?" I'd repeated over and over again. I'd hounded him for answers as I crouched down in the puddle of blood, desperately looking for a pulse, any sign that my best friend was still alive. All I'd received in response was unintelligible nonsense.

I push the image of Zoe's hair matted against the wound on the side of her head out of my mind and sit down at the table, letting my head fall into my hands. I can't look at him. I can't. I am furious at him, livid that he could do this. That he has done this.

But equally, I am furious at myself for letting it get this far. It's been hours since I found her and we still haven't called the police. Haven't even discussed it, not properly. Even Myra, good, conscientious Myra, hasn't brought it up.

What does that say about us? What does it say about me?

Aseem is my brother but Zoe was my best friend. My soul sister.

I need to do the right thing.

I rub at my forehead, trying to think.

And then I look at him and any resolve to do the right thing splinters.

"This is my fault," I whisper, my throat thick with tears. I can no longer ignore the guilt that's been eating away at me for hours.

Myra frowns, confused. "What? How?"

"I betrayed her," I say. I force myself to breathe. Swallow. "Zoe told me that as soon as they had the money from the sale, she and Aseem were leaving. She'd had enough of the family interfering in everything and she said Aseem wanted to focus on his own career. They were planning to move to London and cut themselves off from the family." I glance at Myra. "From Mama and Papa. She didn't want them to have anything to do with the baby."

Myra slumps back in her chair and looks at me, eyes wide. In most families, something like this would be considered extreme. In our family, it would be nothing short of catastrophic.

"Right after she told me, I—I went and told Papa. Mama's already so fragile and whether he admits it or not, Papa's become extremely reliant on Aseem as well. I knew what Aseem leaving would do to them and I thought Papa would feel blindsided if he found out later. I thought I was doing the right thing. I had no idea he would take it so badly," I say. "Next thing I know, he's announcing that the sale is off and—and . . . Mama's pressuring Aseem into staying . . ."

"And then Aseem is telling Zoe they have to stay in Delhi," Myra says, finishing my sentence. A beat of silence, then Myra asks, "Is that what you think happened? Why—"

"It's the only thing they ever argue—argued—about. The family. If I'd just kept my mouth shut. What happened to Zoe . . . it's my fault. If I'd just kept her secret, Papa wouldn't have known what they were planning, he'd have agreed to the sale and none of this would've happened."

Shame and regret pierce through me. Because it wasn't just my conscience that made me speak up, was it? It was my selfishness. Whether we like to admit it or not, our parents are aging. I knew that if Aseem left Delhi, Myra and I would have to pick up the slack. We'd have to spend more time at home. Look after our parents. And that would mean giving up my life in LA. It would mean giving up Gabe.

Myra reaches across the table and squeezes my hand. "Don't go down that route, Aisha. We need to stay focused," she says, her gaze sliding sideways to Aseem.

Aseem's sitting on the floor, his knees pulled to his chest. He hasn't said a word since he got back. It's as if he's in a trance. He's rocking back and forth, eyes glazed, while Mama crouches next to him, talking to him in low whispers, trying to comfort him. She's got blood on her clothes as well, the initials on her thick fleece dressing gown barely visible under the streaks of red.

Papa fills a couple of glasses with water and hands them to Mama, whispering something to her, before coming back into the kitchen. He sits down next to Myra.

"Mama's going to get him cleaned up." Papa's voice is tight.

The mood at the table changes in an instant.

"We can say it was an accident," Myra suggests.

Papa rubs his face, pinching his eyes with his fingers.

"That won't work." I look at my hands, twisting them together. "I think Aseem might've hit her with something. There was a wound on the side of her head."

Myra turns her gaze to me.

"I don't know where the weapon is. Or what it is. I looked, but there was nothing there."

Myra sucks in a loud breath.

"Okay, okay." Her eyes linger on Aseem for a few seconds before returning to Papa. "What do we do?"

We sit silently for a few moments, the question, its implications, too big to wrap our heads around.

In the end, Papa takes over.

"The only thing we can do," he says. His face is inscrutable but his voice is decisive. Definite. "We protect our family."

53

MYRA

My mouth tastes bitter, acrid.

How did I miss it? I'd known that something wasn't right in their marriage. I'd sensed it, but I'd kept my attention focused on Zoe, when instead I should have been looking at Aseem.

I run my hands through my hair, twisting it up into a bun. Even though it's the depth of winter, my skin feels hot and clammy.

I don't know what to do, how to reconcile the kind, considerate brother I know with the man sitting in the corner, covered in his wife's blood. It's one thing to snap in a moment of extreme pressure and make a mistake, but to then have the presence of mind to drag the body for several meters . . . I feel a chill run up my spine, realizing for the first time the cruelty and callousness that must lurk underneath his calm exterior.

Except I knew it was there, didn't I?

I'd seen what he'd done to Javier. I have no doubt in my mind that if Owen hadn't stepped in when he did, Aseem would've killed him then and there. I'd seen how quickly the switch had flipped and the daze he'd gone into afterward, barely coherent, exactly like the daze he's in now.

I should've done more than dismiss it as a drunken mistake. I should've forced him to get help, see someone. Aseem has had to witness more than his share of trauma, had to carry more guilt than he was due, and his response to it has always been to bottle it all up. We've all seen it. The hot flashes of anger, the simmering resentment, the violence. Any one of us could have tried to help him, except that's not how we do things in our family. It would be far too middle-class to talk about our feelings or, god forbid, our trauma.

Panic spews through me. There is no mistaking what Papa's saying. He's asking us—asking *me*—to conceal evidence. He wants us to obstruct the course of justice. Which in itself is a punishable offense.

And it's not as if we can simply bury the body and move on. Zoe is one of us. She can't just disappear.

The only way to protect Aseem is to frame someone else. I know this, as does Papa.

I glance at Aisha, trying to work out if she's clocked it yet.

Get it right and you ruin an innocent person's life.

Get it wrong and we *all* go to prison.

I turn to Papa. "What you're suggesting is impossible," I say. I push the chair back and get up. "We should call the police."

Papa twists in his chair and grabs my arm. "If you do that, you will be sending Aseem to prison for decades." He forces me back into my seat. "Look at him. *Look at him.* Is that what you want?"

Aseem's sitting on the floor, his head in his hands. He hasn't stopped crying. Whatever happened out there, whatever led to this, he regrets it. I can tell he regrets it.

We should turn him in. Save ourselves. It would be crazy not to consider it.

Then I look at Aseem, my baby brother. The one whose life has been full of more trauma than he deserves and who's done more for the family than any of us. We make excuses, insist we all share our familial responsibility equally, but the truth is we've exploited him for years. Aseem's had this deep need to do the right thing after his one mistake cost Ishaan his life and we've all capitalized on it to lessen our burdens.

I should've taken over the business when Papa had the stroke. I am the eldest. It should've been my responsibility. It *was* my responsibility. But I had other things to focus on. Then Aseem offered and that was that.

We might not have delivered the blow but we're all equally responsible for what happened to Zoe. And whatever happens to Aseem, it'll be on all of us.

Looking at him, I have a moment of clarity. We will see this thing through; we will do whatever it takes to protect him, and this time I will make sure he gets the help he needs.

"Zoe can't just disappear. There will be an investigation," I say. "A murder investigation. They will question our alibis, go through our finances, interrogate our motives, look at forensics, everything. This will not be easy. If we do this, we all need to be on the same page."

Papa nods.

Aisha looks up, understanding dawning.

I swallow, continue. "There are only three people here who aren't—"

"Two," Papa interrupts. "Owen is family. And with his family's connections . . ."

Surprising as it is, I do my best to hide the utter, complete relief that floods through me.

"Stu then," Aisha says. "He's already made threats."

Papa and I exchange a glance.

"The threats were against me."

Aisha shrugs. "Maybe he thought Zoe was you. It's so dark out there."

"Okay," I say slowly, taking my time to think it through. "But if he did it, why is he still here? That's the first thing the police will ask. Wouldn't it make sense for him to run? He has no alibi, a reasonable motive. He has nothing to gain by staying here."

"You don't even know if he is still here," Aisha objects.

"We'll check but I can't see why he'd take off in the middle of the night."

"But—"

"And from a purely logistical point of view, we have no possible way of planting any evidence on him. Not safely, anyway. Even if the police arrest him, without forensics, the entire case will fall apart."

My knowledge of criminal law is limited to a short module on criminology and office banter, but I do know this.

Tears fill Aisha's eyes. "What are you saying?"

Despite everything, it breaks my heart that we have to ask this of her.

"Gabe," Papa says. "We need to pin it on Gabe."

"Have you lost your mind?"

I reach for Aisha's hand under the table, my fingers twisting around hers. "We have no choice, Aish," I say. "The only way this works is if it is one of us."

"No, please. Not Gabe. Please," she says, her voice hysterical, pleading. Tears are leaking out of the corners of her eyes, her panic increasing with every word. "We'll say it was Stu. It's not our job to find evidence, it's theirs. Or we'll tell them it was a stranger."

There is nothing I can say to comfort her. I slide my chair close to hers and rest my head against hers. A gesture from a lifetime ago.

She turns her pleas to me, her words punctuated with sobs. "Myra, no. I can't. Please. *Please.* Gabe means everything to me. I can't do that to him."

"I know how difficult this is, Aish," I say. "But this is our brother we're talking about. We can't let Aseem . . . I wish there was another way. I really do."

Aisha wipes her tears with the back of her hand. "It's never going to work. Why would Gabe kill her anyway? Don't they need motive?"

"He was a bit . . ." I pause, searching for the right words. This man is still her fiancé. "He was inappropriate with Zoe earlier; she told me he commented on her body. Owen noticed it as well. And there is the fact that Zoe knew what really happened with Annabel. We can build on that. The police will do the rest."

I sneak a look at Aisha, thinking of the argument I'd overheard earlier. The set of her jaw confirms what I already suspected: he's probably done a lot worse than just flirt with other women before, and what's worse, Aisha's put up with it. It's not unlike her. Almost all her past boyfriends have cheated on her and yet for some unfathomable reason, when it comes to men, my baby sister, the entitled, overconfident brat I'd go to the end of the world for, seems to lose all her bravado. I can't tell if it's some deep-seated insecurity or her overriding need to shock, but she settles for the ugliest of toads when she could have her pick of the princes.

Papa's voice draws me back to the crisis at hand. "You're sure that'll work?"

I nod. It always works. Sex. It can drive people to madness. To murder.

"What do we tell them?" he continues.

"The truth. Or as close a version of the truth as we can manage," I say. Nine times out of ten a witness's testimony falls apart when they try to overembellish—it's too easy to see through. "We tell them that after the party, we all went to bed. Then early this morning, Aisha went for a run. She found the body and raised the alarm. We don't hide how we feel about Gabe or that we've had arguments with him, but we don't point the finger at him either. This is important. They have to arrive at Gabe themselves; we have to let them work for it, even if that means that for a little while each of us become a suspect ourselves. The only way this works is if they believe that we are a normal, fucked-up family with grudges and resentments, no better than their own but no worse either. If we try to play happy families, they'll see right through it."

Papa nods, slowly. "What about evidence?"

I try to remember everything I know about homicide. DNA. They will be looking for fingerprints, blood samples, skin cells, fibers. Forensic evidence that will bind the killer to the crime.

"If Aisha can get us some of his things—"

"What if I say no?" she demands.

"That is not an option," Papa says.

Aisha tilts her chin, eyes sparkling with defiance.

"Aisha . . ." I start, but Papa holds up his hand, the signal enough to cut me off.

He lets out a long breath, looks her in the eye.

There is a moment of complete silence.

Papa opens his mouth as if to speak, then shakes his head. He could threaten to cut her off. He could blackmail her, but he doesn't do any of that. There is no need. He shifts his gaze to Aseem, then back to Aisha, and in that one gesture, it's done.

Aisha lowers her head, nods.

"So we're agreed then?" I ask, casting a glance around the table, even as a knot of guilt twists in my throat.

No one speaks, our agreement written in silence.

Papa sighs. "We need to do this and we need to do it right."

54

MYRA

I've seen dead bodies before, but nothing could have prepared me for the sight that greets us when we arrive. Zoe is on the ground, her limbs bent at an awkward angle, her eyes still open, staring straight at us. Her skin is waxy, her lips are blue, her hair is caked with blood.

Blood. So much of it. Pints and pints spilled on the ground, shimmering in the dim moonlight. It's everywhere.

I put a hand on my mouth, sure that I'm going to be sick on the body. Not the body. Zoe.

Zoe. The girl who had walked around wide-eyed when she first visited me in Edinburgh, touching the walls, fingering the silk curtains. The woman who had brought more laughter into my brother's life than I thought possible. The woman who was pregnant with his child.

I set the bin bag down and hold my hands out, trying to stop them from trembling. I'm not sure I can do this. I'm not sure I *want* to do this.

"You okay?" Aisha asks.

I shake my head. It's one thing to theorize how to get away with murder, quite another to have to look at the smashed-up skull of someone you once loved.

"How could he? What was so bad that he had to do . . . this?"

I look up at the sky, trying not to cry. Already I can see the light filtering through the clouds, the edges of the sky getting lighter.

We're running out of time. I need to snap out of this. I need to think of it as a crime scene, nothing more.

There will be time for questions later. We need to finish this before Owen or Gabe wakes up.

Once the decision's made, it's easy. Or rather, it's mechanical.

I try to keep my eyes away from Zoe's body as I snap on a pair of rubber gloves and pull out Gabe's shoes from the bag. I set them on the ground, then hand the disposable shoe covers to Aisha.

It's her turn to wince.

"I can't," she says. Her voice is pleading, broken.

"It has to be you, Aish," I say. "If they find any of my skin cells, any traces of DNA . . ."

I don't finish the sentence.

She nods, understanding. It wouldn't surprise anyone to find Aisha's DNA on Gabe's things. Mine, however, is another matter.

Aisha sighs and puts on the shoe covers and then Gabe's shoes, then walks over to the body, stepping purposefully into the puddle of blood near the head, stomping around until the shoes are filthy with it and the surrounding area is covered in impressions of Gabe's boots.

She looks at me and I nod. She will have to walk back in his shoes, but for now, that's enough. In an ideal world, the investigators would be able to trace Gabe's entire journey to the body and back, but that's next to impossible for us to orchestrate. Plus, after all the hikes and walks we've been on, all of our footprints are all over the place anyway.

I hand her Gabe's coat and jeans, bile rising up my throat as I watch her bunch the clothes up and dab the body with them, finishing up by touching them to the ground, until they're drenched with blood and dirt and Zoe's DNA.

Next, the hair. I crouch next to Zoe and place a hand on her head. I have to look away as I do it, wincing when I feel the snap. I carefully place the strands of hair in a Ziploc bag and get up.

That's it. Hard part's over.

Or that's what I tell myself anyway.

It's nearly seven a.m. by the time we get back. Aseem's showered and dressed in a pair of rumpled pajamas and Papa's burned his clothes, the ashes safely disposed of in the loch. Mama's kneeling on the kitchen floor, a bottle of bleach in her hand. Thankfully, Owen and Gabe are still asleep.

I hand Aisha the Ziploc bag, then go to deposit Gabe's bloodied boots in the mudroom, but she stops me.

"What will he get? What's the—the sentence?"

A knot of guilt twists around my throat. "Depends. Manslaughter is a few years. Murder is more."

She looks at me, waiting for me to elaborate.

"Fifteen to twenty years is standard. But we'll help him find a lawyer," I say. I look at Papa; it's the least we can do.

"The best one we can find," he adds.

"And if they work it out?"

I take a breath. "Then we all get charged with perverting the course of justice."

The silence that stretches between us seems to hum.

No one says it but I know we're all thinking the same thing. We don't have a choice.

"He wouldn't leave them like that," Aisha says, her voice barely a croak. "If—if he'd really done it, he wouldn't leave his shoes like that."

I nod. She's right.

I take the boots on to the patio and hose them down. I leave specks of blood embedded in the grooves on the soles. Barely visible to the naked eye, but there nonetheless, waiting to be discovered. I smear a bit of dirt across the leather, then put the shoes in the mud room.

Next I get to work on Gabe's clothes. I can't imagine anything being more conspicuous than not having a winter coat in Scotland at this time of year, but just to be safe, I put the fire out before everything turns to ashes. I want them to sift through the fire pit and find fragments of Gabe's clothes in it.

I want them to look at Gabe and think: here is a man who killed a pregnant woman, tried to destroy the evidence, then went upstairs and got into bed with his fiancée. All because she rejected his advances and threatened to tell the family.

I want them to look at Gabe and think: here is the monster.

55

MYRA

I t worked.

After the floor was spotless and the evidence in place, I went to get Owen. I hammered my fists on his door, shouting for him to wake up. Across the hall, Aisha was putting on a very similar act as she roused Gabe from sleep, while downstairs, Papa was on the phone to the emergency services.

"It's Zoe," I yelled when Owen emerged from the guest bedroom, rubbing his eyes. "Papa's called an ambulance but you need to come now."

I led him to her, all the while pretending I didn't know she was already dead, acting like I genuinely believed he could help. That wasn't even the hardest part.

The hardest part was seeing her there, seeing how quickly her body had deteriorated.

"Aisha found her," I explained. "She was out for a run."

Owen looked up at the sky, still a swirl of velvety blue, sunlight slowly leaking through dense clouds. I wondered then if perhaps it would've been more believable to say that I'd been the one to find her; anyone who knows me knows I enjoy running in the semi-darkness, but Aisha . . . the girl hasn't seen a sunrise in her life.

Owen looked at me, then back at the body.

If he had any questions, any doubts as to the timeline or what really happened, he didn't voice them. He simply shook his head and said what I already knew.

"We need to call the police."

Things moved quickly after that. Despite the remoteness of the island, the police arrived within a couple of hours. Zoe's body was transported to Fort William for a post-mortem exam while CSIs in tell-tale white suits took over the island, laying out yellow markers and taking endless photographs, searching for evidence I knew they would find. After the initial interviews were complete, we were all brought to the Fort William police station for even more questioning. We stuck to the plan. Stuck together.

The detectives zeroed in on Gabe within hours. They'd spotted the blood on his shoes and questioned him about the fact that his coat was missing, but to my knowledge, they never found anything of value in the ashes, and the strand of hair Aisha had planted on his jumper could easily be explained away. In the end, it came down to motive.

Zoe had been right: Gabe had been the one who cheated on Annabel and he was desperate to keep that fact secret. Another thing he was desperate to keep secret: he'd spent months researching our family before he "ran into" Aisha in Singapore. His search history alone could constitute a dissertation on the Agarwal family.

When they questioned him, Gabe insisted that the only reason he'd been researching us was because he wanted to know what he was walking into and ensure he made a good first impression.

No, I didn't believe that either.

The prosecution painted him as an ambitious man who made a habit of targeting young women with social capital. They argued that for someone as financially savvy as Gabe, money itself was never a driving factor, it was always about access to people with money. He targeted families whose names commanded respect and inspired trust and then he embedded himself within those families. The police rolled out theory after theory, but what ultimately sealed the deal was Annabel's testimony. She spoke of how keen he was to move in her circles from the moment they met and how he'd insisted that they have a large engagement party with the who's who of London high society present. All he took from Annabel's bank account was ten grand, but the investors he managed to reel in after just three months of being engaged to Annabel? Those investors made him a millionaire. The fact that Zoe knew all this made her a threat, the prosecutor argued. A threat that needed to be eliminated immediately, which Gabe did with a single strike to the side of Zoe's head.

With a motive and priors like that, even with a heavyweight solicitor working his case, Gabe never really stood a chance. He got life. Fourteen years. No bail.

I try not to dwell on it too much. During the trial, I refused to look at Gabe's family. I refused to bear witness to the agony they were being forced to endure. It's the only way I can live with what I've done.

What happened on Kilbryde that week, what we did, it's unforgivable.

But here's the thing I keep coming back to, what I imagine I'll say to the jury if I ever have to defend myself:

If it was your brother, your family, wouldn't you have done the same?

MYRA

I wake to the faint sound of running water. I push my eyes shut and try to will myself back to sleep, telling myself I need the rest, but the noise only gets louder as the shower pump kicks in. I twist on to my side and reach for my phone. Six a.m. Why on earth is he showering at this time?

I lie there for a moment before pushing myself upright, remembering suddenly what day it is.

I leap out of bed and run into the bathroom.

Ten minutes later, we're in the taxi, anxiety mingling with anticipation as we speed toward the interview that will determine our future.

I'm not going to lie: it hasn't been easy. How do you even begin to move on from something like that? A murder in the family. Our names plastered all over the media. There is no script for it, no manual that tells you how to handle things. We managed to stick together through the investigation, but after the trial and that unbelievably difficult memorial, the family fragmented. Knowing what we did, the lengths that

we each had to go to . . . Suddenly the thing that was binding us together was not love or familial responsibility, but a truth so dark, the
only way to survive was to brush it under the carpet.

As soon as the trial ended, Aisha announced that she was moving to
Belize. I haven't heard from her since. She didn't even attend Zoe's memorial.

Papa retired and sold the company to his old rival, Malhotra, after
all, splitting the proceeds between the three of us equally. He and
Mama are still in Delhi but their life isn't what it used to be, in part
because of Aseem.

I spoke to Aseem about getting help, but he was unwilling, and in the
end I decided not to press him on it. Therapists are bound by confiden-
tiality but not when it comes to criminal behavior. He's living in London now, in the house that Zoe picked out for them. We text every now
and again but he hasn't spoken to our parents since the trial.

As for me, I hired the local developer Stu recommended to work on
the island and moved back to Edinburgh. I realized I was no longer
afraid to confront the friends and colleagues I'd been avoiding for years.
Their wholeness, their happiness no longer frightened me. Instead it
opened the door to a new understanding of motherhood. In mourning
Zoe and playing with my friends' children, I learned how to mourn Misha and Jay. I learned how to hold them close and set them free at the
same time, and somewhere through it all, I found my way back to love.

To Owen.

Thank you," the lady says, ushering us out of the building and into
the busy London street. "We'll be in touch."

I suck in a lungful of the wet air, then look at Owen, a small smile
playing on my lips.

"What do you think?"

He wraps his arm around me, pulls me in close. "I think we're getting a baby," he whispers in my ear.

We have lunch in a small restaurant off Kensington High Street. Between discussing the meeting and the additional paperwork the adoption agency requested, Owen brings it up.

As I knew he would.

"So will you see him?" he says, swirling spaghetti around his fork.

I look at him over the rim of my wine glass. Owen's been circling this for weeks, nudging me toward a reconciliation that, if I'm honest, I have little interest in. It's not that I don't want to see Aseem. I miss him desperately, but I'm not prepared for the unpleasantness a real conversation might dredge up. The crime and what covering it up did to us; it's not something we discuss. We are Agarwals after all, masters in the art of avoidance.

But this time I don't have that option. I promised Mama I'd see him.

I set my glass down and stab a piece of lettuce with my fork. "I'm meeting him for coffee later."

Owen reaches across the table and gives my hand a small squeeze, before returning to his pasta. A tiny gesture, but one that reminds me of the depth of his feeling.

One that reminds me of how lucky I am to be with a man who will do whatever it takes to keep me and my family safe.

Aseem looks exhausted, as though the mere act of living, of taking one breath after another, is draining. We're in the park near his flat, both of us clutching cups of takeaway coffee and making small talk about the weather, when really all I want to do is look into his eyes and ask if he's okay.

"How come you're in London? I would've thought the practice is keeping you busy."

"Not half as busy as I'd like," I say. It's the truth. Business has been hard, clients few and far between. I shoot him a look. "I'm here because Owen and I . . . We're adopting a baby. We had the interview today."

Aseem says nothing for a while, just continues staring into the distance. When he turns to me, his eyes are wet. "You'll be a great mum." He takes a sip of his coffee. "She would've been a great mum, too, you know. Zoe."

I look at my brother. His pain is still so raw, it makes my heart break. "Yes, she would. Are you okay?"

"I'm okay. Or as okay as I can be, anyway." He shrugs, gives me a sad little smile. "Mama sent you, didn't she?"

I nod. "She wants you to come home. She's falling apart without you, Aseem."

He sighs. "It never ends, does it? She's still trying to control me." He looks at me. "Control *us*. You haven't replied to my texts in weeks. And yet one call from Mama and here you are."

I shake my head. "That's not fair. I've been busy and as for Mama . . . She misses you and she's worried about you. We all are."

He nods. "Worried about me. Right." He looks up at the sky, squeezes his eyes shut. "Zoe was stealing from me." He darts a quick look my way, then corrects himself. "Us."

"Really?"

"I didn't know," he says. "Mama told me that night . . . It seems she had known for months."

"How could she know something like that?" I ask, genuinely baffled. Mama has never taken any interest in the family's accounts.

"Mama said she had a hunch that Zoe was exaggerating about her brand sponsorships, and then when one of Mama's friends told her that they saw Zoe buying a designer bag she claimed was 'gifted,' Mama asked our accountant to keep an eye on Zoe's accounts."

"Why didn't she say anything?"

"She was waiting for the right time. Mama likes leverage. She knew she could hold that over Zoe. And she did."

I look at him, genuinely confused. He's implying Mama was black-mailing Zoe, but to what end?

"In the last few months before she died, Zoe was terrified. She was being trolled online. Zoe didn't know it, but the troll was Mama."

"I'm not sure I understand. Why would Mama do that?"

"Mama's too smart to resort to blackmail. She knew how much Zoe valued her work online, so she set up a fake Instagram profile and started trolling Zoe anonymously, insinuating she knew things about Zoe that could destroy her, threatening her with—" he takes a breath "—frankly, disgusting things. Zoe tried to tell me she was getting abuse online but I just told her to ignore it."

"How do you know all this?"

"Mama asked me to wipe her phone. After she—after the incident. That's when I saw the messages she had sent Zoe. She called herself *NB_Lurker* and the things she wrote . . . It sickened me."

I shake my head. This is not a conversation I need—or want—to be part of. "I should go."

"Should you?" he says, turning that piercing gaze on to me.

I sigh. This is it, the reason I've been avoiding Aseem, and he knows it. "I don't know how to talk about this, Aseem. I've tried, but . . ."

He silences me with a hand on my knee. "How about I talk?"

I nod.

"I've been seeing a therapist." He pauses, notices the alarm on my face. "Don't worry, I've been careful."

"Has it helped?"

"To an extent. Though it's funny, we hardly talk about Zoe or the baby. Somehow most of our conversations seem to circle back to Ishaan." He looks at me for a minute. "He was your favorite."

"He was everyone's favorite."

"I hated that."

I look at my brother, taken aback by this admission that's so unlike him. It hits me again how much I let him deal with on his own. "I'm sorry I didn't do more. Back then. You had to go through that all by yourself. It wasn't right."

"No, it wasn't."

That surprises me. Aseem doesn't complain. He never apportions blame. Or at least, he didn't used to.

"Why did you leave that day?" he asks. "In Greece."

I frown. "I wanted to see my friends."

"Yes, but why on that day specifically? Your friends had been there for a week and you hadn't even bothered to meet them for a coffee. Yet that day you fought tooth and nail with Mama until she agreed to let you go. Why?"

"I don't know, Aseem. It was probably something to do with some boy. I can't remember."

"Can't you?"

There it is again, that look, the sense that he can see right through me. And I wonder if he knows. If he saw the same things I did growing up.

It's not inconceivable. Aisha and Ishaan were too little but Aseem was old enough to understand.

I close my eyes, trying to remember if Aseem was there when I first found out. It was a few weeks before the holidays and we were still in Delhi. I can still feel the urgency in my steps, the tight anxiety in my chest as I went looking for Mama, phone in hand, knowing already what her answer would be. I'd been grounded for two weeks for skipping school. With Papa I could usually get my way, but Mama never let me get away with things like that, not when it came to schoolwork. It was a Bryan Adams concert though. And all the girls from school I'd been so desperately trying to impress were going. I had to try.

I went straight to her bedroom, ready to charge in and do whatever it took to convince Mama, but the door was locked. Strange, because our parents *never* locked their bedroom door, not during the day.

I knocked on the door. "Mama, Sabah has spare tickets to see Bryan Adams. Everyone's going. Noor says she can pick me up in an hour."

Silence.

"Mama?"

I knocked again, loudly.

"Please?"

She opened the door a crack, for less than a second. "You're not going anywhere."

I still remember the heavy weight in my chest. Perhaps it had to do with the expression on her face, the bra that I could see draped over the armchair. Or perhaps it was something vaguer, one of the teenage fears that felt life-altering back then. Of being left out, of losing my status within the group, of Noor and Sabah choosing to take that new girl, Alia, instead of me.

I looked at my mother, the weight morphing into something different as I realized the power I held over her. She couldn't stop me. I looked at the shadow I could see in the mirror behind her. She *wouldn't* stop me.

I felt the frisson of defiance in my entire body.

"I'm leaving. I'll be back in the morning."

I have no memory of how she responded, but I remember clearly the disgust I felt in that moment, as much for her as for me. Right at that moment, I hated her more than I've ever hated anyone. Even though she was furious and I knew there would be a price to pay for my defiance, I walked away. I spent the entire night thinking about what I'd seen or what I thought I'd seen.

My relationship with Mama never quite recovered from that. I've spent the past twenty years pushing the image into the darkest corner of my brain, refusing to acknowledge what I'd seen, or rather, who I'd seen.

Papa's friend.

The same man I saw a year later in Greece, the day Ishaan died.

Aseem's memories of that day are far more vivid than mine. Just as I've spent the past twenty years trying to erase my memories, Aseem has spent them trying to reconstruct his, to try and pinpoint the exact moment when things started to go wrong.

Like me, he doesn't remember much of what was said, only the anger he felt when he realized what he'd seen, his feeling of terror knowing what would happen if Papa ever found out, his instinctive feeling that what happened to Ishaan was his fault. He was supposed to stay with the twins and he didn't. His shock at seeing our mother draped around another man was so visceral he had thrown up, the nausea rising in his stomach uncontrollably as he bent over, vomiting over his new trainers. He remembers thinking that if he confronted Mama he wouldn't be able to control himself. He might do something he would regret. He ran away hearing, at first, Mama's moans, then her cries as she called after him.

Later, he tells me, it was those screams that he heard in his dreams. Mama calling out to him, begging him not to leave.

Those are the screams that haunted him for years. They cemented his shame and with that, his role in the family.

So much remains broken, so many details blurred, but what's clear is that after Aseem stormed off, Mama ran after him, trying to explain or perhaps ensure that he didn't tell Papa what he'd seen. When she went back to the hotel minutes later, there were fire trucks lining the driveway, an ambulance parked to the side. The place was brimming with police. Had she known then that it was her children who had caused such a commotion? Is that why she ran straight for the play center instead of her room? Or was it merely a stirring, a realization that something terrible had happened?

By the time I returned, it was all over. The fire trucks had gone, but there was the smell of smoke in the air. I remember still the cold that seeped through me as I walked in, despite the oppressive Greek heat. The way my heart seemed to have escaped my chest. The deep knowing that whatever had happened would change my life forever.

We'll never know the details, never know exactly what happened that day, why the fire alarm didn't go off until it was too late and why no one noticed the flames. All we'll know is the part each of us played.

"Why didn't you say anything?" I ask him.

"What could I have said? I was furious with Mama, but I didn't know what to do with my anger. She had just taken the blame for me and the police were already giving her a hard time. I couldn't direct it toward her, not when she was so broken already. I turned it all inward. All the anger, hatred, disgust. I blamed her to a degree, but I also knew that ultimately what happened was my fault. Affairs are fixable. My mistake cost Ishaan his life. It cost Mama her son."

I look at Aseem, for the first time realizing how deep his scars from that day run, how much he has carried with him. "You know that's not true, don't you? We did things differently back then but that doesn't mean we did them right. Mama should never have left you alone with them. You were a kid, Aseem. She took the blame because it was her job to look after us, not the other way around."

"You know what's funny? That's exactly what Zoe said."

"You told her?"

He nods. "The night she—that's what she was trying to explain to me."

I suck in a breath, the picture finally completing itself.

"I didn't want to hear it. For years, I'd been trying my best to do whatever I could to ease Mama's pain and here was Zoe, trying to show me that Mama was somehow benefiting from my guilt, using it even to keep herself protected. It was—I couldn't wrap my head around what she was saying, you know? It was too much."

I nod. Aseem has always been so protective of Mama. It's one thing for me or Aisha to criticize her, but for Zoe to do that . . . that would've been enough for him to lose it.

"That—that would be enough for anyone to snap. To have your entire childhood reframed like that . . ."

"Is that what you think happened? I snapped, then struck Zoe with a rock because she questioned my childhood?"

He looks at me. I shrug.

He turns his eyes skyward. "My therapist says we all play roles within our families. And once you become accustomed to playing a specific role, you find ways to repeat the same patterns into adulthood."

I frown. I don't understand what he's getting at.

"None of you ever asked me. You never once asked if I'd done it, if I'd killed the love of my life, if I'd killed my own baby. Not once. I've always been the hothead, the one most likely to snap so you all just assumed." Aseem looks at me, his eyes searching my face for signs of understanding. "I'm also the one who spent his entire life protecting his mother, sacrificing what I wanted for the good of the family."

It has to be made that obvious before I finally get it and I still can't articulate it. I don't want to articulate it. I look at Aseem, speechless.

"I didn't kill her, Myra. I did snap; you got that right. When Zoe started talking about Mama like that, I got angry, really, really angry. I was too used to seeing Mama as the victim. I didn't want to believe that, intentionally or not, Mama had been manipulating me for years. We were fighting, saying all sorts of things to each other. But I didn't kill her. I could never kill her. I held my dead wife in my arms knowing what it would look like if anyone found us. And when Aisha did, she didn't ask how long I'd been there or if anyone else had been out there with me. She just assumed. And by the time I came back to the house, you had all made up your minds. I took the blame. I let an innocent man go to prison because that's what I've been taught to do." He sighs. "Family first, right?"

It's like watching pieces of the world realign themselves around me. Aseem's right. Mama never really recovered from Ishaan's death and perhaps that's why she loves Aseem to the point of obsession. But her love for her remaining son, her vulnerability, her fragility—none of that changes the fact that she's also manipulative. Always has been. Aseem has always been the martyr in the family. There's nothing he wouldn't do for our mother and she has always known that.

"I didn't kill Zoe," he says.

I nod, understanding.

And yet, I need him to say it. To utter the words that I already know, in my heart, are true.

"It was Mama."

Acknowledgments

I feel very lucky to have three outstanding agents in my corner. Jonny Geller, Viola Hayden, and Ariele Fredman: thank you for your brilliance, thoughtfulness and determination, and for working your magic on my books.

Huge thanks to my editors, Selina Walker and Jeramie Orton, who understood the twisted world of the Agarwals from day one and helped bring their story to life with their intelligent and intuitive comments, attentiveness and enthusiasm.

Thank you also to the wider teams at Century and Pamela Dorman Books, and to the teams at Curtis Brown and UTA who work so hard on my behalf, especially Jazz Adamson, Emma Jamison, Atlanta Hatch, Ciara Finan, and Laurie-Maude Chenard.

This novel took longer to write than any of my others and I owe a huge debt of gratitude to the authors and mentors who took the time to brainstorm plot holes and character motivations along the way. Sophie Hannah, Tash Barsby, and Louise Ford, thank you for your generosity, your encouraging words, and for always telling me the truth. I can't ask for more than that.

The hardest part about writing novels is getting the words on the page to match the vision in your head and every writer needs at least one first reader who gets it. I'm lucky enough to have two. Anvi Mridul and George de Freitas, thank you for your tireless reading of drafts and for understanding not just every layer of the story and its characters but also my ambitions as a writer.

When writing a book about the nature of family, it helps to have such a solid example of the real deal. To my parents, my brother, Rishabh, and my sister-in-law, Prachi: thank you for being nothing like the Agarwals. I would be lost without you. Myra and Saira, thank you for letting me be the one who gets to spoil you rotten. I take my position as the favorite bua more seriously than any job I've ever had.

And finally, thank you, dear reader—I was just a writer with some stories and a dream. You read my books and made me an author.

Dear Reader,

I started writing *The Inheritance* in 2020, shortly after the first COVID lockdown was announced. I was living alone in London at the time, and with every passing day, my fear and worry for my family in India grew more and more intense.

And I wasn't the only one.

I've always been fascinated with the reasons that compel good people to do bad things. Over the next two years, as the world navigated lockdowns and unprecedented medical emergencies, it seemed as though even the kindest, gentlest, most honest people I knew were being forced to do terrible things. I heard of civil servants smuggling oxygen cylinders so their grandparents could survive. I learned of a distant cousin who had been forced to bribe hospital staff so his mother might find a bed in an overflowing ward. I heard of a COVID-positive father who broke every lockdown rule and put countless lives at risk to attend his daughter's last rites—the same daughter who had succumbed to her symptoms while fighting to get her father the treatment he needed.

Everywhere I looked I saw people doing despicable things in the name of love.

And yet, I kept asking myself if I wouldn't have done the same—or worse—for my own family.

I already knew the setting and the premise for *The Inheritance*, and as I started writing, that question became the heart of the idea. What do you do when someone you love has done something terrible? What is it like to do something terrible yourself and yet still demand loyalty from the people you love? And how do you live with yourself knowing you've done something utterly unforgivable?

The Inheritance is a story about a family with a dark history; it is about greed and unfulfilled desires; it is about the life choices that shape us and make us who we are. It is about the ferocity of love and hate within the sibling relationship and how it's often impossible to pry the two apart. It is, I hope, a taut page-turner that you would have struggled to put down.

But above all, dear Reader, *The Inheritance* is a meditation on family and loyalty.

It asks a question I hope you will examine yourself. When faced with the impossible choice, what would you choose to protect: your conscience or your family?

Let me know.

Love,

Trisha ♥

Trisha